ALSO BY R. C. SHERRIFF

Fiction

The Siege of Swayne Castle

The Wells of St. Mary's

King John's Treasure

Another Year

Chedworth

Greengates

The Fortnight in September

Journey's End

Nonfiction

No Leading Lady: An Autobiography

Plays

A Shred of Evidence
(or The Strip of Steel)

The Telescope

The Long Sunset

The White Carnation

Home at Seven

Miss Mabel

St. Helena

Two Hearts Doubled

Windfall

Badger's Green

Journey's End

Mr. Bridie's Finger

The Feudal System

Cornlow-in-the-Downs

Profit and Loss

The Woods of Meadowside

A Hitch in the Proceedings

Film Scripts

The Ogburn Story

The Night My Number Came Up

The Dam Busters

Cards with Uncle Tom

Trio

No Highway

Quartet

Odd Man Out

This Above All

That Hamilton Woman

The Four Feathers

Goodbye, Mr. Chips

The Road Back

One More River

The Invisible Man

The Toilers

The

HOPKINS

MANUSCRIPT

a novel

R. C. SHERRIFF

SCRIBNER
New York London Toronto Sydney New Delhi

Scribner

An Imprint of Simon & Schuster, Inc.

1230 Avenue of the Americas

New York, NY 10020

Originally published in Great Britain in 1939 by Victor Gollancz

First Scribner trade paperback edition January 2023

SCRIBNER and design are registered trademarks of The Gale Group, Inc.,
used under license by Simon & Schuster, Inc., the publisher of this work.

For information about special discounts for bulk purchases,
please contact Simon & Schuster Special Sales at 1-866-506-1949
or business@simonandschuster.com.

The Simon & Schuster Speakers Bureau can bring authors to
your live event. For more information or to book an event,
contact the Simon & Schuster Speakers Bureau at 1-866-248-3049
or visit our website at www.simonspeakers.com.

Interior design by Kyle Kabel

Manufactured in the United States of America

1   3   5   7   9   10   8   6   4   2

Library of Congress Cataloging-in-Publication Data is available.

ISBN 978-1-6680-0394-7
ISBN 978-1-6680-0396-1 (ebook)

The

HOPKINS
MANUSCRIPT

FOREWORD

From The Imperial Research Press, Addis Ababa

When the Royal Society of Abyssinia discovered "The Hopkins Manuscript" two years ago in the ruins of Notting Hill, it was hoped that some valuable light would at last be thrown upon the final, tragic days of London.

But a careful study of the manuscript has proved these hopes to have been raised in vain. Edgar Hopkins, its author, was a man of such unquenchable self-esteem and limited vision that his narrative becomes almost valueless to the scientist and historian, and is scarcely mentioned in the Royal Society's massive and masterly *Investigations into the Dead Civilisations of Western Europe*.

But despite all its shortcomings, "The Hopkins Manuscript" possesses one unique feature. It is the only personal day-by-day record yet discovered that gives us the intimate feelings of an Englishman during the days of the Cataclysm. Our ignorance concerning the History of England has caused much comment in recent scientific debates, but it should be remembered that for a hundred years after the collapse of the "Western Civilisation" the peoples of the reborn nations of the East indulged in an orgy of

1

senseless destruction of everything that existed in their own countries to remind them of the days when they lived in servitude to the "white man." Every printed book, every vestige of art surviving from Western Europe, was systematically hunted out and destroyed. The damp climate of England completed this work of destruction in the seven hundred years that followed, and the tragedy of our revival of interest in the long past nations of Europe is that it has come too late. Our knowledge of England may rest forever upon such inadequate fragments as "The Hopkins Manuscript" that have survived by a miracle of chance.

A word may be said here concerning the romance of its discovery.

The mainland of Western Europe, once inhabited by the French, Germans, Italians, and Spanish, has long since been colonised, and every vestige of its past civilisation swept away. In the Island of Great Britain alone there remained some hope of recovering evidence to reconstruct the lost glory of the "white man."

The damp British climate has not attracted the peoples of the East, and for nearly a thousand years, since its last wretched inhabitants starved to death amidst the ruins of their once noble cities, the Island has remained a deserted, ghost-haunted waste—its towns and villages buried ever deeper beneath encroaching forest and swamp.

The difficulties facing the pioneer expedition of the Royal Society of Abyssinia were sufficient to discourage the most ardent explorer, and it is not surprising that it returned almost empty-handed.

The English recorded their lives and achievements upon paper so flimsy that every vestige has perished in the perpetual dampness of the Island, and their inscriptions upon metal and stone are of the poorest quality.

An extremely rusted iron tablet was found twelve miles south-west of London. Its inscription has been deciphered by Dr. Shangul of Aduwa University as KEEP OFF THE GRASS and it is now lodged in the Royal Collection at Addis Ababa.

The rectangular column of stone inscribed PECKHAM 3 MILES can be seen in the Imperial Museum of Afghanistan.

The only other inscription found in England raised great hopes when first discovered. It had many names engraved upon it, but it proved to be the greatest disappointment of all. The tablet, which commemorates the opening of a swimming bath in North London, records in detail the names of the Borough Council, the archi-tect, and the sanitary engineer, and omits the name of the ruling monarch and Prime Minister—an example of urban vainglory that appals the modern mind.

"The Hopkins Manuscript" was discovered by a pure stroke of chance. While cutting brushwood for the fires lit by the expedi-tion every night to protect themselves against the packs of wild dogs that roam the Island, a young scientist discovered a much-decayed wall of red brick that collapsed under pressure, revealing in a recess a small vacuum flask. The manuscript within it had survived where millions of books, exposed to the climate, had perished.

And so "The Hopkins Manuscript" comes to us—a thin, lonely cry of anguish from the gathering darkness of dying England—infinitely pathetic in the pitiful little conceits and self-esteem of its author. It raises the shadows from the dead limbs of a once powerful nation as the glow of a match might dispel the darkness from the desert of Sahara, and yet it is all that we have—all that we may ever have to remind us of a people that once lived in glory.

We know that Julius Caesar invaded Britain, for this is recorded upon imperishable stone in Italy, but what happened after the invasion of Julius Caesar remains a mystery that our men of science are never likely to solve.

This popular edition of "The Hopkins Manuscript" is published exactly as it was written, but a fully annotated edition by that brilliant scholar of English, Dr. Shangul of Aduwa University, who has corrected all the author's grammatical mistakes, has been published by the Royal Society of Abyssinia.

CHAPTER ONE

I am writing by the light of a piece of string which I have pushed through a fragment of bacon fat and arranged in an egg-cup. I shall write by night, partly because I can no longer sleep through these ghastly, moonless chasms, and partly because by day I must search for food, and the days are short.

It is hard to believe that this is Notting Hill, and the inky, silent void beneath me is London. There was a time when I could see a million lights from this window, with the Bayswater Road and Oxford Street piercing the heart of London like a blazing, jewelled sword. There was a time when the roar of the traffic would come up to this window like a lulling sea beneath a dying storm, but now I seem to be suspended in this broken wooden chair between unheavenly darkness and unearthly silence.

An owl was hooting just now in Ladbroke Square, but it stopped abruptly as if suddenly ashamed, like a man who has laughed in a cathedral.

Earlier this evening I saw a few fitful little yellow lights beneath me—flickering and disappearing as people in their ruined houses tinkered with their gimcrack home-made lamps and gave them up in despair. Only a few still try to fight these horrible black nights with their feeble home-made lanterns. The majority have turned into savages and crawl into their sleeping-holes at sunset, and lie there in a kind of stupor until dawn.

I wonder what they think about as they lie there—for most of them are quite alone and none of us has any hope. We are all just waiting for the end.

A man I met yesterday in Kensington Gardens as I was drawing my bucket of water told me that there were only seven hundred people alive in London now, and every one of us can own a street-ful of houses if we want them.

An old lady who used to live opposite me at No. 10 Notting Hill Crescent has gone to live in the National Gallery. She heard that it was empty, and wanted to gratify her love of art and lust for possession during the last days that remain to her.

I went to tea with her today. She lives upon the pigeons that fall dead from the Nelson Column in Trafalgar Square. She cooks them over a fire which she keeps blazing with Dutch masterpieces upon the stone floor of the entrance hall. She dislikes Dutch masterpieces and enjoys the fire as much as the pigeons.

After tea she took me around the galleries to show me her collection of Turners, Constables, and Gainsboroughs. She had grown tired of one or two and tore them down for her fire that evening. She gave me a little medieval panel worth £5,000. I accepted it as politeness suggested, but threw it away upon my walk home. Nobody disputes her possession and I am glad there is one happy soul in this dying city.

But there is no time for anecdote. I must write my story, plainly and simply, while I have the strength, and sufficient light to see by. The idea of writing my story has given me quite a lot of happiness.

I alone, of all these hopeless people, shall die with the knowledge that I leave something behind that may one day be found and valued as highly as the Rosetta Stone or the priceless manuscripts of Egypt.

In those happy, peaceful days before the Cataclysm I spent much time in searching for the relics of people who lived before history began. History has ended now, but one day it may begin again—one day my story may be found and I shall stand amongst the immortals. Tacitus, Ptolemy, and the Venerable Bede produced work that lit the dark ages of the past. My story may be the solitary torch that lights the dark age that followed the Cataclysm, for when it is finished I shall screw it tightly in my thermos flask and conceal it behind the bricks of my fireplace.

I am a bachelor, aged fifty-three. My name is Edgar Hopkins and I come of an old and honourable family of Worcestershire squires. The fortunes of my family have declined somewhat in recent years, and in 1912 my father sold our old family estate at Stoatcastle to the Victrix Sand and Gravel Company and retired to Chislehurst.

I was educated at Winchester and Jesus College, Cambridge. Upon taking my degree of Bachelor of Arts, I accepted the position of assistant arithmetic master to Portsea Grammar School, a post which I held, I think, with distinction for twenty-three years until the death of my father at last provided me with a small but sufficient legacy upon which to retire.

I have always taken the keenest interest in poultry breeding. For three successive years I carried off first prize for Rhode Island Pullets at the Portsea Poultry Show, and my brochure upon "The Successful Breeding of the Domestic Fowl" was very favourably reviewed in the *Poultry Gazette*. A carping and small-minded criticism in *Our Feathered Friends* did not dismay or surprise me, for jealousy is unfortunately as rampant amongst poultry breeders as it is amongst metallurgists, in whose grudging world I also, I might say, ranked as an expert.

My retirement afforded me the opportunity of gratifying my interest in poultry breeding to a wider extent. In the summer of 1940 I purchased a small but charming estate upon the outskirts of the village of Beadle in Hampshire. It was known as Beech Knoll and consisted of a nice little house upon the summit of a small hill 580 feet above sea level (a fact to which I owe my life). The terraced gardens, rich in old hollies and yews, sloped pleasantly down to a well-drained, sheltered meadow of five acres—a veritable paradise for poultry.

I brought my best hens from Portsea, secured six excellent cockerels from a good breeding farm in Kent, and settled down to a life of simple but vigorous purpose.

Nature has provided me with a happy gift for friendship, a witty but not unkind tongue, and, I think, a restful, pleasant personality. I soon became well acquainted with my neighbours, from whom I selected Dr. Perceval and Colonel John Harrison as my most intimate friends. I spent many happy evenings with these two gentlemen, discussing my poultry until long past midnight, and it was a great regret to me when both of them decided to go and live farther away.

But before he left, Dr. Perceval engaged my interest in a hobby which was destined to play a remarkable part in my life, and without which I should never have gained the knowledge and authority to write this story.

Dr. Perceval was a keen amateur astronomer, and had constructed a small observatory in the summerhouse of his garden. My eager imagination was quickly stimulated by my first glimpse of the moon through his magnificent telescope. I was fascinated by that brilliant, crater-pitted little world of rock-strewn silence, and I spent many hours with my eye fixed to the telescope as the old doctor patiently explained to me those far-off mountains and awe-inspiring chasms.

Within a few months I became, through the doctor's influence, an associate member of the British Lunar Society—a learned body devoted entirely to the study of the moon.

The Society's headquarters were at 76 Barbara Street, Covent Garden, and consisted of the whole top floor. There was a large lecture room, a small office for the Secretary, and a refreshment room that quickly became famous for its sandwiches composed of chicken supplied from my estate.

On the second Tuesday of every month we met to hear a paper read by a distinguished visitor or member of the Society. A stimulating debate would follow, and the evening would close with a pleasant, informal adjournment for coffee and sandwiches in the anteroom. So easy and happy was this final half-hour of the evening that the distinguished visitor would frequently unbend and almost become one of us. Upon one occasion I engaged Professor Rolleston-Mills of Greenwich Observatory in conversation for nearly twenty minutes. I explained to him that the unusual whiteness of the chicken meat in the sandwiches and their exceptionally delicate flavour was due to a deliberate inbreeding of a selected strain of Wyandotte. We had a hearty laugh when he described me as a "man of many parts"!

This monthly meeting of the British Lunar Society became the most looked-forward-to event of my peaceful life. Upon the second Tuesday of each month I would rise especially early, complete the necessary attentions to my chickens as quickly as possible, snatch a hasty lunch, and catch the 2:14 train for London.

This train reached Waterloo at 4:23 and gave me the opportunity of attending a cinema theatre before our meeting began at 6:30. We usually departed at about eight o'clock, and there was time for me to dine quietly at a pleasant little Soho restaurant before my train left for home at 9:52.

It gave me a "night out" which I enjoyed the more because I had become rather a "country cousin" in the past few years, and I never failed to return home with a sense of mental well-being.

I am afraid old Police Constable Wilson used to look askance at me as I strutted up Burntash Lane towards my home at well past midnight, and perhaps it is an understandable vanity that made me cock my hat at a jaunty angle and swing my umbrella with a touch of abandon as I wished him goodnight.

I not only gained stimulating mental refreshment from my monthly visit to the British Lunar Society; I also secured a new respect from the "locals" by being "a bit of a lad"!

My story really begins upon a summer evening, seven years ago. Can it only be seven years? It seems an eternity, but careful calculation proves it to be true. Even the words "summer evening" come haltingly from the pen and look strange upon paper in a world from which summer evenings have long since sped.

There are no evenings—no twilight in a land from which the sun plunges in one ghastly, blood-red torrent. It is burning yellow day—then suddenly black, utter night.

I remember, upon that summer evening, that I had walked into the village after tea to see Mr. Flidale, the carrier. I had been to discuss with him the transport of my three outstanding Wyandotte cockerels to the Brigtree Poultry Show, and it was arranged that he should collect them next evening after sundown. It is my firm belief that a finely trained domestic bird should never be transported except at night, when its drowsy condition prevents that undue excitement and concern which actuates so seriously against a bird in a highly strung condition, and prevents it from looking its best next morning.

As I reached the turn of the lane upon my homeward journey, I saw Mr. Barlow, our village postman, about to enter my gate. It was a steep climb up the path to my front door, and as Mr. Barlow was an elderly man I called out to him that I would take the letters myself and save him unnecessary exhaustion.

Mr. Barlow was grateful, and we stood for a few moments, chatting by the gate in the mellow light of the sunset.

"Lovely evening, Barlow," I said (for I believe in being affable at all times with the honest folk of the village).

"Lovely indeed, Mr. Hopkins," replied Barlow. "Lovely sunset—but rusty again."

Our heads turned towards the glow that fretted its way through the ancient beeches of The Manor House, and for a while we were both held in a strange silence.

"Rusty again." It was the first time I had heard expressed in words the strangeness which I had felt towards eventide on several occasions in the past few weeks. . . .

"I never seed that rusty colour in all my life afore," added Barlow.

I nodded in silent agreement, but could not dismiss the phenomenon so easily as Barlow did, as a mere freak of nature. There was no difference in the actual appearance of the sun, nor in the shape of the little clouds that surrounded it as it sank gently behind the trees. But, as it passed, it left a great sombre tarnish in the sky—a feverish glow of poisoned blood that had no beauty in it—that oppressed and disturbed me.

The newspapers, so quick to note and record all oddities of nature, had apparently overlooked the phenomenon, nor had the village folk done more than pass a casual remark across the bar of the Fox & Hounds.

But my keenly developed astronomical eye had led me to an observation of this strange phenomenon more close than that of my neighbours. At first I had noted it with curiosity and scientific interest—and then, as it persisted, I was drawn each evening into my garden with an increasing sense of wonder and a growing disturbance of mind.

Upon one evening in particular I returned to my house with a genuine sense of fear. The sky, upon that night, was overcast, and the sun, since midday, had been lost to view. But as I watched the sky beyond the beeches I saw the same rusty glow appear—indistinct because it was swathed in cloud—and yet it seemed to pulsate behind its covering like some horrid, festered wound beneath a dirty yellow bandage.

I felt so uneasy that I sat down after dinner and wrote a letter to *The Times*. I registered the letter next morning, but I watched for its appearance in vain. And then for a little while the phenomenon had disappeared and the sun had set once more in its old, friendly gowns of gold and crimson. I had begun to believe that the strangeness had been, after all, a mere passing illusion: I had ceased to search the sky at evening—I had almost forgotten it—and now, here it was, "rusty again," as old Barlow so aptly put it.

"It disappeared three weeks ago," I said. "It'll disappear again." I took my letters, bade the old man goodnight, and closed my gate.

Halfway up my hillside path lay an arbour shaped from fine old yews. It was a favourite resting place of mine with a lovely view across the countryside, and upon clear days I could glimpse a silver strip of sea.

I paused at my arbour and sat down to read my mail. There were three letters that night. The first was an invoice for £18 12s 3d covering the new poultry houses I had recently purchased from Haggard & Jackson of Winchester. The second was an invitation card to the Annual Prizegiving and Latin Play at Portsea Grammar School—an invitation I always appreciated and frequently sacrificed important engagements to accept. The third contained the letter that ended my days of peace: happy days that have never since returned, and never will again.

Often, in the past seven dreadful years, I have looked back upon that evening; often I have lived again the last hour of happiness that I was ever to know upon this earth: that peaceful stroll to the village—my quiet chat with Mr. Flidale, the carrier, in his cottage by the bridge—a moment's pause to watch the boys at football on the green—the country sounds, the smell of the hay—the peaceful stroll home and chat with old Barlow at my gate; the last hour of my life—the last hour in which I was to know the meaning of repose . . .

I have that letter in my pocketbook today, worn and battered by the dreadful misfortunes that I and my personal belongings have suffered. I copy it down in its entirety:

THE BRITISH LUNAR SOCIETY

Secretary: 76 Barbara Street
Humphrey H. Tugwall   WC1
                                          18th September 1945
Sir,

I am instructed by the President and Committee to summon you to a special meeting of the British Lunar Society to be held at the Society's headquarters on the 8th October at 6 p.m.

As the subject of this meeting is of the most highly confidential nature, no guests will be permitted, and members are requested to keep both this notice and the matters announced at the meeting most secret and confidential.

Yours faithfully,
Humphrey H. Tugwall

Twilight came, and I sat without moving with the letter in my hands. The invoice for the poultry houses, the invitation to the Prizegiving, fluttered to the ground, forgotten.

I felt suddenly cold and sick, for the thing that I had secretly dreaded for the past six months had apparently happened.

In the spring of that year Professor Hartley, our President (a brilliant astronomer and a charming man), had put before the members of the Society a bold proposal.

In his opinion, he said, the Society should not be content with a monthly meeting for reading papers and discussing lunar topics. The Society should possess its own observatory and its own telescope.

In a simple but masterly statement of finance, he explained that a lease could be obtained of the roof of a tall radio factory upon high ground at Hampstead. The rental would be £90 a year, the cost of the observatory £800, and the price of the telescope, instruments, etc., £750: an outlay of £1,550 and a yearly rental.

Our existing inadequate premises cost £120 a year and subscriptions from our 109 members at two guineas was £230. We had a satisfactory balance of £194 in the bank, and as the observatory was certain to lead to a large increase in members we could confidently look forward to a higher revenue.

He explained a sinking fund to defray the cost of installation, and as I listened I was thrilled by the courage and enterprise of the scheme.

I shall never forget my growing anger as member after member rose to his feet to tear the scheme to pieces with ridicule, cowardice, and spiteful criticism. Their sluggish little brains were content with what they had: their timid little minds dreaded the dangers of expansion. They didn't want a telescope! Apparently they were content to read about the moon and listen to cleverer men than themselves lecture upon it. To study it for themselves would be too big a call upon their intelligence! They disguised their cowardice by enlarging upon the financial risks and predicting bankruptcy for the club.

Neither shall I forget the part I played upon that historic evening. With a surge of white-hot anger I rose to my feet and spoke as I have never spoken before. By nature I am a quiet, retiring man, too prone to allow men with louder voices and lesser intelligence to have their way. But as I sat there watching our President's brave, patient face as his carefully made plans were ridiculed and destroyed I became as a man beside himself.

In a loud, firm voice I accused my opponents of rank cowardice, narrow-mindedness, and base disloyalty to our fine President.

I dwelt vigorously upon the untold advantages of possessing our own telescope. "We call ourselves the British Lunar Society," I said, "and yet we do nothing but listen to strangers who tell us what we should see with our own eyes!"

Well do I remember the stupid, ironical laughter that became fuel to my ungovernable passion. Well do I remember the voice that shouted: "Who's going to pay the bill if the scheme's a failure?"

And never shall I forget my reply. "I will!" I shouted, crashing my clenched fist into the palm of my hand. "I am not afraid to face the consequences of enterprise and courage!"

I was too angry to realise what I was saying, and in the next moment could have bitten my tongue off for its rashness.

There was a moment of silence and then a burst of vigorous, sincere applause from the members present. Before I realised what was happening, Dr. Willoughby, an old and highly respected member of the Committee, was standing up, addressing the meeting.

It was an inspiring moment, he said, when a wealthy member of a society came forward as sponsor and guarantor in the noble cause of science. Personally he considered the scheme a risky one for a small society, although he applauded its courage. Now that those risks had been so generously covered by Mr. Edgar Hopkins, he looked forward with a restful mind to the completion of the scheme.

I had come out in a cold, clammy sweat, but what could I possibly do? Around me sat the men who had tried to kill the scheme—who were angry with me for saving it. If I were to stand up again and say that I did not mean what I had said, what would be the reply of the men whom I had accused of cowardice? I should be discredited and laughed out of the Society.

I am prepared to admit that it was my inexperience in public speaking that had led me into this rash outburst. Had I been a rich man with money to spare, the position would have been different. But I was not a rich man. After purchasing my house and poultry farm I had £9,000 of invested capital that produced an income of £400 a year. It was just sufficient to meet my modest expenses but gave me not a penny to spare.

What might be the consequences of this reckless outburst of mine? The failure of this observatory scheme might throw the Society into debt to the tune of £2,000! The loss of so much of my money would mean the end of my present home—the end of my cherished poultry farm. It was more than I could bring myself to think of. I sat in my chair, the hero of the evening, but limp, bewildered, and helpless, applause ringing in my ears. I could not

THE HOPKINS MANUSCRIPT

draw back now if I were to retain a vestige of pride and respect amongst these men around me.

I heard, as through a disordered dream, the voice of our President, thanking me for my generous guarantee; I heard him put the scheme before the meeting and I saw a sea of hands lifted in favour of it. The scheme was carried by forty-seven votes to nine.

How I summoned the strength to walk to the anteroom I do not know. I vaguely remember someone handing me a cup of coffee and biting a sandwich which seemed like dry cotton wool in my mouth when I tried to swallow it. I remember my hand being shaken—I remember smiling faces and words of praise.

And as I went out into the night to catch my train, my teeth were chattering in impotent misery.

The scheme was put in hand without delay, and it was as if an evil spirit had cursed its progress.

Everything seemed to go wrong. It was not until the Committee had purchased a seven-year lease that the borough architect inspected the premises and pronounced the roof unsafe in its present condition for an observatory.

The Committee was ordered to strengthen the roof at the additional cost of £217. Hardly had the shock of this blow abated before the telescope makers announced an increase of 10 percent upon the telescope and instruments owing to the rise in the cost of materials.

I was not upon the Committee at this time, although I was assured that my generosity would gain me a seat at the next election. I therefore only heard what was happening through my old friend Dr. Perceval.

My enemies—the opponents of the telescope—naturally heard of these troubles and did not conceal their malicious pleasure at our monthly meetings, but one evening Dr. Perceval told me in confidence that the Committee was struggling bravely against its difficulties and was doing its utmost to achieve success without calling upon my financial support. He told me that if the scheme failed a General Meeting would be called and that I could consider no news as good news.

How I prayed that the scheme would overcome all troubles and succeed! Not only for the sake of my own fortune and my own future, but for the sake of the triumph over my enemies!

How I would smile upon those fools at the brilliant opening ceremony! How I would chuckle as the British Lunar Society went from strength to strength as a result of its splendid observatory—the result of my courage and the generosity that despite my opponents had not been called upon!

Every day that passed meant greater assurance that the scheme was succeeding, and during that summer I achieved a serenity of spirit and happiness that I had never known before. I felt the joy of a gambler whose gamble had succeeded—the joy of being a man of courage—the satisfaction of feeling that my friends believed me to be a very wealthy man. . . .

And now, like a bolt from the blue twilit sky of that autumn evening, had come this fateful letter.

"We shall call a General Meeting if the scheme fails." Dr. Perceval's words beat upon my ears like totem drums as I sat in the arbour upon the hillside of my garden.

What else could the letter mean? Private—Confidential—Matters of the highest importance.

For the last time I seemed to see my beloved poultry farm as my own: that deep-green meadow and those olive, aged yews. I could scarcely look at my home as I walked up the hillside with a heart of lead. That little house, no longer mine, was so beautiful, so infinitely friendly in the twilight that a glance at it would have been insufferable.

I had no appetite for the excellent sole and cheese soufflé prepared for me by Mrs. Buller, my housekeeper. After toying with the food I went into my library and mechanically picked up a new book that I had so eagerly received that morning—*The Craters of the Moon* by Professor Herman Parker of Harvard. I opened it, then flung it aside with repulsion. I strode to the window and wrenched the curtains together to conceal the thin, silver crescent that was rising placidly and smugly above the meadows. I loathed the moon: it was the cause of my ruin. I hated the moon and everything to do with it.

I heard the gloating laughter of my enemies: I heard the tap of the auctioneer's hammer—knocking down my poultry at pitiful prices. For a moment I thought of running away—absenting myself from the hateful meeting on the 8th October—but even as the thought came I knew that it was unworthy of me. I determined to attend and face the consequences. Better to be a pauper and keep my honour than live with my money in shame.

I went to bed, and saw the dawn come without closing my eyes.

CHAPTER TWO

The reader can well conceive the misery I suffered during those weeks of suspense before the fateful Meeting.

One morning, no longer able to bear the cruel uncertainty, I telephoned to Humphrey Tugwall, the Secretary of the Society, and asked him to tell me in the strictest confidence the nature of the meeting.

Tugwall replied curtly that the matter could not be discussed and cut me off with an abruptness that told its own story.

For the next ten days I was drenched in a gloom that nothing could dissipate. On the 7th October, my hen Broodie won the Egg Laying Contest for two-year-olds at Little Bramble Poultry Fair, but the triumph was a hollow mockery. I received the diploma from the Hon. Mrs. McNaughton and accepted the Challenge Egg Cup with a smile that needed all my courage to produce. I expect those country bumpkins in the audience attributed my pale face and haggard eyes to the drawn-out anxiety inevitable to a poultry owner during an egg-laying contest. How little they suspected the truth!—How little they knew that upon the morrow, in the great

City of London, I was to face a hundred men of science and receive my dreadful sentence—to be stripped of my small fortune as a disgraced officer is stripped of his sword.

The horrible part of it was that I had no idea—no conception of the sum that I should be forced to pay. Too late I realised that I might at least have compromised by limiting the extent of my guarantee. I had failed to do so, and a hundred tragic possibilities loomed like spectres before my sleepless eyes on that last night before the meeting.

Supposing the Committee had become involved in some hideous lawsuit? Supposing, in the course of altering that building for the observatory, the roof had collapsed, killing men beneath and causing untold damage? The liability of the Committee was my liability: I visualised claims running into thousands, and a sickening twist of my brain suddenly presented an even more terrible fate than financial ruin. If my whole fortune failed to meet the heavy claims I might be convicted of false pretences and imprisoned, for fifty honest witnesses could be brought forward to prove that I had guaranteed the Society's losses without limit!

The loss of my fortune seemed now a little thing compared with this new, ghastly possibility. I think I was near to madness upon that awful night. I truly believe that I should have lost my reason had nature not stepped in to give me a few hours of restless stupor.

So dawned that Thursday: that fateful day of 8th October—the day that was to end everything of tranquillity and happiness that life had given me.

It was a lovely autumn morning, filled with a pale, crisp sunlight. Frost sparkled the meadows and rimed the hedgerows as I dragged my weary limbs down the hillside to feed my pullets.

Now that the day of the meeting was upon me I felt a curious repose—a philosophy that gently dethroned my worldly troubles and prepared me to face my fate with dignity.

To retain my peace of mind I clipped the yew trees of my arbour, although within my heart I no longer thought of those sturdy trees as mine. At midday I returned to the house. I dressed myself with care in the blue suit which I kept for business occasions, ate a light lunch of sweetbreads and braised celery, and walked to the station to catch the 2:14.

As the train ran through the familiar, sunlit countryside, I recalled many a happy journey to past meetings of the British Lunar Society and sadly reflected that this might be my last. If, as I now felt certain, the observatory scheme had failed, I knew that I could never again face those jeering men who would say: "I told you so." I recalled hot summer evenings with the Society's windows wide to a twilit sky and the drowsy hum of traffic floating up to us—and evenings when the big fire blazed behind the President's table and I had trudged home through the snow—happy evenings that would never come again.

I was too restless to make my usual visit to a cinema theatre when I arrived in London. I walked up Regent Street and along Oxford Street, blind to the happy, home-going crowds of London workers. Although the night was cold I sat for a while upon a seat in Hyde Park, hunched grimly in my greatcoat, counting the minutes that hung like lead.

Towards six o'clock I began to make my way towards our head-quarters in Barbara Street. I had no desire to arrive too early and stand through an agony of suspense in the anteroom. I peered aimlessly into shop windows, timing myself to arrive at the doors at five minutes to six. I passed an old ragged man selling matches: I saw a little bunch of raw, shivering fingers protruding from a ragged mitten—and shuddered. In a little while, I, too, might be penniless and homeless.

But as I came within sight of our doorway I saw something that diverted my attention and stirred my anger. For who should be advancing from the opposite direction but Mr. Winchelsea, a clever but mean little science master from a school at Hornsey who had been one of the most spiteful opponents of the observatory scheme, and who had been foremost in tormenting me with idiotic jokes about "my telescope" at the past few meetings.

My first impulse was to turn upon my heel and pointedly walk away until he had gone in, but second thoughts urged me to show restraint and unconcern. I walked steadily forward and we entered almost together. In fact, he waited for me and, to my great surprise, instead of giving me the malicious grin I had expected he nodded with a grave face, and said: "Good evening, Mr. Hopkins. Keeping well?"

I was puzzled, but replied courteously and walked up the narrow steps beside him.

He said nothing until we had reached the floor beneath our lecture room, and then suddenly he turned his face towards me.

Beneath the pale, unshaded lamp upon the landing I looked into the most haunted, piteous eyes that I have ever seen.

And when he spoke, his voice was high-pitched, almost hysterical. "It isn't true, is it?" he cried. "I mean—it's only a silly mistake?—it must be—it's impossible! I . . . I mean, the greatest astronomers make absurd miscalculations, don't they? DON'T THEY! . . ."

I was astounded. His last words came almost in a scream. Winchelsea, the one man above all others who should be gloating and chortling at the collapse of the telescope scheme, was actually trembling, and nearly hysterical with anxiety!

My first reaction gave me a gleam of respect for the man. It occurred to me that in his heart of hearts Winchelsea had longed for the success of the scheme as sincerely as I, and had only opposed it out of jealousy for my fighting speech.

But second thoughts made me sick with a new twist of horror. Supposing the scheme had collapsed even more tragically than I had anticipated? Supposing the Committee had by some means assessed my poor little fortune and realised that it was so far short of covering the loss that other members must sacrifice their savings, too? I nearly fainted at the sight of Winchelsea's thin, tragic face. He was a poor, struggling schoolmaster with a large family: every spare penny was needed for his children's well-being. In that dark moment I saw myself not merely ruined financially, but ruined in character—the man whose reckless promise had dragged others to poverty and tragedy.

I saw myself, not merely the poor match-seller with the frozen, quivering fingers, but a convict in penal servitude with the ruin of my friends upon my conscience.

The reader may feel that I was taking an absurd, exaggerated view of my misfortune, but every normal, honest man will sympathise when he calls to mind how some trivial misfortune, such as a minor motoring offence, has preyed upon his mind until it has enlarged itself to tragedy.

I think it was the jovial voice of my old friend Dr. Perceval, who had overtaken me on the stairs, that forced me to take a grip upon myself.

With a hearty clap upon my shoulder he cried out: "Hullo, old boy, how are the chickens?"

I stuttered a grateful reply, but I noticed that even the old doctor's face was unusually grave and careworn as we ascended the last steps towards our lecture room.

My heart went out towards the old man as I walked beside him. Here at least was a stout friend who would stand by me and defend me. Here, too, was a man from whom I could at least secure some inkling of what lay in store for me. . . .

I took him by the arm and drew him into the alcove at the head of the stairs.

"Perceval," I said. "You're on the Committee. Tell me the truth! Is it . . . is it very bad?"

The smile left his face and he answered with a curtness that I had never received from the genial old man before.

"How did you know?" he demanded.

I was angry. "I imagine I've a right to know," I snapped. He looked at me keenly and his eyes softened.

"Of course you've a right. Every member has a right." He paused, then spoke with his eyes upon the moonlit window behind my head. "It is bad. The President will tell you everything—but it's better to face it than stick our heads into the sand."

This gave me very little comfort, and as I miserably followed the doctor into that big, familiar lecture room I felt at once a subtle difference from anything that I had known in that room before.

At other times you would have heard the high-spirited ring of conversation before you were halfway up the stairs—the jovial laughter and greetings of old friends. At other times not more than half the members, about 50 of us, would meet—but tonight I think every member was present, every one of the 109 of us, and although the room was filled there was something uncanny in its quietness.

Usually we entered freely, bringing our friends if we so desired. Tonight, for the first time in my experience, Humphrey Tugwall, our Secretary, stood beside the door and requested us to show our cards of membership. He scrutinised each of us and ticked our names upon a members' list before we were permitted to enter.

Instead of the carefree ebb and flow around the room, members were gathered in groups together, talking almost in whispers.

The reader can well imagine what I suffered as the clock ticked off the minutes to the hour of six. I had never belonged to any group, or "clique" of members, and had always preferred to extend a general good-fellowship to all and sundry. Never in the past had I found myself in want of someone to talk to during this interval between my arrival and the hour of our meeting: but tonight I felt like a leper. I was utterly ignored: utterly alone.

I approached a group in which Walter Archer, whom I knew quite well, was standing. I mastered my feelings and with a smile called out a cheery: "Hullo, Archer!—how goes it?" The man did not even reply—he seemed to look right through me—he did not even grant me a nod of recognition, and I saw that his head was twisted in an endeavour to hear what a doddering old professor was mumbling to a little ring of members.

I went from group to group with the same result: an impulse came to stride out into the night and leave them to their troubles, for they were putting me upon the rack—torturing me before my trial.

But I knew that I must face it like a man. I determined that I, who had the most to suffer and the most to lose, should appear the calmest of them all. I strolled to the window and nonchalantly lit a cigarette, but nobody seemed to notice this gesture of defiance.

The street beneath me was almost deserted in the oasis that lies between the departure of the day's business and the arrival of the night's pleasure. A full moon, silver and aloof, rode above the rooftops of Drury Lane. I looked at its silly face and hated it again as the cause of all my trouble and despair.

After an eternity—with unspeakable relief, I heard the clock strike six. I crushed out my cigarette and turned towards the room

27

to witness the time-honoured little ceremony that preceded our meetings.

From the private office of the Secretary came three brisk knocks. This was a warning to members to be seated. After the space of a minute, during which members took their places, the door was thrown open and the Secretary appeared, calling out: "Gentlemen, the President!"

It was then the duty of members to rise and remain standing until the President had taken his place upon the platform. On nights when a visitor was speaking, the Secretary would also call out: "Gentlemen, give welcome to our guest!" and all would applaud heartily until the visiting speaker, in company with the President, had mounted the platform and prepared himself to speak.

It was a simple, amusing little ceremony of which we were quite proud, and we never failed to carry it through with meticulous attention to detail. Upon this night there was of course no visitor. The President entered alone, followed according to custom by the Committee who took reserved places in the front row.

Even in the Secretary's voice I caught the note of tension that had pervaded the whole room since I had entered it. By nature Humphrey Tugwall was a bluff, hearty man who played his part at meetings with gusto. But tonight he said: "Gentlemen, the President!" in a thin and hollow voice from lips that were pale and strained.

I began to wonder how much longer my mind could bear this torture—whether I should ever leave this gaunt, ghastly room in possession of my sanity. I had come prepared for an unpleasant meeting. As the member most responsible for the telescope scheme going forward—and in consequence most to blame for its tragic collapse and failure—I was prepared for members to act shyly and self-consciously towards me.

But never in my worst nightmares had I expected to be treated in this dreadful way—as if I were dirt—as if I did not exist.

It seemed wrong that I should even sit amongst my fellow members. I should be in the dock: nay, rather in the condemned cell—for already I knew myself to be condemned. Except for Dr. Perceval, not a soul had even smiled at me that night.

I had found a place between two members whom I had never seen before. I am sturdy rather than tall, and as we stood there I could not see the President as he walked to the platform. I heard in the silence of those standing members a shuffling of footsteps; then, as the Committee took their places and became still, the solitary tread of one man, the President, as he mounted the steps of the platform.

I judged that he was now beside the reading-table, for there was complete silence for a moment, broken then by the subdued rustle of members seating themselves.

I sat there, cold and limp, completely resigned to my fate. Upon my right, oozing slightly over the edge of his seat, was a large fat man who breathed rhythmically and ponderously through one nostril only—for the intake of air was audible and under great pressure. He folded his fat, warty hands across his waistcoat and began slowly to rotate his thumbs.

I could now see the President quite clearly. He was arranging a sheaf of notes upon the table: he adjusted the green-shaded lamp and glanced around the room.

I had an immense admiration for Professor Hartley. He was not a handsome man upon conventional standards, but his rugged face was full of character and power. I used to think of him as rather like Oliver Cromwell. I should judge that he was in his early fifties, for his wiry reddish hair was greying over the temples and the strong lines around his mouth were deepening with maturity of thought and responsibility. For the past five years he had held the Burnholm Chair of Astronomy at London University and he had done much to popularise the study of the heavens through his brilliant broadcast lectures.

I think the only calmness in the room at that moment lay in the grey pools of Professor Hartley's eyes. I caught one glimpse of the strained profiles around me—of the lines of rigid bodies sitting upright in their chairs.

The President glanced at us, and then over our heads. He bent forward and whispered to the Secretary who sat to his right, at the foot of the platform. The Secretary nodded, rose to his feet, and all eyes followed him as he went to the back of the room, to the door that led to the stairs.

Quietly he turned the key in the lock and pulled the green baize curtains carefully across the door to subdue any sound that might escape to the outside world.

There was something horrible—something irrevocable in the tiny grating of that key and the thin, metallic twitch of the curtain rings. Never before had I seen it done: not even at the memorable meeting when the telescope was first discussed. I felt trapped. I had no escape. I believe that I should have broken down and screamed if the President's calm voice had not come to me through the silence.

I remember that quiet, level voice as if it were speaking to me now from the black stillness of ruined London beneath me.

"Gentlemen," began the President. "The majority of you have guessed the purpose of this unusual meeting. I do not wish to dramatise what I have to say, but you must know that I speak tonight by the authority of the Prime Minister who binds one and all of us, upon our honour, to the most absolute secrecy. From the outset I must make it clear that not one detail of this evening's business must be divulged either by word of mouth, the written page, or by inference. If any member present desires not to accept these conditions, I would ask him to leave the meeting now, before anything further is said."

The President paused: there was a deathly silence: not a muscle of those hundred bodies moved. For my own part I could not have moved had I desired to. My body was paralysed, my brain was numbed by the appalling revelation that the disaster of the telescope and our observatory had become so serious that it was receiving the attention of the Prime Minister himself.

"Thank you," said Professor Hartley. "I am glad that every member of this Society is prepared to accept the responsibility that I am bound to place upon him."

He paused, and glanced down at his notes.

"Some of you," he proceeded, "by reasons of your professions, are more conversant than others with the facts, or—shall I say—the rumours that have been whispered in scientific circles during the past few months, but for the sake of all present here tonight I will relate these facts from the beginning.

"You will remember the eclipse of the sun on the 24th August 1940—just over five years ago. You will no doubt recall to mind the amusement aroused by the Press when it was announced that the moon was three seconds late in its arrival. There were some good-natured digs at the astronomers, who were told to go away and find out where their calculations had gone wrong.

"For several months the observatories of all nations tested their instruments and checked their calculations. In that December, at an International Congress held in Berlin, these results were compared and proved unanimous. The calculations were correct. It was not the scientists, but the moon that was wrong. In August 1940 the moon was travelling three seconds behind its time.

"The scientists were puzzled, but not unduly disturbed. It was agreed to delay public report until further observation could be made upon the eclipse of the 12th February this year.

"This eclipse was best observable from Mount Wilson Observatory in California, and the foremost scientists of the world gathered in conference upon this anxiously awaited occasion. Conditions were perfect and the finest equipment in the world was available.

"The result, gentlemen—the result beyond all regions of doubt—was that the moon was twelve seconds late. Not only was it late, but the cause—which had been suspected but hitherto unconfirmed—was definitely established.

"Some gigantic force had disturbed the moon from the path that it had pursued from the dawn of time: it had slowed up the moon's progress through space and forced it upon a journey towards the earth.

"At midnight on the 12th February this year the moon had drawn nearer to the earth by 3,583 miles."

"The Congress remained in session for five weeks and observation was made by all assembled scientists.

"It was ascertained that the moon was returning to the earth at the steadily increasing speed of 8 miles in every twenty-four hours. It was nearer by 128 miles on the 13th February—by 136 on the 14th—by 144 on the 15th.

"The moon, as you are aware, was normally, at its maximum, 250,000 miles from the earth. Tonight, at midnight, it is 217,500 miles away; tomorrow night it will be 470 miles nearer, and each night it is drawing closer at a speed increasing by 8 miles per day.

"The Congress at Mount Wilson Observatory broke up on the 15th March. It was decided unanimously to keep its proceedings a strict secret until the governments of the world had been consulted.

"As a great deal of public curiosity had been excited, the Congress issued the report which you may still remember: a report that announced everything to be normal and that the moon was in its correct position. It was a deliberate lie—but a lie for the sake of humanity, as I think you will all agree.

"When the results of the Congress were placed before the responsible governments of the world, the decision of the statesmen in favour of secrecy was as unanimous as that of the scientists. A conference was held at Paris upon the 3rd May this year and a definite course of action agreed upon.

"It was recognised by all that the publication of what could only mean the destruction of the world would lead to a condition of affairs too horrible to contemplate. The number of people in the world with the strength of character to accept the news with calmness and philosophy would be in the minority, and the last months of human existence would become a welter of anarchy, debauchery, and famine. It was of vital importance to keep the truth a secret until the last possible moment and only then to publish the facts by means best calculated to allay panic.

"An International Committee of Control was established. Each government held a secret conference at which the leading men of science, politics, church, and press were told the truth and bound by oath to secrecy.

"It is calculated that the change in the moon's course will not be discernible to the human eye until February or March of the coming year.

"When it becomes impossible to conceal what the public will obviously discover with its naked eyes, the newspapers will take action upon lines universally agreed upon. They will announce that the apparent increase in the size of the moon is due to a phenomenon—a refraction of light that gives an illusion of greater size.

"It will then be for the church to play its part, for by no other means can the truth be told with more hope of arousing the courage and assuring the calmness necessary to save the world from agony."

"That, gentlemen, is all. I realise that those who are hearing these facts for the first time must feel as I did a week ago when I heard them from the President of the Royal Society. I wondered whether I were in a nightmare or whether I had lost my senses. I have tried to place the truth before you plainly—but I realise that words are incongruous—an absurd little jumble of sounds in the face of the facts which they have tried to explain.

"It is recognised that the time has now come to bring all men of standing and knowledge in the scientific world within this 'conspiracy of silence.' It is your duty not only to keep these facts secret to yourselves: if rumour gets abroad it is your duty to deny it. You are men whose word upon such matters will be believed and even if you are forced to lie, you will do so as part of your duty to preserve the peace and happiness of the world to the last possible moment.

"When my own courage began to fail me upon first hearing the news, I regained it through the knowledge that I was a privileged man—one of an infinite few to be trusted as you are tonight.

"I am afraid it sounds a little incongruous to revert after this to normal procedure, but the meeting is now open to questions, and I shall answer them to the best of my ability."

*   *   *

The President was silent. He glanced for a moment, half-questioningly, at the audience, then sipped from the glass of water beside him and took his seat in the big armchair behind the speaker's table.

The reader can well imagine how my surprise at the President's first words had gradually changed to unspeakable relief as he had proceeded. Slowly it dawned upon me that this meeting had nothing whatever to do with the telescope. The telescope was not even mentioned, so apparently everything was going on all right. There was every hope now that the Committee had surmounted its financial difficulties. Instead of being a ruined man I would be, after all my fears—the hero—the man whose fighting speech had turned the day! In my fevered imagination I had already given up my small fortune and all my personal property as lost by a reckless promise, and now in one glorious moment of relief it was all returned to me!—my beloved home on the Hampshire hills—my poultry—my careful investments—everything!

It can readily be understood how this torment of mind and sudden, unexpected relief had blurred for the moment the significance of what the President had been talking about. I could scarcely be expected to care what happened to the moon so long as my fortune was saved and my enterprise vindicated.

It was not until the President had taken his seat that I began to realise the significance of this new turn in affairs. If the moon returned to the earth, or disappeared into space, the telescope would be a pure waste of money. It was just the kind of thing that would happen, I bitterly reflected. How was I to have known that by the time the telescope was delivered by the makers, there would be no moon to look at? It was scant consolation to tell myself that this was a pardonable miscalculation that even the biggest astronomer might make.

I was upon the point of rising to ask the President what the Committee was going to do about the telescope when my attention was attracted by something that was happening around me.

It was as if a monkey wrench had been thrown suddenly into the wheels of time. Time had stopped dead, and every one of those men around me sat as if embalmed for all eternity. There was not a sound. The fat man beside me had apparently ceased to breathe, for the whistling intake and exhalation through his effective nostril had died away. I stared at the pallid, rigid profiles around me, and it seemed as if death had already brushed its fingers across those stark cheekbones.

And in that icy silence the terrible meaning of it all crashed into my brain and sent it reeling for support.

Many a time, in moments of morbid reflection, I had pictured this mighty, uncontrollable earth of ours plunging through space like a great liner ploughing at full speed through the dense fog of an iceberg-ridden sea. Always I had shuddered away from the thought of a ghastly collision with some dead, roaming world and applied my mind to healthier things.

And now—if this were true—if this meeting and these words from the President were not the twisted ravings of a nightmare, the horror was in fact staring us in the face.

A mighty mass of dead, ice-cold rock—two thousand miles in thickness and two thousand million tons in weight—was plunging towards us through the night.

No one could stop it. Death was facing us, and something worse than death. For always I had believed that when I died, the unquenched vitality of my body would mingle with the reservoir of life-giving power that lay within our atmosphere—to be used again and again to give animation, intelligence, and happiness to living creatures forever. My body would die but my life would survive, and now the horror that was approaching us would blast the earth to fragments. It would not only destroy our flesh and bones but would swirl this glorious life-power into the blackness of eternity.

The lecture room, with its tawdry, glaring lights—the President resting in his chair—that audience of rigid bodies—all become unreal and hollow—a cheap tin toy that tapped against my brain and set my teeth on edge.

Out of the silence came a tiny voice: the distant, quivering voice of Humphrey Tugwall, our Secretary. He rose to his feet and I stared at him. I knew his face, but I could not remember his name—nor his purpose in life.

"The President will answer any questions," said the voice.

And then, without warning, came the incident which I think restored to all of us the knowledge that we were facing reality. And indirectly it restored to us our courage and control.

A small, sharp-featured man with dead-white face and mop of black, dusty hair, sprang up from the back of the room and began to shout in an almost incoherent voice. Out of the babble of cascading words I caught remnants of coherency:

"It's all this damn monkeying that's done it," he yelled. "All this damn monkeying with wireless and television and radio and aircraft rays!—I said it would!—you can't monkey with things eternal and get away with it!—all this bloody monkeying with—"

The President had risen. He had taken up the small ebony mallet that lay beside him: he tapped sharply upon the table and the hysterical little man collapsed with a strangled sigh. There was something symbolic and exalting in those three sharp knocks upon the table: the first skirmish of reasoning courage against panic and disruption: courage won and panic collapsed.

"Questions were invited," said the President. "No good can be served by useless proclamations. I would ask members not to speak too loudly: the walls are thin and a women's welfare club is meeting next door."

There were murmurs of approval—even a ripple of laughter—and with it the tension snapped.

It eased rather than snapped, for the action of one of our number in rising and making an exhibition of himself did us all a power of good. It had been another man and not ourselves who had shown himself the coward. The terror of that little black-haired man had made the rest of us brave.

There came the rustling of a hundred bodies relaxing in their chairs. Someone lit a cigarette: someone cleared his throat, and a soft whistling beside me showed that my neighbour's unobstructed nostril was at work again.

And then, as if further to bring us back to sanity, came the clear, jovial voice of Dr. Perceval. He stood up, jingled a few coins in his pocket, and spoke as if he were opening a discussion upon the Butterflies of England.

"I am sure that I voice the feelings of all members of this society when I tell Professor Hartley how much we have admired his courage, and his ability in placing this matter before us so clearly and calmly." He raised his head and spoke directly to the President. "You have given us, sir, a fine example, and I hope we shall prove worthy of it."

Professor Hartley inclined his head in acknowledgement: there were some subdued "Hear! hear's!" and a little applause that died away directly Dr. Perceval spoke again.

"I would like to ask the President a question. It may be a futile question, but I think it is one that lies in the minds of all of us.

"To what extent can the President give us hope? What hope is there of the earth surviving? What hope is there of life surviving? I realise that hope under such conditions is not easy to discover—but even in the gravest peril there must be a loophole for it."

The President rose from his chair.

"Thank you, Dr. Perceval," he said. "I expected that question, naturally. I did not refer to this in my speech because I felt it better to confine myself to fact and leave theory and conjecture to discussion."

Without conscious intention Professor Hartley gave proof that this question was expected by drawing towards him some notes which he had not yet consulted. He glanced down at them and proceeded.

"Science, as you may well guess, is divided upon the question whether the earth can survive this concussion, and if so, whether life in any form can survive. There are those that believe that the explosion and destruction of the earth is inevitable. This I might describe as the 'official' view. The earth, as you know, is no more than a stout crust that encases a furnace of molten rock. It is generally believed that the impact of the moon will split the earth to such an extent and to such a depth that this subterranean furnace will explode and blow the cool outer crust of the earth into fragments. Or it may burst from the ruptures in the earth's surface in the form of great ridges of volcano. Upon this theory, the earth may become as it was in the beginning: a ball of fire that in the course of eternity will once again form a crust upon which life will begin afresh.

"Another school of thought led by the great German scientist Franz Mulhause believes that the moon may strike the earth a glancing blow and ricochet, as it were, into space again—once more becoming a satellite of the earth or vanishing altogether into the limitless spaces of the universe. This view is based upon the theory that the moon is not being drawn back to the earth by magnetic power: that the moon, for reasons unknown, has been forced from its normal path and is not necessarily bound to strike the earth a fatal blow. This theory may sound fantastic, but we are facing fantastic problems.

"If this 'glancing blow' occurs, the chances of survival of life upon the earth are dependent upon the severity of the impact. If it is no more than a slight 'graze,' then we may reasonably hope that life, even some fragment of human life, might survive.

"A development of this 'grazing theory' is that the impact of the moon against the earth's surface may force the earth itself out of the path that it has followed from the dawn of time. In this case it is obvious that one of two things must happen. We shall either travel towards the sun or away from it. If we travel towards the sun we shall no doubt be drawn into it and become part of the great furnace which we have enjoyed so frequently from a comfortable distance. If we travel away from it, then we shall suffer a period of darkness and cold until possibly we may join up with another of the many millions of suns in the universe, become its satellite, and life may start from the beginning once again."

"Thank you, sir," said Dr. Perceval. The old man struck a match and the silence was broken by the gentle popping of his lips as he drew at his pipe.

A tall, stooping man, whose name I think was Wilkins (although I cannot be quite sure), rose from his seat near the door.

"If the best happens, and the earth receives such a slight graze that its crust remains unbroken, can the President give us any indication of its effect upon the atmosphere—the tides of the sea, etc.?"

"We cannot predict that with the remotest hope of certainty," replied the President. "But we can assume that the shock would displace the earth but not its atmosphere. Crudely stated, the earth would be jolted out of the skin of air that loosely surrounds it—but that skin would return and settle evenly around the earth again. We should suffer tornado and flood upon two sides of the earth as it slides out of its atmosphere, and a temporary disappearance of air upon the other sides. But I repeat that everything would depend upon the nature of the impact."

To my surprise I saw my stout neighbour rise to speak.

He had appeared so completely stagnant and devoid of intelligence that I had not believed him capable of understanding a word of what was going on. But when he spoke his features suddenly became alert and mobile, and his voice was deep and cultured.

"Mr. President," he said. "I agree—I am sure we all agree—upon the wisdom of keeping this matter within the knowledge of a selected few. But you spoke of a faint hope of survival.

"Cannot something be done—even if only to increase this hope by a tiny fraction?

"I am thinking of dugouts. It may seem ludicrous to suggest such a puny endeavour, but assuming this 'graze' to be so slight as to permit the earth to survive, would it not be worth constructing very deep dugouts, reinforced with steel and concrete, supplied with oxygen and other necessities of life for several days while conditions upon the earth's surface may possibly return to normal?"

When the President rose to reply there was a slight smile upon his face—the first smile that I had witnessed in the whole of that strange meeting.

"I am glad to speak of something constructive and hopeful after so much gloom. I am glad to say that this suggestion has already been put into action with the greatest energy. The engineering corps of all armies are at work upon subterranean strongholds, built with the utmost strength and fitted with every possible protection against shock, flood, and lack of air. The positions of these strongholds have been selected with scientific care and they are being built in secret. The officers and men employed believe the dugouts to be against air raid and gas attack from foreign powers.

The number of people to be protected in this way cannot be more than the smallest proportion of our population, and the selection will of course rest with the Government."

A few other questions were put and answered, but I do not remember them as being of much importance. A fat man with a grating voice began a rambling speech to the effect that the Government must not be allowed to take political advantage of the dugouts by leaving all persons of socialist leanings outside. He went on to suggest that no person who believed in otter hunting should be allowed in the dugouts, but the President pulled him up sharply and asked if any further questions were desired.

Somebody wanted to know whether the approach of the moon had anything to do with the strange colour of the sunsets that we had recently observed, but the President was unable to give a definite reply. I began to notice an increasing restlessness in the audience, as if the strain of the meeting was bringing a reaction that cried for movement and freedom. The President announced that the Society would meet in two weeks' time, instead of the normal month, and that he would then report anything further that had been imparted to him through official channels. It was just after seven when he closed the meeting, and I think that the adjournment for coffee and cakes in the anteroom was the weirdest experience of my life.

I suppose we were all affected, far more deeply than we realised, by an intense, overpowering reaction. Or possibly it was the result of the President's reply to the last question of the evening when he had stated that, upon present indications, the moon would strike the earth upon the evening of the 3rd May at about eight o'clock.

The 3rd of May! Seven months ahead! One and all of us, I think, experienced the exultant, irrational joy of a man condemned to die at dawn, who learns at the last hour that his execution has been postponed for seven months. In the course of those first calm, terrible words of Professor Hartley's every one of us had felt the awful imminence of death, and in that last reply had come the sweet breath of postponement. The fact that this would only mean seven months of agonising suspense occurred to none of us in our utterly unbalanced condition of mind.

Whatever the reason, I only know that, as we rose and pushed back those hard wooden chairs and trooped into the refreshment room, a low murmur began—a murmur that was pierced by a sudden laugh—a sudden babble and buoyancy of spirit that gave every appearance of intense well-being and happiness.

You would not have recognised those pale, drawn faces and haggard eyes of ten minutes ago. There came the familiar rattle of the shutter that ran up to reveal Mrs. Ayling behind the big brass coffee urn in the recess that was called "The Bar." True to tradition the Committee gathered around to pass out the coffee and plates of sandwiches and buttered scones. There was a great deal of laughter over the fact that there were not enough coffee-cups to go round—our economical Committee having failed to visualise the possibility of every member turning up at the same meeting!

A member shouted out: "What about a vote of censure upon the Committee!" and there was such a shout of laughter that you would have thought the best joke of the century had been made!

I believe what really gave us this extraordinary feeling of bravado was the self-esteem that every one of us was conscious of. We were amongst the chosen few: we were members of a little band of intelligent men who alone amongst millions had been entrusted with this unearthly, awe-inspiring secret.

It may seem a little childish, but I think all of us began to show off deliberately before the unknowing Mrs. Ayling as she kept twisting and untwisting the tap of the coffee urn. Here before us was the first member of that mighty, ignorant public that did not share, and must not share, our secret.

I observed one member, with an eye upon the old lady, talking loudly and elaborately about the chess tournament at Hastings—another held forth upon the coarse flavour of American tomatoes, and another upon yesterday's fog. I am sure that all our conversation was a lot further away from the moon than the moon, at that moment, was away from us.

For my own part I was conscious of an indescribable joy. The telescope scheme had not collapsed into financial chaos. It had not even been mentioned and my fortune and prestige were untouched. I found myself telling a complete stranger that the chicken in the sandwiches had come from my estate—my estate!—still mine! For no particular reason the man threw back his head and laughed with such abandon that he revealed his plate of false teeth in greater detail than he had probably ever done to any living person except his dentist. But now and then a little shaft of terror shot through the glow of my exultation—as a man drunk with champagne might feel for a second a drink-dulled abscess in his cheek. For a fleeting second I realised that my friend's false teeth would look very much the same as the pupils of my eyes when they all revolved together as the dust of a destroyed world. There was something macabre about this babble—a dance of death. I shuddered, gulped some scalding coffee, swallowed a piece of buttered scone, and laughed out loud although nobody had said anything to me. Nobody noticed. It seemed quite normal and I felt in no way embarrassed.

Finding myself beside Humphrey Tugwall, our Secretary, I took the opportunity of enquiring how the new telescope and observatory were getting on. He said: "Swimmingly!—swimmingly!" and pushed through the crowd with an imbecile smile fixed on a top corner of the room.

Everybody squeezed about in the crowded space as if the friction of jostling shoulders struck new sparks of courage. Eight o'clock chimed but not a man gave sign of leaving. Generally by eight o'clock the refreshment room was deserted, everyone having hurried away for home, but it seemed this evening as if none of us desired to break the queer spell of herd-like courage. None of us desired to be the first to go down those steep, narrow steps into a world made strange and lonely to us through the secret that we must not share with it.

The coffee urn was empty and Mrs. Ayling, bewildered beyond doubt by the unusual demand, stood behind her bar, shaking her head as members squeezed up and presented their cups for more. But although there had been a fierce demand for coffee I noticed several plates of untouched, neglected cakes—principally of the puffy, "éclair" type that need calmness and deliberation in their consumption.

And then at last came a sudden dropping away of the staccato sound of voices: it turned into a drone that reminded me of a gramophone record running down: it revealed with brutal clearness how artificial it all had been.

The reason for this sudden change was the appearance of the President from the committee-room in his hat, smartly tied silk muffler, and overcoat. He gave me a friendly smile as he passed me, and at the door he turned and waved a gay farewell.

"Goodnight, gentlemen!—until Thursday week!"

There was a chorus of farewell that expressed the depth of our feeling for the calm, courteous man who had set us such a fine example. There was a moment of embarrassed silence: a few members attempted to revive the conversation and gaiety, but the falseness of it was too pitiful for words. We fell back to a cold bedrock of silence and began to gather up our hats and coats.

In the cloakroom I noticed a new and quite unusual regard for one another. Normally we would all jostle in, and if another hat were dislodged with ours we would not always feel obliged to pick it up. Tonight all kept saying: "After you. No—no! You first!" Everybody helped each other to find umbrellas and complete strangers helped each other on with their coats. I liked this unconscious friendliness far more than the unhealthy heartiness of the coffee-and-cakes period. There was something genuine about it: a tiny signpost towards the nobility that springs from a common peril.

At the street door a member asked which way I was going, and when I said, "To Waterloo," he offered me a lift although his route lay north. I thanked him but declined, for now that it was over I wanted to be alone. Had I realised the desolate solitude I was to feel in those crowded London streets I should have accepted the offered lift to secure for a few moments longer the fellowship of one who shared the Secret.

I was bewildered by the blaze of traffic and the surge of people. It was just upon eight-thirty and the theatre rush was at its height. As I stood watching those hurrying, smartly dressed people, I could not resist a smile. How colossally important was this trivial little round of amusement to a world of unsuspecting, ignorant people: how different they would be if they knew what I knew!

A young man paused beside me with an attractive fair-haired girl upon his arm. As they stood waiting for the traffic to allow them to cross the road, the young man glanced up at the clear black sky, then down at his companion with a smile.

"Gorgeous night," he said. "Hunter's Moon."

Suddenly I had a horrible impulse to laugh: to take him by the arm and say: "Yes!—it is hunting the earth!—and the kill will be in the fields of eternity!"

It was upon the tip of my tongue to say it, and only with an effort could I choke myself to silence. I, a tiny speck of humanity, had it in my power to evoke a world panic! I struggled with a devilish temptation to become at one stroke a figure famous in history as the man who told the world of its impending fate!

But my better feelings took possession of me: I remembered my solemn vow: I suffered the young man and his fair companion to pass on to their fool's paradise and took the steep road down to Hungerford Bridge.

The bridge was almost deserted at this hour. The city workers had long since crossed and taken their trains for home. Halfway over I paused in an alcove above one of the buttresses and stood for a long while gazing at that lovely, moonlit panorama of London with the sullen river oiling its silent way to the sea.

The great sweep of lights upon the Embankment gave enchantment to the dark, ghostly buildings that loomed above the fringing trees: the sounds of traffic were lulled to a sleepy murmur, and the foot taps of the little ant-like stream of people were muffled by the distance.

I looked up at the moon. Its stupid, placid face was cocked to one side in an expression of mild desire. There was no menace in it: no hint of the awful thing that was to happen in the spring of the coming year. The 3rd of May!—I pictured my meadow spangled with spring flowers—I saw them dancing in the wind—a great ear-splitting roar—and eternal darkness.

I gripped the parapet of the bridge, for my whole body was quivering. Seven months of waiting!—too ghastly for the human brain to bear! I looked down at the river—at the silver beam that sparkled and danced across it towards the setting moon. There was no one in sight: it would be an easy thing to slip over into that friendly river. I had paddled too often along its friendly stream—picnicked too often in its quiet backwaters to be afraid of it. I would go swirling up that moonlit path: I would challenge the moon by going up to meet it!

I would be hurting no one. Mrs. Buller, my housekeeper, would wonder for a bit and tell the police, and my uncle at Notting Hill would inherit my little fortune. No one would grieve my loss, and I would save myself the aching terror of seven months of living death. I had all but made up my mind: I was about to climb onto the parapet when by chance I turned my head and saw through the girders of the railway bridge the great floodlit face of Big Ben. Slowly it began to strike the hour of nine, and as its deep note floated down the river I saw the big shadow-haunted building beneath it—I saw the Members of the House of Commons—all sharers of the Secret—all calmly carrying on the business of State without a flicker of hesitation.

I was ashamed—then proud. Ashamed that I should think of leaving those others to bear the awful burden: proud that I was numbered amongst the select and trusted few. I pictured the Prime Minister of England, planning the great subterranean strongholds to salvage a drop or two of British blood to build the Empire again. The Prime Minister!—and me! We knew—while untold millions were ignorant!

With a surge of renewed pride I strode across the bridge and was just in time to catch the 9:18. I had felt no desire for my usual little dinner in Soho, and the 9:18 was, on the whole, a better train than the 9:52. It did not stop at Basingstoke, where frequently the 9:52 had a tedious delay to take off empty milkcans.

I was lucky to secure a compartment to myself, and settled down to read the latest number of the *Poultry Times*.

I was very pleased indeed to find an authoritative article recommending at last the tubular metal perches that I had advocated so persistently for the past seven years. It is my firm conviction that a hen's laying capacity is undermined by long hours of sleep upon a cold perch.

By a simple device of a small, inexpensive boiler it is possible to keep a steady flow of warm water through these metal perches. This not only warms the feet of the fowl and prevents loss of vitality, but my experiments have proved that the fowl sleeps longer and more soundly—awakes refreshed and full of strength and lays, within ten to twenty minutes of rising, an egg of far greater quality than one generated under vitality-lowering conditions.

I advocated this in a long letter to the *Mulcaster Wednesday Echo*. The letter was published, but the only result was a ribald and indecent reply (which the Editor should never have published) suggesting that hot chicken perches would cause the eggs to hatch inside the hens, causing them unnecessary embarrassment and discomfort.

I never took the *Echo* again—and now here before me, in no less a paper than the *Poultry Times*, was my own idea, smugly presented under the pseudonym of "Ego."

It only went to prove the unspeakable meanness and dishonesty into which a man can be led by professional jealousy.

CHAPTER THREE

I am very much a creature of habit. It was my invariable custom to say: "Good morning, Mrs. Buller," when my housekeeper brought my tea at eight o'clock—and "Thank you" as she placed the morning newspapers upon the counterpane beside me.

It was a simple little ritual, so deeply engraved by years of habit that frequently I spoke the words in my sleep. I know this to be a fact, because upon apologising to Mrs. Buller one morning at breakfast for not acknowledging my early cup of tea she assured me that I had said "Good morning" and then "Thank you" just as usual, although my eyes had been closed.

But if ever that habit was broken it was upon the morning after the fantastic meeting of the British Lunar Society. So drugged was I by the deep, unwholesome slumber which had come to me at dawn that the first sound to penetrate my bemused brain was the clock in Beadle Church tower striking nine, and the first sight to greet my aching eyes was a stone-cold cup of tea on my bedside table with an unappetising pink-brown scum upon it.

Even so I could not move. One leg of my pyjamas, grim token of a restless night, was rucked tightly above my knee, but I had neither the energy nor the inclination to adjust it. Vaguely I knew that something had happened, but I was far too tired to reason what it was.

I think that my uppermost, conscious mind was trying hard to persuade me that I had experienced a most unpleasant nightmare and that I had only to arouse myself, jump out of bed, and pull back the blinds to make everything all right and normal again. The nightmare, said my befuddled, conscious mind, would vanish with the daylight as the meadow mists before the morning sun. But all the while my innermost, subconscious mind was warning me that nothing so simple as a nightmare had occurred—that very soon I must summon the energy to face a most unpleasant truth.

When the chimes of Beadle tower came clear-cut across the valley it meant that the wind was from the north. I was pleased about it this morning because it would dry the scythed grass in the meadow and enable us to stack it before the leaves began to fall. I was pleased—but I knew that I was silly to be pleased, and tried to wonder why.

I think it was the sight of my blue serge suit, lying carelessly, almost flauntingly across the armchair, that brought me to full consciousness and reasoning. It was a suit reserved for special occasions, and I usually folded it neatly and hung it in my wardrobe before retiring. The crumpled carelessness of those sprawled clothes reminded me of the large double whisky I had taken upon my return home, and with a cruel lash-cut of recollection the whole incredible business of the night before came back to me.

In the spring of the year the world would end, and that was why I had been silly to think about stacking the meadow grass. Fully awake, I lay there for a while, my eyes upon the bright crack of sunlight that filtered through the drawn curtains.

I lay there and wondered what I ought to do. Seven months of life remained to me—two hundred days. A lot could be done in two hundred days. How ought I to change my mode of life to get the best from those precious remaining hours? It would give me pleasure, and others pleasure, if I were to give my money away. There would be no point in giving it to charity in a lump sum, for it would simply remain invested. I could draw it in the form of half-crowns and go around giving it to poor men and poor women and poor children, and receive a hundred surprised, grateful smiles a day for the rest of my short life on earth. The idea appealed to my impulsive nature, but after reflection I discarded it. It was my duty to avoid arousing any kind of suspicion, and if I were to give my money away people would naturally wonder why, and possibly guess the truth. I could not risk divulging the Secret in this way. Besides which, if anything miscarried and the world did not end after all, I should simply feel a fool. I could hardly expect my money back.

No. I must do my duty by carrying on exactly as if nothing had happened. Not by one hair's breadth would I deviate from the routine of life which I had so carefully constructed for myself. I got up and shaved: I took my bath and dressed and breakfasted.

I gained fresh confidence as I stood admiring the view from my breakfast-room window. I was happily placed in this lovely, secluded backwater of England. There were scarcely a hundred people in the village and the nearest town was over six miles away. If panic came it could scarcely touch us here. If famine descended upon us, my vegetable garden and poultry farm would amply supply the needs of Mrs. Buller and myself. Even if mankind ceased work in the face of approaching death, my pullets would carry on until the end: my pullets would keep up their average of seventeen eggs per day until their very nests were whisked to eternity.

But even with the knowledge of our President's words so vividly in mind, I believed in my heart of hearts that nothing very serious would happen to the earth. The moon would go back to its place:

it would not hit us—could not hit us, for reason told me that the Divine Power that controlled our destinies would not so suddenly and callously lose interest in us. God would not permit His handiwork to be blasted to senseless destruction. I could well imagine a certain hysterical type of preacher crying out that God was destroying us because we had proved ourselves unworthy of Him, but I had no patience with this silly stuff. If God could create us then God could control our brains and minds: if we had failed it was because He had been unable to make better creatures of us, and that was His fault—not ours. God must have as much reason and as much sense as the visible beings that He had created, and it was most unlikely that He would advertise His own shortcomings by destroying us.

It did not occur to me that this all-important world of ours was one of a thousand million worlds eddying in the great hive of the universe. It did not occur to me that God had an intense, burning interest in them all—that even as we seethed and strutted on our own little earth, God might be planning and creating life upon a million others. If two of His thousand million worlds were to collide and destroy each other, there was no special reason why He should be more concerned than I should be if two specks of dust ran into one another in my breakfast-room when Mrs. Buller was sweeping the carpet.

But these thoughts have come to me only in the bitterness of the past seven years. Upon that sunlit autumn morning I am afraid my vanity persuaded me that God would never permit the world to end until I personally had finished with it.

Anyhow, the principal fact remained that I was a bachelor aged forty-seven, of set habits and comfortable circumstances. Even if I had wanted to, I could not have altered those habits upon my own accord. It needed more than a mere threat: it needed a complete, head-on collision with the moon to alter what I considered to be my rightful mode of life. The Burhampton Poultry Show was on Saturday and I had a reputation to keep up. I had entered six handsome Wyandotte cockerels, and my first duty after breakfast was to remove their portable run (with the assistance of Haggard, my gardener) to a clean spot in the meadow where they could benefit from the sweet grass and nutritious insects that infested it.

It was a magnificent autumn morning of crisp sunlight and refreshing northwest wind. As I worked with my gardener, Captain Alec Williams, the riding master, came along with one of his grooms and a waggon to stack a load of grass.

I had an arrangement with Captain Williams by which he paid me four guineas a year for my meadow grass, he being responsible for scything and stacking it in a corner of the field and collecting it as necessary. He paid me half-yearly, in June and December, and it occurred to me, as I watched him at work, that if the worst happened on the 3rd May he would get four months' grass for nothing.

I did not resent this personally, but knowing what an honest man he was I realised that he would never forgive me if I allowed him to die in my debt. I decided to drop him a line suggesting that he paid me quarterly, so that his guinea upon the 25th March would practically cover the grass to the end.

It is remarkable how quickly a fine sunlit day can dissolve one's cares. As the morning drew on and the sun grew warmer, and the bracing wind blew away the remnants of my headache, I found the trouble about the moon receding right into the background. For ten minutes at a time I completely forgot about it, as a man working in the sunlight of a garden around a haunted house might forget the ghost within until the shadows lengthen across the lawn.

I had a half-bottle of my favourite claret for lunch, and as I sat smoking a cigar and reading *The Times* beside my fire I felt prepared to argue against the greatest scientist in the world that the whole business about the moon was an absurd hoax—that everything would be all right and that I should continue to enjoy life upon my little estate for years and years to come. It was too absurd to believe.

During the afternoon I had one difficult moment when Haggard, my gardener, was helping me to clip my shaped yews. Without any warning he asked me whether my meeting had gone off all right on the previous evening.

It was upon the tip of my tongue to tell him that it had gone off quite unexpectedly: gone off, in fact, with a considerable explosion, when I remembered my oath and replied lightly that it had been a pleasant meeting at which we had discussed the action of the moon upon the tides of the ocean. It was my first lie for the sake of humanity and I was pleased with it.

He asked me whether the tide went out farther at Southend than it did at Brighton because Southend was nearer the moon. I replied that this was no doubt the reason and tactfully changed a subject which I did not wish to pursue by making a suggestion concerning the shape of one of my yew trees.

When I had purchased Beech Knoll five years ago, the yew trees lining the path to the front door were trimmed into the shape of rabbits sitting up on their hind legs. By carefully training and clipping each summer I had altered these figures into hens sitting upon nests. I had achieved this by allowing the lower portions of the rabbits to bush out a bit (to form the "nests") and by training a small piece of foliage in each tree to resemble a hen's tail.

I now suggested that in one tree, as an experiment, we might entirely cut away the foliage that formed the nest, trim down the base until we had two parallel stalks, and so make a very passable gamecock.

Haggard agreed enthusiastically, but in doing it we had the misfortune to cut the stem that supplied the foliage for the head. We had no alternative but to trim the tail into a head, with the disappointing result of what appeared to be a small fat man with his trouser legs turned up, paddling in the sea.

Those who know the slowness of a yew tree's growth will realise what this meant. For years I would be forced to look at this grotesque monstrosity and explain it away as best I could to my friends. My nerves were no doubt upon edge and I am afraid I lost my temper when Haggard suggested trimming it neatly all round and having a cannonball.

"Leave it alone!" I said. "Let it grow out and we'll do what we can next year."

Even as I said the words I felt a sudden, sick bewilderment. It needed something definite, something intimate like this mutilated yew tree to give me a full sense of proportion. Yews were late starters and seldom made new growth until mid-May or June, and there was never to be another May, or another June. The old trees stood before me—olive green in the fading light: for five years I had known them as the faithful, unsleeping sentinels that lined my path—that greeted me in the morning and rustled a "goodnight" to my bedroom window. And now they were over. Most of my trees would have awakened from their winter sleep and clad themselves in a sheen of delicate spring leaves to meet their death on the 3rd of May—but my yews were ended forever—they had thrown out their last green tips of growth this summer and were doomed never to grow again: the end would come before the spring life stirred in them—they would die in their sleep . . . it was bewildering, and horrible. . . .

"You all right, sir?" enquired Haggard.

"Of course I'm all right," I snapped. "Why?"

"You're looking quite pale, sir. Turns cold quick in this wind at sundown. Better be careful of chills, sir."

I was angry, and made no reply. Haggard apparently thought me a weakling—chilled by a puff of wind. How quickly his contempt would have changed to wonder had he known the truth!—had he known the awful reality that I had faced with no more than a passing paleness!

I had been very proud of the terrible secret I had carried away with me from our Meeting: proud of the trust reposed in me—proud of my supreme knowledge over ignorant millions—but steadily my pride was turning to impotent annoyance. What, after all, is the pleasure of holding within oneself a colossal, awe-inspiring secret when nobody around one even knows that you are keeping it? No more good than a brave smile to hide a toothache when nobody knows you've got a toothache!

I had no heart for further work. As I glanced up from my darkening yew trees I saw that the sun was setting, and once again there had crept into the sky that pulsating, rusty glow. I felt utterly miserable as I watched Haggard striding down the hillside with an armful of tools. Out in this carefree, sunlit garden I had been able to cast aside my thoughts of dread reality, but the beauty of this dying autumn day was making more horrible the knowledge that never again upon this earth would there be another summer—never again a haze of violet blossom in May—never again the spangle of June roses.

As I walked towards the house I felt for the first time in my life a dread of my library—the room in which I had spent so many peaceful evenings of solitude—the room that suddenly loomed before me as the cell of a friendless, condemned man.

By nature I am a sociable fellow with a ready gift for making friends, but my numerous hobbies had of late years taken possession of me to such an extent that I had quite lost touch with neighbouring society. Night after night I was perfectly happy by myself in my well-stocked library. My poultry accounts, my notes on botany, and my foreign stamp collection filled the winter evenings until dinnertime, and the after-dinner period was never long enough for all that I had to do. So much of a hermit had I become that my housekeeper had strict instructions never to disturb me once I had risen from dinner. But now, as I entered my library, its very "cosiness" repulsed me.

Deliberately I had furnished it with dark, heavy curtains and solid, enduring furniture to give it an atmosphere of solitude and repose. Suddenly it took upon itself a suffocating oppression. I realised that I had made of this room a dark, soft-footed servant rather than a friend in need.

The fire was crackling brightly and nothing could look more inviting than the tray of tea that stood on the table in the flickering light. But I had no appetite. I toyed with a slice of seed cake but my mouth was so dry that the seeds almost rattled inside it, and I had to gulp some tea to dispose of them.

I had determined, in the false optimism of that sunlit morning, to make no change in my normal routine of life, but the shadows of an autumn evening threw a sadly altered light upon my vow. How horrible to sit alone in this room through the steadily lengthening darkness of the winter evenings! How terrible to sit alone, counting away the minutes that divided me from a ghastly end! There seemed no alternative: I could not suddenly begin a series of unexpected calls upon my neighbours, for that would arouse the surprise and suspicion that I was in duty bound to avoid.

But I knew that I must do something to preserve my sanity, and after long thought I resolved upon what may seem a pathetic attempt to alleviate my awful loneliness. I resolved to read from beginning to end the works of Sir Walter Scott. I possessed these in thirty volumes, and one a week would carry me far into the winter—even until the day when I should no longer need to nurse my secret.

As I rose and went to my bookshelves something happened to warn me of the dire state of my nerves. Mrs. Buller had orders to pull my curtains firmly when she brought my tea, in order to give comfort to the room, but tonight these curtains worried me—I desired a sense of freedom, and I paused by the windows to draw them apart.

As I did so I glanced into the night. I saw the moon and nearly cried out in terror. It was rising over the valley—inflamed—diabolically swollen—hideously menacing! I dragged the curtains to, staggered to my chair, and crouched over the fire. My forehead was cold and slimy with sweat. The scientists were right after all, but hopelessly wrong in their calculations, for the moon was already upon us!—I sat there quivering—waiting for the end: waiting for a rending crash in the beech trees—earthquake—tumult—blackness—eternity! By a strange twist of the brain that I have known so often since, I found myself struggling to decide whether there was any last thing I wanted to think about before the power of thought was beyond me forever.

My jagged nerves had robbed me of the reason to reflect that the waning moon on a frosty October night was often yellow and distorted in size, and when presently I crept to the windows and peered through the crack of the curtains—when I saw it there—silver and serenely normal above the meadows—I cursed myself for an idiot and a coward.

I glanced at my watch. It was half-past six: an hour and a half before dinnertime: a lonely dinner with more eternal time before I could go to bed. I could stand it no longer; I had to do something, and in desperation I decided to walk down to the village to buy some stamps at the post office.

I was happier out there in the clear, frosty night. I took the path across my meadow and climbed the stile to the village street. I had no fear of the moon out there beneath it: the moon and I knew all about each other now.

As I passed the gate of the Vicarage a new thought occurred to me. Last winter we had played one or two evenings of bridge. Hubert Edwards, the Vicar, his wife and I, and Major Willoughby from The Grange as a fourth, had arranged a weekly game, but the Major fancied himself a good player—insisted upon 6d a hundred and was so exceedingly difficult to get on with that the arrangement collapsed after three weeks, I having lost seventeen shillings and the Vicar and his wife nearly a pound between them.

Nothing had been said about bridge this winter, but here was a ray of hope—a chance to break the endless monotony of the empty nights that loomed ahead of me.

The Vicar was at a meeting, but Mrs. Edwards was delighted to see me. She was quite sure that Hubert would enjoy a game on Tuesday evenings and suggested Mr. Fayne-Higneth, Lord Burgin's new agent, as a fourth. She and the Vicar would be happy to dine with me on Tuesday next at seven and would bring Mr. Fayne-Higneth with them.

I was so pleased with this quick success that I decided to postpone my purchase of postage stamps until the following evening and to drop in to the Fox & Hounds instead.

At one time, when old Joe Sparling was proprietor, I had frequently dropped in for a glass of sherry before dinner. There was a comfortable little saloon bar where I would usually meet Alec Williams, the riding master, and one or two of my other neighbours. After a chat we would stroll into the public bar and please the good-hearted farm hands by playing a game of darts with them.

But I never liked Murgatroyd, the new proprietor. He was a bustling, bullying type of fellow, far more concerned with how much you drank than with how long you stayed. One evening three years ago I had been drawn into an unpleasant and undignified argument with him over the feeding of Bantam cocks of which he professed to be an expert. Since then my visits had grown less frequent and now for over a year I had never even crossed the threshold of the Fox & Hounds.

But it now seemed to me a duty to go there. Our President had impressed upon us the necessity of keeping careful observation upon the public and reporting immediately any sign that they were receiving rumours or otherwise learning facts that must be kept from them.

The Fox & Hounds was a pleasant, half-timbered little place that lay back from a small green in the centre of the village. I felt almost shy as I pushed open the saloon door, and something akin to physical pain as a blast of strident music hit me in the face. The large, ornate radio installed by the new landlord was one of the reasons why my visits had ceased. I had disliked the automatic piano of Joe Sparling's day but that at least became silent after the consumption of each penny. I hoped that the radio might have worn out, but it seemed healthier than ever.

The saloon bar was occupied by a solitary fat man in gaiters who eyed me up and down with impudence. For some years past I had deplored the decay of country "types." When I was a boy, a farmer was a farmer and none could mistake his hearty, weather-beaten face and breeches and gaiters. Today there were crowds of "half-farmers" who aped the gentleman—who wore anything from corduroys to canary-coloured jerseys—who scraped impatiently about in the fields and lived on petrol pumps.

This fellow in the bar was not the type of farmer that I admired, but he was obviously connected with the land although he debased a sturdy profession by carrying an umbrella.

"Good evening," I said.

"Evening," he grunted.

Murgatroyd, the proprietor, was nowhere about—he had probably gone to the pictures at Mulcaster—and the barmaid who served me with a glass of ale was a stranger to me. I regretted more than ever the self-centred interests that had drawn me in the past few years from the village people. At one time, when first I came here, I knew them all by name, but now when I so desperately needed companionship, they were all strangers to me.

I tried to engage the girl in conversation. I thought it would be a good idea to arouse her alarm about those strangely coloured sunsets so that I could do my duty by calming her fears with an elaborate (but untrue) explanation of them.

But I had scarcely started when someone called to her from the public bar and she turned her back on me.

I sat in a corner opposite the fat man and again attempted to begin a conversation about the sunsets. But he was a dull, surly fellow who took no interest in it whatsoever. He complained bitterly about the decay of the potato market, and when I endeavoured to interest him in my scientific theories of poultry breeding he grew violently angry. He said there wasn't a farthing left in English eggs and a man was a damn fool who pretended there was. When I began to explain the effect of water-heated tubular metal perches upon a hen's laying capacity, he got up and went out without saying goodnight.

My loneliness surrounded me like a shroud. The radio in the public saloon was making such a row that I could not recognise any of the voices or judge how many men were there. Nor could I summon the courage to walk in. One needed a companion when one strolled from the saloon into the public bar, and in my dejected state I could not face a crowd of strangers alone. I listened for a while to the *plonk* of darts and occasional rounds of laughter—then I put my glass down and left the saloon. The Fox & Hounds had failed me: my thoughts were thrown back upon that lonely hillside home of mine, and with something verging upon panic I knew that I could not face that silent, curtained library. I would walk: I would take the road towards Lullington and not return until the stroke of eight. I would go straight in to dinner and perhaps the soothing effect of a meal would help me to tolerate those dreaded hours to bedtime.

Some youths were lounging outside the general shop: they were laughing and chattering raucously together, but stopped to stare at me as I passed. One was the boy who worked for the butcher, and although he knew me quite well he made no attempt to touch his cap. The old country custom of touching caps and bidding good-night had died out except amongst the older men, and the country was rapidly becoming a drab, thin imitation of a London suburb.

Something about those aimless, chattering youths infuriated me. I longed to wheel around and lash them into silence and awed respect with my secret. I was ignored by everybody, yet I had only to stride into the Fox & Hounds, hold up my hand for silence and tell them what I knew to become the centre of amazed attention! My house would be besieged by the countryside!—group after group of round-eyed people would be ushered into my library to receive a ten-minute speech and a message of encouragement and hope! My name would be upon the lips of everybody and my house would become the Mecca of all Hampshire!

But a vow was a vow. In honour bound I must hold my tongue, but as I walked that winding lane to the ridge of the downs I began to long for the day when the Secret would be broken—when the whole village would know that for long, terrible months I'd carried the incredible truth so calmly that none even suspected it!

I walked for a long while in companionship with the waning moon: I stood for some moments at the edge of Cheddow Wood, looking down at the silver streak of the Arun as it wound through the water-meadows of the valley. I drew from that peaceful scene a wistful serenity that gave me courage to turn back upon my homeward journey.

Had I known of the things that lay ahead of me: had I a glimmering of the living death that was to come in place of the oblivion I expected, I believe that I should never have returned to my home that night. I believe that I should have gone down the hillside to the River Arun and died while there still remained distinction between life and death.

CHAPTER FOUR

As if to pay compensation in advance for her approaching madness, Nature presented us with a succession of perfect autumn days. Dawn after dawn rose up in clear-skied radiance: mellowed afternoons pursued the sunset and bathed in its glow until the shadows of the beech trees were stretched like fine elastic to the full breadth of the meadow, only to be snapped with the nip of twilight.

The lovely weather helped me to recapture a semblance of my past life and habits. The moon had waned, and its passing brought relief. Time began to gather something of its normal progress and the Lullington Poultry Show was upon us before you could say "Jack Robinson."

The Lullington Show is amongst the most important of South Hampshire and I invariably sent my best exhibits.

I do not believe in priming my pullets artificially, but there are some exhibitors who go to what I consider unscrupulous lengths in preparing their birds for show. They give them stimulants to enrich the colour of their combs and drugs to incite an artificial jauntiness of bearing. For my own part I depend upon honesty, upon birds prepared under normal healthy conditions, and this policy never fails with judges of experience.

But at Lullington this year the judges of the Wyandotte pullets were men of the poorest quality, if not of downright dishonesty. I had entered a brood of six of the handsomest little birds that ever strutted in a judges' ring. I had bred them from chicks and they possessed not only beauty of appearance but a wonderful esprit de corps.

But a scandalous thing happened. I had the humiliation and disgust of seeing the judges completely misled by an exhibit of palpably unhealthy, abnormal pullets. They were dull-faced, incubated chickens—totally devoid of the vivacity and character that is present only in birds raised by a mother hen. Their plumage was fluffed up to make them look like clowns: their feet and legs, I am certain, had been treated with yellow varnish, and one bird gave such an exhibition of hysterical clucking that I knew it had been deliberately intoxicated.

The owner (a local man, I might mention!) carried off First Prize and a silly woman in breeches (also local and, I subsequently learned, the wife of the judge of the Bantam cockerels) was awarded Second Prize.

Never before, in a reputable show, have I been witness to such unashamed favouritism, and I told the Secretary that I would never exhibit at Lullington again.

But adversity brought a strange and touching result.

So moved was I by the plucky effort of those game little birds of mine—so stirred was I to pity by those puzzled, beady eyes that I no longer thought of them as a mere exhibit in a poultry show. They were my faithful little friends: friends that had been insulted and victimised by a local oligarchy.

I had intended to bicycle home the six miles from Lullington, but upon a sudden impulse I slung the bicycle upon the back of the carrier's van and travelled inside with my birds.

As the van jolted through the winter sunset I pushed my finger through the crate and rubbed them one by one upon their combs and sleek white necks. I saw their eyes cocked up at me as if in apology for their defeat—as if in gratitude for my sympathy and forgiveness.

And when, in the twilight, I put them into their little home, they did not, in their usual way, wander stiffly and sleepily to their perches. Instead, they gathered in a corner and looked up at me through the wire. They stood there in a group as I walked away, and when I glanced back I saw them still as I had left them—a silent little grey cloud of friendship in the gathering twilight of the meadow.

I felt quite touched by this spontaneous little gesture of affection, and although, on the following morning, I realised that in my emotion I had forgotten to give them their evening meal, I honestly believe that they, too, had forgotten their meal, and had been moved to a devotion that few suspect in the domestic fowl.

My dinner party for the Vicar and his wife and Mr. Fayne-Higneth was a great success and pronounced delightful by all concerned. Mr. Fayne-Higneth, Lord Burgin's new agent, was a shy young man with a slight stammer that only became marked in moments of stress. When, for instance, I doubled his three clubs in the first rubber there was an embarrassing pause, and he had to struggle quite hard before he could say that he redoubled. But I quickly set him at ease by laughing heartily when one of the doors of my bookcase flew open by itself. It frequently did this, but I said it was the family ghost and he was so amused that his stammer left him for the rest of the evening. The Vicar told me that Fayne-Higneth was a distant relative of Lord Burgin himself—an old Oxford man and in every way a suitable acquaintance. I felt an immediate friendship for him and told him to drop in whenever he liked.

Considering how rarely I entertain, I think the dinner prepared by Mrs. Buller was excellent. I like to be modern in every way, so sherry and small cheese straws were served in the library before going in to dinner. The party went with a swing from the very beginning. The Vicar and his wife read over an article I had recently written upon "Metallurgists of the Nineteenth Century," and while we waited for the dinner-gong I showed Mr. Fayne-Higneth my egg chart for September.

Dinner was a few minutes late because the village girl who helped Mrs. Buller dropped the gong stick behind the radiator in the hall, but the party was too happy to notice a trifling delay and the gong sounded just as well with a tablespoon.

The meal itself was practically "home-produced." An artichoke soup was followed by an excellent boiled fowl (which was in fact Victoria III, the prize hen that caused such a stir in South Hampshire poultry circles in the spring of the previous year). There was a sweet omelette of damson jam and a fine Camembert cheese which was included, as the Vicar wittily put it, "to show our French allies that there was no ill feeling."

After dinner we drew a table up to the library fire and played bridge until after eleven. Habit was beginning to make the keeping of my secret an easier matter now—I behaved quite normally at the card table and discussed the Summer Bazaar as if nothing were likely to happen!

And this was not entirely a matter of play-acting. My belief that the whole "moon business" was nothing but an absurd scare upon the part of a few super-clever "experts" was growing firmer every day. I called to mind the numberless "experts" who had predicted hard winters that had turned out warm: "experts" who had predicted Stock Exchange slumps which turned out to be booms. I despised the experts: I snapped my fingers at them. For the future I would trust my own common sense that told me the moon was temporarily misplaced and would find its proper course again without trouble.

I lost 3s 9d and Fayne-Higneth 2s 6d, but I was glad the Vicar and his wife returned home 6s 3d the richer, for the living is a poor one and the Vicarage much too big an expense for them. I walked down to the gate with the party, all of whom readily accepted my invitation to dine again on the following Tuesday.

I returned to my house much happier than I had been for a long time. The dear old Vicar and his wife gave such confidence, such symbolism of the permanency of English life that I slept sounder than for many nights and did not wake until my tea came up at eight o'clock.

My growing belief that everything would be all right caused me to look forward to the next meeting of the British Lunar Society with the keenest relish. I sincerely believed that the President would apologise for arousing our alarm: that he would announce the discovery of a scientific miscalculation: that the experts were wrong and that the moon, the good, steady old moon, was as right as rain. My arrival at the meeting on the 22nd October fully confirmed my optimism. As I ascended the narrow stairs I heard the old familiar buzz of cheerful talk. As I entered the room I saw happy, excited faces upon all sides and the same old-time jollity of members greeting one another. So buoyant was the atmosphere that I believed the news must already have spread—the news that all was well with our good old earth.

I suppose the truth was that everybody had reacted as I had done. Everybody had persuaded themselves in their own ways that the whole thing was a scare and that we should hear the fact confirmed in a few moments.

Nothing else can explain the buoyant confidence and heartiness of our arrival—or the ghastly, sickening silence that fell upon us as the President spoke his first words. . . .

"There is not much to report, gentlemen—except that the moon continues to approach the earth at the same increasing ratio of speed. . . ."

It seemed as if the very lights of the room grew pallid as the blood drained from two hundred cheeks. So pitiful are the limits of human reason that I believe this casual confirmation was a ghastlier shock than the first news of two weeks ago.

The significance had been too vast for us to understand in that one short statement of words at our first meeting. The meeting of the 8th October had passed sentence of death, but still left us the right of appeal. The counsel of our dreams had given us high hopes of a reprieve. This second meeting was the Court of Appeal: judgement was confirmed: there was no reprieve.

The President continued, but there was none of that rigid, incredulous alertness of the first meeting. There was a limpness of despair in those silent bodies, hunched in their cane-bottomed chairs. I doubt if many of us were really listening to his words in detail. Through a haze of despair I heard the President say that two nights before he had attended a meeting of the Royal Society at which the Astronomer Royal had amplified his earlier statements. The moon was now 203,800 miles away and the rate of its approach had risen to 1,238 miles in twenty-four hours. One small miscalculation had arisen concerning the time of the moon's collision with the earth on the 3rd May. It would be at 8:15 p.m. instead of 8:03 p.m. as originally calculated. Somebody murmured, "More time for dinner!" but the joke fell as flat as mud.

I felt no gratitude whatever at the gift of an extra twelve minutes, and as the President embarked upon a long and technical explanation of Magnetic Attraction I found myself growing impatient and angry. What did all this scientific rot amount to if we were blasted to eternity in six months' time!—I grew furiously angry at this imbecile waste of precious life. Here sat a hundred healthy, intelligent living creatures—stagnant and useless—doing utterly nothing with precious minutes that were relentlessly ticking away! Yet what else was better? How could I face some bawdy musical comedy—or the silence of that dreary curtained library in my home?

As I glanced at those hopeless, sunken faces I realised for the first time how lucky I was to be alone—how infinitely more terrible for those with wives and children—who had to keep this awful secret from those who by instinct could see far into their husbands' minds. . . .

If only we men in this room could live henceforward together—could talk each day together! . . . it was the terrible loneliness of our separation that brought the cruelty of hell.

The President told us that shortly after Christmas the moon would have approached within 150,000 miles. Its increased size and general appearance would then become so obvious to the naked eye that no further concealment from the public would be possible. The full moon of the week beginning Boxing Day might pass without comment if weather conditions were against clear visibility, but the moon at full in the third week of January was certain to end the Secret.

That would be three months before the end. What purgatory had those three months in store for us? I squeezed up my eyes to suffocate the contemplation of it.

The adjournment to the anteroom was horrible in its silent, oppressive gloom. Only a few attempted a display of normal conversation to reassure the round, puzzled face of Mrs. Ayling behind the coffee urn. As I took my cup of coffee she asked me "What was up with them all?" I replied that grave difficulties had arisen over the construction of our new observatory at Hampstead, and her face immediately lit up with reassurance and happiness. She was against the telescope from the beginning, for she lived at Sidcup, and the journey to Hampstead would have been a long and tedious one for an old lady.

Upon this evening the news of confirmation was broken to seven other scientific societies in London. Just before midnight a man named Dr. Burgoyne, a teacher of physics at a provincial university, went mad, and ran along Regent Street shouting: "The world is ending!—the world is ending!"

He was arrested by a policeman on point duty at Piccadilly Circus, certified insane, and sent to Walthop Hill Asylum. It was not reported in the press.

CHAPTER FIVE

A few days after that wretched meeting of the British Lunar Society, the Prime Minister made a remarkable speech in Parliament.

The headlines in the newspapers startled me. They announced: "DUGOUTS FOR ALL," and for a moment I thought the Secret was out. But as I read the speech I realised what a clever move had been made.

The danger of air attack by foreign enemy, said the Prime Minister, was at last to be given vigorous attention and every town and village in Great Britain was to have its dugout for the protection of its citizens against bombs and gas.

Every community was immediately to set up its "Dugout Committee" and work was to begin at once under the supervision of local engineers, who would receive full details and specifications from the Ministry of Defence.

The work as far as possible was to be done by voluntary labour and the newspapers put the scheme over in such a fascinating way that no sensible citizen could withhold his enthusiasm for a long-delayed necessity. Extracts from the official directions proved how skilfully the real purpose of the dugouts had been disguised. Modern bombs, it was announced, had such deep penetrating power that the dugouts should be thirty feet deep. Hillcrests and valleys were to be avoided and the sites selected should be upon hillsides protected as far as possible by the natural folds of the ground. This, it was explained, was to give security from aircraft observation and at the same time to place the dugouts out of reach of poison gas which naturally accumulates in the valleys. I knew, of course, that hillcrests and valleys were to be avoided because of hurricane in the one case and flood in the other.

It was evident that immense preparations had been under way for some months, for the Government announced that large quantities of oxygen cylinders and steel doors were already available and would be delivered immediately the local authorities announced the completion of their dugouts.

Personally I was delighted with this vigorous and sensible move. It meant that preparations would proceed in an orderly manner, free from the risk of panic, and when the truth had to be told the dugouts would be so far advanced that the news would act solely as a stimulus for completion.

It also made my secret infinitely more exciting and important, for everybody in Beadle would be talking about the impending disaster without actually knowing about it. I personally would be the only man in the village who knew the real reason for all this activity, and I could undoubtedly assist (without divulging the secret) by suggesting the best place to put the Beadle dugout.

Our village lay in the rural district of Makleton and Dr. Hax was our local Member upon the Council. I accordingly went down to see him directly after breakfast and was lucky to find him in his surgery on the point of departing upon his rounds.

Dr. Hax was a big, dusty-looking man with a flat white face and a clumsy, ambling walk. He was respected in the village but not greatly liked. He always carried a shabby little black bag of imitation, shiny leather which looked to me a perfect hotbed for germs. A stethoscope generally dangled out of his pocket and his bedside manner was poor to say the least of it. He had a habit of abruptly turning his back upon his patients that annoyed them but often cured them. He also had a small private income that was resented by old ladies with nothing the matter with them because he was sufficiently independent to tell them they weren't ill.

"Morning, Doctor!" I said. "Seen the papers?—The Government's waking up at last!"

He looked at me vaguely for a moment, then began stuffing his unsavoury little bag with cotton wool.

"The great Dugout Scheme?" He gave a short laugh. "Yes—most important! I hear the Germans are organising a big attack on Beadle Gravel Pit to put it out of action."

"Is that the way to treat a vital move towards national safety?" I sharply rejoined.

"Volunteers to build dugouts," he jeered. "If they got volunteers onto bringing some of our waste land under potatoes and wheat, they'd be talking sense!"

I was appalled by this despicably narrow but typically "local" attitude.

"I came to offer my services as a good citizen with a respect for the safety of England!"

He looked at me curiously. "Sorry, Hopkins. Didn't mean to offend. I'm a good citizen, too—or I hope I am. What d'you want to do?"

"I thought," I replied stiffly, "that I could be of service upon the Dugout Committee. I'm not exactly a yokel. I've knowledge of geology—particularly of these parts—I might be able to advise upon a suitable position for the Beadle dugout."

He shut his bag with a snap. "That'll all be dealt with by the Makleton Council," he said. "They'll be responsible for the villages in their area. There's a meeting on Thursday week and I'll know more about it then. They've got to discuss a big new drainage scheme, but maybe they'll bring up the dugouts if there's time. Come along down and see me in a fortnight. Maybe I'll have some news and you can come and dig and bury yourself. Now I've got to get over to Horley Farm to bring a baby into the world."

I was too astonished and appalled to make a reply. I stuttered something and watched him drive down the lane in his ramshackle little motor car. Thursday week!—and they might discuss it if the Drainage Scheme gave time! How ghastly the whole thing was!— Here were a hundred good honest Beadle folk, frittering away precious moments upon sweeping roads and ploughing fields and playing darts when they might be doing something to save their lives and save humanity!—and there went that pitiful fool of a doctor to bring a baby into the world!—might as well bring a dewdrop into a blast furnace.

I was determined to arouse the public conscience, and strode down to the Fox & Hounds. Murgatroyd was there, lounging behind his bar, and he was naturally surprised to see me after so long an absence. "Morning, Mr. Hopkins—glass of sherry? You haven't been in for quite a while."

"I was in a few days ago," I replied shortly, annoyed that the barmaid had not recognised me and reported my previous visit.

There were two or three men lounging by the bar, including Mr. Bewdley who kept the grocery store, and I was pleased to find that they were discussing the "Dugout Scheme."

"Where's ours to be?" asked Mr. Bewdley.

"I'll let 'em have my cellar," said Murgatroyd. "Turn the air raids into a nice little business boom for the Fox & Hounds—beer's better than oxygen tubes when it comes to keeping alive!"

"I've just seen Dr. Hax," I announced. "He casually informs me that the Dugout Scheme may be discussed by the Makleton Council on Thursday week!—if the Drainage Scheme allows time!"

"We been waiting for that Drainage Scheme these eighty years," said an old fellow behind a tankard in the corner. "If that goes through it'll put all Hanley Marsh under the plough. Drains first—dugouts second, I says."

"Hear!, hear," said the other imbeciles.

"The defence of our country comes first," I declared. "What protection have we? What's the good of draining Hanley Marsh if the whole of Beadle is wiped out—by bombs and gas?" (I quickly added).

For some reason this aroused an inane laugh.

"Got the wind up?" enquired Murgatroyd, winking at one of the loungers.

"I got an old tin hat I'll give you," said the old man in the corner.

I left the Fox & Hounds with laughter ringing in my ears and a grim determination to let the whole village be swept to eternity as reward for its stupidity. Criminal stupidity of this type deserved but one thing—destruction.

I learnt a few days later that the Makleton Council had called a special meeting. It seemed that the Government had anticipated the wretched slackness that I had discovered in Beadle and had sent out a skilfully worded Memorandum, hinting at the possibility of a sudden war and urging immediate construction of the dugouts.

I had a silent laugh at the doctor's expense but did not put myself to the indignity of offering my services again. Later I heard what I had expected: the Dugout Committee for Beadle had been formed—without me.

It consisted of Dr. Hax as Chairman, Major Willoughby (our unpleasant bridge player of last year), Pawson, a retired police-man, and the Vicar. It was too ludicrous for words. They had as technical adviser some fellow who had been a railway engineer in India, and they began the dugout in the grounds of Burgin Park one Sunday afternoon.

I ignored the whole thing. It was so utterly ludicrous. The one man in the village who knew everything was excluded from the Committee! I simply had to laugh.

But one day I could not resist the curiosity to walk by and see what they were doing. They had dug a big clumsy hole in the hillside and a dozen or more men were wheeling barrows of chalk and tip-ping it into a hollow. Some children were playing about on a pile of timber, Dr. Hax and his wonderful "committee" were fussing about in an aimless way, and a stranger, presumably the "expert," had a lot of coloured poles stuck up and was peering at them through an instrument. I stood nearby for some while, but naturally they were all too busy and self-important to notice my smile of amused tolerance.

My knowledge of the true facts had lifted me above the petty trivialities of the village: more and more I ignored these silly people as if they had already ceased to exist and took the moon—that suffering, struggling moon—as my sole companion. I no longer regarded it as an enemy—I understood it for what it really was: a calm, lovely thing that had shed its sublime beauty upon the earth since time began—a faithful servant, wrenched from its divine course by a devilish power that had sent it plunging against its will to its own and the earth's destruction.

During the early days of the November moon the skies were overcast, and only upon one night was I able to see the thin crescent high overhead. It shone through a film of tarnished cloud and seemed very much the same as usual. But never shall I forget the Tuesday night of that November moon's third week. It was at about half-past eight when I left my house to walk down to the Vicarage for our evening of bridge. I was just passing through the wicket gate that led from my garden into the meadow when I chanced to look up into the sky.

For the first time in several nights the sky was partly clear, and as I looked upwards, the clouds suddenly drew aside to reveal the full moon riding for a few moments in a deep, unrippled pool of blackness. In that one glance the whole of my carefully assumed sympathy and understanding with the moon was shattered, and I prayed for the clouds to draw their merciful veil. I can swear that it was bigger than ever I had seen it in my life—but there was something far worse than that. Its familiar, benevolent smile seemed gone forever and in its place I saw a hideous, pockmarked face, blazing with fever—a hungry, silver-bleached skull that raved for blood. And when a ragged mantle of black cloud submerged it, it was as if the light in a room had been flicked out and we were plunged in blackness. The silver birches in the Vicarage garden were like pale slits of light shining through the drawn curtains of a darkened room.

Mrs. Edwards glanced at me in surprise as she let me in, for try as I would, I was unable to disguise the panic that had sent me floundering for the friendly shelter of the Vicarage. My boots were muddy and my trousers splashed, for I had taken no account of the pools that lay beside the road. But Mrs. Edwards was too well-mannered to make remark, and by the time we were seated for the game I had recovered sufficiently to joke about the wet weather of the past few days.

It took me a long time to concentrate upon my cards. My distorted imagination pictured the whole world outside staring in horror at that blazing white monster in the sky. My ears were cocked towards the windows—I expected to hear sudden cries—the pounding of running feet—a terrified banging at the Vicarage door. But the minutes passed and there was nothing but the distant hooting of an owl. . . .

That evening, as we sipped our coffee during an interval in the game, I began to regard the old Vicar with a new interest. I wondered how that simple, gentle old man would play his part when it became his duty to announce his terrible message to the little congregation of his church.

It had been vigorously advocated in scientific circles that as the first news of the impending calamity was to be announced from the churches, every clergyman should be admitted to the Secret at once in order that he should have more time to prepare his message. But this had been opposed upon the grounds that many might find it incompatible with their calling to keep such a secret, and possibly be forced into lies and deceptions should their people become alarmed before the facts were announced.

Hubert Edwards would have barely a week to prepare his message when the time came; but as I glanced over my cards at that fine, careworn face and calm grey eyes, I had little doubt that the Vicar of Beadle would discharge his awful task with dignity and humanity.

I met Wilson, the policeman, as I left the Vicarage gate upon my journey home. He bade me a cheerful "Good evening" and walked beside me with his bicycle to the stile that led me to my meadow. We spoke of casual things—of Parsons, the goalkeeper of Beadle

Football Club, who had sprained his ankle in the game against Makleton last Saturday, and of Burton, the lad who was to play in his place. Carefully I turned the conversation to the weather—to the cloudy skies—to a delicate question:

"I don't suppose we've hardly seen the moon this month!"

The remark caused no reaction—Wilson hitched up the electric torch on his belt and said:

"We had a clear patch around nine o'clock. Quite bright for a bit."

I breathed again. Wilson had noticed nothing, and the nights that followed were shrouded in dark cloud. When the skies cleared with the frost in the first week of December the moon had gone, and we were saved for another month—for one last happy Christmas!

CHAPTER SIX

In accordance with my usual custom I arranged to spend Christmas with my Uncle Henry and Aunt Rose at Notting Hill.

On the 20th December I was up early to give Haggard, my gardener, his final instructions concerning the care of my poultry, and towards midday I took my bag and drove to the station with a cheerful heart. I always enjoyed my Christmas week in London and this year, for obvious reasons, I had looked forward more keenly than ever to my annual diversion.

And we were promised a really old-fashioned Christmas. The unsettled weather had turned to snow and I journeyed to London over a lovely mantle of whiteness.

At Waterloo Junction there was a scene to warm the heart. A train had just arrived with a load of happy, excited children returning home for the Christmas holidays, and nothing in the world compares with that joyful medley of parents, porters, pigtailed girls, and straw-hatted boys all struggling with luggage and shouting eager enquiries about home. I saw behind every little group the vision of a snug house upon the borders of London that would presently resound with the happy voices that were echoing into the roof of the great railway station. Usually I look on at such a scene with a wistful loneliness, but today a pleasant incident occurred that drew me into the turmoil and made me for the moment a genuine part of it.

As I walked down the platform towards the barrier I nearly collided with Colonel Parker, who lives at The Manor House opposite to me across the valley at home. With him was a tall boy of about sixteen whom I recognised as his young nephew Robin.

My retired life had never brought me into close touch with Colonel Parker, whose interests lay mostly in the country gentleman's pursuits of hunting and fishing and the like, but whenever I had met him in the village or upon the downs he had always greeted me with a friendly smile. Since early childhood his nephew and niece had lived with him—their father, a Major in the Indian Army, having been killed upon the North-West Frontier, and their mother, I understood, having died when Robin was born.

I had watched the boy and girl grow up: I had seen them galloping across the downs with a contemptuous disregard for their necks, and I had always admired them for their abundant gaiety and vigour.

I had not actually spoken to either of the children until this moment, and as Colonel Parker called out a cheery "Hullo!" he introduced the boy, who had grown so much since I had last seen him that I scarcely recognised him.

"Where are you off to?" asked the Colonel. "Deserting the village for Christmas?"

I explained my customary visit to my aunt and uncle.

"D'you know my nephew Robin?" enquired the Colonel, and I found myself looking into a pair of clear, friendly eyes that in later days I was to know so well, and under conditions so terribly different from this gay Christmas homecoming.

"How d'you do, sir!" said the boy.

"Pat—my niece—arrives at Paddington at five," said the Colonel. "She's one of those undergraduettes at Oxford. We're just going to dump the luggage and get some lunch. Then Robin wants to see a picture called *The Black Pirate*—sounds awful to me! Well—so long! Happy Christmas!"

"Happy Christmas!" called the boy.

"Happy Christmas!" I called back—and they were lost in the crowd. That scrappy, hectic little meeting pleased me. For a moment I, too, had belonged to it all and I hoped the people around us thought that I was an "uncle." It may sound a little absurd, but as I walked through the crowd I glanced anxiously to right and left. I wanted people to believe that I, too, was searching for a nephew or a niece, a son or a daughter.

By the time I had arrived at Notting Hill the menace of the past months had faded completely into the background. I refused to believe, as I sat lunching with my aunt and uncle in their cosy dining-room, that anything could possibly go wrong with the earth while people as permanent as Uncle Henry and Aunt Rose lived upon it.

They were a delightful old couple: connoisseurs of happiness, and we used to revel in the Christmas Pantomimes like three overgrown children. Uncle Henry was in comfortable circumstances and had been retired from the Office of Works for several years.

During his prime he had done much to add dignity and decorum to the public spaces of London, and it was through his untiring endeavours that the hands which pointed to the public conveniences in Hyde Park had a short length of sleeve and white cuffs painted onto their naked wrists. Aunt Rose had grown stout in recent years, but she possessed the finest collection in England of old coloured prints of stagecoaches that had overturned in snowdrifts.

Clemnestria, their house at Notting Hill, stood upon high ground and from the library window upstairs one enjoyed a lovely panorama of London at night. It was romantic and fairylike to look over that stardust of twinkling lights into the heart of Theatreland, especially when one sat there for a last moment, sipping one's port, clad in evening dress and preparing to plunge into that warm, friendly whirlpool of gaiety.

Immediately after lunch I departed for the City upon a mission that I had been considering for a long time. I went to see my stockbroker concerning my investments, and lest my motives should appear mercenary I will explain the underlying facts of the matter.

The day after the scientific societies were secretly informed of the approaching calamity, there had been a sharp fall in the stock markets. Government securities had lost three or four points and nearly all industrial shares had weakened.

The reason given in the City was the approach of Christmas and the liquidation of funds to pay Income Tax in the New Year, but I am convinced that many scientists and others who knew about the approaching disaster were selling out their stocks and shares to enjoy their money while they could.

It did not appeal to me to sell my securities and spend my last days in a debauch of senseless extravagance, but I did feel I could do something that would benefit me very greatly in the event of the moon only "grazing" the earth and giving it a severe shaking without actually destroying it.

I am not by nature a businessman, but I think I hit upon a clever idea. I gave the most careful consideration to the lists of Stock Exchange securities and came to the conclusion that the company that would benefit most definitely by a collision with the moon would be Wigglesworth & Smirkin, the big manufacturers of china crockery.

The more I thought about it, the more interesting my scheme became. I would sell £2,000 of my Great Western Railway Stock and buy 4,000 shares in Wigglesworth & Smirkin which were 10s each. The railways were certain to be shaken to pieces and their shares would become useless, but Wigglesworth & Smirkin would suddenly find themselves called upon to supply new cups and saucers, plates and dishes to everybody in England. A collision with the moon would cause an enormous breakage of china: my shares would soar sky-high and I should make a fortune.

My stockbroker lectured me upon the danger of selling first-class Debenture Stock in exchange for shares in a company that was by no means flourishing, but I laughed up my sleeve at his ignorance.

"Is it my money or yours?" I asked. He shrugged his shoulders and did as he was bid.

I left the City feeling that at last I had been able to do something really constructive and entered into my Christmas shopping with a light heart. For my housekeeper, Mrs. Buller, I bought a neat little alarm clock; to the Vicar's wife I sent a calendar, and for the Vicar himself I purchased a copy of *The Poultry Breeder's Annual*, hoping that it would excite his interest and make him more interesting to talk to.

The conquering spirit of Christmas had thrown a dreamlike unreality over the future, and as I walked with that crowd of people along Regent Street I felt that such an irresistible tide of happiness must surely triumph over the gloomy prophecy of science and send the moon reeling back in shame to its appointed place in the heavens.

Only once was the pitiless horror of it thrust back upon me. I was passing Hamleys toyshop, and the lights shone full upon the faces of three children, dragging their father and mother to a fascinating display of model engines. I caught one glimpse of those faces, young and old—I saw them brimming with the best that life can give—I pictured their return to some quiet house in a tree-lined road—the children climbing upon chairs to decorate the picture-frames with evergreen from the garden—the future blazing golden from a log fire—and I quivered with impotent rage . . . this monstrous thing could not happen in a world that harboured people such as these.

I went on my way with a leaden heart, but happy to know that at least a fragment of joy was left to that little family—if only a month—if only this one magic evening of glittering shops.

And as I boarded the bus for Notting Hill I caught one glimpse of the thin crescent of the fateful December moon. I saw it as I took my seat . . . I saw it over my left shoulder, and through the glass. . . .

We had a delightfully boisterous Christmas dinner at Clemnestria. Several friends came in with their children and we played quite ridiculous old-fashioned games. The snow was falling softly outside. We played "Postman's Knock," "Blind Man's Buff," and "Consequences." The children were sent home at ten o'clock, and as I stood upon the doorstep to see them off I almost expected to see Father Christmas come jingling through the snow to bear them home in his sleigh.

On Boxing Day I went with my uncle and aunt to see the Pantomime at Drury Lane with Sidney and Jessie Philpotts. The Philpottses were old friends of my family, Jessie being distantly related to my aunt. Sidney was an analyst with the Metropolitan Water Board and although he had once played chess for Hertfordshire, he was quite a modest, unassuming fellow.

Jessie, however, always offended me a little at theatres, for being over-anxious to show her sense of humour she did not laugh while the rest were laughing, but waited and laughed heartily by herself when everybody else had finished in order that none should doubt that she had seen the joke. But she was a good-natured soul and it was a wonderful evening—an evening that is enshrined in my memory because it was the last—the very last upon which I heard carefree laughter around me. I have heard laughter since, but it has been the laughter of heroism or the laughter of insanity.

I can shut my eyes and see that great theatre on Boxing Night of 1945—I can see those serried ranks of happy faces. Those mighty gusts of laughter eddy through the arid years and bring a lump to my throat that nearly overwhelms me.

For it was in this very room in which I write—this ruined, mould-stenched room of darkness and broken furniture—that I dined that night before leaving for the Pantomime.

The table was softly lit by a dozen candles under charming amber shades (if only I had but one of those candles now!): the maids moved quietly in the shadows by the wall, serving hors d'œuvres that lay in neat glass dishes upon a silver-crested tray—serving a cool hock in amber glasses: a finely cooked chicken with mushrooms . . . it tortures me to write these words, yet somehow it squeezes those sweet memories to a flicker of life . . . life that I hunger for . . . life that is gone forever . . .

We laughed until our sides ached at that last Pantomime at Drury Lane: every song was encored and the final curtain did not fall until almost midnight.

My uncle had hired a car for the occasion, but knowing from our journey to the theatre how uncomfortably crowded it was with five persons in it, I insisted upon walking part of the way home and picking up a taxi at Piccadilly Circus.

Jessie Philpotts called out, "Behave yourself!" as she climbed into the car, and although her husband exclaimed, "Jessie, dear!"

I did not resent the pleasantry, with its implied suggestion that I was a dark horse when left alone.

It was the loveliest night imaginable. A crisp frost lay underfoot and the rooftops glistened with the fine sparkle of snow that had fallen in the afternoon. All along the Strand went merrymakers, singing together, arm in arm, and people were gushing from the theatres amidst a chorus of hooting taxis. The whole scene was intoxicating, and I lingered amidst it, reluctant to end a delightful evening.

It is strange how the things which we visualise as happening in a hundred different ways so often discover in the end a totally unexpected means of surprising us. Upon that hilarious Boxing Night my mind had never been so far removed from the horror of the future—then suddenly I turned a corner and it was upon me—upon me in all its stark, staring reality.

I turned the corner from the blaring gaiety of the Strand and entered the broad quietness of Trafalgar Square. I decided to cut straight across the Square, to walk up Haymarket and find my taxi in Piccadilly.

The Square was almost deserted, but my attention was drawn to a silent little group beneath the Nelson Column . . . an incongruous little group of a dozen people drawn together in the common bond of curiosity. There were a couple of ragged wayfarers, on their journey, no doubt, to a night's rest in the sanctuary of St. Martin's; two or three ordinary-looking men, who may have been clerks on their way to night duty; a messenger boy; and some people in evening dress. And all were silently staring into the sky.

I stared up with them. Heaven knows I should have expected what I saw, and yet of all that group I must have been the most surprised and horrified. For the past week the snow-laden clouds had permitted the moon to grow to its full in secret—and here it was, blazoning its awful message to the earth at last.

No longer was it the flat, silver disc that man had known since man began to live. It was a ball—a great shining ball whose centre seemed nearer to us than its rim. It was no longer set firmly in the sky: it had broken loose from its time-rusted moorings in the heavens and seemed to hover in quivering uncertainty between sky and earth.

It was not appreciably larger in size, but its old familiar face had gone and in its place were those craters of awe-inspiring beauty that until now the telescope alone had revealed.

I think the silence of that little group was more torturing than the sight above me. Here stood humanity—facing at last its awful test, and it neither moved nor spoke. I had to speak . . . I had to make some sound to break that uncanny stillness. I turned to one of the unshaven men beside me.

"What is it?" I asked.

He turned a pair of dull, hollow eyes towards me and jerked his head upwards.

"Ask yourself," he said.

There was no more to say. Presently the little group began to disperse. A man in evening dress buttoned his coat and relit his cigar.

"Funny," he said. "Come on, Joan. It's late."

A girl slipped her arm through his and they walked away.

From the surrounding streets came the sound of singing. Big Ben, down by the river, began to strike the hour of midnight; cars purred around the Square, and I walked on alone.

At the corner of Pall Mall and Haymarket a policeman on point duty paused from his work and stared into the sky. A taxi hooted and he waved it on: he was upon earth, at work again.

I sat huddled in the taxi that drove me westward towards my uncle's house in Notting Hill. The secret was out. It was no longer my secret. It belonged to the world.

CHAPTER SEVEN

Today, when all attempt at organised Government has long since passed, I look back in admiration at the skill and foresight with which the authorities handled matters in those critical weeks of the New Year.

I do not know to this day whether the December moon caught them by surprise. I rather think that it did. I believe that they had hoped for it to wane without exciting undue curiosity, but the clear sky of Boxing Night, aided by the exceptionally dry air and a snow-covered land, all but wrecked their carefully arranged plans.

A Committee under the Chairmanship of the Prime Minister had for months been preparing the steps by which the public were to be made conscious of the approaching calamity. It consisted of certain Members of the Government and Opposition, the heads of the great newspapers, the Church, and a few others selected by reason of their special knowledge of mass psychology. One false step might have set loose an avalanche of panic from which no rescue could have been possible. After the moon of Boxing Night the Committee decided that delay would be fatal, and acted at once.

The morning press was silent, but the news "broke" in the evening papers of the 27th December. The selection of the evening papers was perfect, and the news was deliberately "stunted."

"Unusual Lunar Phenomenon," announced my paper. Owing, it stated, to an exceptionally clear sky and a rarely experienced refraction of light from the snow, the public had been given the opportunity of seeing the features of the moon more clearly and brilliantly than in many years past.

"The Moon in Festive Mood," announced another paper, giving the same explanation and remarking that our chief satellite had apparently decided to compete against the seasonable illuminations beneath it. It was further stated that, given clear skies and a continuance of the snow upon the ground, the phenomenon should be visible for at least a week, until the moon waned.

This deliberately jocular means of dealing with the matter did far more to allay suspicion than any amount of carefully sugared scientific explanation.

The phenomenon caught the public imagination. The two following nights were brilliantly clear, and the whole of London turned out, as it always will turn out, to enjoy a free show.

On both nights I walked with my aunt in Hyde Park. My uncle had severely bruised his head upon a bookcase while playing "Blind Man's Buff" on Christmas night and preferred to rest at home.

The Park was an astonishing sight. Thousands paraded to and fro as if it were a Sunday morning in June—soldiers with their girls—children with their mothers—old gentlemen muffled in greatcoats. Here and there an amateur "expert" stood with a group around him as he described the craters and mountain ranges usually invisible to the human eye, and an old man with a telescope on a tripod was coining money at a penny a look.

Upon all sides one heard exclamations of delight. "Isn't it beautiful!"—"If only it always looked like that!" I nearly laughed out loud. Never before had I enjoyed my secret so hugely. I longed to jump onto a seat and tell the truth to these open-mouthed stargazers, but never by word or inference did I arouse suspicion in Aunt Rose's breast. When we got home we sat up till past midnight describing the scenes to Uncle Henry.

Upon the third day the weather broke. A thaw set in, and for a week the sky was filled with heavy cloud. By the time it had cleared the moon had gone, and the newspapers dropped the matter. They concentrated upon the trial of Lord Heskerpool, who had shot his gardener and put the body into the back of a guest's car. The unsuspecting guest had driven the body about for a week, and when he discovered it he was so terrified that he tried to throw it into the river. The police caught him and arrested him, but Lord Heskerpool's guilt was discovered in time. It was revealed that the gardener had been blackmailing his master, and altogether the whole case was so sensational that the moon was forgotten and England saved for another month to go upon its normal way. The governments all over the world, apparently, only explained away that December moon by the skin of their teeth.

A week after Christmas I returned to my home on Beadle Hill. In some absurd way the passing of that moon and the disappearance of the phenomenon from the newspapers and from the public mind lulled me into a feeling of security. I suppose it was due to my return to the humdrum village life after the excitement of Christmas. I cannot tell. I only know that for a few days I practically forgot the whole thing: the scare had come and gone and all was well. My extraordinary calmness of mind is proved by the fact that on the 2nd January, according to my diary, I actually bought six little Bantam hens and proceeded to bring them into condition for showing!

But it was a very short-lived armistice with the truth. On the 9th January I attended my last meeting of the British Lunar Society, and from that night onwards events were to move with ever-increasing rapidity towards their climax.

The meetings of the Society following the two that I have already described were dull in comparison, and something of an anticlimax. The President had merely endorsed his previous statements and provided us with lengthy and rather tedious résumés of current scientific opinion. The meeting on the 23rd December had, in fact, been quite sparsely attended, no more than half the members appearing. Whether this was due to the diversion of Christmas shopping or an inability to face these macabre gatherings I do not know, but there was no doubt about the 9th January. Members were obviously curious to hear about the "phenomenon" of Boxing Night and every seat was taken.

The President hardly mentioned the "scare" of those three clear-skied nights at Christmas: he dismissed them as unimportant—as something past and done with—and from my seat in the third row I listened to the last announcement I was ever to hear from Professor Hartley.

In eleven days' time—upon the 20th January—the new moon was due. The Government realised that further deception would be impossible. Even if given cloudy sky and poor visibility, the moon, at some period of its phases, was certain to be seen, and nothing could explain away its increased size and brilliancy. On the 27th December it had been 183,000 miles distant from the earth: upon the 25th January it would have drawn nearer by 32,000 miles and would have decreased its distance from the earth by almost one-half: it would appear at the end of January twice its normal size. . . .

The dead silence of our first fantastic meeting was upon us once again. There was something akin to physical pain in the tension that surrounded me. I felt a bead of perspiration trickle down my forehead as I sat there with my eyes upon the calm, grey-haired man at the speaker's desk.

Grey-haired!—only now did I realise how much our President had changed. Two months ago his red hair had been flecked by a touch of grey around the temples: tonight it was almost pure white. In October he had been a sturdy, youthful man of maybe forty-five—tonight he was an aged man of seventy. For the first time I realised what men of science—men who knew far more than us amateurs—must have suffered. I had believed that I, and these amateurs around me, had shared all his secrets—and now I knew that this prematurely whitened head bore secrets more terrible than any that we, his listeners, had been keeping with such self-importance from an ignorant public.

The calm, measured voice announced the dreadful programme as if it were a list of events at a sports meeting. . . .

"Sunday next will be the 14th. The new moon will be visible six days later—upon Saturday the 20th.

"It has been decided that the Church shall break the news from the pulpit on Sunday morning. By this means six days will elapse before the public will have visible evidence in the appearance of the moon: six days that may be invaluable in establishing calmness. From the morning after the announcement in the churches, the burden of guiding public thought will be upon the shoulders of the press, whose course will naturally be governed by circumstances as they arise.

"The Government will, from time to time, make official statements, but these will be limited to bare necessity. . . ."

There was something verging upon the comic in this extraordinary programme. Only today do I realise the consummate

wisdom of it . . . how heroically the world responded, how pitifully it culminated.

On the evening before that epic Sunday I walked down to the
Vicarage to see Mr. Edwards. I knew that the old man had received
his instructions and that he would now be struggling with the
terrible task of preparing his message to the people of Beadle at
tomorrow's service.

I felt that the knowledge of my having been acquainted with
all the facts for the past three months would help him, and that
my courage in carrying on so calmly in the face of death would
give inspiration and courage to the villagers if the Vicar were to
mention my behaviour in his announcement.

The housemaid took my name and returned to say that Mr.
Edwards was very busy upon tomorrow's sermon and would I
excuse him. I sent back word that my mission was one of the gravest
importance, and presently I was shown into the Vicar's study.

The old man rose to receive me in his courteous, kindly way. He
invited me to be seated, offered me a glass of sherry, and pushed forward the biscuit jar. I admired him beyond words in that moment.
No doubt he believed that I had called upon some trivial village
matter and yet he was prepared to listen with courteous patience.
He betrayed no sign of the awful burden that lay upon his shoulders: his fingers were quite steady as he broke a biscuit—there
was no tremor in his hand as he raised the sherry to his lips, and
although my admiration for him was soon to disappear, I silently
saluted him at that moment as a man whose courage and self-
control were equal to my own.

He asked me what he could do for me, and gently I broke my
secret.

"I know what you are striving to write at your desk tonight, Mr. Edwards: I know what you are called upon to do tomorrow. I have known for three months."

His face filled with alarm, and I hastened to explain. I told him that I had been numbered amongst the select few to share the secret from its birth.

To my surprise, he showed little interest in this. He asked none of the eager questions I had expected. There was a dreamlike, far-away look in his eyes, and a wave of pity swept over me. The poor, gentle old man was pitifully unequal to his task and I was glad that I had come so opportunely to support him.

"I think that I can help you," I went on. "I am, as it were, a 'veteran' of this secret: I have already suffered the worst that the terrible truth can inflict and I have survived. If you tell this to the people of Beadle tomorrow, it will help them to master their own terrible fears—"

The old man raised his hand to interrupt me.

"It is not terrible," he said. "Nor will my people think it so. If God has ordained that our work upon this earth is finished, then it is not for us to question Him. In His mercy He will relieve us from suffering; in the place of suffering he will grant happiness. The sadness of death lies with the lonely ones that are left to grieve—the children that are left without guidance. If God has ordained that we shall depart together—there will be none to grieve . . . we shall all be happy. . . ."

I was moved by the simplicity and sincerity of the old man, but his old-fashioned, stereotyped ideas irritated me. He would not be quite so smug and philosophical if he could visualise the full horror of it all, the horror that had turned white the hair of that brave man Professor Hartley. . . . I felt it my duty to bring him down to earth. . . .

"But the world isn't going to end tomorrow, Mr. Edwards. It isn't going to end with your sermon . . . there's three months ahead . . . three months of torment—"

Once again he interrupted me with a futile wave of his podgy little white hand.

"You needn't fear, Mr. Hopkins. The people of Beadle are honest and brave, and they trust in God."

I was getting angry, but I concealed it as best I could—fortunately the villagers of Beadle whom this futile man was to face next morning possessed imagination even more limited than his own!

And then quite suddenly he changed the subject. He asked me whether any of my early bulbs had taken advantage of the mild weather to peep above the surface of my meadow. He said that a cluster of snowdrops were in bloom in his rockery—an early cluster that never failed him in the first weeks of January, and that I must take a look at them as I went out.

I was really angry this time. I finished my sherry and curtly put down the glass. I would go—but I certainly wasn't going to potter about looking at his anaemic snowdrops. He was treating me like an ignorant villager, and I had ten times more snowdrops than he had, anyway.

He had not troubled to ask me a single question. He had ignored my offer of assistance and seemed quite incapable of realising how much he could have strengthened his message to the people of Beadle by inviting me to describe the whole course of my feelings and reactions during the past three months.

I realise now that he was jealous of me. He had quickly foreseen the importance and prestige that I should have gained at his expense if he were to announce that I knew all about it three months before he did. I do not blame him now—perhaps he was right to keep the importance to himself—goodness knows he needed all the importance he could collect—but I could not resist one dig at him as I turned to go.

"Now you understand why they told you to build that dugout!—clever idea to tell you it was against enemy bombs!"

"It was," he replied. "Quite a clever idea"—and he held out his hand with a gentle smile.

Only as I left the room did my pity return. At the study door his wife met me, took my hand, and bade me goodnight. In her calm eyes I could read that she too knew the secret now. I glanced at the old desk beneath the gaunt, poorly curtained window; at the twisted fragments of paper upon the threadbare carpet. Twisted paper: proof of the poor old man's pathetic inability to master his awful task in words. I saw, too, a fragment of blotting-paper thrown hastily over his feeble notes as I had entered the room.

I took one last glance at that peaceful, book-lined study: at the biscuit jar with an engraved message from some little Welfare Club of which the Vicar had once been Secretary—at a faded old football cap upon the wall and his rack of blackened old pipes beside the mantelpiece.

After this rebuff I scarcely expected ever to enter this room again. I realised that I was saying "farewell" to the first of many long-familiar scenes; that for three months to come I would often gaze upon some corner of my life and say: "I shall never see that again."

I walked straight past the Vicar's rockery without so much as a glance at his snowdrops. He had invited me to look at them as a man might humour a frightened child. My anger was redoubled when I thought how Dr. Hax had rebuffed my offer to help with the dugout and how the Vicar had snubbed my endeavour to assist in phrasing his sermon.

I had no appetite for supper: the little-minded jealousy of these "big men" of the village gnawed at my brain. I had the worst night since the one upon which I had first heard the news of the approaching disaster—three months, I repeat, before the Vicar knew a word about it.

CHAPTER EIGHT

The day upon which the news was broken to the world turned out to be one of the most disappointing in my life. It sounds absurd, but it is true.

As far as the village of Beadle was concerned, the whole thing completely misfired. It was partly due to the weather, partly to the general dullness of the villagers, but the chief blame must rest with the Vicar himself.

I really do not know what I had expected. No doubt I imagined panic-stricken people running screaming down the lanes, leaping stiles and burying their faces in the meadow grass—I visualised a fear-maddened mob smashing down the doors of the Fox & Hounds, bursting open the cellars and drinking themselves into stupor—I imagined others refusing to leave the church and kneeling the whole night in prayer. It was natural for me to imagine a hundred fantastic happenings when at last the ordinary people knew their fate. But I must explain what actually occurred and dwell no longer upon my imaginings.

To begin with, we were extremely unfortunate with the weather. I awoke to the dreary dripping of water from the drainpipe beneath my window and when I drew the curtains I saw my garden as it can only look upon a wet Sunday in January. The bare branches of the trees were slimy with rain and the sodden, wormcast lawn looked bald and hopeless. Even my cheery little Bantams scarcely raised their heads when I went to feed them.

The Sunday papers were unusually dull, and I filled in the time before morning service by heating some glue over the dining-room fire to gum a strip of green baize in my bookcase. The door of this bookcase had a way of opening by itself and I hoped that this would stop it.

The rain had almost ceased by the time the bell began to call us to the service, and a weak, watery sun had edged its way halfheartedly through the clouds.

From my bedroom window, as I dressed for the service, I looked down for the last time upon the placid people of Beadle as they threaded their way along the winding lanes in their Sunday clothes. Never again, I reflected, would they walk so placidly—so free from care.

In my annoyance of the previous night I had nearly decided to ignore the service as a protest against the Vicar ignoring my help, but curiosity had got the better of me and I reached the church with the last peal of the bell.

St. Peter's, Beadle, had none of the charm associated with an ancient country church. Although its vaults burrowed down into the thirteenth century, its structure had been destroyed by fire in the reign of George II. It had been rebuilt with an ugly, light-brown brick from a neighbouring kiln, and while it possessed attractive bells and a passable tower, the soil that it stood upon was so poor that no ivy or creeper had ever mustered the energy to climb its walls and even the churchyard yews lived in a state of perpetual exhaustion. Two stained-glass windows, the gift of the second Lord Burgin, only served to enhance the for-lorn bleakness of the others, and the morning sun had a way of shining diagonally upon the faces of the congregation, making repose most difficult.

The Vicar was respected and popular in a limited way, but despite his twenty-five years in Beadle he had never shaken off the disadvantages of following the fiery old "Vicar Hutchings," who had become almost legendary in the village and its neighbourhood by reason of his terrifying denunciation of every form of evil and most forms of good. When Vicar Hutchings had burst a blood-vessel at the Harvest Festival in 1920, the arrival of the timid, middle-aged Mr. Edwards was scarcely noticed for twenty years, and it was only recently that he had become a part of Beadle. Normally his congregation numbered about 80 of the 130 people in the parish, but only a stalwart 50 braved the weather on this historic Sunday. As I pulled off my galoshes in the porch I glanced at their placid, cowlike faces and wondered what they would all be thinking as they walked home under sentence of death.

Presently the shuffling and whispering died away with the entrance of the Vicar. A few late-comers crept into their places and the service began. The old man showed no sign of strain or distress. I thought that his face seemed a little paler, but his child-like grey eyes were as serene as ever.

The service followed its placid, age-encrusted course: the old man read one or two routine announcements, then cleared his throat and removed his spectacles. I saw the notes before him and I knew that the time had come.

In some respects he delivered his message well. The old man possessed dignity, and a clear, pleasant voice. I learned later that the bishops had issued merely a statement of fact and a few sug-gestions, leaving each vicar to frame his message in words most suitable to his own congregation. But when I say that Mr. Edwards delivered the message well, I only mean that the quality of his voice and his calm behaviour were open to admiration. The message itself was, as I expected, quite hopeless from the start. In his endeavour to avoid alarm, the meaning of it all became misty and obscure, and his attempt to blend it with the old-fashioned forms of conventional sermon made it sound almost exactly like what he had said every Sunday for twenty-five years. He blundered and stammered pathetically at one point when he attempted to explain the scientific aspect of the matter, and was far more at home when he was appealing to his congregation to accept God's will.

He spoke for nearly twenty minutes. When he finished there was a slight rustling of satin Sunday dresses and the hollow pop of a farmer's starched front as he relaxed his position. I do not believe that half a dozen people in the whole of that gathering had the slightest idea of what the Vicar had been talking about. I glanced over my shoulder at the cluster of pink, vacant faces behind me: a thin slant of sunlight fell upon them from the gaunt, unstained windows, and those faces looked like a bunch of moons themselves. But unlike the one the Vicar had been talking about, these moons around me would never in a thousand years draw nearer to the earth.

The congregation knelt in prayer as they had done in Beadle since Richard Cœur de Lion built their church to gain God's favour in his first Crusade: they filed out very slowly as old ladies blocked the way in their search for umbrellas and galoshes in the porch, and as I pulled on my own galoshes I was cheered by a sudden inspiration.

I had expected to leave church that morning robbed of all my superior knowledge of the moon's descent upon us: I had expected that the secret I had held with a chosen few would by now be shared by everyone in Beadle, but owing to the incompetence of the Vicar and the bluntness of the congregation, my secret seemed to be as safe as it ever was.

But with one vital, all-important difference!—I was now free to talk!—I was free to explain it all, clearly and sanely and vigorously—and succeed where the Vicar had so ignominiously failed!

It was twelve o'clock. I would go at once to the Fox & Hounds! No longer would I be a barely tolerated visitor!—In a few moments I would be the centre of a stunned, silent audience: I would play before the people of Beadle the part that Professor Hartley had played before the members of the British Lunar Society. I would become the one man in this village, the one man for miles around, whom everyone would seek! Dr. Hax and the Vicar would become nonentities and I the hero! I would pay these old fools back in their own coin and show them what it felt like to be snubbed and neglected. The reader may feel that I was ungenerous at that moment, but he will readily sympathise and support me when he thinks back upon the treatment I had received from the "big men" of the village.

As I hurried through the lingering congregation, I quickly received my first opportunity. Old Barlow, the postman, was standing at the gate arguing with his wife in a heated voice. He stopped me by laying a hand upon my arm.

"Mr. Hopkins," he said. "What was it the Vicar said was going to happen on the third of May?"

"He said," I replied in a quiet voice, "that on the third of May the moon will strike the earth and the world will end."

To my astonishment, the old man turned to his wife with an idiotic leer of triumph.

"There you are!" he cried. "I told you it wasn't no Bazaar! Nobody ever has Bazaars in May!"

"We had a Bazaar in May six years ago," shouted the old woman. "It was for the new club-room—and it was May because the stalls were got up with lilac blossom!"

I was about to explain in detail but the two old fools went doddering down the lane, abusing one another.

A girl was shouting at her deaf grandmother, almost at my elbow.

"He says the world's going to end, Grandma!"

"Eh?" said the old lady.

"He says," bawled the girl, "the world's going to end!"

The old lady's eyes lit up in a gleam of memory.

"That's more like old Vicar Hutchings," she cackled. "Vicar Hutchings used to say that every Sunday."

I heard the girl still shouting as they turned the bend in the lane.

"He says it's going to end on the third of May!"

"That's what old Vicar Hutchings always said," murmured the old lady. "But Vicar Hutchings never gave no date."

I do think that a lot of the blame must be laid upon the long-deceased Vicar Hutchings. That fiery old man had so often consigned the people of Beadle to eternal flame, wrath to come, etc., that the gentle Mr. Edwards with his plunging moon was naturally a bit of an anticlimax.

I think the average feeling amongst the congregation that morning was that Mr. Edwards, growing jealous of the undiminishing fame of his vigorous predecessor, had tried to pull it off himself with the moon as a novelty in the place of Vicar Hutchings's hellfire, but that he did not possess the personality to get away with it.

But at least a glimmering had apparently sunk into the people after all. A little group, mostly younger members of the congregation, had gathered around the vestry door and Mr. Edwards was speaking to them. I pitied the old man for having to suffer the added torment of explaining it all for a second time, but I really had no patience with him. He should have made it clearer upon his first attempt. I hurried off to the Fox & Hounds, burning to play my own dramatic part.

But apparently I had been forestalled. Murgatroyd, the proprietor, was hurrying out as I arrived. He was dragging his coat on, his hat was askew, and he was surrounded by a group of chattering villagers. He stared at me with his usual impudence and shouted out:

"Have you heard all this claptrap about the moon!"

"It is true," I replied. "I knew it all three months ago."

"Then why the hell didn't you tell us, you damn fool!" he shouted, and then, ignoring me and turning to the villagers: "Come on!—let's go and see this doddering parson!"

His rudeness infuriated me, and for the first time in my long residence in Beadle I lost my temper in public. Had I been a man of lower standing in the village I should have knocked the fellow down. As it was, I ran after him along the road and shouted:

"You were kept in ignorance because a fool like you would have gone off his head with fright!—that's why you were not told!"

I was about to say a great deal more when an old man walking beside the landlord—an old fellow who farmed a smallholding near Tewcastle—laid a hand upon my arm and said: "Keep your head, sonny. It's up to all of us to keep our heads!"

The humiliation of this nearly suffocated me: I strove to reply, but words failed me. I was being told to "keep my head"!—I!—I who had known the truth for twelve weeks—who had held this dreadful secret in such iron control that none had suspected it—was told by a fat-headed farmer to "keep my head"!

Without another word I turned upon my heel and strode away to my hilltop home, thanking heaven that I lived in a little world of my own, remote and aloof from the village yokels. There is something ugly and indecent about smug ignorance. I felt that I needed to wash my hands and face and rinse my mouth before I could return with dignity to my own thoughts.

I had expected with every reason to become the friend and philosopher to every man, woman, and child in Beadle as a result of my inner knowledge of the moon's approach: I had expected to stand with the Vicar as a bulwark of courage and wisdom against the childlike fears of the villagers: I had expected to be given a leading part in the construction of the dugout upon the hillside—and here I was, ignored and insulted, driven back to the solitude that I had endured for twelve weary weeks. To make matters worse, I had omitted, in my hurry to reach church, to remove the tin cup of glue that I had placed upon the fire to mend my bookcase. It had boiled up and overflowed and had stunk the house out. I opened all the windows and doors, and wandered in my garden while the smell blew away—I wandered like an exiled Napoleon upon St. Helena, looking down with infinite contempt upon the people who had repudiated me.

I could never enter the Fox & Hounds again: I doubted if I would ever again see the Vicar, for he would have incessant callers and would probably lose his head completely in his sudden rise to importance. I was thrown back upon Mrs. Buller, my housekeeper. It occurred to me that if I told her everything I knew, she would soon spread it amongst the villagers that I was a man with important facts and unique experiences to relate.

I accordingly detained the old lady when she came to remove my tea-tray. She had been to the morning service and I began by asking her what she thought about it all.

She told me that she hadn't heard it all properly. She had been worried about the sweetbreads that she was going to fry for my lunch, for they had smelt a little strong when she had washed them. But she had thought Mr. Edwards had been "quite good" and quite like old Vicar Hutchings, whom she remembered as a girl.

I explained the whole thing to Mrs. Buller in a few simple, selected words.

She nodded now and then, but did not even put the tray down. I could see that her poor old cottage-bred brain was utterly unable to grasp the overwhelming significance of it. She had never, apparently, visualised the moon as a solid, spherical body revolving majestically in space: to her it was a flat, shining disc sewn to a dark fabric of black sky that moved overhead and took the moon along with it. She obviously had no notion of its size, or its original distance from the earth. Size was controlled by the distance she could see, and she had been short-sighted since a child.

The idea of the moon's return to the earth did not disturb her very much: she was visualising, I could see, a large silver tray hitting the roof with a clang and bouncing down the hillside.

She remarked that she hoped it wouldn't land upon the earth when it was a new moon, because in that case the sharp points might cut somebody. She asked me whether my sweetbreads had been all right, and went off to prepare dinner. She returned a moment later to say that if the smell of the glue upset me, she would set my dinner in the library.

I lay back in my lonely chair, gazing into the fire, crushed by the heartrending isolation that must, I suppose, be the tragic lot of any intelligent man who lives in a village like Beadle.

CHAPTER NINE

My annoyance over the trivial stupidity of Beadle was soon forgotten when I awoke on Monday morning.

So infuriated—so justly infuriated—had I been at my treatment by the Vicar and the publican that for the moment I had almost lost sight of the fact that the rest of the world might be just as badly disturbed by the news as the village of Beadle.

I awoke from a restless sleep at three in the morning, and after lying for several hours rehearsing what I would say to the publican if ever I met him again, it suddenly occurred to me that the morning newspapers ought to be extremely interesting.

Within a very few minutes the Vicar and the publican assumed their correct size in my sense of proportion (in other words, they became small insects and were completely forgotten) and I began to wonder how the newspapers would tackle their frightfully difficult job.

They had got away with the "phenomenon" at Christmas by the skilful expedient of humour, but headlines such as "The Moon in Festive Mood" would serve no longer. They could not make fun of the end of the world, but on the other hand it was their duty at all costs to allay fear. I was still pondering this intriguing problem when Mrs. Buller brought my morning tea, and I could scarcely wait until she had left the room before I snatched up the papers to see what they had to say about it all.

Upon first sight I was somewhat disappointed. I had expected terrific, flaming headlines of the most sensational description: I almost expected the papers to appear with broad edges of black, in advance mourning for the death of the world. But instead I observed in each paper a masterly restraint, and a tone that inspired excitement rather than panic.

Each published an Official Statement of the salient facts, phrased with a calm dignity that somehow stirred one's pride. Each followed this with interviews and articles by famous scientists who enlarged upon every particle of hope with the greatest skill.

The "grazing" theory was the one unanimously adopted. It was explained that the tails of comets had frequently grazed the earth without doing the slightest damage, and although the moon was a solid body, its size in relation to the earth was only that of a cherry compared with a large orange.

If a cherry were to graze the surface of an orange, it was scarcely likely to smash the orange to pieces.

Some papers went so far as to question whether even a graze would occur. The moon, they explained, had simply taken a new course: its gravitational poise had been disturbed and it might now be moving without any relationship with the earth at all. It might pass close to us and then move away forever into the uncharted spaces of the universe: we should miss it, naturally, but it provided nothing that we could not do without at a pinch. The tides, for instance, which were influenced by the moon, were valuable in keeping the seaside beaches clean during the summer season but other means could doubtless be discovered. Shipping would be assisted very greatly: so many big liners were slaves to the tides and frequently lost so much time in waiting for them that the disappearance of the moon would be welcomed in nautical circles. The Oxford and Cambridge Boat Race, which took advantage of the tide upon the Thames, would have to be rowed in the opposite direction, from Mortlake to Putney, in order to obtain the advantage of normal river stream—and so, with extraordinary adroitness, the newspapers led us away from the dangerous, panic-breeding grounds of scientific theory to the homely, amusing details of life without a moon.

One finely written article stressed the awe-inspiring romance and excitement that lay in store for us. The generation upon earth this day would be privileged to witness a stupendous phenomenon denied to the ages past and the ages yet to come. . . . In three months' time would come a terrific thrill . . . the moon would pass literally a few miles from us—it would fill the whole sky—it would pass and leave us, perhaps forever. In years to come old men at their firesides would say to their grandchildren—"I remember the moon . . ."—every ounce of human courage would be demanded: there might be storms and floods . . . there would be danger, but the human race was inured to danger . . . the world must keep calm . . . it was not created to perish . . . all would be well.

Upon one point all were definitely agreed. There would be no "head-on" crash. This was impossible because the moon and the earth were revolving in the same direction. We could no more have a "head-on" crash than two motor-cars could crash head-on when travelling side by side. The only thing that could definitely smash the world was therefore out of the question. . . .

I dressed and shaved with a buoyancy of spirit which I had not experienced for years: I even sang in my bath—a thing I had not done since my college days. I was profoundly affected by the newspapers. This was no mere "eyewash." There was reason and deep thought behind their optimism. I was angry with Professor Hartley for having disturbed us so unnecessarily at the meetings of our Society, but I reflected that all "experts" were tarred with the same brush—they could never resist exploiting their superior wisdom to alarm their listeners. I felt a deep, exultant conviction that the world would survive—that the human race, purified by a common danger, would emerge with all its petty jealousy and senseless strife forgotten. Instead of destroying us, the moon would deliver us forever from greed and cruelty and war by frightening us into an everlasting thankfulness.

Directly after breakfast I went down to the village to ask Mr. Westrop, the postmaster, whether he thought the Widgeley Poultry Show would be cancelled. Widgeley was fortunate in having a keen, efficient Committee and their show, unlike some that I could mention, always went like clockwork. I well recollect one show (which I will spare from naming), at which the judge of the Wyandotte cockerel class appeared in a disgustingly intoxicated condition. After making several absurd remarks he announced in a loud voice that he would give a special prize of five pounds to the hen that could lay the most eggs in ten minutes. He then shouted: "Are you ready, go!" It was a disgraceful scene, but it aroused such deafening laughter from the onlookers that my hen Broodie actually laid an egg on the spot, and it gave me the greatest pleasure to force the drunken sot into delivering a five-pound note.

Mr. Westrop, who shows Rhode Island pullets in a modest way, agreed with me that the Widgeley Committee were most unlikely to cancel the show, particularly as they had already booked the County Hall. The show being on Thursday, I arranged to share a van with Mr. Westrop to convey our exhibits. I was showing my six little Bantam hens for the first time, and although I had not possessed them long enough to bring them into winning condition, I was very anxious to see how they would compare with thoroughly trained birds.

After leaving the post office I had to pass the Fox & Hounds. I was giving it a wide berth (for I had no wish to see its surly proprietor again) when I heard someone call my name, and to my surprise saw Murgatroyd himself approaching me.

I was about to turn away and ignore him when something in his manner detained me against my will.

Normally his big, shapeless face was the very embodiment of smug self-indulgence: his fat red cheeks were so thoroughly embalmed in alcohol that I had pictured them blooming unseen beneath the soil of the churchyard forever and ever. And now, with a shock of surprise, I saw a face that had aged by twenty years in a single night: a face that in a night had fallen to a wreck beyond repair. Those crimson, blooming cheeks had become grey, flabby pouches filled with hundreds of little wandering blue veins. Those bulbous, self-satisfied eyes were flickering now in deep, dirty-yellow pits that symbolised an eternity of sleepless nights.

There was stark, ugly death in the face of the proprietor of the Fox & Hounds and I recoiled from it in horror.

I should have prepared myself to meet a certain number of men who would collapse pitiably like this, but the serene calmness of the Vicar and his wife and the homely stolidness of my housekeeper had misled me.

There was something infinitely pathetic in that quivering bulk of flesh with all its arrogance stripped from it: something pitiable in the way he approached me, almost shyly, with his haggard face twisted into the burlesque of a smile.

"Sorry about yesterday," he said. "It ain't my way to be rude. Shall we call it quits?"

Why it should be called "quits" I do not know, for the rudeness had been entirely upon his part, and never in my life had I been rude to him. But the big trembling hand was before me; I took it, and shook it warmly. I loathe bad feeling and was very glad that the incident was over. He had capitulated completely, even if in a pathetic little attempt to save his pride he preferred to "call it quits."

The fat coward was in such a state of repressed terror that I felt it my duty to reassure him and put new heart into him.

"That's all right," I said with a smile. "We were all a bit over-wrought yesterday, but it's better now."

"What d'you mean—'better now'?" he said abruptly, his eyes full of groping suspicion and resentment.

"I mean it's not going to be so terrible after all," I replied. "Haven't you seen this morning's newspapers? We're all going to live to tell the tale!"

The man's feeble smile had disappeared: the sunken, jaundiced eyes had a horrid leer in them and he spat a harsh, unpleasant laugh at me.

"You needn't treat me like a kid," he snarled. "You ain't such a damn fool as not to know it's the bloody end." He dragged a crumpled newspaper from his pocket and flourished it in my face. "D'you s'pose any man with half a brain believes the blab in these papers?—They talk about a 'graze'!" (His voice was rising: he was almost inarticulate, and as he shouted at me he crushed the paper into a ball and flung it over the hedge.) "A *graze*!—have you ever heard such bloody rot? D'you suppose a mighty great thing like the moon can give us a 'graze' without smashing millions of us to bleeding pulp and jerking the rest of us to kingdom come? They've got the nerve to tell us the moon's the size of a cherry!"

"They don't say that," I began, "they—"

"They *do* say that," he shouted.

"It's just a comparison," I went on.

"Comparison!" he yelled. "The moon's the size of Europe!—What kind of a mess would you be in if somebody hit you over the head with Europe?" He looked at me with a contempt that I had never seen in a human face before. "You talking about having a tale to tell!—Try dropping Westminster Abbey on top of a cheese-maggot and see what kind of a tale it's got to tell! O' course the bloody papers 'ave got to say something! Any fool knows that!"

With an effort I quenched the angry retort that sprang to my lips. I do not believe that he had any direct intention of comparing me with a cheese-maggot: I prefer to believe that it was merely his clumsy way of putting it.

"Anyway," I said with an attempted smile, "we've all got a right to our opinion. What about a little drink to wash the moon away?"

He shook his head. "Not me. I ain't drinking no more. With three months to live I reckon a man's a damn fool to knock chunks of his time away with a gin bottle. I'm just walking into Lullington to see my old ma. She's near ninety and won't understand nothing. I'd rather be with them that can't understand than those who don't try. You go inside. Tell Mabel to give you a glass on the house. There's plenty of nitwits in there who believe them papers like you do!"

With that he turned away, and walked off down the road.

I had done my best to keep calm before him, but as I watched that waddling, tight-trousered figure disappearing around the corner, I could have thrown impotent curses after him. I nearly ran after him and shouted my anger at him as I had done the day before. It was not his obscene tongue that had angered me—nor his contemptible terror; it was the horrible conviction that this man was right—that every word he had said, despite his stumbling coarseness, was pitilessly true. I was angry because he had revealed me as a fool. I had surrounded myself with a feeble little screen of self-deception which this drink-sodden creature, in a few lashes of his crude tongue, had shattered beyond repair.

But worse still, this bloated publican had destroyed with his foul tongue every particle of heroism that might have sustained me against the horror that lay ahead.

With Professor Hartley I had faced death and been unafraid—for death in the company of a fine man can become a brave adventure. I had faced death in the presence of our Vicar because no man could sink to fear in the presence of pure courage and unquench-able faith. But death in company with a swollen, craven creature that smelt of whisky and perspiration was a revolting, terrifying thing—an obscene thing that carried me to the brink of suicide . . . to anything that would spare me from dying at the same moment as that nasty man.

For the first time in my life I craved alcohol—by bitter irony I craved forgetfulness in the very thing that had made the propri-etor of the Fox & Hounds such a loathsome creature to die with!

I had to do it. If I had restrained myself I do not believe I should ever have seen another day in my right mind. I stumbled blindly into the saloon bar, elbowed my way through the chattering crowd, and called for a large brandy and soda.

I dislike the taste of brandy and rarely drink it, and to this fact I owe its almost instantaneous and stimulating effect upon me. In a few minutes I was able to take note of the scene surrounding me with a calmness that I would never have believed possible again.

The saloon bar was crowded with farmers who had come in to discuss the news as their forefathers had come to talk of the death of Queen Anne and the victory at Trafalgar. Nobody was drink-ing to excess and if any felt concern they concealed it well. For a time I sat wondering where I had witnessed such a scene before: that full-throated, excited murmur was vaguely familiar—and suddenly I knew. I was witnessing again, with uncanny similarity, that scene of strange elation in the refreshment-room of the British Lunar Society, when after the stunning shock of our President's announcement we had reacted over our coffee and sandwiches into something very near to exultation. I saw again those same eyes, stirred to brightness by the fascination of a threatened danger that still lay reassuringly in the future: I heard those same excited voices that mirrored the pride in a brain that was suddenly grappling with something far bigger than anything that had come within its ken before.

I could quickly see that the majority had accepted without reserve the reassurances of the newspapers. The average farmer so completely exhausts his store of pessimism over the future of farming that he has no alternative but to be optimistic about everything else. The news about the moon was obviously producing plenty of wit. The "grazing" theory had caught the popular imagination, and one old fellow raised a hearty laugh by expressing the hope that the moon would graze his barley field and save him a week with the plough. Another raised a still louder laugh by calling out that it wouldn't leave anything for his sheep to graze.

I began to feel so much better that I was almost moved to join in and turn the conversation to my long-preserved secret and the dramatic meetings of the British Lunar Society. But reflection warned me that scientific details would be out of place amongst these simple, slow-witted fellows: out of harmony with the defiant, carefree atmosphere.

I suppose I am unduly swayed by the feelings of my fellow men, for when I left the Fox & Hounds I was so completely restored to my normal state that I went straight home and telephoned to Pomfret

Wilkins, Secretary of the Widgeley Poultry Show, to confirm that everything would be carried through as usual on Thursday. His cheery, booming voice quickly reassured me. The Widgeley Poultry Show would be held as arranged—moon or no moon. He told me that there was an unusually heavy entry for the Bantam cockerel section, but fewer hens were being shown than last year. When he told me of the keen interest aroused by the news that I was showing my Bantams for the first time I especially asked him, if he had the chance, to let it be known in Widgeley that the entry was purely a sporting gesture upon my part, as I had not had the time to bring my Bantams up to the standard expected of me. I explained to him that I was entering merely to compare the progress of my birds with prize entries and had no expectation whatever of carrying off an award.

Between ourselves, I was anxious for this to be clearly understood on account of the jealousy that was at that time so prevalent in the poultry world. As the most successful breeder in South Hampshire I was naturally the principal target for this jealousy, and a failure upon my part would lead to a chorus of delight from the less successful. By making it clear that I was not seriously competing for a prize I was forestalling these jeers in the event of my not winning. Pomfret Wilkins promised to do what he could: he was attending a Rotary lunch next day and it would give him the chance of explaining about my exhibit. The news would quickly get around Widgeley and the facts concerning my Bantams would be quite well known by Thursday.

An amusing thing happened that evening. I felt so much better disposed towards everybody in Beadle after my cheerful visit to the Fox & Hounds that I decided to let bygones be bygones and go down to offer my services upon the dugout. I accordingly set out to see Dr. Hax and offer to help in any way I could.

At his gate I met Pawson, the retired police sergeant, who was a member of the Dugout Committee.

I greeted him jovially, but to my surprise I discovered him filled with disgust.

"Damn waste of time," he growled. "Just the kind of thing that *would* happen."

"What do you mean?" I asked.

"Why, this blooming dugout! Here we've been breaking our backs on it—and now this!"

I was completely puzzled, and again asked him what he was driving at. He nearly lost his temper.

"Well—use your common sense! Here we spend weeks of our time building a whacking great dugout to get into if there's a war—and who d'you suppose is going to waste time having a war with all this moon business coming on?—Damn waste of time!"

At first I was astonished—then I simply had to laugh out loud. The poor fool had never realised what the dugout was really for!

"Use your *own* common sense!" I cried. "The dugout's to save the village from the moon! That war story was just a blind!"

He was completely unconvinced, but soon afterwards he apologised most handsomely, for Dr. Hax, as Chairman of the Dugout Committee, had now received full official instructions. We were to press ahead with the dugout at full speed and have the excavation complete by Wednesday week, when a sapper of the Royal Engineers would arrive in Beadle to instruct us upon the final details.

The doctor was more self-important than ever now. He felt completely responsible for the lives of all Beadle and was like a general preparing for a battle. He accepted my services in rather an offhand way and told me to report in Burgin Park at nine o'clock next morning.

I went home far happier with active and useful work ahead, but I could not sleep for laughing at that poor dunderheaded fellow who never realised the purpose of the dugout until he was told!

CHAPTER TEN

The newspapers on Tuesday morning were not quite so pleasant. It is true that they published special articles by foreign scientists that confirmed the optimistic statements of our own astronomers, and the cartoonists had even dared to compare the moon's approach with current political matters, but I noticed a stern undercurrent that was missing from the almost holiday-like atmosphere of the Monday papers.

As a dentist puts comic papers upon the table of his waiting room, so the newspapers cheered us up on Monday to make us the stronger to meet the facts on Tuesday.

There was, for instance, the Government order against "malingering" that surprised and disturbed me. A special Act of Parliament declared it to be an offence, punishable by imprisonment with hard labour, for any man to absent himself from his work without a medical certificate of illness.

It seemed that in certain districts, under the influence, no doubt, of individuals with strong personality, large numbers of factory workers had decided that it was a waste of time to work anymore, and had gone home at lunchtime.

It was a harsh law that deprived those who sincerely believed the end to be near from spending their last days with their wives and children—particularly for those engaged upon work of a kind so obviously useless as, say, making hats, when there were more than enough hats in stock to last until the 3rd of May. Nobody in his right mind would bother to buy a new hat which, even if not totally destroyed by the moon itself, would obviously be blown away in a hurricane that accompanied the moon's passing. But the official attitude was right in all the circumstances. Far better to make superfluous hats than be idle under such conditions. In any case there would be few with sufficient money saved up to last the three months until the 3rd of May: idleness would lead not only to moral collapse, but in the end to thieving, looting, and anarchy.

I think that the newspapers exercised a great deal of voluntary censorship in those early days of excitement, for although they stressed the heroic calmness with which the news had been received all over England, I know for a fact that the Rector of Chadley was thrown into the village duck-pond.

It appears that the Rector, in an excess of righteousness, had blamed the evil ways of his villagers for the moon's threat to destroy the earth. The villagers naturally felt it was absurd to suggest that God was destroying the world in order to teach Chadley not to play darts on Sundays, and they showed their irritation in the manner above mentioned.

If a thing like that could happen within seven miles of Beadle, I am pretty sure that even more serious incidents must have occurred here and there in other parts of the world. But the newspapers did not report these disturbing incidents and no doubt they were right in suppressing them. "Business as usual" became the slogan, and it was emblazoned upon all the posters.

*   *   *

The newspapers also urged on with all speed the work of defence, and I could scarcely force my way through the crowd when I reported at nine o'clock that morning for work upon our dugout in Burgin Park. The whole village was there to watch, partly because the dugout was now so exciting and partly because, under normal conditions, Burgin Park was private.

The Vicar and Dr. Hax were fussing about with ridiculous importance. They were both wearing enamelled blue badges inscribed COMMITTEE which had been bought the previous year for the village sports, but I soon realised that Mr. Murdoch, the engineer from Makleton who had been made "technical adviser," was the real boss of the show. He was a thin, bleak-looking Scotsman with a drooping black moustache and a broad accent, but he obviously knew his job and had got the work far better organised than anything achieved by Dr. Hax at the Beadle athletic meetings.

A large hole gaped in the chalky hillside and broad steps led down into the bowels of the hill. I was told that Mr. Lanbury, the blacksmith, with his son Richard and old Peter (who broke stones for the Rural Council) were down below with miners' picks, and two lusty farm boys were hauling sandbags full of broken chalk up the dugout steps.

Dr. Hax introduced me to Mr. Murdoch and I was detailed to join the "wheelbarrow gang." I was given a zinc barrow and my job was to trundle the excavated chalk down the hillside and dump it into a disused quarry. It was pleasant work, for the full barrow practically ran by itself downhill and it was an easy matter to wheel the empty vehicle up the slope again.

At twelve o'clock old Lady Burgin sent her butler and pantry boy down with a large canister of tea and we knocked off and had a picnic lunch beneath the trees. While we were lunching a load of timber struts arrived in a lorry from the Cakebridge Saw Mills, and during the afternoon we unloaded them so that John Briggs, the carpenter, could begin strutting the dugout steps. I was told that the whole of the interior was to be lined with timber, a packing of old sacking and cloth being thrust into the cavity between the chalk walls and the lining to act as a shock absorbent.

It was a lovely day with a hint of spring in the air and I enjoyed it all immensely. The mild weather had encouraged the bulbs: the crocuses were spangling the glades of the Park with a sheen of gold and blue, and as I lay under the trees eating my sandwiches I could picture these woods in a few weeks' time with their glimmering carpet of daffodils.

There was a grand spirit amongst us, too. We had always been a friendly, peaceful village, but I had never before felt such a fine bond of comradeship. We were all so happy at having something novel and valuable to do. The men all called each other by their nicknames and I was almost tempted to tell John Briggs, the carpenter, that my Christian name was Edgar. I decided upon reflection not to do so, for if nothing fatal happened on the 3rd of May he might fail to appreciate his duty to call me "sir" again.

All the same, I felt so happy with my wheelbarrow that I was quite sorry to have to ask Mr. Murdoch for leave off on Thursday afternoon to attend the Widgeley Poultry Show. For two pins I would have cancelled my entry and stayed in Beadle, but I well knew that this would be interpreted by my rival exhibitors as a confession of weakness, and I had to go.

I spent that evening preparing a few words that I should be called upon to say when my champion Wyandotte hen Broodie was awarded her fiftieth First Prize. I have scarcely mentioned Broodie in my story until now: I could not resist holding her name back and dwelling upon her fame at this point as a surprise to my readers who might by now believe that they were fully acquainted with every branch of my success as a poultry breeder.

Broodie was born in the early hours of the 14th June two years previously. She was one of a brood of nine, and it is remarkable that none of her brothers and sisters emerged from mediocrity. Nature lavished all her gifts upon her, and I was quick to single her out for special care. She became my "chef d'œuvre": her first appearance at the South Hampshire Poultry Show caused the biggest sensation in years: by the age of eleven months she had carried off twenty-three First Prizes and her photograph had appeared in three papers in Denmark. She was in a class by herself—so much so that in many cases, upon news of her entry, the other exhibitors withdrew their hens in a body and Broodie secured a triumphant walkover. At the age of nineteen months she was, if anything, in finer condition than ever, and this will afford reassurance to the reader who may have considered my action in preparing a speech in advance as over-confident, even vainglorious.

I prepared an amusing little speech, giving Broodie all the credit and finishing with the remark that she had been offered a big prize to star in a film! I knew that this would cause a great deal of laughter, and went to bed looking forward to the Show the next day.

But for some extraordinary reason I had a most disturbing nightmare. I dreamt that when the time arrived for Broodie to be taken before the judges at the Show, I found to my horror that she had shrunk up to the size of a sparrow. The judges were waiting—everybody was waiting—and I was at my wits' end what to do. Desperately I carried the poor shrivelled little creature into the Market Square, hoping that the fresh air would revive her and restore her to her normal appearance, but she escaped from me and ran back into the County Hall. I rushed after her, but too late—for there was the poor, tiny bird strutting up and down with the other Wyandottes to the deafening laughter of the onlookers, all of whom were delighted at Broodie's downfall and my embarrassment.

I awoke with a dry, burning mouth and beating heart. It puzzled me, and worried me, for I had eaten a very light supper.

I have since thought that my digestion had been disturbed by the heavy and unaccustomed work with those wheelbarrow loads of chalk. Hard physical labour soon makes us conscious of tired arm and leg muscles, but we are inclined to forget that our digestive muscles are equally tired and unable to do their normal work. I have frequently considered the matter, and am now convinced that my nightmare about Broodie was due to that wheelbarrow.

CHAPTER ELEVEN

I had not been in the market town of Widgeley for ten minutes before I began to wish that I were back in the calm, unchanging atmosphere of Beadle. I suppose town folk are more sensitive to fear than village people, or possibly their less active lives provide a more fertile breeding ground for morbid thoughts. I can only say that the atmosphere of Widgeley was far different from the trustful optimism of my native village, and there was an unhealthy flavour about the place which I did not like.

People seemed to be wandering restlessly in the streets with no definite purpose, and as I entered the Unicorn for my customary lunch before the Show I had to stand quickly aside to allow a strange and pathetic scene to pass before me.

A handsome woman, obviously of good social standing, was helping a grey-haired chauffeur to lead an elderly man along the passage, and behind them walked a pretty girl of about eighteen, carrying the man's hat.

There was such pitiful dismay and shame in the eyes of that girl and woman that I knew them to be the wife and daughter—and the man was helplessly, revoltingly drunk.

I could see at a glance that he was not an ordinary drunkard, for there was pride and intellect in the finely chiselled face even as it lolled hopelessly to and fro. I could visualise quite easily what had happened—that quiet country family driving to the market town—that wife and daughter leaving to do some shopping—the father, in a fatal moment of inactivity and loneliness, breaking suddenly under days of hideous, pent-up strain . . .

From the coffee-room window I watched the little group cross the Market Square to their waiting car. I saw a party of loungers gather round and snigger while the woman held her husband's arm as he vomited in the gutter. As I watched the sedate old Daimler drive away there came a chuckle at my elbow, and I turned to find Tim, the waiter, standing by me.

"Major Hildesley," he remarked, "one of our Magistrates." And then he chuckled again. "Not much chance for him on the Bench again!"

I had little appetite for lunch. I could not detach my mind from that pathetic scene. I could not bear to think how that proud family would pass the rest of the day—and the long days to come.

There were scenes in the dining-room that disturbed me, too. A young man came in and loudly ordered a grilled steak. Within a couple of minutes he was abusing Tim, the waiter, for not bringing it, and as Tim was explaining that all grills took ten minutes the man crumpled up his newspaper, flung it upon the floor, stamped out of the room, and did not return.

A fat, red-faced man, to whom meals must surely have been an absorbing pastime in happier days, was finicking and fussing with a helping of steak-pie. He turned the cubes of meat over this way and that in an aimless, helpless way that so got on my nerves that I could have shrieked at him. At last he pushed the plate away with a heavy sigh, called for a large whisky and soda, and gulped it like a thirsty animal. I was very glad to leave the Unicorn for the more familiar atmosphere of the Poultry Show.

As far as I was personally concerned, things could not have been better. Broodie defeated her three mediocre rivals with laughable ease and carried off her fiftieth First Prize. This I expected, but what pleased me so much was the fact that my little Bantam hens received an Honourable Mention. When the reader bears in mind that I had not entered these little birds with any thought of a prize, he will readily understand the pleasure I felt.

But my personal success was really the only bright spot of the whole afternoon.

The Poultry Show itself was a mockery of former days. It seems that the courage of the Committee in deciding to carry on had aroused a lot of stupid amusement amongst the rougher elements of the town, who had gathered at the door and were cheering and laughing as the hens and cockerels were carried in. It is the worst possible thing to disturb highly trained birds in this way and I was justly angry.

When I entered the Hall I found it barely a quarter full, and Pomfret Wilkins, the Secretary, greeted me with an exuberance that seemed, in the circumstances, a little overdone. He told me that a number of entries had been cancelled at the last moment, and several had simply not turned up, without a word one way or another, just as if the Show had slipped their memory as something of no importance whatever.

It was all terribly depressing, and I was furiously angry that Broodie should achieve her fiftieth victory under such unworthy conditions. Some of the exhibitors put on a kind of swaggering bravado as if they were heroes to have come at all, and the judges carried out their responsible duties with an impatience and a care-lessness that was a lasting disgrace.

There were scarcely a dozen people remaining in the Hall when the prizes were distributed, and the Chairman's mind was so hopelessly off his duty that he completely forgot that it was customary to invite an exhibitor to say a few words when one of his hens achieved a specially notable distinction.

He apologised when I reminded him, but there were only eight people left when I began my speech. Although I spoke for less than fifteen minutes, three of these people actually left in the middle of it, and the others turned out to be the five men who were waiting to take the platform away when I had finished. In the circumstances it is not surprising that my carefully prepared joke, about Broodie receiving big offers to star in a film, completely misfired. It was received in silence, and I was very glad, as I have already said, to start back to my own brave village of Beadle again.

But as I watched the towers of that once friendly, happy town fade into the twilight, I knew that the last effort to keep up the old traditions was over forever: the last happy, normal event had been bravely attempted, and had dismally failed.

After dinner that night I went out into my garden to see the new moon: the February moon: the last moon but two. I sat in my arbour of yew trees where four long months ago I had first opened the fateful letter that called me to the memorable meeting of the British Lunar Society. The thin crescent was high above the beech trees of Burgin Park. Except for its brilliancy it seemed little different from usual, but as my eyes grew accustomed to the night sky I perceived the darkened portion of the moon looming huge and venomous against the thin bright crescent. I think, in its concealed darkness, it was more terrible than ever it seemed when later it emerged in its full brilliancy—it was like the foul black head of an octopus rearing its way through a dark, weed-slimed ocean.

I could not bear to be alone with that bloated thing for long. As I stood there I half expected to see it move and change before my eyes—but it lay so firmly, so serenely in the sky that I could scarcely believe that in every second it was plunging upon its dreadful, relentless journey towards us.

I drew the curtains in my library and tried to lose myself by entering into my Poultry Journal the hollow victories of that afternoon. I turned the six closely written folios that recorded Broodie's triumphant rise to fame, and a lump rose in my throat as a procession of happy days came back to me—starlit evenings, riding home in Mr. Flidale's van with Broodie in her crate beside me. Perhaps it will all seem paltry and trivial to the man who finds and reads this manuscript in the long-distant years of the future—but it was something real and honest and thrilling in those happy, sunlit days.

CHAPTER TWELVE

As the weeks passed by I discovered that the people of Beadle had divided themselves into three definite schools of thought.

The first school, and the one that claimed the largest following, was influenced by the country gentlemen whose views upon the matter reached the Fox & Hounds by way of their grooms and gardeners and chauffeurs.

In the opinion of the country gentlemen, "the moon business" was all a scare. Nothing would happen, but if it did, it would happen in China where that sort of thing always happened. In their opinion, it would not affect England. Things like that did not happen in England. We should "muddle through" as we always had done in other troubles. We had a Government with a strong majority and the police were equal to anything.

I liked this view. It was healthy and defiant, and I sincerely wished that I could subscribe to it in full sincerity. It was the view most likely to assist in keeping law and order to the end, and I invariably supported it in public.

The second, or "middle" school of thought was that which followed the opinion of the newspapers. The moon would "graze" us: it would give us a big thrill, a severe jolt that might cause some damage, and bounce off again into space, never to return.

I think the people who believed this were the happiest, for they had something genuinely exciting to look forward to. They were prepared to see the stately beech trees of Burgin Park come crashing down like nine-pins: they were ready for a deluge, a hurricane, a terrific blowing about of dustbin lids, and a very fine sight as the moon passed overhead almost within touching distance. They did not, I think, associate any of this damage with themselves, and they talked vigorously and endlessly in the Fox & Hounds until closing time. And even after closing time they would stimulate the cool night air with their fantastic imaginings, frequently forgetting the huge, glittering ball in the sky above.

The third school of thought, the members of which I at all times endeavoured to avoid, were those who were known at the Fox & Hounds as the "prepare ye for the end" crowd. They mustered, I should say, about one in ten of the population of Beadle and were drawn from all classes irrespective of calling and creed. These people were quite certain that the moon would destroy the earth completely, and they reacted to their terrible conviction according to their characters and temperament.

I have since realised that these were the genuinely brave people of the world. The majority of the rest of us preferred other opinions because we could not face the thing that was most likely to happen.

This school of thought was represented in its highest form by Hubert Edwards, our Vicar. From the evening upon which he first received the news I believe that Mr. Edwards was convinced that the end had come. He did not accept it as a dramatic gesture of God's wrath: he humbly and reverently believed that God in His wisdom had decided that the earth had served its purpose as an abode for His creatures, and that He was about to place it amongst the milliards of dead worlds that had, in their own time, played their inscrutable part in the Universal Scheme. His faith was unshaken, for Heaven, in Hubert Edwards's mind, was not local to the earth; it embraced every living creature that had played its part in every world in the unfathomable spaces around us. Nor did he lapse into religious heroics. He pursued his work in the village serenely and cheerfully: he well knew that many of his parishioners believed that the earth would survive, but never by word or inference did he seek to influence their views. Although he must have known the dugout to be a pitiful waste of time, he was there every day, frequently with his coat off, wheeling a barrow: he was here, there, and everywhere with a cheery joke and a large bottle of fruit tablets which he distributed as thirst quenchers. Perhaps the greatest tribute that can be paid to Hubert Edwards is that everyone attended his services every Sunday, and everyone secured renewed hope from them, no matter whether they belonged to the "all is well" school, the "moon will graze us" party, or the fatalists. He spoke as he had spoken for twenty-five years in Beadle Church, simply because he had spoken his best from the day he came to us. To this last school of thought, but at the opposite and most revolting end, belonged Murgatroyd, the publican. He, too, believed the end to be upon us—but it was an end that reeked of hearses, musty black plumes, and grave-clothes. In his haunted, jaundiced eyes there lurked the mould of new-dug graves—in his hunted brain gleamed the spade of the sexton—the toll of the bell—blackness—dirt—and corruption.

He was rarely seen in the bar of the Fox & Hounds. Mabel, who tended the wants of customers, said that he brooded for hours by the fire in his fetid little bed-sitting room upstairs: she said that he read the Bible and *Whitaker's Almanack*, and moulded grotesque little figures out of putty. If he drank any longer he drank in secret, and almost every evening, when the spring twilight fell across the meadows, he would put on an old bowler hat that he used to go to the Races in, and walk the six miles through the valley to his bedridden old mother at Lullington. The old lady was senile and understood nothing: it was doubtful whether she even knew who he was, for he had neglected her for twenty years. But they said he would read scraps from old magazines to her, and sit there in silence until she had been asleep for hours, then wander home beneath the midnight sky.

The February moon grew to fullness and waned without creating undue excitement in Beadle; it was very large, and golden more than brilliant. Its face had given place to the mountain ranges of the telescope, but it behaved in an orderly manner and in some ways, I think, aroused disappointment and a good deal of crowing from the "all is well" school. There were some who even asserted that it was smaller during its last days, and that it was going away again. We were now in the midst of March, with a bare six weeks to the fatal night of the 3rd of May. I no longer attended the meetings of the British Lunar Society. Scientific calculations had ceased to interest me: the sharp edges of my hopes and fears had worn smooth by their frequent and painful friction against reality, and I no longer suffered acute feelings of any kind. I had fallen into a state of resignation, but I was not altogether unhappy. Orders had come from the Government that we were to make three separate entrances to our dugout as precaution against one, or even two of them becoming blocked. This provided plenty of healthy work, and I had never felt fitter in my life. I toiled all day with my wheelbarrow, and in the lengthening spring evenings I even found heart to potter in my garden. I actually mowed the lawn, but thought it too absurd to weed it. The daffodils were very beautiful, clustered in the corners of my meadow, and I spent many evenings in my yew tree arbour gazing wistfully upon their sheen in the fading sun.

Something happened one evening towards the end of March which must have been fate's recompense for all that I had suffered—a friendly whisper of fate that urged me, towards sunset, to take my stick and walk across the downs. It was so trivial and casual in its beginning, and yet it was to bring such happiness to the tragic days ahead.

At the northern corner of my meadow I had cut a way through the thornbushes and laid a plank across the deep surrounding ditch so that I could walk straight up the hillside to the springy turf of the downs. This little ready-made bridge had always been the starting point of my favourite evening stroll. It led me for three miles along the ridge to the edge of a pine wood from which the whole plain lay before me, and on a fine spring evening I could watch the sun set over the meadows and still be home in ample time for dinner.

It was a boisterous evening of dark cloud that scurried in the rising wind, and as I neared the end of my journey I saw two solitary figures approaching me: two dark, striding figures against the narrow, lemon-tinted strip of sunset that lay squeezed against the horizon beneath the gathering storm. As they came towards me I saw them to be a girl and a boy. Their coats were fluttering and their heads were bent to the fierce gusts that moaned across the downs, and suddenly the girl's beret blew off, and the boy chased it over the crest of the hill. I could not help admiring the girl as she stood there against the sunset: there was something in the manner of her bearing, something in the way she stood with her legs planted against the power of the gale, that told me that she would stand up against far more than a howling wind if need be.

I am a man of retiring nature with an absurd instinct to circle right around a fellow mortal who happens to be as solitary as myself, but a friendly fate was guiding me that evening: I walked straight on, and as I was about to pass, the girl turned with a merry laugh and spoke to me.

"He's got it!" she cried.

In my embarrassment I replied with a singularly futile remark. "Lost your hat?"

She nodded towards the boy upon the slope beneath us. "Do him good," she said. "He's getting too fat."

The boy was returning with the little blue beret clenched in his fist, and I would not have said from his lithe, striding figure that he stood in much need of exercise. And as he came up with us I recognised Robin Parker, Colonel Parker's nephew, of The Manor House—the boy whom I had met with his uncle at Waterloo Station a few weeks ago when he was returning for his Christmas holidays.

The recognition caused me to glance quickly back to his companion, and I realised that this tall, pleasant girl must be his sister. I remembered her quite well as a child, riding her pony across the downs, but I had lost touch with her since she had been away at school. Children have a most startling way of suddenly growing up. The boy recognised me at once. "D'you remember me, sir? . . . at Waterloo Station? . . . You know my uncle . . . my name's Parker."

I was pleased to be remembered so easily by a boy whose crowded schooldays must bring so many and varied faces before him. . . .

"Of course I remember," I said, and wished that I could think of some easy, amusing thing to say. But my life had brought me very rarely into the company of young people and I'm afraid I could only add the rather silly, drawing-room visitor's remark: "I remember you even although you are growing up so fast. . . ."

"He's much too fat," repeated the girl, "look how he's puffing!"

"I'm not too fat!" retorted the boy. "I might have been once but I'm not now! Anyway, you'd be out of breath if you'd chased a greasy little hat for half a mile."

Suddenly the boy became conscious of his social duties.

"I'm sorry," he said. "This is my sister Pat"—and I felt the firm pressure of the girl's cool hand.

"I remember you quite well," I said, "when you used to ride your ponies up here on the downs."

"Adam and Eve!" The girl laughed. "They're pensioned off now. Adam's older than I am . . . he's nearly twenty-one."

I should say that Pat was about nineteen, and her brother a couple of years her junior: she was pressing her little beret upon her head and it was a slander upon her brother's part to call it "greasy." It was surprising how quickly she made it look so neat and attractive: an ordinary woman would have taken an hour to achieve that carefree, jaunty tilt before a looking-glass. She just rammed it on, pushed her hair up, and there it was.

"You live in the house that looks across at us from the other side of the valley, don't you?" she asked. "We've often argued about it."

Why on earth such an obviously polite remark should have pleased me so much I do not know, but it certainly *did* please me to think that Pat should have argued about where I lived.

"That's mine," I replied, "and the meadow below, in the valley."

"With all those neat little chicken-runs?" she enquired. They were not "little" by any means, nor should one describe them as "runs," but anything that this girl said was pleasant, and very far from objectionable. If Dr. Hax or the publican had called them "runs" it would have been different: they were "poultry houses"— scientifically designed—scientifically heated and ventilated according to my own patent. . . .

"Yes," I replied with a smile, "all those neat little chicken-runs!"

145

Without formal arrangement or accepted invitation I found myself strolling back with the boy and girl across the downs. They were so charmingly natural, so easily friendly that I felt within a few minutes as if I were an uncle upon a visit to The Manor House. Pat and Robin had only returned home that afternoon. "Pat's at Oxford," said Robin, "pretending to read History."

"Reading History like mad," corrected Pat.

Robin was at Eton. It had been hoped to keep the schools and colleges open until the normal end of term, but parents had made such urgent appeals to have their children with them for every moment of these last, pitiful days that nearly all the big public schools and the universities were closing that week.

"The Vice Chancellor of Oxford," said Pat, "announced that owing to present circumstances Hilary Term will end a week earlier than arranged, but if anything miscarries, and the world refuses to end on the third of May, then Summer Term will be extended two weeks until July fourth to make up for the loss of time. Isn't that perfect Oxford!"

"Perfect!" I replied. "But I was at Cambridge—and I'm sure Cambridge will ignore a trivial matter of this kind!"

They laughed. It was delightful to hear the way they laughed at my jokes which are normally too subtle for stodgy, ordinary people. But as they laughed I wondered what thoughts lay behind those steady, fearless eyes. Could they understand? They were of an age to understand, and I knew in that moment that never again, no matter what terrors came to me, would I be afraid.

"Could I persuade you to stroll across to see my poultry?" I enquired. "I've got some rather nice little birds over there."

Robin stole a glance at his watch. "Sure!" he said. "But we must be back by seven. Uncle's a stickler for boiled shirts at dinner. If I were to sit down in a sweater, he'd say, 'Let the world end and be done with it!'"

The wind was whistling through the thorn hedge as I led Pat and Robin across the plank bridge to my meadow. Pat fell in love with Broodie at first sight and Robin was immensely struck by my game little Bantam cockerels. Broodie, who had grown a little sedate beneath the load of her many honours, grew quite skittish when Pat dangled a tuft of groundsel above her head, and Robin showed me how to mesmerise a Bantam by holding its head beneath its wing and revolving it in rhythmic circles in his hands. I did not like this altogether because the other Bantams pecked the little mesmerised bird when it came to, but I was not preparing them for an immediate show so it did not matter.

I persuaded Pat and Robin to come into my library. It was the first time I had ever entertained such young and amusing visitors, and it was lucky that I could produce a bottle of ginger beer for Robin, and a tin of chocolate biscuits that I had purchased for my bridge evenings. Pat, the grown-up young lady, accepted a glass of sherry and sipped it as though she had taken it all her life!

I showed them my stamp collection and they were both very envious of my three-cornered Cape of Good Hopes. I was about to read them an article I had just prepared upon Migrating Birds when Robin leapt to his feet like a jack-in-a-box and exclaimed: "Good heavens!—it's nearly seven!"

I watched them stride down my hillside path in the dusk: they waved to me from the gate, and were gone. My library seemed very cheerless and empty when I returned to it. I could almost have wished to have left that little sherry glass upon the fireside table, just as Pat had laid it down. Those little balls of silver paper which Robin had pulled from the chocolate biscuits shone in the fender more brightly than my fire.

CHAPTER THIRTEEN

In the first week of April, Sapper Evans arrived, and quickly became the hero of the village. Sapper Evans was a dynamic little Welshman, detailed to assist the village of Beadle in completing and fitting out its dugout.

Not until Sapper Evans appeared amongst us on that April evening did I realise the wonderful organisation that was working for us so rapidly and secretly behind the scenes. While the newspapers kept us amused with skilfully composed articles about the interesting and exciting time that we were shortly to enjoy, the Government was throwing every ounce of its giant resources into the grim preparations for a fantastic gamble against death.

The Army, Navy, and Air Force had been mobilised into one huge Defence Corps: machine-guns, aircraft, and battleships had been laid aside, and the implements of mining had taken their place. For the first time in history the threat of war had ceased to exist and the whole of Europe—the whole of the world—was in alliance against the same dread enemy.

Every skilled mechanic, and thousands of semi-skilled soldiers, sailors, and airmen, were rapidly passed through a "school of dugout construction," and as they qualified they were drafted into the cities, towns, and villages of Great Britain. The large cities received a Defence Corps of twenty or thirty men under specially trained officers who mobilised the civilian volunteers, and even the smallest village like Beadle received one man who thoroughly understood the task ahead.

We were lucky in getting Sapper Evans. Not only was he a dynamo of energy, but he had tact as well, and a cheery understanding of men that gave all of us renewed inspiration and energy. Although he was a sapper in the Royal Corps of Engineers, he came from South Wales and mining was in his blood. He so obviously enjoyed his work that all who came into contact with him were infected, and gave of their best.

He arrived with a lorry containing three immensely impressive steel doorways and sliding door panels for the entrances to our dugout. They were airtight and watertight: their dimension had been announced with the original orders three months ago, and the openings to our dugout had been made accordingly. With the help of the blacksmith and his son, Sapper Evans began fitting these doors on the night of his arrival. He worked all night by the light of car lamps trained upon the entrances, and by next morning the work of cementing them into position had begun.

Nobody in living memory had worked all night in Beadle, and it created a great impression of importance and urgency. He explained that he wanted everything finished well before the 3rd of May so that we could have a full dress rehearsal before the night.

Every man and woman in the village now volunteered their help, and Sapper Evans divided us into three shifts to work in eight-hour spells, day and night. Dr. Hax and Pawson, the retired police inspector, who were on the Dugout Committee, and Mr. Murdoch, the engineer in charge until the sapper's arrival, were inclined to be a little difficult at first, for they felt their authority had been somewhat rudely usurped by this bustling little Welshman, but Evans soon won them over by putting each in charge of a shift. The Vicar, in the meantime, was perfectly happy running about with chewing gum and a bottle of fruit drops for relieving thirst.

One day I was promoted from my wheelbarrow to help Sapper Evans and a local electrician to lay the electric cable from the village to the dugout, and this enabled me to make my first visit to the interior.

I was greatly impressed by its size and workmanship. The entrance was narrow to take the steel doors, but as one descended, the steps widened out and gave a wonderful feeling of safety and spaciousness.

The rooms themselves were thirty feet beneath the hillside and consisted of three large compartments, one for women, one for the men, and one as a kind of "control room" to contain the oxygen supply, stores, water, and lavatories. I was astonished at the amount of work accomplished in the last four months and felt a little ashamed at my original attitude of contempt towards it all.

It may seem strange to say how thoroughly I enjoyed those vigorous, purposeful days. I was on the shift that worked from eight in the morning until four in the afternoon, and I never felt so well in all my life. Class distinctions and petty jealousies were forgotten, and there was a superb comradeship between us as we toiled side by side in wind and rain and sunlight. The women brought lunch to their men at midday. At first I used to bring a small attaché case with sandwiches and a bottle of cider, but later on, in order to be completely at one with my comrades, I got my housekeeper to bring my lunch as the other women did.

I would return at four o'clock for my tea. I would rest for an hour, and then at six o'clock would stroll down and join the "timber club."

This curious title arose from a pile of timber that had been cut for the strutting of the dugout. It became the habit, on fine evenings, for the men off duty to stroll back to Burgin Park and sit upon this pile of timber in the shade of the beech trees, throw jokes at the men at work, and smoke their pipes and talk. There was something very attractive and romantic about that gathering in the twilight: the glow of pipes against the darkness of the trees and the drone of sleepy conversation. The attraction was increased by the casks of ale that old Lord Burgin had ordered to be kept in readiness for the thirsty villagers. Primarily it was there for the men at work, but one night Lord Burgin had come down in person to view the work, had seen the "timber club," and asked them to drink a glass with him each night whether he were there or not.

Barely four weeks now remained before the critical night, and by this time not only every man in Beadle, but almost every man in England had been partly withdrawn from his normal occupation and was engaged upon some work in connection with defence against the coming cataclysm.

Much of this work was probably futile in the light of scientific reasoning—even the dugouts themselves, however deep, however strong, were like protecting a wine glass against a cannonball with a piece of tissue paper. But the Government was alive to the vital need for occupation, and made us believe that our dugouts were giving us a "fifty-fifty" chance. They organised "flood defence" upon the seacoasts and riverbanks: "storm defence" in removing structures such as large hoardings, and dangerous trees: they were "streamlining" the whole country against tornado, and although the work done was barely one-millionth part of all that would be needed, it provided the vital, sanity-protecting medicine of hard physical work. I have not previously mentioned the Misses Cheesewright, for they were relatively minor figures in the life of Beadle. The Misses Cheesewright owned the little drapery store at the corner beside the Village Hall. They had inherited the business from their father, but their prosperity had always been handicapped by the difficulty experienced by their customers in opening the shop door. In 1897 old Mr. Cheesewright had fitted a cumbersome rubber contrivance to the bottom of the door to prevent draughts, and for fifty years the business of his two hard-working daughters had languished in consequence. When you pushed the door the rubber contrivance was caught by the mat, and only the most powerful inhabitants of Beadle were able to shop with the Misses Cheesewright. The rest were forced to take the bus into Mulcaster; but one morning, after years of unfailing hope, the Misses Cheesewright enjoyed a glorious week of boom business.

Sapper Evans announced that the cavities between the timber framework of the dugout and the chalk outer walls were to be packed with every kind of shock-resisting material that could be obtained. The villagers were instructed to bring old clothes, old blankets, old sacking—anything that would help to prevent a fall of chalk from bursting the timber frames. The village responded generously, but the cavities in the roof and walls of the stairways still remained unfilled.

The Dugout Committee, who were now in possession of Government funds for all emergency, thereupon purchased the whole of the Misses Cheesewrights' stock of soft goods.

The shop door, for the first time in Beadle history, was wedged fully and permanently open for a whole morning while a lorry was loaded up with bales of cloth, a vast quantity of outmoded ladies' petticoats and knickers, some black shawls unsold upon the occasion of Queen Victoria's funeral, and other articles whose names have even faded from the modern dictionaries. I liked the Misses Cheesewright and was very happy at this belated stroke of fortune.

CHAPTER FOURTEEN

One morning a pleasant surprise awaited my arrival at the dugout in Burgin Park.

Colonel Parker, of The Manor House, was naturally one of the leaders in the work. With a battered old Ford car he had become the Transport Officer, and spent much of his time in helping the men who lived at a distance from Burgin Park by driving them to and from their homes. Frequently I had met him rattling along the country lanes with one of the workmen beside him, and he had always given me a cheery wave of the hand. As I arrived at the gates of the Park that morning I stood aside to allow him to drive by, and he pulled up to ask me whether I would dine at The Manor House on the following evening.

My pleasure at this unexpected invitation was twofold. It was a great compliment to dine with "the Village Squire," but it gave me even greater pleasure to think that it must have been Pat and Robin who had asked their uncle to invite me.

I saw my two young friends almost every day, for they were valiant workers upon the Beadle dugout. Robin delighted in proving his muscular powers and volunteered for every job that threatened to break the human back. I caught a glimpse of him straining at a rope around the trunk of a mighty beech tree that Lord Burgin's forester was felling for some timber planking, and he was so vigorous with his wheelbarrow that one day it ran away with him down the hillside and he nearly killed himself by going headfirst into the quarry.

Dr. Hax sent him home to bed, but he appeared next morning, very proud of a large white bandage around his head. I think he showed off a little too much as the "wounded hero" that morning, but he was very young and high-spirited and really no more than a boy playing at building a stockade against pirates.

Pat aroused a good deal of comment amongst the village women when she first appeared at the dugout, for she was dressed exactly like her brother, in grey shorts, cricket shirt, and sweater. But she quickly disarmed criticism with her gay spirit and devotion to her job. She collected wood and built the fires and kept the working parties supplied with piping hot, strong tea: she insisted upon being at her post at dawn each morning to make hot soup for the tired men, and did little first aid jobs to cut fingers and splinter-wounded hands that were beneath the notice of the arrogant Dr. Hax.

We were too busy to talk very much at our work, but when she passed me she had always given me a cheerful smile. I had taken it as the smile that she gave to everyone around her, and had not dreamed that she would one day ask her uncle to invite me to The Manor House. As I passed her that morning she looked up from her fire: the great cauldron of tea was bubbling before her and her cheeks were smeared with grime.

"Uncle's been looking for you," she said. "Have you seen him?"

"Yes," I replied. "Just a moment ago."

"Can you come tomorrow night?"

"I'd like to . . . very much indeed."

"Splendid!" . . . and she gave me that flashing, impish smile.

I tossed my coat beneath a tree, rolled my sleeves to the elbow, and for an hour my happy whistling drowned the squeak of my wheelbarrow.

Remembering a remark that Robin had made upon the evening of our first meeting upon the downs, I got out my dinner jacket and dressed for the occasion and walked across the valley in the haunting glory of the waning moon.

Although but half of it remained, it lit the earth as with a golden sunset: the gaunt windowpanes of the church received it, and filled the old building with a lurid blaze of fire.

Many a time had I passed the gates of The Manor House but never until this evening had I entered that long, winding drive.

Giant cedars and stately beeches stood out against the golden sky and wild banks of rhododendron billowed upon the carriage-way. The gardens were beautiful, but even in that eerie, glowing light I could sense the gathering decay that was encroaching upon them. The Vicar had told me one evening as we were play-ing bridge that Colonel Parker had mortgaged three-parts of his land to send Robin to Eton and Pat to Oxford. The Parkers had been rooted in The Manor House of Beadle since the head of the family had backed the right King at the Battle of Bosworth Field. For nearly five centuries the family had flourished and declined with the fluctuating acumen of succeeding Parkers. The Colonel had no children of his own and Robin was his heir. The Colonel was poor, but that Robin should go to a lesser school than Eton had never entered his thoughts: Eton and one-quarter of his land was infinitely more desirable than the whole of his land to the sacrifice of a great tradition.

It occurred to me, as I walked that neglected, weed-grown drive, that the great schools of England took very little fresh-grown money for their nourishment: they lived upon the mellowed land of the manor houses—the cattle of the squires—the table silver of the country clergyman and many a cherished oil painting of a small boy's ancestor.

Robin himself answered the door in response to my knock. He helped me off with my coat and led me through the wide, dim-lit hall to his uncle's study.

Colonel Parker was at work at his desk as I entered, and he rose to meet me with a friendly smile. I recognised at once the three deep latticed windows that I could always see from my library window across the valley: in summer they were only partly visible through the foliage of the trees, but in winter those three warm, amber panels of light had often, in years gone by, sent a silent message of friendship to my lonely room.

"Typical example of country neighbours!" said the Colonel, as he stood by the windows. "Here we've sat looking across at one another's windows for five years and it never occurred to either of us to take a five-minute stroll across the valley!"

It was an odd sensation to look at my house from a room that I had known for so long but never entered: I felt like Alice, just after she had jumped through the mirror into Looking-Glass Land: I stood staring at my own house as if seeing it for the first time. It was a fairly modern house of red brick and could not, of course, compare with The Manor House in mellowness or dignity. The light over my front door looked rather small and mean and I decided that, if the moon did nothing serious to us on the 3rd of May, I would have an iron lantern fitted, with amber glass that would throw a warmer message to my new friends at The Manor House.

"If you've never been to each other's houses before, it's entirely your fault, Uncle. You were here years before Mr. Hopkins and it was your clear duty to call on him."

I turned quickly at the sound of Pat's voice: I took her hand: she glanced up at me with a smile of welcome and then at her uncle with a charming frown of rebuke.

"My fault entirely," murmured the Colonel. "But excellent excuse! Mr. Hopkins came to Beadle so quietly that nobody knew he was here for a year!"

I laughed at this gentle dig at my modesty as Pat took up the decanter from the side-table and poured me a glass of sherry.

It seems almost ridiculous to admit it, but as I walked home upon the close of that delightful evening I could not for the life of me remember the colour or texture of the dress that Pat was wearing that night. Never before, and never after, did I see her in evening clothes: I think that it was a soft blue—or perhaps it might have been a bluish-grey—I just remember thinking how delightfully simple it was and how perfectly it suited her, but for the rest my whole mind was captured by those three faces beneath the shaded candles at the table: they formed one fleeting, fragrant page from a book that had never been within my reach before—a book that was wrenched from my hand and destroyed even as its fineness was exalting me.

The dinner was simple but I felt that it had been arranged with thought and care: soup with little pieces in it shaped into the letters of the alphabet; a fillet of sole, a roast fowl, and a trifle flavoured with brandy. We were served by a maid who did not appear to come or go: she just materialised in the pool of amber light from the candles and dissolved into the shadows of the big curtained room. We drank an elegant Moselle, and Pat was allowed to remain with us at table as we smoked our cigars.

I had never known that conversation could flow with such effortless pleasure: I had thought that my dinner party to the Vicar and his wife and Mr. Fayne-Higneth had been a success, but it was jerky and artificial compared with this: we had "told stories," some of which had left difficult patches of silence behind them, but upon this evening at The Manor House there were no "stories"—no forced laughter—just a delightful family party of which I had become an honorary member.

We talked of the village, and Colonel Parker referred to every man by his Christian name without a touch of patronage. I found myself talking quite freely about myself. Robin pretended to be immensely frightened of me when it transpired that I had been a schoolmaster—he said: "Please, sir, can I have some more trifle if I spit the brandy out?"—but how different was that boy's "ragging" to the torment of those hateful little creatures of my memory! Colonel Parker spoke of the sacrifices that schoolmasters made for the sake of their duty: how they let the chances of worldly success pass them by in order to devote themselves to a noble calling. With a glance of his kindly eyes he made me picture myself as a man who might have been Prime Minister of England or Governor of the Bank of England had I not turned aside from such mundane things for the mastership of arithmetic at Portsea Grammar School.

Suddenly Robin looked at me and said: "We never think of it really—but it must be pretty grim being ragged." For a moment I felt myself stiffen—who said that I had ever been "ragged"? Nobody had: but all three, in their instinctive understanding, must have guessed. But I did not feel angry: I sipped my port and laughed. "That's what schoolmasters exist for," I said. "We're just a lot of Aunt Sallys at a circus!" And then, for the first time in my life, I spoke freely of all that I had suffered: and the pent-up bitterness of years dissolved like magic in those understanding eyes. When I had finished I felt a wonderful freedom and happiness. Robin was immensely interested. He had never before sat face-to-face with a master who had actually sat on the drawing-pin so frequently prepared for him and so invariably discovered in time: he had never before heard from a schoolmaster's own lips his reaction to a pellet of ink-dripping paper striking the bald patch upon his head.

The conversation swung to Robin himself: he admitted, with a flash of defiance, that his Latin and Greek were a little below par, but he had won the junior steeplechase that year and had covered nearly eighteen feet in the long jump for his House. I could see by his uncle's face, as I wrung these achievements from the boy, that Colonel Parker was well satisfied to let the classics finish second to the steeplechase.

And then, for the first time in the evening, a lull came in the conversation—for the first time in that magic evening I was conscious of the gentle flutter of the glowing logs in the hearth. We sat, in that moment of stillness, with our eyes upon the shaded candles before us. It was as if, with one accord, we silently acknowledged the struggle our companions had waged against mention of the ghastly days so near at hand.

For my own part that evening possessed a dreamlike quality, but unlike a dream its memory has survived every horror of the seven years that followed it. As I gaze now into the blackness beyond my tattered window curtains, I conjure up as clear as yesterday that peaceful, panelled room: I see those lines of care in the strong, grave face of Colonel Parker: I see the clear boyish profile of Robin to my right: I see the soft candlelight upon the little coral bracelet upon Pat's wrist, and I feel the grace and mellowed courtesy of an old proud family.

In that fragment of silence the Colonel rose. I think that he knew that the spell was ended: he knew that an attempt to revive the conversation might lead us into the depths that we had so triumphantly avoided.

The clock was striking ten as we gathered around the fire in the Colonel's study. We talked a little of our gardens—of the Christmas Pantomimes that Colonel Parker had seen with Pat and Robin in the holidays: we talked of the Norfolk Broads, where the Parkers went sailing in the summer: the future kept flickering to glorious life and dying in the little pits of silence that followed our gay words of make-believe.

And then Pat rose to bid goodnight.

"I must be up at four to get that soup boiling down at the dugout," she said.

"You might put that nasty little alarm clock of yours in a sock," suggested Robin.

I caught the gleam of Pat's dress as she stood beside me. I took her hand. I looked into those friendly, lovely eyes of hers, with their strange, fascinating flecks of green: I felt the firm pressure of a hand that told me of steadfast friendship.

Robin's hand was as hard as nails: he made me feel the hardened blisters that he had gained from hauling trees and shovelling the broken chalk from the dugout: he was just offering to take his coat off to display his muscles when Pat hauled him off to bed: how I envied him the hand that lay upon his shoulder as he left the room with Pat! How I prayed that, even now, fate might relent, and allow some other boy to feel that hand upon his shoulder while I, a proud guest of the wedding, was privileged to kiss the bride!

*   *   *

I was alone with Colonel Parker. I began to offer him my thanks for a delightful evening but he detained me.

"Have a nightcap before you go."

I sat once more before his fire as he brought me a whisky and soda. He took a pipe from the rack beside the open hearth. I followed his example and pulled out mine.

I had not until this moment discussed the days ahead of us with a plain, straightforward man in the privacy of his room. The gossip of the villagers was tedious and superficial—the sublime resignation of the Vicar, the arrogant outlook of Dr. Hax, and the ghoulish vulgarity of the publican were not the expressions of the normal Englishman—but I was alone with Colonel Parker; I lay back in the worn leather chair beside his fire, and glanced almost shyly at the man who embodied so much that I admired in the life of my country.

We talked of Pat and Robin first, and I told him of our meeting upon the downs. I told him of my memory of them as small, wild bundles of energy upon shaggy, galloping ponies.

He laughed. "Surprising they're still alive," he said. "They both broke their heads and collarbones before they were old enough to go to school."

"They're splendid," I said—and there was silence. An owl hooted in the valley and the wind brushed the deep windows of the room.

Colonel Parker lit his pipe. "I hear the dugout's ready for testing on Saturday," he said. "Sapper Evans is a good man: lucky to get him."

It had come at last. The subject we had so carefully avoided had arisen quite naturally now that Pat and Robin had left us. I was longing to ask him what he honestly thought about it all—I had a far deeper trust in the opinion of this quiet country squire than in all the scientists in the world, but before I could speak he said something that astonished me.

"We shan't go to the dugout that night," he said. "We've talked it over quite a lot. We shall stay here."

"But surely . . ." I began.

He looked over his glowing pipe and smiled.

"I know," he said, "but it isn't bravado, or anything silly like that. The dugout idea was a grand one and the whole thing's been splendidly done by the Government and the newspapers—it's given people occupation—given them a hope."

"Do you feel," I blurted out, "do you feel there . . . there isn't any hope?"

He puffed at his pipe and stared into the fire.

"None of us can answer that," he said. "Sometimes I just refuse to believe it. You must have felt that, too . . . felt of it like one of those little troubles that hangs over our lives more or less all the time—one going—another coming—but all of them clearing up somehow in the end. . . . Even this one will clear up somehow or other in the end . . . there's bound to be peace and quiet again sooner or later . . . some sort of peace and quiet—because noise and disaster and blazing light and all that has got to burn itself out . . . and peace and quiet wins back in the end."

It was a new idea to me, and for a moment I did not reply. "Some sort of peace and quiet"—it was rather horrible—and yet this quiet, thoughtful man had gained philosophy in the hope of some kind of peace and quiet in the end. Far away from his own life and all our lives, lay peace and quiet that was better to think of, in the last extreme, than gross eternity. . . .

"Don't you think," he went on, "that the quietest thing in all the world is the world itself as it goes rolling through space? If we were outside of it all, and stood watching it go by, it would not make a sound. A marble rolling across the floor must be an unholy racket beside the earth floating along in the emptiness. The moon's the same—it never makes even a whisper as it goes around us. . . ."

"And now it's going to make up for its long silence," I replied rather stupidly, for as I spoke I realised how crudely I was breaking into the Colonel's strange, groping philosophy.

"How do Pat and Robin feel?" I asked.

"They understand," he replied. "They understand better than we do, for they are young, and their minds can bend more easily than ours."

A pall of darkness had fallen upon the valley with the setting of the moon, and for a while I groped like a blind man down the narrow lane. Not until I reached the stile that led me to my own meadow could I see the pallid glimmer of the closed spring flowers. Now and then came a thin, uneasy gust of wind. It came like something jerked from a powerful spring: it hissed through the bushes: twanged through the branches of the elms and sighed away to die upon the downs. And between these strange, unnatural gusts there lay a stagnant deadness, with a thin metallic flavour in the air that seemed to twist the back of my nostrils and bring a pain to my temples. It was the first night of the "disturbances" that the newspapers so lightly brushed aside each morning—the first night of the strange whisperings that were now to remain with us until the end. No one sought to explain them: I doubt if even the scientists understood. The nights began to turn uneasily in their sleep—as if they no longer trusted themselves with the guardianship of the world and were impatient to hand us back to the safety of the day.

It was near to midnight as I sat for a last pipe beside my study fire. The room seemed cheap and musty and artificial beside the mellowed library of The Manor House, and I was glad that I had not risked the pitiable anticlimax of asking the Colonel and Pat and Robin to dine with me.

It was not that I was really ashamed of my home—it was just that I wanted my evening at The Manor House to endure until my death, and to endure it must remain isolated within the cherished groves of memory.

CHAPTER FIFTEEN

Two weeks before the critical night of May 3rd, the dugout in Burgin Park was finished.

Four cylinders of oxygen arrived in an Army Service lorry that Friday night. Sapper Evans installed them without delay and announced a "Dress Rehearsal" for three o'clock on the Saturday afternoon.

The Dugout Committee, accompanied by half a dozen selected villagers, entered the dugout and closed the airtight doors in the presence of a large crowd. The test was only to be for three hours, the supply of oxygen being too precious to waste upon a longer experiment. The Mulcaster Fire Brigade directed a powerful cascade of water upon each door in turn to test them against flood, and at six o'clock the Committee emerged from the dugout to report complete success in every way. Sapper Evans, with his usual resourcefulness, had organised a whist drive within the sealed dugout to pass the time, and I was gratified to learn that Dr. Hax had lost ninepence.

Everything now seemed finished, and nothing remained but to await the fateful day. I was afraid that a sudden lapse into idleness

would have a damaging effect upon the morale of the village, and
Sapper Evans evidently thought the same, for at church next morn-
ing the Vicar announced an important meeting to be held at the
Village Hall directly after tea and before evening service.

Old villagers declared that they had never seen such a crowd in
the Hall since the day it was opened by the Duke of Teck. The Vicar
was in the Chair and the Committee had seats upon the platform,
but it was Sapper Evans's evening from beginning to end.

Dr. Hax began with a silly, pompous speech, obviously inspired
by official instructions from the Government. He explained at
such length that there was absolutely no danger whatever that
his audience began to wonder whether there was more than they
had realised.

"The main purpose of this dugout," he announced, "is to
protect you against the violent atmospheric disturbances that we
may possibly experience. There is a chance that these disturbances
may begin upon nights before May third: we shall be advised of
approaching danger by wireless and the warning will be relayed
to you by a series of short peals upon the church bells. If you hear
this you must take shelter in the dugout until the moon has set.

"But the critical period," he continued, "will most likely be
from six o'clock upon the afternoon of the third until the morning of the fourth. You will be free to take up your positions in
the dugout from four o'clock that afternoon and must be there
without fail by five." He went on to say that nobody must bring
bulky possessions with them, but everyone should bring a flask of
hot coffee or tea—a blanket, and, if desired, a book. Alcohol would
be strictly forbidden, although a supply of brandy for medical
purposes would be in his own care. As the main electricity supply
might be temporarily disarranged, the Committee had provided

an adequate reserve of electric torches, and smoking would not be permissible under any conditions.

He announced, amidst applause, that Charlie Hurst and his Trio had promised to entertain the party with music that night, and the Vicar would bring his gramophone.

Dr. Hax was resuming his seat when the Vicar urgently whispered to him.

"Oh, yes," exclaimed the Doctor, standing up again—"and don't forget, before leaving your houses, to make sure that anything likely to blow about in the gale is placed in a position of safety, or firmly secured. There is no need for the least fear of any kind: you saw with your own eyes how the dugout stood up against the powerful jets of the Fire Brigade: if it is immune to flood, it is doubly immune to gales."

I could not help smiling at these sugar-coated pills of reassurance.

A lady asked whether knitting or needlework would be allowed, and the Committee, after a brief discussion, agreed to the loose, handy type but forbade tapestry frames, etc. Toys for the children were also permitted, and the suggestion of Mr. Barlow, the postman, that progressive games be organised was agreed to on condition that there was no heavy gambling. Darts, however, were vetoed after some forceful opposition upon the score of limited space.

Then Sapper Evans stood up. He received a terrific round of applause, for it was our first formal opportunity to show our keen appreciation of his work. He set aside at once the rumour that he was now to be recalled to military duty, and announced, amidst renewed applause, that in common with all other soldiers detailed to assist in dugout construction, he would remain on duty with the people of Beadle until all danger had passed.

I was glad of this because it was one in the eye for Dr. Hax, who had obviously resented the popularity of the little Sapper and was hoping for his departure in order to become the boss again.

Sapper Evans congratulated the villagers upon the splendid work they had done. "It would be a fine thing," he declared, "if every village was like Beadle!" The applause was deafening, and when it subsided he sprang a surprise on us.

"You may think you've finished your job," he said, "but you haven't! If you think you're going to sit back and enjoy yourselves, you are mistaken!"

There was laughter at this, and a murmur of appreciation, for none of us, in our hearts, was relishing the idea of "sitting back."

"Some villages might stop at what they've done, and be proud of it," he said, "but not Beadle!—We may get floods—we can't tell: we've got to be ready for anything. When we open our dugout on the Tuesday morning, we might find the valley turned into a lake. By that time you'll want to be getting home for a square meal, and most of you live on the far side of the valley. You won't fancy swimming home, so what are we going to do about it?"

There was an expectant silence.

"We're going to build half a dozen good-sized rafts," he declared. "We'll use the spare timber in Burgin Park and lash the rafts against the dugout doorways. I've an idea they'll come in very handy. It's a stiff job with a bare two weeks to do it in. Who's going to volunteer?" Every man in the Hall sprang to his feet: every man clutched eagerly at a few more days of comradeship upon the slopes of Burgin Park—a few more evenings with pipes and mugs of beer at the "timber club."

For my own part I could not help feeling that this raft idea was absurdly far-fetched: I doubt if it would have deceived any but these simple country folk, but its conception sprang from a full understanding of human nature: it would bridge the perilous gap of idleness that might easily have undermined the courage of our village.

"Splendid!" exclaimed Sapper Evans. "We start at seven in the morning. Bring all the rope you can lay your hands on for lashing the timber together." The little man sat down with a cheerful smile: Mr. Flidale, the carrier, proposed a vote of thanks to the Vicar, and the meeting broke up with a buzz of conversation that reminded me of the end of a successful concert.

I honestly believe that if news had suddenly arrived to say that the moon was not coming after all, and that the whole thing was off, the majority would have been thoroughly disappointed!

If this sounds an exaggeration, it must be remembered how remote our village lay from the rest of the world. We were at the end of the valley, and no road climbed the downs beyond. No traffic passed our way, and the village was immune from the disturbing influence of travellers. We depended for our news upon the papers and the radio, both of which were deliberately soothing and reassuring. With few exceptions the people of Beadle believed themselves in for a thrilling experience that would be over and done with in a single night, and even those of us who knew the truth could not help being influenced by the optimism of the majority.

Although I was grateful to live in such tranquil surroundings, I naturally felt, upon occasions, an urge to know what was passing in the outside world, so now that the most urgent work upon the dugout was over, I decided to go and spend a few days in London with my uncle and aunt at Notting Hill. Not only would I get the latest news at firsthand, but it was also my duty to go. They were my only relatives, but I had hesitated about visiting them for fear that it might seem like a "deathbed" parting and cause my uncle and aunt unnecessary alarm. On that Sunday night I dropped a line to Aunt Rose and received a cordial invitation by return.

How deeply I regret that I ever went to London! How sincerely I wish that my last memories of the old world had been confined to those happy days in Beadle!

CHAPTER SIXTEEN

When I left the village on Wednesday morning, I quickly discovered that the organisation of the rest of the world had not stood up to the strain as successfully as it had in Beadle.

The Railways had instituted a "skeleton service" in order to release all possible men for Defence Work, and upon arriving at the station I discovered that the 10:23 was no longer running. I had to kick my heels for nearly an hour, and when at last a long, lazy train crept in, we proceeded to stop at every station between Beadle and London. Most of the passengers reminded me of war refugees, travelling with untidy parcels of luggage. They were country folk, unused to travelling, on their way to spend the critical days with friends and relatives. In my compartment was an old lady with a parrot that kept saying: "Catch 'im!—catch 'im!" with such monotonous regularity that I got absolutely sick of it.

The appearance of the countryside did nothing to cheer me. In Beadle the farmers had sown their land as usual. They had bought their corn, and whatever the future held in store, they had decided that they might just as well sow the stuff as waste it.

But I noticed as we crawled along that, despite strict orders from the Ministry of Agriculture, many fields were weed-grown and neglected. This was particularly noticeable in the regions of towns from which unwholesome influences had spread. Now and then, upon a hillside, I saw the new-turned earth from dugouts, with men and women moving about beside them: here and there I saw labourers lopping tall trees by the roadside in accordance with the "streamlining" scheme, and although I saw a few men wandering aimlessly in the fields and lanes, only once did I see a pair of horses drawing a harrow.

Waterloo Station was more like a deserted exhibition building than a busy railway terminus, and the collector took my ticket as if it were an outworn formality of no further meaning. Even the taxi-driver accepted my instructions as if he were doing me a favour, and meandered along with no apparent desire to return for another fare.

The only normal things in London seemed to be Westminster Abbey, Uncle Henry, and Aunt Rose. My uncle and aunt were delighted to see me, and far from being annoyed at my late arrival, expressed surprise that I should have come up so well. I was hungry for my lunch, but hungrier still for news: I quickly told them my own experiences: under normal conditions I would have dwelt at length upon my adventures as a member of the British Lunar Society, but today I dismissed them in a few words.

"And now, Uncle," I said, "tell me everything—just as if you were speaking to a man from the back of beyond—as indeed I am!"

Uncle Henry was fond of talking, and eagerly seized the opportunity, but what he told me killed all desire for a second helping of Aunt Rose's excellent sponge pudding and made me wish devoutly that I had remained in the blissful ignorance of Beadle.

London, it seemed, had behaved very much like Beadle upon receiving first news of the approaching calamity. The people were stunned and incredulous: they accepted the assurances of the Government, the radio and newspapers because they were not in a fit condition to reason for themselves. They responded magnificently, at first, to the appeal for "business as usual," but as the days went by—as the great March moon had grown and waned—ominous happenings began to wrinkle the smooth surface of the great city's life.

It is not fair upon London to compare it with Beadle: it was clearly impossible to find "defensive work" for more than the smallest percentage of those teeming millions. The construction of the London dugouts was for the most part in the hands of trained men of the Army and Navy, and the people, unlike those in Beadle, were thrown back upon their own morbid reflections. While the novelty lasted, all went well—but as the hideous reality began to dawn upon them, they could no longer concentrate upon their work, and the "business as usual" effort collapsed into chaos.

Thousands, of course, were idle through no fault of their own: who, for instance, was going to keep the shipping agencies busy by booking cabins for a summer cruise?—who was there to keep the building trade in occupation by ordering new houses, or even alterations to an old one?

The most serious aspect of all was something that I had not anticipated. The passing of each moon had brought freakish and terrible convulsions to the sea. On the 23rd February the giant liner *Gibraltar* had disappeared in mid-Atlantic after one frantic, garbled SOS, and not a single fragment had been found to show what terrible fate had befallen her.

The *Queen Elizabeth*, upon docking at Southampton a few days previously, had reported sudden whirlpools, and a towering wave, one evening towards sunset, that spanned the ocean from horizon to horizon. Driving northward with terrible power, it had lifted the giant liner bodily with it—two miles from its course.

Shipping was now almost at a standstill. The Government had foreseen this possibility and had for six months been laying in reserves of food, but the rationing which had already become necessary had not contributed to the public peace of mind.

Still more disturbing were the outbreaks of lawlessness which had increased with terrible rapidity during the past few weeks. Every great city contains, by the laws of nature, a certain number of people who only keep the law through fear of long terms of imprisonment. This fear, in such people's opinion, had now ceased to exist.

"The trouble began," my uncle said, "in the East End two weeks ago, when the March moon was at its full. One night a hundred or so hooligans came together—apparently without any prearrangement. They smashed down the doors of a dozen public houses and drank themselves mad: then looted some restaurants and grocery stores and beat six people to death."

"But the police—" I began indignantly, and my uncle laughed.

"The police are brave men," he said, "but what could a handful of police with puny truncheons do against a gang of raving madmen? They dispersed them in the end, but several were killed. Those hooligans were not only mad with drink—they were crazed with fear as well. It must have been ghastly—in the glaring red light of that moon. . . .

"Martial law was declared next day: a battalion of Grenadier Guards took over the bad areas and it was announced that looters would be shot on sight. That put a stop to the hooligans working together in big gangs, but every night we get a dozen or more sudden riots and violent robberies.

"We're safe enough in our houses: they go for the pubs and drink them out, then career around in twos and threes holding up people for their money: the soldiers and police do what they can, but it happens so suddenly—in such unexpected places—and the police can't be everywhere."

I was getting impatient and rather angry at my uncle's long, disagreeable story.

"But there are millions of decent, law-abiding people to set against these miserable wretches!"

"Millions," agreed my uncle, "and they are magnificent. They just carry on—quietly and stubbornly. If it's done nothing else, this trouble has shown us the meaning of family life. In other days, the boy was at the pictures every night: the girl was at a dance: father was playing billiards at his club, and mother was alone, looking after baby. Every night in these days they gather in their homes. I don't know what they do," he added rather lamely.

I was getting very tired of Uncle Henry. Up to a point his views were interesting, but he had neither the imagination nor the humour to brighten what he said with inspiration or excitement. I began to feel an intense longing to be back in Beadle—to help build those rafts—to hear Robin's merry laugh—to take a steaming mug of tea from Pat—to sit and smoke my pipe with the "timber club" . . .

"They've had to open a lot of emergency asylums," remarked my uncle. "There's a closed van goes by here every morning, with screams coming out of it. They've cleared all the London prisons and filled the cells with lunatics: they're mostly pretty violent and want careful handling."

"Every morning," put in Aunt Rose, "they have to go through all the shrubberies in the parks and cart away the suicides in an Army lorry. They've given up having inquests anymore: they just bury them."

177

I rose from the table. I could not stand this anymore. "I'll go for a walk around London," I said, "and see what it looks like."

"Dinner sharp at seven," called out my uncle. "We've got tickets for *Money Bags* at the Coliseum: they say it's a jolly show!"

"A *show*!" I exclaimed. "Surely the theatres aren't running!"

Uncle Henry gave a booming laugh. "Of course they're running!—and doing jolly well! Cheer up, Edgar!—things aren't as bad as you think!"

I left the house, admiring and yet despising my aunt and uncle. I admired them for their extraordinary calmness: I despised them for that gloating smugness that seemed to say: "We're old, but you are not: we've little to lose, but you have much." I may be doing them a gross injustice: their detached, cold-blooded behaviour may have been an expression of bravery as great as that of Professor Hartley, the Vicar, or Colonel Parker, but I could not help feeling that Uncle Henry had mashed up those suicides and riots with his second helping of sponge pudding and swallowed them with a gloating relish.

It was a typical April afternoon with spells of warm sunlight quenched now and then by sudden, heavy showers.

I put on my mackintosh, took my umbrella, and sauntered out into the Bayswater Road with no set purpose or destination. A casual observer would have noticed little different from the ordinary routine of London life. Although the traffic was sparser, there were plenty of buses on the streets, and through the Park railings I saw nurses upon their afternoon parade with perambulators.

But I was no casual observer that afternoon, and visible evidence was quick to come my way. The windows and doors of the King's Head public house at the corner of Ladbroke Grove were boarded over: through the boards I could see broken windows and a splintered door and beneath the upper window hung a flaunting, rather pathetic notice: BUSINESS AS USUAL!

Massive steel doors, like those to our dugout at home, had been built across the opening to Notting Hill Tube Station. The tube railways had been closed for a month and the railwaymen had been employed in turning the tunnels and underground halls into massive fortresses against the moon. They were designed to hold a million people, and tickets had already been issued to denote the entrance that each holder was to use, and his position in the tunnels.

Massive barriers of reinforced concrete had been built in the tunnels between the stations so that if one entrance to the railway system were broken down, the flooding would be limited to that section alone.

The whole of St. James's Park Tube Station with its adjoining tunnels had been reserved and fitted up for Government use—with offices, radio apparatus, and even a miniature House of Commons a hundred feet beneath the surface!

I was told that a huge dugout beneath Hyde Park, constructed by the Coldstream Guards, would hold a thousand people on its own, and similar dugouts existed in many other parts of London.

If you can imagine an enormous ants' nest, with every ant robbed of its purpose and its powers of concentration, you have some idea of the appearance of London in those final days. It took me some while to understand why the crowds in Oxford Street and Hyde Park Corner looked so much the same as usual and yet so subtly different: it was simply that purpose and concentration had gone from them. They were dressed as any London crowd is dressed upon an April afternoon: I saw no sign of neglect or untidiness in clothing: their appearance had not changed: it was just their manner that was different.

Usually the seats within Hyde Park are occupied by rows of people who seem rooted there for the whole day: they lie sprawled in every attitude of repose. This afternoon there was no permanency in those rows of seated people: always they were getting up, wandering on—getting up—wandering on. I noticed, too, a far greater number of half-smoked cigarettes upon the ground, a far greater consciousness of one another—far more smiles from stranger to stranger—faint, pathetic smiles of brave passengers upon a sinking liner.

The band was playing from the stand in Hyde Park: they played lively, catchy music: a crowd surrounded them, but the seats were almost empty. The listeners stood awhile—wandered away—stared into space, and wandered back.

It was interesting to notice the varying activity of the shops in Oxford Street. Some were completely neglected—others even closed altogether. These were mostly the jewellers' shops, the furniture shops—the shops that catered for wants of permanence that were no longer desired.

On the other hand, the outfitters' shops that sold ready-made shirts and pullovers, socks and underclothes were almost besieged. There was a widespread belief amongst Londoners that, should the world survive in a semblance of its present form, there would certainly be a long period of chaos during which the wardrobe and storeroom would have to stand up to a long siege. Even if the world did survive, money would be useless anyway, so people were buying warm, serviceable clothes, stout boots and shoes, and any tinned food they could lay their hands upon. In Woolworth's I noticed a large crowd around the chocolate and sweet department, while a tray of curtain hooks was quite deserted.

The Government had avoided every possible announcement suggestive of danger or panic: they had put no restrictions upon the banks and everyone was free to draw his money if he chose. Millions of paper money had been printed—for millions desired to have their savings in their hands—but strict orders against profiteering had prevented the panic-stirring effects of inflation. Beyond the purchase of useful things, I saw no sign of reckless squandering.

I returned from my walk with a greater admiration for these Londoners than I had had before. They had so much less to hold them together than we had in Beadle. In Beadle we had our Village Hall, our church and sports clubs, a tight little community in which every member had his place. But in those vast, sprawling suburbs of London there was no such bond of community life: just miles of houses, filled with people who frequently did not even know which Borough they lived in, what Council they came within, or which church served them. Their clubs and interests were frequently outside the districts in which they lived: their families and their gardens were the only communities that they had ever known . . . and yet they held together. I saw no madmen, no suicides upon my long, wandering walk that afternoon. I saw calm people—tired, pale faces—haunted, restless eyes—swinging arms and wandering feet—eager, chattering children staring up at the grave, bent heads of their parents. I saw a woman with a tin of toffee under her arm and a man tightly clenching a little first aid box as he came from a chemist's shop. The only people I disliked were those who laughed and talked in loud, raucous voices, who stared around with eyes that said: "Just look how brave I am!"

And in the pocketbook of every one of them I visualised a small buff ticket with the Government stamp upon it: a ticket that admitted its owner to a little, steel-protected space beneath the ground: a ticket, for so many, to the grave.

CHAPTER SEVENTEEN

I will not dwell upon my visit that night to *Money Bags* at the Coliseum with my uncle and aunt. It was inspiring and pitiful by turns—a make-believe composed bewilderingly of courage and unwholesomeness.

There was something very wonderful in that London night twelve days before the end. Once more I was reminded of a giant luxury liner with every light ablaze: with bands playing—with silk-dressed women and white-tied men with eyes turned resolutely from the fatal gash of an iceberg in the lungs of the ship beneath them.

London blazed with light as if it would squander its glittering wealth before it died. Its outskirts were almost deserted, but as we drew near to Hyde Park Corner we came upon thousands of people surging in and out of the Park and along the pavements of Piccadilly. The crowds were uncannily quiet: they had not come for display: they had come to quench loneliness—to poultice their minds with life and movement—to draw the chill, festering terror from their brains with the warm comfort of humanity.

Through the railings of St. James's Park I saw the pale glimmer of tents and a glow of braziers where detachments of the Guards were quartered under arms, and once, up a dark side street, I saw a patrol moving with slung rifles.

And all the way, in the taxi, my uncle kept saying: "There's no danger—we're perfectly safe," until I began to hate him. I can quite understand that he felt some personal responsibility for my safety because I was his guest, but you would have thought, by the way he carried on, that the armed police and military patrols in the streets were there for his especial benefit.

"We don't need military protection in Beadle," I remarked with some asperity—and Uncle Henry burst out in a rich oily laugh as if I had made a brilliant joke.

One of my saddest reflections is the manner in which Uncle Henry and Aunt Rose declined in my esteem during that last brief visit to them. I try to think of it as little as possible because sometimes my conscience is uneasy and I wonder whether I was unjustly critical. I had always known them to be selfish and pleasure-loving: over-eager for their food and comforts. I imagine it is difficult to be otherwise when two people have lived together for forty-five years in utter freedom from financial stress and the responsibility of children. I had always enjoyed my Christmas visits because they gave me a good time, but I knew perfectly well that I was only welcomed as useful in making up their parties, calling taxis after theatres, and seeing Aunt Rose safely across roads.

And now, in the face of the approaching cataclysm, I saw less than ever to admire in their incurable complacency. I do not believe that it was an expression of philosophy or courage: I believe it was the symbol of a smugness so ingrained by time and habit that nothing, however tremendous, could bring them again into sympathy with the common people of the world.

Uncle Henry was seventy-four and my aunt a year his junior. Both of them had lived for twenty-five thousand comfortable, self-indulgent days. A few days in addition, more or less, could be of little moment to them. But I was only forty-seven, and I could not help reading into the fat, smug laugh of Uncle Henry a gloating pleasure that he had got the better of me by twenty-seven years: the gloating pleasure of a selfish cricketer who has had his innings and made his runs before the rain comes on.

But let me forget it. Let me accept the discredit of ungenerosity and give Uncle Henry and Aunt Rose the doubtful credit of abounding self-control!

I cannot offer a calm criticism of *Money Bags*, the musical comedy at the Coliseum. Conditions were not favourable to a reasoned analysis of its dramatic merits.

For the first ten minutes I thought it was the best show I had ever seen: from then onwards it was as hollow as a blown sparrow's egg.

The audience was far different from that healthy, joyous throng at the Christmas Pantomime. The theatre was full, but there were no children: the onlookers were mostly of the unwholesome "men about town" type, the type that is known as "sophisticated": those poor, hunted, complex-ridden people who have never found the gateway that leads to the crystal sunlight of simplicity.

They came bubbling into the theatre with a kind of breathless exhilaration as if they had been taking secret swigs at the oxygen tubes in the dugouts beneath them. A young man next to me, with a pasty, twitching face, had obviously drunk too much: his laugh was like the bark of a dog, and when he tried to concentrate upon the show he could not sit still for a second—his long white fingers kept side-stepping about his chin and sliding around inside his collar.

I admired the actors, for they worked with defiant bravado. I do not know when *Money Bags* was written, but if it had been composed in the peaceful days of the previous year it had certainly been adapted to suit the conditions of these last pitiful weeks. Every joke of the past fifty years had been added to the piece; the audience roared with laughter, and the actors looked up with surprised smiles as the managers of a bankrupt firework company might greet the unexpected success of a box of mouldy rockets.

My heart went out to those brave little girls of the chorus who danced and sang and smiled in the same old dauntless, glassy way. But within twenty minutes of the rise of the curtain, the whipped-up hilarity had spent itself. Relentlessly the damp seemed to seep into the verbal squibs that were popping on the stage, and long before the interval they would scarcely pop at all.

Even before the interval some people began to edge from their seats and creep out of the theatre. I was thirsty, and tried to get some lemonade between the acts, but the refreshment bar was nearly a riot. "Double whisky!—double brandy!—double whisky!" was being bawled out around me. I stared at those pale, jostling faces, those burning eyes, and hated them. I thought of the cool night air of Beadle: of the warm, amber glow in the windows of The Manor House across my valley—of the Vicar in his study—of Pat and Robin, reading by the fireside in Colonel Parker's library—and I knew that these people around me in the theatre bar were the dregs.

I could get no lemonade: all that I could secure was a very small bottle of soda water peculiar to theatre bars—so fizzy that most of it bubbled out when the girl opened it and the drop that remained tasted like very hot chicken-run wire.

Money Bags, after the interval, was hopeless: all effort at concentration had gone and people were continually sneaking out as if news had been passed quietly around that the theatre was on fire.

I longed to go myself, but Uncle Henry and Aunt Rose seemed to be enjoying themselves in their own incredible way. Uncle laughed richly every time there was a joke and frequently when there wasn't. Aunt Rose watched the audience creeping out with the smug, indulgent smile of a woman immune to seasickness watching the shamed departure of diners from the restaurant of a rolling ship. I knew that if I suggested leaving they would conclude at once that I was afraid. And so we stayed to that bitter end: to that pitiful, empty-seated end. And when the curtain rose for the last time upon that group of tired, brave actors, a lump came to my throat, a mist to my eyes—and I cried: "Bravo!" I was glad, in that moment, that I had stayed.

London had changed ominously in those hours of the theatre. The streets were almost empty, and people scrambled for taxis as if they were rescue boats around a sinking ship. I could see that all feared to walk in the streets alone.

Four policemen stood together at the foot of St. Martin's Lane. When at last I secured a taxi, the driver sat pondering before he would agree to drive us out to Notting Hill. "It's perfectly safe," said Uncle Henry, and the man glowered at him. "Who said it wasn't?" he snarled—and then with a curt jerk of his head towards the door he said: "Get in!"

There was a line of piled rifles in Trafalgar Square and a platoon of soldiers resting beside them. A police car with a radio stood at the kerb nearby, and a tall Captain of the Guards was stooping with his head at the window, speaking to the police officer at the wheel.

A few people still roamed the pavements of Pall Mall—they looked like sleep-walkers—like people dreading a return to haunted houses. But as we reached the Bayswater Road and left the military encampments of the Park, the broad streets were utterly deserted. At the corner of Notting Hill Tube Station I saw a group of six armed policemen—otherwise it was a district smitten with the plague.

The taxi-driver hunched himself over the wheel and flew down the last wide stretch of the Bayswater Road. He jammed on his brakes outside my uncle's house and jerked his head backwards towards the door. "Get out—quick," he snapped.

"There's no danger," declared Uncle Henry, as he groped in his pocket for money.

"No danger!" growled the man. "Three taxis held up since sunset—two men shot dead." He snatched the money, grated his gears, and rattled off into the darkness.

"Absurd," said Aunt Rose. "The soldiers and police are every-where." But I could not conceal a smile as the old lady glanced furtively down the deserted road and Uncle Henry fumbled rapidly for the latch-key.

I could tolerate this no longer. There was nothing for me to do in London. Another walk in those tragic streets would have dragged me to the depths of depression, and another theatre would have driven me mad. Never had I longed so desperately for my home.

I sat with my uncle before his library fire: the night was warm—the curtains were tightly drawn and the room was suffocating.

My uncle was laughing at the panic-stricken taxi-driver.

"It's a disease, my boy—infectious disease. One man gets into a funk and the germ spreads down all the taxi ranks in London! There's absolutely no danger if you keep your head."

He handed me a whisky and soda, and raised his own to the red light of the fire. "Well—here's luck, my boy."

I took the plunge.

"I must go home tomorrow, Uncle—I'm sorry—it's been a very short visit. . . ."

I was astonished at the effect of my casual words upon the old man. The light died from his eyes and his round, rosy cheeks seemed to fall suddenly away into little pouches of utter weariness.

"But . . . but, my dear boy!" he murmured. "You . . . you promised us at least three days. . . ."

"I'm on the Defence Committee at Beadle," I lied. "We've got a very important meeting. I must be there"—but my uncle went on speaking as if he had not heard—in a low voice, with his eyes upon the dying fire.

"We had planned it all, you know . . . quite a programme . . . a motor drive to Hampton Court tomorrow . . . a picnic lunch: we could walk in the Park like we used to, and perhaps a boat on the river for a little while . . ." He raised his head with a last brave rally of gaiety. "And the Trocadero Cabaret in the evening, my boy!—delightful show!—lively music and jolly pretty girls!"

It was a hard struggle to hold my ground. There was something pitiful in those faded, appealing eyes and bowed old head: something pitiful in that dapper, old-fashioned little evening tie and the drooping pink rose in that buttonhole: an old man clinging desperately to the last rending shreds of a self-indulgent life. I thought of the supper he had planned at the Trocadero—the bottle of claret and the grilled sole—the hurried, padding feet of waiters and the memories. . . . I thought of them both when news of my visit arrived—a frantic search for spectacles—an excited scanning of the amusement page of the newspaper—a desperate determination to be true until the end to the name I had once given them: the name which had so immensely pleased them: "connoisseurs of happiness" . . .

But I could not draw back now. "I'm terribly sorry," I said. "I've simply got to go."

I played him a last game of chess before we went to bed: it was deathly still outside, although once, through the darkness, I thought I heard a distant shout, and running footsteps. I am glad that Uncle Henry won the game. He laughed as he cried: "Checkmate!" I never heard that deep, familiar laugh again.

Only two trains were running each day to Beadle now, and for the sake of my uncle and aunt I delayed my departure until the evening.

We went in the afternoon for a short stroll in the Park, and Uncle pointed out some green railings that he had been instrumental in putting up when he was an official at the Office of Works. It was a lovely, warm spring day. The white narcissi were thrusting their way through the fading daffodils, and the trees had a beautiful pale sheen upon them. The birds were bold in their journeys to find food for their hungry young families, and as we sat beside the lake, they hopped around our feet in the hope of crumbs.

We talked a little of old, far-off days. Aunt Rose reminded me of a never-forgotten holiday in a tiny Cornish village when I had been a child—when Aunt Rose and Uncle Henry had been young. With my father and mother we had tramped the sun-baked moorlands and gone at dawn in a fishing-boat around Astral Head and helped the men to haul their nets. Sunlight and springy turf—the tang of salt air, and eggs for tea. I saw my mother and my aunt again: two lovely women who wore blue jerseys in the fishing-boat and hauled the nets like men. The spring leaves in the lime trees were misty as I stared at them, and I became a child again. These plump, white-haired people were all that remained to link me with those happy boyhood days, and now my last hour with them was ending.

They passed from my life with a cup of china tea and a buttered scone in my aunt's old, over-furnished drawing-room: the window stood open: a butterfly hovered over the flowers—and for a second it brought back those Cornish moors of long ago.

The train crept out of London in the April twilight, and the sunset glowed upon the face of Big Ben across the Thames. I said "good-bye" to that calm, stately city, and wished it happiness in the ten days of life that remained to it.

CHAPTER EIGHTEEN

It took me the best part of the following morning to attune myself once more to the calm atmosphere of Beadle.

When I set forth at nine o'clock to report for work at the dugout, I half expected to see groups of armed policemen lurking behind the hedges. I expected every moment to be held up by armed bandits, but all that I saw between my house and the village was the fat, red-faced baker's boy, sliding ponderously to and fro upon the seat of his bicycle in order to reach the pedals of a machine three sizes too big for him. He grinned at me as he passed: he touched his cap, and as I smelt the warm loaves in his basket and listened to his cheerful whistling die away down the winding lane, the peace of Beadle began to seep back into my bones again.

It was fine to walk up the slope of Burgin Park once more and hear the cheery voice of Sapper Evans shouting: "Come on, slacker!" After those haggard, drifting crowds in London and the lurking menace of those city streets, it was a tonic to see the sturdy men of Beadle hauling tree trunks and lashing them together. I was given a saw and was told to cut the branches from the trunk of a young cedar to make one of the rollers for the rafts.

Towards midday a heavy shower drove us for refuge to the dug-out. We sat upon the steps and ate our lunch in the dim, slanting light from the doorway while Charlie Hurst, Captain of our village cricket team and leader of the Beadle String Trio, sang popular songs, and we joined in the chorus.

When the rain stopped, one of the men poked his head out of the doorway and called out: "All clear, boys!—Come on!—the moon's missed us!" How desperately I hoped that this grand comradeship would hold until the final, uttermost moment of these last ten days! I was thankful now that I had suffered those wretched hours in London. They had given me an increased love for the village of my home. When I had finished my job upon the cedar tree, Sapper Evans put me onto lashing empty petrol cans around the sides of the rafts to give them buoyancy. I was sorry to hear that Colonel Parker, with Pat and Robin, had gone off to spend a couple of days in Winchester with an aged relative. I missed Robin's boisterous fooling, and the tea made by the village woman who deputised for Pat was weak and tepid in comparison with the hot, strong brew that Pat had made. But I now had many friends amongst the village people. We shouted jokes to one another as we worked: we whistled and sang in chorus, and although my hands were blistered I quite resented the arrival of the new shift that came to take over from us at five o'clock.

If the people of Beadle were slow-witted and deficient in imagination, they certainly did not fail in practical precautions. As I walked home to my dinner I noticed several people at work, boarding up their windows, and Mr. Westrop, the postmaster, was on a ladder unscrewing the swinging sign that advertised tobacco. The flagstaff had been taken down from the Club gateway and I even discovered Mr. Flidale, the carrier, burying some china ornaments in his garden.

"Wedding presents," he explained. "I nearly lost one of them when they had that big explosion in Mulcaster Powder Mills. Our mantelpiece isn't broad enough for big stuff like this: a real storm might shake 'em off."

I felt inclined to laugh at Mr. Flidale's puny precaution, but on my way home I decided to follow his example so far as taking down one or two of my favourite pictures and putting them in the cellar. I also decided to remove the antlers from above the hall door, as they might cause personal injury if they fell. But I decided not to do these things until the last moment to avoid alarming Mrs. Buller, my housekeeper.

Mrs. Buller puzzled me that night. She seemed absent-minded and preoccupied while she served my dinner—quite different from her usual self, and when dinner was over she surprised me still more. It was an iron rule that I was not to be disturbed in my library once I had retired after dinner, and I was astonished when a timid knock came at the door, long after Mrs. Buller's usual bedtime.

In answer to my summons she entered the room. She had a sheet of paper in her hand, and I had never seen her so nervous and ill at ease.

"What is it, Mrs. Buller?" I enquired.

The poor woman was almost inarticulate, and it needed all my patience to calm her and help her to explain.

It appeared she had received a letter that morning from an old lady in Bristol with whom she had been for many years in service. This old lady had taken the gloomiest view of things: she was convinced that the world would end on Monday week and had written to bid Mrs. Buller goodbye—urging Mrs. Buller to meet her end in a manner befitting one who had served her so excellently for seventeen years.

Mrs. Buller explained to me that she had never realised, until receiving this letter, what a serious thing it really was. She had thought the matter over very carefully all day and felt that it was only right to make her will. She had a little saved up in the Post Office, and wanted to leave it to her favourite nephew, Harry Fuller. She wanted to know if I would help her with the wording.

I was quite touched by the old lady's confidence in me, and although not an expert in legal documents, I offered her all the help I could give.

Mrs. Buller had often spoken with pride of her nephew Harry Fuller. She had told me that he was considered by many people to be the most promising young tram conductor in Cardiff. I drew up a simple, dignified wording, which she signed. I appended my signature as witness, and the old lady retired with many grateful words of thanks.

"I shall sleep happy now, sir," she murmured as she left the room.

It was not until I was getting into bed that I realised with a shock how fruitless the thing had been. If the cataclysm were sufficiently powerful to envelop Beadle and Mrs. Buller, there was every reason to fear that it would also envelop Cardiff, nipping off Harry Fuller before he had the opportunity to benefit by his aunt's will.

I had accepted Mrs. Buller's request that I should take care of the will and had put it in the bottom drawer of my desk as being safer, in the event of a catastrophe, than the top one. It now dawned upon me that Beadle, Cardiff, and every drawer of my desk without distinction would receive impartial treatment from the moon if it hit us.

It took me a long time to get to sleep. The bigness of the whole thing ahead of us was bewildering. It prevented one applying normal common sense to anything.

CHAPTER NINETEEN

How can I describe the last incredible week in Beadle without giving the impression that the whole lot of us were as mad as March Hares? Sometimes I have wondered whether we were, in fact, completely mad that week: at other times I have thought that we behaved as we did because we were all so incurably sane!

The majority of the village, it is true, had no conception of the peril that lay over them, and the Defence Committee, inspired, no doubt, by Sapper Evans, did everything it could to sustain this blissful ignorance. They organised what I can only describe as a "gala" week.

Fate was kind to us in at least one respect, for the critical night was due to fall upon a Monday. Monday was by far the best day of the week for a crisis, because it gave us a last full week in all its glorious freedom, ending with a final Sunday in which to compose our minds.

And so the Committee strove to fill that last week with every possible diversion to keep the villagers from morbid inactivity.

The week began with a "sing-song" around the campfire beside the dugout in Burgin Park, and was designed to celebrate the successful completion of our work. An immense fire was made from the brushwood, and the whole village sat around in a great, unbroken circle with the Committee and some of the special ladies in chairs brought from the Fox & Hounds.

The choirboys opened the entertainment as twilight came. They sang "John Gilpin Was a Citizen of Credit and Renown," "Sweet and Low," "John Peel," and a few old English folk songs as an encore. I thought at first that it was going to be rather tedious, but as the darkness fell, as the boys in their grey flannel suits merged into the dimness of the hillside, all that you could see was a little pale cluster of faces that seemed to flicker and glow with the gentle crackle of the brushwood fire. There was a wonderful cheer as the last notes died away. The boys broke up with smiles of shy embarrassment, and the Vicar's wife gave each a bottle of ginger beer and two sponge cakes as a "prize."

Dr. Hax followed with "Trumpeter, what are you sounding now?" which was not good, although greeted with polite applause. His voice was too loud and assertive, and his manner so condescending that he contrasted very poorly with the sincerity and charm of the choirboys. I was glad when it was over.

But Sapper Evans retrieved the situation and turned the evening from the failure threatened by Dr. Hax's song into an uproarious success. He was acting as "Compère," and when he came into the centre of the circle to announce the next item, someone shouted: "Song from Sapper Evans!" The little man vigorously shook his head, but his announcement was drowned by the whole village shouting: "Song!—song!"

It was quite clear that he could not get out of it, and I was sorry for the plucky little man when at last he nodded in surrender, and silence fell. I was sorry and ill at ease, for it was cruel upon him if he had no voice. I watched him as he screwed nervously at the sheet of paper that contained his announcements, and then he stood back a pace and raised his head, and began to sing an old Welsh song in a sweet tenor voice. He stood as I had once seen a small Welsh boy standing, singing for pennies upon the slopes of Snowdon, in a curious attitude of alertness, with heels together and shoulders squared, with eyes half-closed as if straining to draw the melody from the far-off mountains of his home. Although the song was in Welsh and none of us could understand, every word came as clear as crystal to us, and as he sang, the new moon rose behind the cedars upon the hillcrest of the Park.

I had drunk a pint of strong, sweet cider. I was not intoxicated, but the power of it mingled with the weirdness of the evening to bring a sense of unreality to the scene. I was facing the hillcrest, and as I watched that immense, incredible golden scimitar rise slowly behind the trees it seemed to entwine itself in the branches of the cedars and become part of a fantastic, imaginative backcloth to a stage.

I had no sense of fear: I just sat there admiring it. I do not think that I should have been surprised if a Pierrot and Pierrette had danced across the hillside, climbed the cedars, and sat in the crescent of the moon to sing a love-song to us. It seemed so incredibly near to us: for a moment it appeared to balance itself lightly upon the tip of a cedar branch before ghostly scene-shifters behind the hill hoisted it clear into the pearl-grey sky.

I was so entranced that even the clear Welsh voice upon the hillside died away. It needed the cheers that greeted the final song to bring me back to a conscious belief in my surroundings.

Only for a moment were the eyes of the audience turned from the brushwood fire. In the silence that followed the applause for Sapper Evans, someone called out: "New moon!—wish!" There was a ripple of laughter and a queer sound as if a hundred bodies suddenly and in unison drew a sigh of wonderment. The great moon was clear of the cedars and rising steadily in the sky. It was not, I think, the glowing crescent that awed us so much as the immense, jet-black globe to which that crescent clung—the immense bulk of the moon as yet in darkness. The crescent, vast as it was, seemed merely like a forest fire licking around the edges of the moon, and as I watched I half expected to see the fire spread and envelop the whole bloated body. . . .

And then from the silence came the voice of Sapper Evans: "I now have pleasure in introducing Mrs. Gump, Mrs. Gamp, and Mrs. Gumble, the Beadle washerwomen!"

The audience was at first bewildered as three apparently large, fat washerwomen, with rolled sleeves and white aprons, ran into the circle and bowed, and I honestly believe that nothing in the world could have made us forget the moon more completely than the amazing antics that followed.

The "washerwomen" turned out to be three lusty farm boys. How much of their entertainment was rehearsed I do not know. It was "knockabout" comedy of the broadest type but uproariously funny. They knocked each other about in the most incredible way and only the soft parkland grass saved broken bones. One was a really remarkable acrobat. He twisted himself up in his apron and skirts to such an extent that the other two completely failed to unravel him. He then rolled off down the hillside in a series of somersaults, the audience making way for him as he disappeared into the gloom. The other two pursued him, carried him back in a bundle, and threw him down the dugout steps with such force that I thought for a moment that the Vicar would intervene.

He emerged, however, smiling if somewhat subdued (for I think the other two had rather overdone it in the excitement of their sudden theatrical success), and they finished with a song and a dance. I am afraid it all sounds a little crude and elementary when described in words, but it reduced us all to such helpless laughter that Sapper Evans had to wait at least a minute before he could announce the next item.

The evening closed with a few old, well-remembered songs which the whole audience sang in chorus so finely that I felt tears coming to my eyes, and as I walked home through the fading, tarnished moonlight I thought how strange it was that it had never before occurred to the village to organise an evening like this—and why it should need the end of the world to inspire them to it.

On Tuesday we had a whist drive and progressive games in the Village Hall. It was not so inspiring as our Campfire Concert: the Hall got very stuffy towards the end but everybody was cheerful and I won a packet of marigold seeds.

On Wednesday there was the first Fancy Dress Dance ever to be held in Beadle—another proof of Sapper Evans's genius, for the invention of the dresses had given the villagers of Beadle almost as much diversion as the dugout itself. I went as Dr. Livingstone in a white tropical suit which I had purchased for a cruise to the Canary Islands some years previously, but the majority of the dresses were less conventional, and some almost too daring, such as young Richard's, the blacksmith's son, who came as an Ancient Briton.

This occasion was distinguished by a visit from old Lord and Lady Burgin themselves, who very rarely entered into village amusements owing to their advanced age.

But an awkward incident occurred concerning Lady Burgin. The Vicar, eager no doubt to bestow a compliment, awarded the First Prize for Ladies' Fancy Dress to Lady Burgin and referred in his speech to "the lovely, graceful costume of Early Victorian days." It was discovered afterwards that Lady Burgin had not realised that the dance was to be Fancy Dress, and had come in her ordinary evening clothes. Fortunately she was extremely old and almost stone-deaf and she accepted her prize of a trinket box with a little red balloon tied to it with a face wreathed in smiles.

But nothing in that strange week compared with its extraordinary ending upon the Saturday night. It was so unexpected and spontaneous, so full of brave defiance yet so horribly upon the brink of the macabre, that every detail remains graven in my mind.

A concert had been arranged at the Village Hall that night, but during the afternoon an idea developed in the hare-brain of Charlie Hurst, the Captain of our village cricket team: an idea that caught the imagination of Beadle and swept all thought of the concert aside.

Under normal conditions the opening cricket match of the season was played upon the first Saturday in May, but for obvious reasons the fixture list had not been arranged this year. Charlie Hurst stood at the door of the Fox & Hounds that afternoon. He looked sadly across at the deserted cricket ground—the field of his many triumphs—and the sight of it was too much for him. An idea flashed into his mind that caused him to dive into the crowded saloon bar and hold up his hand for silence.

Within half an hour a large, hand-painted poster appeared upon the gates of the Village Hall. I had been down to the village to settle one or two small outstanding accounts in order to face Monday with a clear conscience, and as I paused in the small crowd to read the poster I did not know whether to laugh, or to be angry at the sheer impudence of the thing:

NOTICE
Tonight at 9 p.m.!
The First Cricket Match ever to be played by moonlight!
Married versus Single Men of Beadle. Losers to stand drinks all round!
Play starts at moonrise. Stumps drawn at midnight!

Charlie Hurst never did anything unless he could do it in style. A gang of boys was already streaming down the road to the cricket ground with the chairs that had been arranged in the Hall for the concert, and as I passed Flidale's barn I saw Charlie himself superintending a party of men as they unstacked the big marquee and hauled the tent poles from the rafters.

I have never been fond of cricket. It is a game too slow for my restless temperament, and after our hectic "gala week" I would have preferred an early bed. But as I sat in my garden that afternoon, as I heard the distant thud of the mallets as the marquee and canvas bowling screens were hammered into place, as I heard the familiar *chock* of bat against ball as the teams practised for the game, I knew that I must go—if only to be with the village upon its last defiant night of gaiety.

After dinner I sat in my hillside arbour and waited for the moon to rise. Twilight came quickly with the sunset and for half an hour the world was swathed in a darkness that was almost terrifying. I could not even see the white gate of my meadow: with trembling fingers I struck a match to assure myself that blindness had not come to me.

Gradually, along the hillcrest of Burgin Park, there came a golden glow as if all the cities of Eastern England were on fire. From the centre of that glow appeared one tiny strip of pure yellow light, creeping out in both directions till it spanned the whole hillcrest from the beech trees to the tower of Beadle Church.

The breathless glory of that rising moon robbed all terror from it and left me humbled and speechless: a blazing, golden mountain range that seemed to press the dark earth from it: clear rays of amber that caught the hills beyond The Manor House and crept down to drink the jet-black darkness of the valley—that flowed over the church and onwards to the cricket ground, emblazoning that shabby marquee and the threadbare bowling screens into a Field of the Cloth of Gold.

A thrush began to sing in the arbour above my head, and beneath me, in the winding lanes, I could see the village people, upon their way to the cricket match—clusters of pale faces staring upwards—motionless and speechless. In olden times the whole world would have been upon its knees.

I walked up to my house to get my coat. Mrs. Buller had turned on the light above the porch, and as I entered I flicked off the pale, incongruous little speck. My chickens had risen with the rising of the moon, puzzled, no doubt, by the shortness of the night. On my way to the cricket ground I paused to cover the wire of their houses with sacking, as one covers a canary cage in a lighted room. They looked at me with perplexed faces as I did so but I heard them returning to their perches almost at once.

All the way to the village the birds sang in chorus as birds only can upon a dawn in May: I think the singing of those birds in the moonlight was the strangest sound that I had ever heard.

As I entered the gates to the cricket ground I expected the same "gala" atmosphere that had marked every evening of the week. But I was surprised at the uncanny stillness. I had to glance around before I could believe that the village was assembled here.

About fifty people sat in the chairs: the white-clad cricketers were assembled in little groups by the pavilion, but the strained quietness told me at once that we had overdone it this time. We had asked too much, even of these trustful, unimaginative people of Beadle, to expect them to enter with gaiety into this weird, unearthly ceremony. For ceremony I can only call it: a farewell ceremony to the game that had graced the meadows and greens of England for so many years and now was over. Those white-clad figures, standing by the pavilion, were no longer men to me—they were ghosts from a forgotten past: memories of summer days that would never come again.

Charlie Hurst, feeling no doubt responsible for a gay prank that had miscarried, did his utmost to enliven the event. He raised a forced laugh from the spectators when he tossed the coin with the opposing Captain—caught it between the back of his neck and his shirt and shook it out of his trouser leg. I could not laugh: I could not take a placid seat amongst those silent awestruck people: I nodded to a few acquaintances and strolled around to the far side of the ground where some old wooden seats stood underneath the trees. As I did so I saw a tall man climb the stile behind the trees: I saw that a girl was with him, a girl in grey skirt and white pullover, and I was glad that I had come. Colonel Parker and Pat were home again. I waved to them and they crossed the field to share a seat with me.

As I took Pat's hand I thought that her face was pale, even in the golden light of the moon, and Colonel Parker's voice was quiet and grave as he spoke to me. Our casual words of greeting were interrupted by some laughter and applause from the spectators. Sapper Evans had appeared from the pavilion in a long white umpire's coat that enveloped his squat figure like a nightgown. Beside him walked Alec Williams, the riding master, as tall as the Sapper was short, and the two umpires made a really comical pair, perfectly selected to dispel the awed silence of the onlookers.

"A gallant effort," muttered Colonel Parker, "brave, but silly, I think—they'd all be happier inside the Village Hall."

"It seemed a good idea—in the afternoon," I answered. "They didn't bargain for such a clear night. If only there were just a cloud or two—to break it."

I had tried to keep my eyes away from the sky above me—I glanced up as I spoke, and once more that incredible thing in the heavens held me in its thrall. I thought of it no longer as the moon: it hung like a great amber, pockmarked lamp above a billiard-table, so vast and enveloping that the little white-clad cricketers moved without shadows to their appointed places on the field.

The voice of Colonel Parker came remotely to me in the darkness of the trees: "I suppose our earth must always have looked as big as that to the moon."

I had never thought of that before: our earth, with its so much greater size, must always have been a huge, awesome thing to our little satellite.

"It's getting its own back now!" said Pat in a low voice. "How terrific we must look from the moon tonight!"

"There was a radio message—just as we left," said the Colonel—and as he spoke on, I understood the reason of his gravity—"there's been some kind of a hurricane—following the moon as it waned over Russia and America—they didn't say much—just warned people to the dugouts."

"When was this?" I exclaimed.

"Five minutes ago—just as we left the house."

I rose from my seat, trembling. "We must tell them," I cried. There was something horrible in the deathly calm surrounding us: in those twittering birds and silent, floodlit trees.

"No!" said the Colonel—and there was a sharp command in his quiet voice that I had never heard before. "Leave them!—If it's a . . . hurricane then it's safer in the open. If they go to that dugout, they won't return to it when they need it most—on Monday night."

I did not understand his meaning, but I felt confidence in this quiet man and accepted his word. I think that he visualised a horror in that sealed dugout that must at all costs be kept until the end. . . .

Pat gave a little laugh beside me. "There's Robin!" she said.

I looked across the cricket field. There was Robin, with Charlie Hurst, walking across the field to open the innings. Charlie was fooling no longer: I honestly believe that he had forgotten the moon: he was back in the dreamland of a summer afternoon—his jaw thrust out, his sleeves rolled to the armpits, his bat gripped in his hand, grimly preparing to defend his nickname—"The Beadle Smiter"—against all comers. Robin, in immaculate white flannels, was wearing the striped cap of his House Eleven: he walked to the wicket as any boy might walk to open the batting of his school at Lord's Cricket Ground in London.

It is incredible that we were able to concentrate upon that eerie cricket match, but despite everything I found myself held by the fascination of it. The village, unaware of the radio warning and growing more accustomed to their surroundings, warmed up with a cheer when Charlie banged the first ball high over the bowler's head to land with a resounding whack against the bowling screen. They responded with their first genuine laugh when Charlie took hold of Sapper Evans's arms and showed him how to signal a hit for six (for the little Sapper clearly knew nothing of the game and soon became a target for good-natured jokes). There was a delightful contrast between those two young batsmen: between Charlie Hurst, Beadle-born and -bred, who slammed the ball by the light of nature, and Robin, playing with the grace and ease of expert coaching. Robin's tall, slim figure contrasted strikingly with the squat, brawny frame of Charlie Hurst—but when the boy stepped out to drive the ball, his perfect timing seemed to throw a giant's strength behind the stroke and the ball would flash across the meadow like a shot from a gun.

I could not help smiling at Colonel Parker's pride. He, too, had forgotten the ghastly menace of that calm night as the magic of the game enthralled him—as he called out: "Well-hit, Robin!"— "Good shot, boy!"

Robin came and sat with us when his innings was over: he had made forty-seven runs in half an hour and his eyes shone with pleasure. "Sheer luck," he said. "I'm not a batsman, really. I'm a wicket-keeper—never make more than a dozen as a rule."

"That last drive was a beauty," said Pat, "a fluke," she quickly added, "but a beauty."

Robin mopped his brow—in the light of that moon his bronzed face was like a Red Indian's.

"Put your sweater on, Robin," said Colonel Parker—and the pathos of the words wrung my heart. We said little more as we sat there together under the elms.

It was nearly eleven when the first innings closed, and everybody gathered around the marquee for cakes and coffee. Beadle was its happy self again: Charlie had knocked up eighty runs in just under an hour, including three mighty hits that landed the ball across the road, and Sapper Evans had delighted everybody with his attempts to conceal a complete ignorance of the rules of the game.

There was an eager buzz of conversation and a chinking of cups in the marquee: the moon had passed its zenith and its dazzling splendour was sinking to a reddish glow as it began to wane. I was hoping that everything would end happily on this last "gala" evening despite the warning issued. I saw Colonel Parker, talking earnestly with the Vicar beside the pavilion at a little distance from the crowd. I imagine that the Colonel was telling the Vicar of the radio warning and discussing the proper action to take. I saw the Vicar standing silently in thought: I saw him glance up, say a word to the Colonel, and begin to walk with him towards the crowded marquee. What decision they had made I shall never know: whether they were going to cancel the game and advise the people to go to the dugout, or whether they had decided to carry on, will remain in doubt, for as they approached the marquee the hurricane was upon us.

I call it a hurricane for want of a better word: it was the strangest disturbance that I had ever experienced. It began with the long-drawn murmur of distant thunder, but the murmur did not die as the murmur of thunder dies. From far across the valley came that deep, gathering growl, and the whole countryside seemed to spring from its uneasy slumber: the treetops quivered, the dogs in the village took up the plaintive howl of the dogs upon the plains.

The strangeness of the hurricane lay in the manner of its leaving us almost unscathed, "licking us," as it were, with an occasional twitch of its dreadful tongue.

With awful swiftness the murmur grew to a roar that passed over the valley like a mighty river in flood—a river through which a hundred express trains ploughed, and as its volume grew it became a long-drawn howl of pain. Swiftly the moon's brilliance faded. It became the colour of an old brown boot as the dusts of the Russian Steppes and the dusts of the plains of America streamed overhead in a vast cascade towards the west—towards the Atlantic and towards the deserts from whence they came.

We stood together on the cricket field in silent wonder until the hurricane gave us its first "lick." Under any other conditions the scene would have been comic as a sudden airspout whipped round us and took a score of hats, cricket caps, trilbies, and bowlers soaring into space. Mine disappeared as if jerked by a string: fortunately it was not my best, but an old one used for evening wear.

Somebody laughed—and then the marquee was hit by a resounding buffet. Every peg upon one side was wrenched from the ground, and for a moment the marquee was like a giantess standing grotesquely upon her head with skirts flying upwards, hanging to the ground by a few surviving pegs. I only saw it for a second because suddenly the hurricane seemed to rise from the very pores of the earth: I felt my trouser legs billow out and rise upwards: I found myself overwhelmed in stuffy darkness as my coat flapped around my face like an umbrella inside-out.

There was a woman's shriek: a crash of coffee-cups—and through the turmoil came the voice of Sapper Evans:

"Get down!—lie down!"

In a body we flung ourselves upon the smooth turf of the meadow, clawing our fingers for absurd protection around the tufts of grass.

And then it was over—as suddenly as it had begun. With a tired sigh the murmur died away: the light of the moon flowed back to us—a golden, waning light. I rose to my feet and pulled down the legs of my trousers. A ripple of nervous laughter came—a woman, crying quietly, began to gather up the broken cups. The marquee hung forlorn and lopsided from a couple of slanting poles, and in the far corner of the field the chairs were heaped like driven autumn leaves.

"Missed us again!" shouted Charlie Hurst. "Now let's see what the other team can make!"

But his attempt at bravado was pathetic: there was no panic, but I saw several little groups standing around distressed old people and leading them quietly home.

Sapper Evans, the Vicar, Colonel Parker, and Dr. Hax were having an emergency Committee Meeting. I cannot believe that they were contemplating a continuation of the match. I think they were discussing the alternative of returning home or going to the dugout. Then Sapper Evans went over to the waiting cricketers.

"No good, boys," he said, "moon's waning. In half an hour we shan't have the light. Better pack up and go home."

It was a sad ending to our heroic "gala" week, but I am glad we played the cricket match instead of having the concert. The hurricane would have been far more terrible in a crowded hall than in an open meadow.

There was a tired smile in Pat's brave eyes as I said "goodnight" to her beside the cricket pavilion. Robin was upon his knees beside his cricket bag, packing his bat and pads and gloves, and Colonel Parker stood by to help him.

Robin stood up, pushed his tousled hair from his forehead, and grinned at me. "Lucky to get my innings before the fun began!" he said. "Look at that heap of chairs!—looks as if there'd been a big speech-day rag!"

I watched them walk across the meadow to the stile that led them to The Manor House. The Colonel was helping Robin with his bag, each taking one of the leather handles. I saw Pat's white pullover: a little pale cloud moving in the shadows of the trees, and they were gone. I felt terribly alone as I turned to make my way back to my home: everything was over now—the "gala week"—the work upon the dugout—my last meeting with those three people whom I loved.

I called "goodnight" to a white-clad cricketer in the lane beside the gate to my meadow—it was too dark to recognise him, but he called out: "Goodnight, Mr. Hopkins!" as he passed upon his way.

CHAPTER TWENTY

A litter of crumpled, wasted paper lies around me upon the dusty floor. For two long nights I have sat in the feeble flicker of my home-made lantern, struggling for words to describe the evening of the Cataclysm and the day that followed. I have been groping for inspiration to paint into my picture the whole agony of England in those stricken hours, but every attempt has led my pen into a flounder of impotence. My supply of paper is growing short and I am conscious of a growing weakness. This afternoon I fainted in the street as I returned from Kensington Gardens with wood for my fire. I have never fainted in my life before and it was twilight when my senses returned to me. I staggered home, fearful lest I should die before my story is finished and all my work should have been in vain.

I must seek no longer for grand words and "purple patches" to describe the things that happened: I must tell my story, simply and directly. The great picture of stricken England that I dreamed of writing must give place to a small, intimate picture of the tiny corner in which I lived. I shall tell everything and conceal nothing: if at times my behaviour seems irresponsible and ridiculous I can only ask the reader to bear in mind the hideous conditions which were influencing my reason through those hours.

I was very tired as I returned home at midnight from the cricket match. The brave, impudent conception of that last event in our "gala week" had been blasted by the hurricane into a pitiful anticlimax. Laughter was over. The people of Beadle returned home in silence to face the end.

I entered my dark house and went to my library. It had been an easy matter to keep cheerful in company with those grand people of the village. What with the hard physical work in Burgin Park during the day and our nightly programme of entertainments, I had scarcely had a moment to myself. But now it was all over, and nothing remained but to wait for the end. With a sinking heart I realised that almost two days still remained: two days that I must spend for the most part in solitude. If only the whole thing had ended that night upon the cricket ground!—ended with the Colonel and Pat and Robin beside me beneath those elms!

I glanced around my library. The old room had meant so much to me at one time. During those autumn days when I alone in the village had known what lay in store, this room had been a prison: sometimes a torture chamber in which I had nursed that dreadful secret in solitude. But I had been in it very little in the past few weeks. So tired was I after my work at the dugout that usually I had gone very early to bed, merely sitting a few minutes in the room to write my diary and yawn my head off. And now, for two final nights, it was to become my prison again.

It was well past midnight. I knew that I ought to go to bed, but there was something revolting in the thought of sleep with eternal sleep so close at hand. I had a desperate yearning to make

the utmost of the few hours that remained to me. A few moments
before I had been wishing these hours away, but now I found myself
counting them like a miser—counting them as a schoolboy might
count the last hours of his holiday. It occurred to me what an
interesting competition a newspaper could organise: "If two days
of life remained to you—how would you choose to spend them?"
How various the entries would be! Some would vote for a pack of
hounds, a sturdy horse, and one last glorious run across the country: others for a box each night at the opera. My own desires were
simple and modest. Tomorrow afternoon I would take my favourite
walk. I wanted to see the trees and the downs and the distant river
from the hillside for the last time. Tonight I would read.

I went to my bookcase. My hands moved instinctively away
from the classics—the heavy books of history and philosophy that
had helped me through unhappy times in days gone by. Instinctively I went to an obscure, untidy row of books in the corner of
the lowest shelf: the oldest friends in my library—the treasures of
my boyhood. I took *The Wind in the Willows*. I drew my chair to the
dying fire and roamed once again in the fragrant meadows with
Badger and Mole and the immortal Mr. Toad. The first streaks of
dawn were coming as at last I arose to go to bed, and as I looked
over the silvering valley I no longer saw a stricken world upon the
brink of eternity.

I thought instead of those myriads of little animals stirring
from their winter sleep: wide-eyed and cock-eared for the Pipes
of Pan.

I slept deeply and peacefully from the moment I closed my eyes.

Sunday was a calm, clear day, incredibly like all other Sundays that
had passed in Beadle. Everyone attended morning service, and in

the afternoon I took the long walk I had promised myself on the night before.

After tea I read the Sunday papers. I have said little concerning the manner in which the newspapers and the radio had dealt with those closing days. Gradually—almost imperceptibly—they had discarded their exciting, almost flippant approach to the crisis. They still kept up their spirit of optimism, stressing in particular the magnificent preparations made by the authorities and the impregnable strength of the dugouts, but a serious undertone had strengthened with the passage of time and I doubt whether any finer messages have ever been published to compare with the leading articles upon that last Sunday. There was an inspiring article by the Archbishop of Canterbury entitled "Courage," and straightforward messages from famous men in different walks of life, all stressing the theme: "There's a fighting chance!—keep your spirits up!" Millions must have become brave again and renewed their faith as they sat with their newspapers upon that calm Sunday afternoon.

At evening service the Vicar reminded his congregation of instructions already issued for the following day, and ended a touching little sermon with the words: "We shall meet again tomorrow night."

There was no storm that evening to break the quietness. Towards sunset the sky was filled with a deep blue glow. Then heavy clouds banked up from the east, bringing a few big, leaden drops of rain. The moon, when it rose, was hidden by the clouds, although its fierce light seeped through the lighter places like molten bronze.

That night I took from my bookcase another of my boyhood's friends. For many hours, until the dawn came, I journeyed down the Mississippi with Huckleberry Finn, his friend Tom Sawyer, and Jim, the negro. Once more I conjured up those brooding, limitless plains with the little lamplit shacks in the groves beside the river. As I undressed in the grey quietness of my bedroom, I realised that Monday had come: Monday the 3rd of May.

The reader may feel that I have dwelt over-long upon these last eventless hours. That may be true, but there is reason for it. Even though seven years have passed: even though I have been approaching this day through the softened light of memory, a growing horror has been stealing upon me as I draw near, and I have sought with my pen to postpone this dreadful day as once I sought to postpone it with books and work and every possible expedient.

Every night, as I have lain down my pen I have sighed with relief and whispered to myself: "You are still a month away"—"You have still ten days"—"The 'gala week' remains." But now nothing remains, for the 3rd of May has dawned.

I awoke at eight when Mrs. Buller brought my tea. I drank the tea and slept again till nine. I drew back my curtains upon a dark, leaden morning, more like November than the first week of May. It seemed as if even the normal functions of weather had ended, and the country lay embalmed beneath a dusty glass case. As I returned up the hillside from tending my poultry I found myself panting for breath. I cannot describe the atmosphere of that morning: it was neither warm nor cold—damp nor dry—a dead, fetid sickliness surrounded me like a pall.

The newspapers were published upon four pages only that morning. It would have been a mockery to produce Society News, the City Page, or the Garden Corner. And there was little beyond some final official instructions, a few messages, and some advice concerning "after precautions." There was a cartoon by Bridgnorth: an effigy representing the world facing the moon—behind the world lay all the dead crises and terrors of the past which the world had faced and triumphed over, suggesting that the world could face and still defeat its most terrible trial of all. On the front page of every newspaper appeared short messages of hope and courage from the heads of every great nation upon the earth. For the first time in history the whole world stood as if clasping hands—quarrels forgotten, friendships remembered in a last great "Auld Lang Syne."

I had intended to spend the day in quiet, reflective solitude, but towards midday the awful monotony of that dead grey atmosphere and tomblike stillness became intolerable. I had an aching hunger for companionship—for somebody—anybody—to speak to. I could scarcely go into the kitchen and talk with Mrs. Buller, for she was busy preparing lunch, so I took my hat and stick and walked down to the village.

I went slowly and deliberately, for any hurry, even the slightest stumble, brought suffocation upon me as if an iron band were tightening around my throat.

The village was deserted: everyone, I imagine, was preparing for their journey to the dugout in a few hours' time. My footsteps echoed down the silent street: a woman peered at me in surprise through a cottage window. I felt a fool and a coward, and silently retraced my steps for home.

As Mrs. Buller was clearing away my lunch I enquired whether her preparations were complete for going to the dugout that afternoon.

"Everything's ready," replied the old lady. "I'm filling two flasks with coffee and taking—"

"One flask will be sufficient," I said—and then I broke to her the news that I had kept from her as long as possible. "I shall not be coming to the dugout myself, Mrs. Buller. I have decided to stay here."

My decision may seem a reckless one: the wilful casting away of my slender chance of survival, but for months the thought of that dugout had haunted me. Ever since childhood I had had a horror of closed-in places. I can face a violent thunderstorm upon an open hillside without a tremor, but I have never been able to face an underground train and will walk up a dozen flights of stairs to avoid a self-controlled lift.

The thought of being shut inside that dugout for hours on end without hope of escape was horrible, and when Colonel Parker told me that he, with Pat and Robin, had decided to remain at The Manor House, I had breathed a sigh of thankfulness. If those brave souls could stay, then I too could stay without suggestion of cowardice.

Another thing that revolted me from the dugout was the thought of being penned up for hours without end with Dr. Hax, who was bound to throw his weight about and would drive me mad.

Mrs. Buller was surprised at my decision, but not in the way that I had anticipated. I had expected her to regard me as a reckless lunatic, but instead she stared at me with disapproving eyes and asked: "How could I do such a thing?"

As a result of the fatalistic letter she had received from that silly old lady with whom she was once in service, Mrs. Buller had completely given up hope of survival and had accepted this night as definitely the end of the world. She was one of those simple, tidy souls to whom a decent burial was the only essential luxury of life. She had frequently told me that her father was taken to his grave in a hearse with two men standing upon the ledge at the back of it and I knew that she hungered after a similar dignity. It had gradually dawned upon the poor old lady that, if the world ended, there would be no one to bury her, and the dugout had become to her the next best thing. She had not been keen about it at first, but when she heard that the Vicar would be there her mind was content. His presence would consecrate the dugout and the honour of being buried with the Vicar made up for the disappointment of being denied a grave to herself.

That I should wilfully refuse the only decent form of burial now open to me filled her with reproachful disappointment. I became, I think, a pagan in her eyes and no longer her master.

"Just as you think, sir," she murmured, and left the room. In a little while her loyalty got the better of her. She returned to say that she had laid out my tea in the drawing-room.

"The teapot's on the stove, sir—with the caddy beside it: you'll remember to give the pot a rinse with hot water before you put the tea in?" She stood by the door, her fingers roving up and down its side: "You sure you won't come, sir?—the Vicar said everybody was to go."

"I'm quite sure, Mrs. Buller. This is my home. I would rather stay here."

At four o'clock I walked with the old lady to the garden gate: she had been my housekeeper for over six years—I had never known any other servant in this house. At the gate I shook her hand—the first time in all those years that I had touched those thin, worn fingers.

"It'll be all right, Mrs. Buller."

"It's in God's hands," she replied.

I watched her go down the winding lane—a blanket over her arm, a little basket in her hand containing her flask of coffee and a book to read—her Bible. Something told me that I should never see her again. As I returned to my home and entered the gloomy hall, it was a home no longer. That frail old woman had taken its spirit and soul with her down the lane.

I could not stay in that house alone. I went out to my tool shed and emptied some flower-pots onto my stack of mould. I took my pruning scissors and began to cut back some shrubs that encroached upon the drive. I had to do something: something with my hands to hack a few resisting minutes from those ghastly, silent hours.

From my garden I could see the village people coming from their homes and going in little groups towards the dugout in Burgin Park. I should have stayed indoors during that heartrending hour, for as I watched them go I had a desperate longing to be with them. The horror of the sealed dugout suddenly became trivial beside the horror of my approaching isolation. I tried to keep my eyes away from the village—blindly and senselessly I clipped at the shrubs—but the lifeless atmosphere had made the stems so soft and flabby that my scissors twisted them in vain.

From the crest of my garden I could just see the dugout between the trees. I could see Sapper Evans bustling about, closing two of the doors. One door alone remained open and the Vicar and Dr. Hax stood beside it welcoming the people as they arrived. Two or three of the younger men, including Charlie Hurst, were acting as "reception clerks." They were conducting the people down the dugout steps, presumably to show them their appointed places, for presently the people would come up again without their blankets and belongings and sit down upon the grass. A woman moved amongst them serving tea and biscuits and the children seemed happy and high-spirited as they played upon the hillside. I looked at my watch: it needed ten minutes to five: there was still just time for me to get hold of a blanket and run wildly to the dugout before the doors were closed. I was in a torment of indecision and only the thought of my friends in The Manor House across the valley sustained my resolution to remain.

And then a sickening thought came to me. Supposing Colonel Parker, with Pat and Robin, had decided to go to the dugout after all? Supposing that I were alone—the only human soul upon the face of the earth? Panic seized me: utter solitude became a horror ten thousand times worse than a crowded dugout. I nearly ran shouting to the crest of my garden to wave my arms at the dugout and beg them to wait for me.

But it was too late: even as I looked I saw the Vicar and Sapper Evans calling to the people. I saw them rise from the grass and file down the steps, and I could bear to look no longer. I went into my house and threw myself into my library chair. I lay there sobbing for breath, for the air was suffocating. I threw open the window and the air that flowed in to me was like a freshly opened tomb: it was cold and evil-smelling—horribly stagnant. I went round my house and closed and bolted every window to retain as long as possible the air that was at least sweet enough to live in.

Presently I went out into my garden. A stubbornness in my nature urged me to see whether I could still breathe outdoors. It was difficult but not impossible. The hillside around the dugout was deserted now: deserted save for a solitary figure standing by the dugout door—the squat little figure of Sapper Evans. He was gazing around as if searching for a late-comer who might be upon his way. Was he waiting for me? He came out a little way and looked into the sky: he went back, adjusted something above the entrance, and closed the door behind him. As the door closed, the clock in Beadle Church tower pealed the hour of five. The Sapper had been true to military punctuality until the last.

It was still two hours from sunset, but a heavy, turgid twilight had begun to fall. The closing of that last steel door in Burgin Park had at least ended my torment of indecision. Nothing on earth could gain me entrance now: whatever my feelings I must face the night alone, but as I turned to go back to my house I was filled with relief and thankfulness. A square of amber light struck through the gloom. It came from across the valley, from the windows of The Manor House, and I knew that my friends were there to keep me company. Almost light-heartedly I went to the kitchen to make my tea. Within sight of me—practically within calling distance—were Pat and Robin, and the Colonel.

As I drank my tea I considered my position. If the forecast of the experts was correct, I still had two hours of safety in which to make my plans, and after careful reflection I decided to meet the crisis in the dining-room. The hurricane on Saturday night had come from the east: and the moon also would come from the east. My dining-room was open to the west side, and while the side of a house was not in itself much protection against a falling moon, I gained a lot of moral comfort by selecting a room as far away from its approach as possible. Built into the wall of the dining-room—well away from the windows—was a deep alcove. It had the additional protection of an arched roof, and there was a snug, safe look about it. I removed the sideboard from this alcove and placed a sofa there: I brought pillows and blankets from my bedroom and made a rough but serviceable bed.

I then went right over the house, taking down the pictures—removing china ornaments and stacking them into cupboards. I began to feel excited, almost elated as I carried out this work. I was the solitary defender of a besieged fort and the spirit of adventure gripped me. I was determined to make my stronghold impregnable. Having "streamlined" the house, wrapped all the kitchen crockery in tablecloths and packed it safely in the drawers, I gave thought to the windows. The air outside was growing steadily more stagnant and unbreathable, for when I crossed the few yards to my tool shed to get a screwdriver it was like passing through a sickly, muddy fog. So long as I could keep the house airtight I should be all right, and I spent an hour gumming strips of stout brown paper around the frames of the windows. I stuffed the chimneys tightly with wet towels, and even had the foresight to gum a square of paper over the letter-box.

The clock in Beadle Church struck seven. It was uncanny to hear that solitary old clock, placidly chiming the quarters to an empty world. There was not much longer to wait now, and there was little else for me to do. Several times I had paused in my work and gone to my library window to stare at the light in The Manor House across the valley. I saw a shadow move across the window and I wondered what they were doing in that old raftered room to pass those leaden hours.

The night outside was incredibly quiet: once I thought I heard a purr of a motor-cycle away up the valley, but I could not believe that anyone was abroad. At nearly half-past seven I mixed a strong whisky and soda, placed it upon a small table beside the alcove, and lay down upon the sofa to read.

In times of great nerve strain I have always been thankful that my recourse to alcohol is rare. Had I been accustomed to a whisky and soda every night, the stimulant I took that evening would have been to little purpose. But as it was I quickly felt its warm peacefulness come glowing through my veins, and despite the perilous nearness of the crisis I found it possible to read, even to enjoy, the first chapter of *Treasure Island*.

Occasionally I lowered my book to listen, but the world outside was deathly still. Once I was startled by a sudden plop as the wet towel I had stuffed up the chimney fell into the fireplace. I pushed it back and sustained it with the poker, but even as I did so a sickly, tomb-like odour flowed down from the outer world.

Half-past seven struck from the church tower. I went to the windows and met utter blackness—just my own reflection with the book in my hand. I sniffed around the frames to assure myself that I had thoroughly sealed out that fetid air. It seemed all right. I returned to the couch to read again.

I finished my whisky and lay staring at the arched ceiling of the alcove. I could hear the clock in the hall knocking away the seconds, and suddenly a thought occurred that almost made me laugh out loud. What a joke if nothing happened!—what a joke if the moon just disappeared and dawn came back to an unscathed world! Early in the morning I would put my hat on, rakishly, to the back of my head: I would go down to Burgin Park, and wait for those steel doors to open slowly and fearfully. As Dr. Hax came crawling out I would saunter up to him with my hands in my pockets and say: "Hullo!—what have *you* been up to?" What a wonderful joke!—but how infinitely more wonderful if fate allowed me to play it!—if nothing happened after all! Every minute that passed in quietness increased my exultation: my conviction that the crisis had come and gone, leaving us unharmed. As I lay there with hands clasped behind my head, the whole glorious future that I had given up surged back to life again. I was only forty-seven, I had many happy, energetic years ahead: this strange interlude and pause in my life would add fire to my ambitions. No longer would I be content to sweep the board at worthless local poultry shows—I would thrust my way into the National Class: even to the International, and triumph with my pullets in Paris and Stockholm and Amsterdam: the strains that I bred in Beadle would bring regeneration to the poultry of the world!

*   *   *

I may have dozed: I do not know—it may only have been those absurd imaginings of the future that distracted my attention from the first strange sounds that broke the stillness: I can only say that when gradually I became aware of them I knew that the sounds had been gathering for some little while in my subconscious mind. I sat up and listened: my book slipped to the ground: I rose from the sofa and went to the window.

It was just as dark, just as quiet outside, but there was a subtle difference in that impenetrable stagnation. It was as if my home lay fathoms deep in a stagnant, murky lake: as if, after many hours of calmness, something had come to ripple and worry the placid surface far above me. At first it was a feeling rather than a sound: when the church clock struck eight, each note came to me in different volume and varying quality: some strokes came clear and resonant as if a slight north wind were carrying them, and then a note would quiver strangely and be followed by one so muffled that it scarcely reached me.

Something very strange was happening, but even as I grew conscious of that encroaching, nameless horror, I clung with all my power to the obstinate hope that the danger time had passed.

I was more angry than afraid. I was so delighted about the idea of meeting Dr. Hax and laughing at him as he crept out of the dugout in the morning that I became furious at the possibility of anything happening to prevent it.

But there was little time for thoughts of Dr. Hax. I could deceive myself no longer. Definite sounds were above me now—a long-drawn, wailing sigh like an animal in pain. It died away—then came again more fiercely: it became a groan: a shriek—and the hurricane was in the valley.

At first it was like the hurricane of Saturday night when the wind had howled above us, leaving the cricket ground almost unscathed, but nothing on that Saturday compared with the first "buffet" that struck my house. It felt as if a huge sea monster had swung its tail and struck my house a resounding blow in the face: I heard something crash and roll upstairs: the glass fell from the table beside the couch and bounced upon the carpet.

My house no longer lay beneath the storm: as the tempest rose it lashed away the darkness. Light returned—but not the steady, golden light of yesterday: it came in a dirty-brown, diseased glow that pulsated with the morbid rhythm of a totem drum. For the space of a second I saw the light in The Manor House across the valley—then suddenly it was gone. With its going my own lights flickered. They struggled to life again: for a little while they seemed to pulsate in horrid mesmerism with the brown glow of the sky— then went out completely. I staggered to my table and gripped the torch placed there in readiness, but I had no need to use it now. The dingy brown sky became wild and luminous: through its dirty brownness came a blood-red streak: swelling and pulsating until the whole sky was filled by it. The heavens seemed to pant and bleed like the shattered lung of a dying giant.

The wind no longer came in scattered, thudding blows: it came in a torrent—one shrieking, ceaseless torrent of maniacal fury. I stood by the window fascinated: I could not move: there came a great rending as if the whole hillcrest were being torn open from horizon to horizon—I saw the giant elms brace themselves—quiver and fall like corn before a scythe. One, seized in a freakish eddy, stood for a few seconds completely upon its head with its roots waving like branches before it collapsed downwards into its own tangled foliage. Something came with a mighty crash against the back of my house: the whole structure swayed and I heard a cascade of falling tiles.

Stupefied by the shock I found myself wondering whether my "all in" insurance policy would be of any use. Mercifully the hurricane was coming from the east: my house was built a little below the hillcrest upon the western side, and but for this protection nothing could have saved it from being swept bodily away. The downfall of those giant elms upon the crest had not ended their torment: as I watched I saw huge limbs torn from them, whipped up, and spun grotesquely to eternity. Something dark and square, that looked like a shed, came flying up the valley, rolling over and over in the air at least a hundred feet from the earth. Around it, like small planets, whirled a number of fluffy balls—my chicken house!—my poultry!—dead, helpless, fluffy balls—and I had known them all by name!

I could bear it no longer: my head was throbbing like mad: horribly it seemed to throb in harmony with the red, pulsating sky. I staggered to the sofa within the alcove—I threw myself onto it, turned my face to the wall, dragged the blanket over my head, and lay sobbing like a child—I cried aloud: as loud as I possibly could to drown the agony of that shrieking tempest.

How long I lay there I do not know: it seemed a year, but I do not think it was for more than half an hour. I thrust my fingers into my ears and the roaring of my own blood drowned the devastation of the earth.

Slowly I became conscious of a new and weird sensation. Once, years before, on my cruise to the Canary Islands, our little ship had struck a violent storm in the Bay of Biscay, and one moment of that storm had lived vividly in my memory. We were lifted onto the crest of a huge swell and had then descended to the very bottom of a gulley: the fall had seemed endless and we appeared to sink and sink to the very bottom of the ocean.

And now, as I lay upon my couch, the sensation came again, but magnified a thousandfold. My body seemed gradually to become as light as a feather. I hardly felt the couch beneath me—we were sinking, and sinking. The whole house—the whole world was sinking.

There was something very peaceful in it: and suddenly I understood the reason. The tempest had left us. The raging inferno had passed as a tortured soul might pass from a shattered body, leaving a miracle of stillness and peace behind it.

Peace . . . and stillness?—Was there nothing else?—Was there not also death?

My terror had given place to relief and overwhelming gladness. The lightness of my body upon this couch . . . the fading of all sound from my ears could mean but one thing . . . the gentle passing of my life. In a little while I should feel my body no longer—the drop of the lids over my aching eyes: the throb in my temples—all pain, all torment, would be gone forever. I lay there waiting peacefully for some final sign—some subtle change to tell me that bodily life was done with, conscious only of a thankfulness that, much as I had suffered, I had been spared at least the agonies of a body maimed and shattered by a falling house.

Just as I was becoming certain that I must now be dead, I was startled by the rudest and most unexpected shock of the whole evening. Suddenly—without warning, the window burst. I cannot say that it broke: it just burst as a bottle of beer might burst if placed beside the fire. The force that burst the glass did not come from outside: it came from within as if an invisible elephant were in the room and had leaned against the pane. The glass flew outwards but made no sound as it fell, and then to my astonishment a pile of notepaper and envelopes upon the writing table whisked up and flew in a stream through the window. They fluttered up a few yards, then dropped like sheets of lead onto the path.

Strange flashes of comprehension sometimes come in moments of extreme danger, for despite my astonishment I realised dimly what had happened. The atmosphere had left the earth—I remembered the words of Professor Hartley, spoken months ago: "The earth may be jolted out of its skin of atmosphere." That accounted for the sudden silence, for without air there can be no sound. But the thought was gone within a second, for almost at once I was struggling in that room like a drowning man. As the air had left the outside world the pressure of the atmosphere in this room had burst the window and was whistling away into the night. I was suffering agonies of physical pain: my head seemed to swell like a balloon and my limbs felt horribly big and bloated. I staggered to the door: I heard the air whistling through the keyhole from the outside hall and as I turned the handle the door flew open, almost stunning me. As the air rushed from the hall towards the shattered window I was able to take one great, God-sent breath of it that gave me the strength to struggle onwards to the door of my library.

As the door opened inwards I had to throw my whole weight against it before it would give against the pressure of air within. I fell into the room and the door crashed to behind me. I lay panting for breath upon the floor, blood gushing from my ears. But there was air in here, and I quickly recovered. The windows of the library were latticed in lead, with thick diamond-shaped panes that had withstood the strain. But I could hear the precious, life-giving atmosphere whistling under the door like water through the sluice gates of a mill. I dragged up the hearthrug and wedged it along the crack: it was easier to keep air within the room than to keep it out, for the pressure drew the rug tightly against the leak and the hissing stopped.

I was thinking calmly and logically again: for greater safety I closed the shutters over the windows to lessen the pressure against the glass. I examined the chimney and was glad of my foresight in blocking it with a wet towel. The room seemed airtight now. How long I could live in it I did not know—I scarcely cared: I was almost angry with myself for allowing that frantic instinct for self-preservation to turn a quick death in my dining-room into a slow death by suffocation in my library.

I dropped into my armchair—inexpressibly tired—clammy with perspiration. I wiped the blood from my ears and tried to coax saliva into my parched mouth.

I think that I must have fainted, for it could not possibly have been sleep. I returned to consciousness with a ghastly headache that seemed to be forcing my eyes from their sockets: my tongue was swollen—I could not swallow. I faced a slow, agonising death, pitifully different from the peaceful end that I had hoped for upon the couch in the dining-room a few hours ago. I looked at my watch and struck a match to see the time: the flame burnt red and stale in the used-up air: it was ten o'clock—a bare two hours since the agony began. In normal times I would not yet be thinking of going to bed!

As I sat there with fuddled brain, breathing slowly and lightly to preserve the fetid air to the uttermost, I thought that I heard a sound. I listened and it came again—the faintest ripple of something like water. Hope surged within me: if there was sound there must be air!

I went to the door and determined to open it. In any case it would be better to die at once than to bear the slow agony of suffocation in this room.

I drew the hearthrug from the bottom of the door. I knelt and held my hand against the crack. There was a slight movement, whether of air going out or coming in I could not tell.

I summoned my courage, took hold of the handle, and pulled. The door opened with ease—there was air upon earth again!

It was bitterly cold, with a sickly, sulphurous taste—but it was air—and breathable. I stood there for a moment, taking deep thankful draughts of it. It made me cough. I retched and was slightly sick, but I felt better for it. Across the dark hall the dining-room door stood open: beyond, through the broken window, I could see a faint grey light. I walked through the hall and into the drawing-room. I went to the broken window, threw it open, and looked out.

What I saw should not, I suppose, have affected me as strangely as it did, but my nerves were wrecked and my brain incapable of further strain.

I was prepared to look from that window upon a shattered world: I was prepared to see the valley heaped with wreckage and the whole village of Beadle swept away. But I saw no valley before me: I saw instead what seemed to be a flat field almost level with my eyes: a limitless plain upon which some light crop like clover rippled in a steady wind.

To say that I could not believe my eyes is an understatement. I could not believe my brain or my intelligence. For a moment I wondered whether the whole house had been lifted bodily from its foundations and carried by the tornado into the Steppes of Russia, but I discarded the idea as too absurd.

The sounds came to me: the *ripple-ripple* that I had heard so lightly in the shuttered library was louder and more constant here. It was very dark: I found my torch upon the floor and flashed it onto the plain beyond the window.

It was not a plain: it was water, a vast expanse of inky, sluggish water moving slowly by the window within a few feet of the walls. I had heard a lot about lost men upon the desert—in the last delirium of thirst: stumbling onwards and onwards towards calm sheets of water that tantalised their maddened brains. I was sure now that I was mad. Floods I could imagine—floods that might even penetrate this inland valley—but before me was an ocean: moving placidly 500 feet above the level of the sea!

I stood there without thought: I stood with dull eyes and deadened brain until a huge black shape came slowly within my vision and quenched the faint greyness of the night. It looked like an immense ship, sleepily nosing its way to harbour. For a moment its vast bulk seemed within touching distance and I thought that portholes passed me. The water was closer now: it was lapping against the very walls of the house: what I had taken to be the ripples of wind across a field of clover now showed themselves to be long, rhythmic waves, advancing steadily—each wave adding a little to the rising surface of the ocean.

I do not remember going back to my library—I have only a hazy recollection of sitting for a long while in my armchair, drumming the armrests with my fingers and saying out loud again and again: "Mad!—quite mad!—raving mad!—solitary raving madman in an empty world!"

When I awoke I felt something upon my knee: it was an open book, with my torch lying upon it. There was a little light coming through the open door. I sat puzzling over it for a long time—puzzling where the book had come from and what it was. I flashed my torch upon the title page: *Downland Rambles in Hampshire*. It conveyed nothing. It baffled me.

Dimly I began to remember. I had gone to my bookshelf to get a book to see if I could read. I had argued that if I could read, I might not be mad after all. With trembling fingers I opened the book and flashed on the torch:

. . . the track becomes difficult to follow as the summit of the downs is reached . . .

The words made sense and I understood them! I rose from my chair, quivering with excitement: I flashed my torch around, saying: "Fireplace!—bookshelf!—cupboard!" I knew the words and the purpose of each thing! I threw myself down beside my chair and gave thanks to God for the blessing of sanity.

I went to the cupboard. A syphon was there. I pressed the nozzle to my parched lips and felt the cool, sweet water hiss into my burning throat.

I went to the window and threw the shutters open. Dawn was coming over the stricken hillside: the sweetest dawn that I have ever seen. The valley was still deep in darkness, but that ghostly ocean had gone as weirdly as it came.

I ran across the hall and flung the door wide to the glorious sunlight: I ran into the dining-room, flung myself upon the couch, and lay there laughing and sobbing. I was alive!—the sun was rising!—the world was saved!

CHAPTER TWENTY-ONE

I must have slept for nearly seven hours, for when at last I opened my eyes the tilt of the sun upon the dining-room carpet showed me that it was close upon midday.

Even so, I lay there in a blissful doze for another hour—utterly regardless of what had happened to the rest of the world in my own surpassing gratitude for life. I desired no greater happiness than to wriggle my toes and to feel the gentle pulsing of my heart.

But gratitude is the shallowest and most transient of all emotions: within the space of an hour it began to grow thin and break up in the face of an increasing desire for breakfast.

Where was Mrs. Buller? She ought to have been out of that dugout hours ago. I began to listen impatiently for the opening of the kitchen door—for Mrs. Buller's footsteps in the kitchen and the pleasant clatter of breakfast cups. But the silence continued, and my impatience grew to annoyance. Nothing is more irritating to a middle-aged man than the dislocation of long-established habits. While I had been through a most horrifying experience, my housekeeper had spent a comfortable, sociable night in the dugout protected by steel doors from the privations I had myself endured. Instead of returning at once to renew her duties she was probably gossiping in the village, bursting with self-importance over her adventure, totally regardless of my comfort and callous of my safety! I began rehearsing a few sharp, sarcastic remarks for when she condescended to return.

"It's perfectly all right, Mrs. Buller! I spent a most restful night and am quite content to make my breakfast upon air!—*Please* don't hurry yourself!"

My watch had stopped, and I had no notion of the time, but the sun was now shining upon the end of the table as it shone when I sat down to lunch at one o'clock. I could contain my hunger no longer. I resolved to shame Mrs. Buller by getting a meal for myself. The pots and pans that usually hung upon the kitchen wall were scattered upon the floor, but thanks to my foresight in storing the crockery there was little damage done. I cut some bread and butter, opened a tin of sardines, and began to enjoy the novel experience of "doing for myself."

But when I returned to the stove to make my tea I received my first shock: the first indication of the state of affairs that I was now to face. I had filled the kettle, turned on the electric stove, and given it ten minutes. I now discovered the stove to be stone-cold: there was no electric heat.

The lights had failed in my dining-room at eight o'clock on the previous night. It was now past midday. A sixteen-hour failure in the electric supply suggested a more serious state of affairs than I had imagined. Because I had survived the night in safety, and because my house had withstood the storm so well, I had been lulled into the false belief that the rest of the world had suffered no worse than I had.

But there was coal in the scuttle and sticks prepared by the methodical Mrs. Buller for the morning fires. I went back to the dining-room, laid the fire, put a match to it, and placed the kettle there.

While it was boiling I decided to make a full inspection of the house. The crash I had heard upstairs during the height of the tornado had prepared me to meet with some disorder in the bedrooms, but I was completely unprepared for the appalling sight that faced me as I reached the upstairs landing. My own bedroom, which faced westward, was in moderately good condition: the window was broken and the floor strewn with books and papers, but when I entered the best spare bedroom on the eastern side I was stunned with dismay. The whole roof had collapsed in the northeast corner and the room stood open to the sky: whatever had hit the house on the previous night had torn a jagged hole ten feet wide. The window had been blown inward bodily with its frame and lay splintered upon the bed, and the room had become the receptacle for masses of filth and rubbish from the tornado-stricken night.

The second spare bedroom was almost as bad: here again the window had been blown bodily from its socket and the debris lay a foot deep on the floor, rising breast-high against the inner wall. I have never seen such an astonishing collection of rubbish: there were two dead rabbits and a Russian soldier's cap in one corner, and in the fireplace I found a toy trumpet and a seed catalogue printed in Swedish. I had not realised until then the terribly widespread nature of the storm.

As I stood meditating upon this doleful mess I was alarmed by columns of black smoke coming up the stairs. I rushed down, fearing that the house was on fire, and discovered to my chagrin that when I had lighted the dining-room fire I had forgotten the wet towel I had pushed up the chimney on the previous evening. I was almost suffocated as I got it down with the tongs, and it was a good half-hour before the fire burnt up sufficiently to boil my kettle.

Food and hot tea revived me a little, but it helped in no way to dissipate my growing concern. Although the sun shone brightly it was deathly still outside: no sound of cars came from the road beyond the valley—no voice of man from the village or song of bird from the downs. I seemed to be as isolated now as I had been in the awful twilight of the previous evening. In retrospect I know that my attitude was childish and unreasoning that morning, but no man can gain full comprehension, in the space of a few short hours, of the complete dissolution of a world that he had taken for granted since childhood. Only by coming face-to-face with each hard fact in turn could understanding grow.

I had been looking forward to my first excursion into the outside world, but now I began to dread it. I had looked forward, in that first blissful hour of my awakening, to going down into a battered but cheerful village and being something of a hero to the villagers who had spent the night in the dugout. I could tell them the whole story of the tornado as an "eye witness" and take a rise out of Dr. Hax who had seen nothing.

But now the worst forebodings were oppressing me. The continued absence of Mrs. Buller no longer annoyed me: it filled me with increasing concern. I went to the hall, took my hat and stick, and threw open the front door.

The first thing I noticed was that my yew trees, cut to the shape of sitting hens, which had lined the path to my front door, had completely disappeared. I was surprised at this, but not altogether sorry. Since my gardener had ruined the uniformity of them by his clumsy cutting when we had tried to turn one of the chickens into a gamecock, the whole line of trees had been an eyesore to me and I was rather pleased that the tornado had removed them so completely and so neatly.

But I quickly discovered that the weird ocean outside my window on the previous night had been no ghostly apparition of a fevered brain. My garden was in a ghastly mess—thick with slimy mud, seaweed, and the kind of rubbish one sees upon the beach of a seaside resort after a Bank Holiday—sodden newspapers, a pair of trousers . . . I will not dwell upon it.

Even this did not depress me as much as the reader might suppose. I was fond of hard gardening, and the obliteration carried out by the flood would afford me the opportunity of designing the garden upon entirely new and refreshing lines. The seaweed in particular would be a good fertiliser when dug well into the topsoil.

My thoughts were now upon my meadow in the valley, where I kept my poultry. I knew that one of my chicken houses had gone because I saw it blown by in the storm, but I still had hopes that a few at least had survived in the comparative shelter of the valley. I walked over the hillcrest and looked down upon the piece of land that had always been my pride and joy.

I blinked my eyes—took off my spectacles and wiped them: what in the world had happened?

Was it an enormous mound of mud? . . . was it a stranded sea monster?

Sprawled in my meadow, almost covering the whole five acres of it, lay a huge black shape. I went down the hillside in mute bewilderment, and as I drew nearer I saw to my amazement that it was an enormous ship.

Its great hull lay facing me—towering above me—its three immense funnels stuck out upon the other side, their tops resting upon the gentle slope that rose towards the downs.

The sun was glinting upon the great bronze screws as I stood staring up at them like a man in a trance. I walked to the bows and, by twisting my head, was able to read the name upon the vessel's side. It was the *King Lear*.

The phenomenon is not difficult to explain. My meadow lay at the head of a great valley that widened southward to Southampton Water. When the huge backwash from the Atlantic Ocean struck the southern coast of Britain, the tidal waves took the line of least resistance up valleys that had once taken broad glacial rivers to the sea.

The greatest ships in the world had been like bottle corks in the face of those mighty waves. The *King Lear*, wrenched from her moorings, had ridden up this Hampshire valley until the lip of the downs had ended her nightmare voyage. The wave had receded as rapidly as it had come, leaving its wrack behind it.

It is useless to argue reason in the face of a thing like this. I had already suffered more in one night than any man before me had suffered in a lifetime. I was blind to the awe-inspiring power that had wrought this miracle: I was conscious only of a consuming, overpowering rage! What had I done to deserve it? . . . Nothing! This was *my* meadow!—my freehold property! I had paid £600 for it and reared in its quiet seclusion the finest poultry that had ever stepped in Hampshire! This lovely meadow had been the pride and the joy of my life, and here, sprawled upon it like a drunken giant, crushing and obliterating my life's work, lay somebody else's property—without my permission, without a word of apology! Of my poultry houses there was not a sign—of my cherished pullets not a feather. . . .

I scrambled up the slimy hillside, panting—sobbing with impotent rage. I strode into my house and took up the telephone:

"Give me the North Star Shipping Company immediately!" I shouted.

The telephone was dead: as dead as my electric stove: as dead as my Bantam hens and Wyandotte pullets: as dead as the whole of this silent, barren world. I collapsed onto the sofa and burst into tears.

My breakdown brought infinite relief to me: the pent-up strain of many months released itself in those floodgates of despair. Gradually I grew calmer: a philosophical calmness came which I had never felt before, and my anger gave place to shame.

I had been so insanely obsessed with my own trivial misfortunes that I had given no thought to other tortured souls that might have survived. When I had left my house I had been so concerned about my garden and my meadow that I had not even glanced at the village beneath me. I had a duty—an urgent duty—towards my fellow beings. I might possibly be the only survivor: in that case there was nothing to be done but live like a Robinson Crusoe—Emperor of a dead world—until I, too, was dead. But there might be others, and my duty was to give them every hope and comfort in my power. I rose from the couch and went once again to my front door, determined this time to meet with courage whatever lay in store for me.

I walked down the slope of what had been my garden until the village came in view. I saw now that the flood which had left the *King Lear* in my meadow had not entirely gone. A grey, stagnant lake submerged the lower part of Beadle Valley, and the ruined houses stood waist-deep in mud and slime. The tower of the church was broken off—possibly by the great liner as it had passed overhead—a solitary black bird, which might have been a crow, was wheeling forlornly over the shattered roofs, but of human life there was no vestige nor sign. I walked up the slope until I could see the doors of the dugout in Burgin Park. Two doors were closed, but the third, the farthest from the main door, stood open. My hope surged up at the sight of that open door, but as I glanced around my bewilderment increased. Close upon a hundred people had entered the dugout: the open door suggested their escape and safety, but where were they? . . . where had they gone? Surely a few of them at least would have stood by the village to salvage what remained of their homes? It baffled me.

I was about to go and get my binoculars to search the surrounding country when I saw something which brought a shout of joy to my lips. I yelled like a madman and waved my hat.

Standing upon the opposite hillside was a solitary figure. It did not move—it did not answer my shout—but it was alive, and human. I felt in that moment as a shipwrecked man must feel when a wisp of smoke appears upon the distant horizon. I shouted again—ridiculously concerned lest the man should turn and go, as a ship might turn and leave the shipwrecked sailor.

This time the figure made a sign. An arm was raised, suspiciously and uncertainly, as if its owner doubted my existence.

I slithered down the muddy hillside and raced across the valley, but fast as I went my brain was racing ahead of me. Who could this stranger be with whom, quite possibly, I was to share the world? What a sorry anticlimax if it turned out to be Dr. Hax or Murgatroyd the publican! I would rather live in solitude than share the world with Dr. Hax, who would promptly make himself King and expect me to serve him. But I was across the valley now—I was scrambling up the other side, and as I drew near I saw that it was Robin Parker.

It was magnificent to find another fellow creature, no matter who it was, but it overjoyed me to find someone whom I knew to be a friend. As I hurried the last few yards I prepared to wring the boy's hand and clap him joyfully upon the shoulder—and then I stopped in front of him. I did not take his hand. My greeting was never uttered.

It was Robin Parker, but only by his features did I recognise him. Nothing else remained to tell me of the carefree boy who had worked beside me in Burgin Park a few short days ago.

He took an uncertain step towards me: I think that he recognised me, although he seemed doubtful whether I were a real person or a vision of his anguished mind. He was terribly pale: an ugly, open wound ran from his cheekbone almost to the jaw, and the shirt was dark with blood: his hair lay matted upon his forehead and his eyes were upon me like those of a tortured, beseeching animal.

I felt quite powerless. I could not greet the boy. I could only stand before him and say: "You're hurt, Robin."

He made no answer to my obvious and futile remark: his eyes wandered vaguely, without any sense of surprise or curiosity, towards the great ship that sprawled across my meadow—then he trembled, and looked me up and down as if seeing me for the first time.

"Will you come and help me?" he said.

I took his arm as we turned to climb the hillside to The Manor House, for he swayed and nearly fell, but he roughly shook my hand away and spoke in a harsh voice that I scarcely recognised: "I'm all right!—can't you see!"

We walked slowly and in silence. Only as we reached the garden gate did the boy speak to me again.

"My uncle's dead."

For a moment he looked me in the eyes, then turned and walked towards the house.

The terrible question upon my lips was only partly answered by the boy's brief words, but in a moment the rest of the answer was given me. With intense thankfulness I saw the figure of a girl come from the house, and walk down the hill to meet us.

Pat smiled and took my hand.

"I'm so glad you are safe," she said. "Has Robin told you? . . . it's good of you to come."

She was deathly pale: I saw that her hands, like Robin's hands, were torn and bleeding, but she walked with a firm step and her eyes were clear and calm.

I followed them to the old panelled room where on a memorable evening I had dined with them so happily. The tragedy needed no words of explanation. The giant beech tree that stood upon the lawn had snapped from its base and crashed through the roof of the house, and the body of Colonel Parker lay crushed beneath the broad oak beam that had spanned the room. The force of the fall must have been terrific, for the tree had ploughed its way through the room above and its trunk loomed through the shattered ceiling—a glossy, satin-faced trunk, filled with the saps of spring.

A mass of fallen wreckage had been thrown to one side in a frantic effort to release the poor, broken body, and I understood the reason for those torn, bleeding hands.

I could think of nothing for the moment. I stood there in helpless silence.

"I don't think that he suffered," said Pat, and her voice seemed to come to me from far away. "I think he was numbed . . . he tried to help us a little, and then it was over."

There was a moment more of silence, and then I was startled by Robin's voice.

"Aren't you going to *do* something!" he shouted. "Can't you see!"

Pat was quickly beside him. "Don't! Robin" . . . and she turned to me appealingly. "I'm sorry," she said, "he's badly hurt."

The boy's eyes were wide and racked with fever. "We must see to Robin first," I began . . . then suddenly the boy was calm.

"I'm sorry," he whispered. "Will you help us? . . . could you . . . d'you think you could help us lift this beam?"

I am not physically a powerful man but I threw every ounce of strength into that terrible task. Little by little we raised the great beam, thrusting a brick beneath it as a wedge, until at last, as Robin and I gave one superhuman effort, Pat was able to draw the body from beneath its prison. I admired her beyond words for the calm gentleness of those arms as they took their ghastly burden.

Only now would Robin allow us to dress his wound: the exertion of lifting the beam had caused the gash to bleed again. We led him to the kitchen. I washed the wound as Pat went away and returned with bandages. We gave him some brandy and forced him to lie down upon the couch in the wreck-strewn library.

"Will you come outside?" said Pat.

I followed her to the garden and she paused beside the skeleton of a great cedar that once had spread its dark foliage far across the lawn.

"He was fond of this tree," she said. "It was a favourite place of his."

I understood her meaning, and gently laid my hand upon her arm. "You must go back and look after Robin," I told her. "Leave me here."

I found a spade beneath the ruins of a shed, and the sun was setting as I finished my sad task. Robin helped me to carry the body to the grave, and Pat followed with a coat upon her arm.

"I think he would have liked this, too," she said.

It was the Colonel's old military greatcoat, with tarnished crown and star upon its shoulders. I looked for the last time upon that proud, drawn face as Pat gently laid the coat across it. It was hard to believe that he was dead, for there was no sign of injury, and the rough tweed suit gave an eerie sense of life. I felt that I was saying farewell to an old, tried friend, and yet I had only twice been to his house: once to dine with him and once to dig his grave.

Twilight was coming as we laid the turf in place, and when it was over Pat looked at me with a grave, grateful smile.

"Thank you," she said. "You must be very tired. I've something ready for you."

The girl had not been resting, as I had hoped. She had made a valiant endeavour to clear the ruined kitchen: she had lit the fire and made some tea. She had even laid a cloth upon the table with a plate of biscuits, some hot Bovril for Robin, and a small bottle of wine for me.

Over that simple meal, as darkness came, we found it possible to speak for the first time of other things.

"Do you know what's happened?" asked Pat. "I feel awfully selfish . . . just our own affairs . . . there must be thousands . . ."

"There's time for everything now, Pat"—(and I spoke that name for the first time). "I know nothing more than you. Tomorrow we shall find out what there is to know—for the time being you must rest, for we shall need all our strength. . . ."

"We shall," said Pat, and her voice was scarcely above a whisper. There was a little silence, and I felt the deathly stillness of the world. Then Pat spoke again.

"If we could live through it, others may have lived. . . . Oughtn't we to . . . to see if we can help?"

"There was no one in the village," I replied. "The dugout was open, I could see it from my garden: one of the doors stood wide open."

"Then they must be safe!" cried Pat.

"They must be," I said. "The door could only be opened from inside."

"Where are they, then?"

"That I can't say. We will see tomorrow."

I looked around that stricken, stone-walled kitchen: a huge fracture gaped in the wall beside the fireplace—an ugly, open crack from floor to ceiling. As I had worked upon the Colonel's grave I had paused now and then to look at the house, and I knew that it had suffered far more than mine. The whole upper floor lay ruined and open to the sky—no one could remain in this house with safety, and shyly I put the invitation that I had been planning all that afternoon.

"I've been wondering," I said, "whether you would come and share my home for a little while? My house was lucky: it's not badly damaged, and I'm quite alone. I should be very happy if you would come until . . . until things get straight."

I saw the boy and girl exchange a quick, enquiring glance: I was very happy to see the spontaneous relief and agreement in their faces.

"That's awfully good of you. We'd like to come."

I tried to dissuade them from clambering up those dark, ruined stairs, for the walls seemed to totter and parts of the broken roof were hanging by a thread, but they insisted upon a few things to bring along with them. I stood in the hall beneath and caught pyjamas, toothbrushes, and various odds and ends, and rolled them up in a tablecloth.

The stars were shining as we crossed the valley. "In an hour we shall know whether we've still got a moon," said Robin.

In the troubles of the day I had entirely forgotten about the moon. "Of course," I said, "it'll be interesting to see."

"Did you see it last night?" asked Robin.

"No—I saw lots of strange lights—nothing of the moon."
"Nor did we."

The spirit of adventure springs eternal. Despite all our sufferings I honestly believe that all three of us enjoyed that weirdly exciting first evening in my desolate home. The leaving of The Manor House, with its personal tragedy, seemed to lift the veil of gloom from the boy and girl. I knew that much of their cheerfulness was a bravely acted part, but as they busied themselves in preparing supper they became again the Pat and Robin that I knew and loved.

We tried to persuade Robin to go to bed immediately but he stubbornly insisted upon playing his part. While Pat went with me to the kitchen, Robin relit the library fire, drew the curtains, and set the table with plates and cutlery in a clumsy, boyish way.

I discovered a packet of candles in the kitchen drawer, but for economy we lit only two: one for the kitchen and one for the library table. Pat was surprised at the wide selection of preserved foods in my larder, for I had given much thought to laying in a proper supply. To take her mind from her own tragic home I made her decide what we should have for supper. She selected a tongue, with a jar of preserved pears to follow, and the romantic little feast that followed has lived always in my memory, for romantic it was, in the deepest sense of the word.

Romance is not easy to find in the placid conditions of civilised life: we strive to capture it by artificial means—through books, from the stage of the theatre, and from the screen. But on that night, in that old book-lined room of mine, it came to us without conscious striving. Without our bidding, despite all that we had faced that day, its thrall enwrapped us. The fire gave us its golden glow: the candles sent our shadows creeping to and fro across the wall, and the curtains, drawn warmly against the stillness of the night, were symbols of defeated terror.

Robin had changed his blood-soiled shirt: he was wearing an old school sweater and grey flannels, and Pat the white pullover that she had worn at the cricket match. I was in my rough tweed walking suit: I felt my bristling, unshaven chin and apologised.

"I must look a frightful tramp!"

"You look like a Wild West pioneer," corrected Pat.

"Perhaps all three of us are pioneers," I said. "Tomorrow we set out to discover a new world."

I saw Robin's eyes light with a sudden dawn of excitement, and I smiled across at him.

"We've suffered," I said. "You two have suffered far more than me, but we shall have our reward, I think—in the days to come. No matter what havoc lies out there—the world has survived: the moon may have gone, but the sun's in the sky and the earth is full of life. Those of us who have survived will have a great duty ahead of us. We have to build the world again, and perhaps in doing so, we shall find little ways of improving it. All three of us have been reborn today—I at forty-seven—you at twenty, Pat . . . and Robin at seventeen. I may not live to enjoy the fruits, but you two have the best years of your lives ahead. Before you are old you may be living in a world much finer than any you would have known if this . . . cataclysm had not come to us."

I was speaking to bring hope and encouragement to the tired, brave girl and boy before me, but even as I spoke I thought of my Uncle Henry, of how he had chortled over his years of full-spent life without consideration of my own desire to live. With Uncle Henry I was young, with years ahead of me, yearning to be lived, but with Pat and Robin I was old, with my best years gone. I had always been a lonely, self-sufficient man. At a pinch I could eke out an existence and even be happy in solitude—growing my own food—fishing in the river and perhaps snaring an occasional rabbit. With sufficient food, and my books around me, I would lose very little if I were to be a Robinson Crusoe for the rest of my life—but what of Pat? . . . this lovely girl upon the verge of womanhood? . . . what of the gaiety and travel and social life that were the due of her youth and charm? . . . where could marriage be found in a shattered world? . . . where could be found the peace and happiness of home life—and children? . . . And what of Robin, at seventeen? . . . with a year still due to him at Eton? . . . a last year that should have been filled with the interests and responsibilities of a senior boy? . . . where were his years at Oxford now? . . . and his cricket blue? . . . He was intended, I knew, for the diplomatic service. Where could Robin find, in this ruined world, a career to be worthy of his birth and character?

But these thoughts came only as a background to my words: I do not think that Pat and Robin had begun to consider the deep, bewildering problems that lay ahead of them, and even if they had I doubt if they would have been dismayed. Their eyes never left mine as I spoke to them, and the light in those eyes kindled fresh admiration in me: a resolve to live for them—to do all in my power for them.

Dog-tired though we were, Pat insisted that we should clear away the meal and wash up before we went to bed.

"Men in the jungles put on dinner jackets every night to keep civilised," she said. "We're going to wash up tonight for the same reason!"

I gave Robin a glass of port and made him rest by the fire while Pat and I worked in the kitchen, for I could see that his wound was giving him great pain. I knew that it should have been stitched and properly sterilised, and I could only trust to his youth and health to heal the gash.

Even so, he would not keep quiet. As Pat and I returned from the kitchen Robin was standing at the front door, staring up into the night. He came in, grinning through his bandages.

"There's no moon," he said. "It's disappeared. I wonder where it's gone to?"

"We'll have a look for it tomorrow," I said. "Now, you be off to bed!"

I gave Robin Mrs. Buller's room, which lay upon the western side and was not badly damaged. I insisted that Pat should have my room and only persuaded her by declaring that I would not sleep at all unless she did.

But the girl refused to sleep until she had brought the sheets and pillows from one of the wrecked spare rooms and made my bed upon the library couch.

I took up the candle when she had finished. "Take this," I said. "I can see quite well by the light of the fire."

And then she took my hand in hers. She held it, and I saw that tears were in her eyes.

"You've been wonderful today," she said. "If it hadn't been for you . . . for your help . . . I don't think Robin and I could have faced it alone. You saved us."

I had to turn my head away: a lump came throbbing into my throat and I had to struggle before I could reply to her.

"You and Robin are the wonderful ones—you saved me."

There was a moment of silence: I heard the fire rustle in its glowing bed.

"What are we going to call you?" said Pat. "'Mr. Hopkins' sounds all wrong, doesn't it!—we'll call you 'Uncle'!"

She laughed. She kissed my cheek and was gone before I could reply. I felt like a silly yokel, standing there.

Tired though I was, I sat a long while by my library fire. I sat there until the last coal glowed and died. I listened to the quiet voices of Pat and Robin overhead, I listened to their footsteps until all was silent.

It was the first time that youth had ever moved in those bedrooms overhead: the first time that young life had ever come to me for help and offered me its gratitude. It seemed a little strange that the desolation of the world should have brought to me the first love and happiness that I had known since boyhood: the first great chance to live and strive for something beyond my own indulgent comfort.

I threw back the curtains and undressed myself in the steel light of the stars. I drew aside the neatly turned sheets that Pat had prepared for me, and slept.

CHAPTER TWENTY-TWO

It was beyond reason to expect my romantic exultation to survive the night and live on to the dawn. I had crawled beneath the sheets of my makeshift bed and fallen asleep with a sense of nobility and inspiration that had never entered my life before, but I awoke in the chill, grey hours with a stiff neck and a feeling of discomfort down one side of my throat that suggested the onset of a chill. I had no idea what time it was, and my head throbbed painfully when I got up to put the hearthrug over my couch for greater warmth.

I crept back between the crumpled sheets, shivering all over, and began to consider my situation a little more practically than I had done on the previous night. Nothing, during dinner, had mattered beyond the thrill and adventure of starting out to build a new and better world—but there were many less exciting things to consider in the cheerless light of dawn.

I was still glad that Pat and Robin had come to share my home, but I began to develop an extreme reluctance to face them in my present condition. The encrusted habits of long and self-indulgent bachelorhood were reasserting themselves. I liked being silent in the morning, particularly at breakfast, but the presence of this charming girl and exuberant boy was going to call for a higher standard of morning behaviour than I was accustomed to. If I were to hold their affection and respect I must be buoyant and amusing at all times, but it was going to need all my resolution to be buoyant at seven in the morning with a stiff neck.

There is a prevalent idea that it does a man a lot of good to be shaken out of his rut of self-complacency, but I have never quite understood how it benefits him except to make him uncomfortable and irritable. I would gladly have exchanged the youth and charm of Pat and Robin for the middle-aged stolidity of Mrs. Buller, who needed no living up to, and who accepted me as placidly without my false teeth as with them.

The business of being "self-supporting," which had seemed so novel and exciting over a glass of good claret at dinner, now began to disturb and oppress me. There would be no hot shaving water this morning, and no hot bath. Pat and Robin were probably accustomed to cold baths, but to me a cold bath was a certain inducement to sciatica, and with my present sore throat and stiff neck . . . the prospect would not bear thinking of. . . .

And how were we to live if, as I imagined, the whole fabric of civilisation had collapsed? No butter, no milk, no bread, no meat? I had a few potatoes stored and some carrots and beetroots earthed up in my vegetable garden, but a diet of vegetables and water would not sustain our strength for long. The grim, unanswerable problems paraded before me in the dawn like spectres: no electric light—no sanitary services—no pure water—thousands of dead, festering bodies that we had yet to see . . . flies . . . rats . . . disease . . . had we survived so bravely to meet slow death from hunger—or swift death from typhoid?

I missed the morning paper, too: I missed the dawn song of birds in spring. And even the cheerful whistling of the milkman.

The morning was as dead and as silent as the previous day—a heavy, suffocating silence that pressed and throbbed against my aching head.

I must have dozed, for I heard no movement in the room, nor the opening of the door: I suddenly started up in surprise at someone standing beside my couch.

It was Pat. Pat in a blue silk dressing-gown—as fresh and as lovely as when first I had met her upon those windswept downs, and in her hand was a steaming cup of tea!

"Pat!" I blurted, "my dear girl!—what on earth! . . ."

"What on earth—what?" she laughed.

"What on earth have you been doing?" I added rather lamely. "Hot tea!—how did you do it?"

"What a man you are! Didn't you know there was a wood stove in the kitchen? A grand little fellow—burns like fury . . . the bathwater's nearly boiling."

Her voice turned suddenly to concern: she was looking at the hearthrug and began to draw it over me. "You poor darling!—you've been freezing all night while I slept like a log in your bed!"

I laughed. All my distaste at letting her see me in my crumpled, unprepossessing condition melted away in the warmth of that friendly smile. I knew that my eyes looked small and bleary without my spectacles and that my hair, when rumpled, looked much balder than when properly brushed—but it seemed to matter nothing: Pat had seen me at my worst and her eyes told me that I had lost nothing by it.

"I wasn't cold in the slightest," I assured her. "Hearthrugs are useless things as a rule. I thought I'd make it do a job of work for once!"

I sipped the tea and she watched me closely. "How is it? . . . sweet enough?"

"It's grand," I said. It brought back the memory of those hot, strong cups of tea that Pat had made at the dugout. She went away, and returned with my dressing-gown and slippers.

"How long have you been up?" I asked. I remembered now that through my drowsiness I had heard movement in the kitchen, but subconscious habit had connected it with Mrs. Buller, my housekeeper.

"About an hour," she said. "I wanted to dress Robin's face."

"How is he?"

"Poor kid," she said. "It's badly swollen and hurting him like mad. It needs a doctor, really . . . but Robin's tough . . . he'll be all right."

I swung myself off the couch and pulled my slippers on. "I feel a lazy brute . . . lying here . . . you doing all this . . ."

"You look like a gangster with that scrubby beard!"

"In half an hour you won't know me!" I declared.

I went to the bathroom and shaved. The tea had soothed my throat, and as I lay stretched in a piping hot bath, feeling my stiffness dissolving like magic, I thought with wonder of the girl who had wrought this miracle. I had thought of Pat as a delightful, modern girl who could ride well, play games with vigour, and talk charmingly of casual, modern things: I had not expected depth or seriousness in her, or an understanding of things that her happy, protected life had never called for. But as I thought of her now I flushed with shame at my cowardly misgivings in the dawn. If but a few more girls like Pat had survived, then this world of ours, however sorely wounded, would live and vibrate with strength and pride again.

Never again would I allow cowardice to assail me: whatever lay in store for us, whatever horrors, whatever privations lay ahead, I knew that I could face and defeat them with Pat and Robin by my side.

I felt a new man as I dressed into easy, comfortable flannels, and a stimulating smell of frying bacon was coming up the stairs as I went to Robin's room.

"How goes it, Robin?"

The boy was huddled upon his side, his hands pressed tightly to his bandaged face, but he sat up quickly as I entered.

"Hullo!" he said.

"How's the wounded hero?"

"I'm all right."

His forehead looked hot and flushed and I could see that his wounded cheek was badly swollen, but his eyes were clear and healthy.

"Pat's been fussing around like an old hen. Says I've got to stay in bed. I'll stay till you're ready to go exploring and that's that!"

I promised to tell the boy when we were ready to go out, and went down to my breakfast.

Pat had laid the meal on the kitchen table: the eggs were a trifle hard and the yolks broken, but it is ungenerous to criticise. I was loud in my praise of the bacon, although it lacked the crispness that I was accustomed to.

"I'll improve," said Pat. "Seems a bit luxurious, having eggs and bacon, but we've got to eat the fresh stuff first."

We delayed our journey of exploration in order that Robin might rest, and it was nearly midday when we started out.

We were very silent as we picked our way across my wreck-strewn garden and stood upon the slope that commanded a view of the village: our keen anticipation was mingled with a shrinking dread....

It was a dull, dispiriting morning. A queer brownish haze filled sky and air, a relic, probably, of the great dust-storm of Monday night: myriads of minute particles were floating in the clouds, obscuring the sun and giving a tinge of autumn to this day of early spring.

From the hillside the view beneath us gave little food for encouragement. The brown tints of the sky found harmony in the earth beneath it: the receding flood had slimed the valley and the lower slopes of the downs with a muddy silt: the lines of the hedgerows were marked by ridges of dark debris. It was like a drawing in sepia, with no contrasting colour—no trees to soften the grim, storm-swept edges of the downs. The lake that had submerged the village on the previous day had partly drained off down the valley, but many pools of muddy, stagnant water remained around the silent, ruined houses.

Deserted, too, was this landscape before us—shorn not merely of its trees and hedgerows, but of life itself: a village of no-man's-land: a village that might have stood beneath an ocean for a thousand years. Not a living soul: not a sound came from that tragic little cluster of houses as we descended the hillside.

The village street was deep in half-dried mud, and we made our way behind the houses where gardens had once been. Now and then we stopped to peer through a paneless window or broken door. Although I knew the village intimately, it was extraordinarily difficult to identify the houses now: it seemed that the hurricane or the first waves of the flood had carried away the roofs of nearly all the buildings, so that hollow cups were formed, receptacles for the mud to settle in. In some cases I saw the mud still trickling down the stairs and through the doorways, horribly like blood oozing from the wounds of fresh-dead bodies: the church was recognisable from its ruined tower and the Fox & Hounds by the open space that lay before it, but the rest were brown, grinning ruins, featureless and impossible to name.

Now and then I called out, "Hullo!" or "Anybody there?" but my voice sounded small and stupid as it echoed off the sodden walls and up the silent valley.

We came to the end of the poor, broken street, and nothing lay ahead but empty stretches of mud. We looked at one another with puzzled eyes.

"Where *are* they all?" said Robin.

"Possibly they came down from the dugout . . . saw all this and . . . and went away." My last words sounded so lame that Pat laughed. "Where to?" she asked.

"Ask me another!" I replied.

Pat and Robin had turned their heads away from me: both were staring up at the silent dugout in Burgin Park.

"Hadn't we better go up there?" said Robin.

I would gladly have returned home: our journey through the village had been eerie and depressing, but at least it was relieved by everything being open and clear to see. My whole instinct recoiled from those grim doorways in the hillside above us: I hated the thought of going up to face the nameless horror of them.

But Pat and Robin were waiting: it was my duty to give them a lead.

"Come on," I said.

It was less than half a mile, but it seemed an endless journey. There was something horribly menacing and sinister in those two closed doors, and the one that stood half-open beside them.

I stole a glance at Pat as we walked in silence: her face was very pale, her lips firmly set: she too was feeling the horror that was stealing through my limbs.

We passed the two closed doors without a glance and made straight for the one that stood ajar. I shuddered even as I gripped it and pulled it fully open. It was like taking the shoulder of a corpse and turning it upon its face.

The dullness of the day helped little to dispel the gloom as we peered down the steps.

"Got a match?" said Robin.

I drew a box from my pocket and Robin took them from me. We watched him anxiously as he began to grope down into the darkness.

"Mind how you go!" I called.

A little flame spat out: we saw the boy's body silhouetted against the light and heard his exclamation of surprise.

"It's full of water," he said.

I groped down and stood beside him. Level with the sixth step lay an inky surface of water.

As we returned to the doorway, Robin picked up something from the steps.

"A woman's scarf," he said.

We stood together beside the door, talking in hushed voices as if people slept nearby.

"*Somebody* opened the door," said Robin, "somebody from inside.

If they could open it, they could come out."

"Perhaps they opened it before the flood had gone," I said. "The water inside suggests that."

"Nobody could open the door against the weight of a flood."

That was true. I could think of nothing else.

Pat was staring at the scarf. "Do you recognise it?" I asked.

"No," replied Pat. "But it's bone-dry."

I struggled to make my thoughts run clearly and logically. My terror of that silent dugout was lost in the baffling problem of that open door and dry scarf.

The fact that the dugout was filled with water made it obvious that, for some unknown reason, it was opened *before* the flood arrived. If it were opened afterwards, how could the water have got in? On the other hand, if the dugout had been flooded by water pouring through the open doorway, how on earth could one account for the dry scarf lying on the steps?

Above all—where were the people who had opened the door? "There's nothing we can do," I said at last. "It's useless to stay here."

Before we took our departure we hammered against both of the closed doors and called out, "Hullo!" I knew that it was a fruitless effort, but somehow it seemed part of a ceremony that we must perform before we could go.

"I suppose we shall know one day," whispered Pat as we went together down the barren slopes where bluebells should now have thrown a haze around us.

Pat was right. In due time we were to learn the solution to that baffling mystery—but it must come in the proper sequence of my story.

The reader can well imagine our feelings as we retraced our steps through the lifeless village and climbed the hillside to my home. What we had expected to find upon that journey of discovery I cannot truly say: at least we had hoped for *something*: some tangible clue: some evidence to give us a better understanding of what had happened to the world.

We had been spared the horrors of drowned, mutilated bodies, but even a body would have broken this terrifying solitude: even a cry of agony would have eased this ghostly silence.

"What are you thinking about?" asked Pat.

We had paused beside the front door of my home and were look-ing back across the ruined village: the setting sun gave shadowed depth to the trail of our footsteps across the drying silt.

"I was thinking," I replied, "how terrible it would be if my companions were a hysterical girl, and a boy without any guts."

Directly I had spoken I felt hot around the ears at having made the sort of remark that Robin would consider "bad form," but Pat saved my embarrassment by laughing. "Or worse still," she said, "if it were Dr. Hax."

I looked up in surprise. "How did you know I didn't like Dr. Hax?"

"Who does?" she answered, "or perhaps I ought to say 'who did?'" . . . her voice dropped almost to a whisper: "Poor Dr. Hax . . . poor old Vicar . . . where are they?"

"We mustn't think of that," I said. "The thing to consider at the moment is a cup of tea. We've earned it."

Robin had borne up wonderfully throughout our long and tiring expedition, but on entering the house he almost fainted. I took him to his room: I made him lie down and pulled the blankets around him, for he was shivering.

"Your job," I said, in reply to his protests, "is to get strong again, and to get strong you must rest."

I went downstairs and found Pat in the kitchen. She had built up the fire: she had put the kettle upon it and spread the cloth upon the table. She was standing by the window, her eyes upon the gaunt crest of the downs that were dark and pitiless against the setting sun—and she was crying.

I had not seen Pat cry before. I laid my hand upon her shoulder and she started violently—her tortured nerves were stretched to breaking point: she looked up at me in confusion and shame.

"I'm sorry," she whispered. "Fine thing to do after . . . after what you said just now!"

"After what I said?"

"About me not . . . not being hysterical . . ."

"My dear . . ." I felt such a hopeless, clumsy fool. Some men would have found wonderful words to cheer that brave, pitiful girl:

I could think of nothing. I just stood there patting her shoulder like a foolish old man.

It was characteristic of Pat that she did not try to stifle her tears: nor did she embarrass me by completely breaking down. I stood in silence until it was over, until she looked up at me, smiling through her tears, and slipped her arm through mine.

"I'm terribly sorry," she said. "I'm all right now . . . you won't think I'm . . . I'm giving up, will you? It isn't that . . . it's just that it . . . it takes so much understanding, and I'm not *clever*, if you know what I mean—I can't realise it all at once. Do you like Russian tea?"

Her final words were so unexpected that for a moment I had a horrid fear of her mind giving way.

"Russian tea?" I stammered.

She nodded. "There isn't any milk—but there's a lemon."

I laughed out loud in relief. "Pat!—what an unexpected person you are!" And then I grew concerned. "But surely there's tinned milk in the larder?"

She shook her head. "I congratulated you on your organisation too soon. Lots of sardines—plenty of tinned tongue—no milk."

This was an unpleasant surprise. I'd counted upon sufficient of everything to last a siege of at least a month—and I could not stand tea without milk at any price.

"I'll go down to the shop and get some!" I said.

It was a crazy remark, designed more to cheer Pat up than anything else, but there was a wild possibility of finding something in the ruins of the shop. I told Pat to rest for a while, took my hat, and retraced my steps to the ruined houses in the valley.

I knew the general store of Mr. Thatcher because it stood upon the corner, almost opposite the church. The door was still shut but the glass panel was broken, and up to the level of the glass the shop was filled almost waist-high with liquid mud. It was impossible to open the door against the weight of this morass. I kicked the panel until it split and had to jump hastily aside as the mud gushed out like water through a mill sluice. I watched it ooze away down the road and had the fright of my life when, as I opened the door, the little bell clanged overhead. It was the eeriest sound I had ever heard, and I stood there for quite a time, half-expecting to see the mud-encrusted corpse of Mr. Thatcher walk from his little back room to serve me.

The counter and shelves behind it were completely bare, but when I went into the small room behind the shop my mission was rewarded beyond my wildest dreams. A big cupboard stood in one corner, the key still in the lock, and when I opened it, out of curiosity rather than hope, I was almost stunned by a cascade of tins and packages that descended upon me.

The shop was a general one in the widest sense of the word: there were tins of herrings in tomato sauce by the dozen, curry powders and butterscotch, soup squares and lunch biscuits: the treasure hoard of a fairy tale.

I emptied out a box of cocoa tins and filled it with a varied selection, including, to my immense satisfaction, three tins of condensed milk.

I struggled up the twilit hillside with the box upon my shoulder, my spirits higher than they had been for many months: I was forced to put the box down and rest for a moment before entering the kitchen in a calm, offhand manner to impress Pat the more.

I stood by with a smile as the astonished Pat unloaded the booty upon the table: there were two tins of herrings in tomato sauce, a box of chocolate biscuits, a packet of candles, half a dozen cubes of compressed soup, and numerous smaller delicacies, including a bottle of Bovril for Robin.

"Magician!" gasped Pat. "How on earth did you do it?"

"Just waved my wand," I replied.

While Pat opened the tin of milk and made the tea, I took a steaming cup of Bovril to Robin's room, with biscuits arranged around it in the saucer.

"You seem to spend your whole time saving my life," said Robin, as he sat up in bed sipping the beverage and munching the biscuits.

"You'll get plenty of chances to save mine," I told him. "Turn over and have a sleep and be down to dinner at seven. Pat's going to make a stew. If that doesn't kill you, nothing will!"

There was magic in the twilight of those brave, early days. With the coming of darkness the barren solitude around us was robbed of its menace: we would light the candles, draw the curtains, make up the fire, and feel the spell of adventure sweep in triumph through anxiety and care.

If fate had given to me, as my companions, a couple of quarrelsome old ladies or even the Vicar and Mr. Murgatroyd the publican, the situation would have been completely different and I have no idea how I should have faced it. But the youth and spirits of Pat and Robin were of a quality beyond the infection of danger and solitude: courage and gaiety were bred in their bones: it bubbled out of them as naturally as spring water from a mountainside. Robin had a constitution that rebounded from exhaustion like a rubber ball. Long before dinner was ready he was in the library persuading me to go across to The Manor House with him to fetch his portable gramophone and a pile of records.

We followed our tracks of the previous day across the valley, for there were no other signs to guide us. We followed them in the pale light of my dying torch and the sparkle of the undying stars above us. Robin clambered over dark heaps of wreckage to a cupboard beneath the stairs, and as we staggered back to my house with our heavy burdens we were met by the savoury odour of Pat's much-debated stew.

I still believe that stew was a lucky, glorious fluke, for Pat admitted to me afterwards that she had never made a stew before. For my own part I had never tasted anything so delicious in my life. Into the casserole had gone the remains of the tongue, the four surviving slices of bacon and a hard-boiled egg, a beetroot, and a spoonful of Bovril, three onions, a parsnip, and some other vegetables I had brought in that morning. Within ten minutes nothing remained except the carrots, which were the only failure, and which Robin referred to as "goldfish stuffed with cement."

We followed up the stew with tinned pineapple and coffee brewed by Robin over the library fire.

The meal was taken with orchestral accompaniment. Robin's selection of gramophone records was bright if somewhat upon the same plane, consisting mainly of American minstrel songs, and I am not sure whether I did not prefer the quietness of the previous evening with its peaceful unbroken conversation.

But there was magic in that evening: a magic that even now surrounds me as I think of it in my solitude—in this dusty, ruined room in which I write. I think of the high hopes—the unquenchable courage of it all, and my hand trembles with weak, impotent rage at the senseless manner of its end.

Now and then my thoughts would wander from that warm, happy room, into the desolate world beyond those curtained windows. I thought how strange and wonderful it would be for some lonely survivor, wandering through what he thought to be a dead world, suddenly to hear the music of an American minstrel band in the distance—to see a chink of light—to hear the clatter of knives and forks and the laughter of happy people.

And then a remark from Pat or Robin would draw me back to the room again: I would feel the warmth of the fire upon my back and see those lively faces with the candlelight upon them.

When we had washed up I produced the port and pulled my chair up to the fire.

"Now!" said I. "Committee Meeting!"

Pat and Robin pulled up the couch, and over the glowing logs, far into the quiet night, we planned the new life that lay before us. "It would be silly to drift along in an aimless way," I began, "waiting for something to turn up. If we face the worst, here and now, we shall have nothing unpleasant in store for us. We've got to make our plans as if we are absolutely dependent upon our own resources—as if we are the only people in the world."

"I don't care if we are!" said Robin rather brutally, as he drank the remains of his port.

"Our first needs," I went on, "are food, water, and as much comfort as we can make for ourselves. Of water we have plenty—the well that supplies my house is deep and good, and has never failed. Of preserved food we have enough for two months if we bring up the rest of the provisions from the shop: our job is to protect ourselves by organising our resources against the future, and providing our larder with fresh food."

"Hear! hear!" said Robin.

I took pencil and paper from my desk, and we wrote down in detail our respective duties.

Robin was to be Minister of Fresh Food Supplies. Next day he was to get his fishing tackle from The Manor House, together with a gun and cartridges, and become our hunter. He was to ply the river for fish, snare rabbits (if any), and keep an eye open for game. It was to be his duty to supply some fresh meat or fish to the household every day.

Robin was delighted with his job. It was, he said, "completely down his street," and he spent the remainder of the evening utterly oblivious to Pat and me—his mind far away in the river valley—over the downs to the Hackwood spinneys—to the burrows and the coverts.

Pat was to be in complete charge of the house. Quickly and methodically she jotted down her duties. She would cook our food, wash and repair our clothes, keep the rooms clean and tidy, and take an inventory of our stores.

I was to be Minister of Fruit and Vegetables and keep the house supplied each day with all that I could produce. Pat herself suggested this, and I think I became as excited and as preoccupied with my job as Robin was with his. I had always loved gardening, and my endeavours in the past had only been marred by the cheapness and abundance of vegetables in the markets. It was thrilling to realise that from now onwards our health, indeed our lives, depended upon my efforts: upon the fresh vegetables and fruit that must come from my skill and enterprise.

Tired though I was, I could only sleep that night in restless snatches. My hands were itching to take my spade and fork to prepare new areas of my ground for food: every time I closed my eyes the darkness was filled with big, juicy turnips—purple beets—and the slim hands of Pat as they placed upon the table a bowl of luscious, home-grown salad.

CHAPTER TWENTY-THREE

It is strange how, in a game of cards, three aces will sometimes turn up, one upon the other, without design or reason.

Three aces suddenly turned up for us in Beadle Valley—just when I was beginning to think there were none left in the pack. Nearly four weeks passed by in complete, eventless solitude, and then, upon the twenty-seventh day, came three remarkable events, all within the space of a couple of hours, bewilderingly on top of one another.

In those first four weeks we adapted ourselves swiftly and happily to our new conditions. It was a good idea of mine to arrange clear, definite duties for each of us, for we became so eager to make a success of our job for the sake of the others that we had little time for introspection or disturbing thoughts.

Every morning, directly after breakfast, Robin went off with his fishing-rod and gun. His wound healed quickly, although I knew that he would carry the ugly scar of it to the end of his days. He revelled in his work as hunter, but for three days he returned at twilight, depressed and empty-handed.

I was beginning to grow alarmed at the boy's lack of success. It was grimly possible that the earth had been swept of every living thing that might have been fresh food for us. Our tinned meat could not last beyond a month and I knew that life depended upon something more than vegetables.

But on the fourth day the boy returned, to my astonishment and consternation, with a hedgehog. He had caught it amongst the willows by the river and he declared that hedgehogs were delicious when baked in gypsy fashion, complete with skin and bristles, over a brushwood fire.

Pat and I had a bad half-hour as we waited in the kitchen, listening to the crackle of Robin's fire outside and trying to overlook the horrid odour of burning quills. We agreed, for the boy's sake, to eat a bit of it, and I was just getting out the brandy as a precaution when Robin came in, red-eyed from the smoke, to make the curt announcement that hedgehog was off the menu. The creature had looked so uncanny without its bristles, he explained, that he could not go on with it. But that was our darkest evening, for next day a far different Robin—a triumphant, jubilant Robin—came in with three small fish. We fried them in sardine oil and ate them like smelts: they were rather tasteless but at least they were fresh, and we drank to Robin's first success in port that night.

Then came the evening when we saw him scrambling breathlessly up the hillside, waving a small brown object in the twilight and shouting: "Hi!—look here!"

It was a young rabbit. Miles away, in a cleft of the downs, he had come upon a thicket almost unscathed by the hurricane, with standing trees and shrubs in blossom, and best of all, the burrows of rabbits.

We stewed it and it was delicious. I was inexpressibly relieved, for where there is one rabbit there are many. Robin never returned empty-handed again: a rabbit almost every day, and fish that we quickly learned to cook most palatably with Worcester sauce. Once he even shot a crow, but I cannot describe its appearance when plucked, and we buried it beside the hedgehog.

I loved my work in the garden. I had enjoyed growing vegetables even when they were plentiful in the markets, but grim necessity now gave double zest to my work. In the past I had bought my seeds in packets, but now I had to preserve my own. I had, of course, to draw mainly upon my stores at first, but the seedlings were coming on well and I dug several new parts, once used as flower-beds, for extra potatoes and brussels sprouts. I made the most careful calculations and was confident that with reasonable luck I would not fail the kitchen for a single day in the year.

Best of all was the time when Robin and I returned home at twilight, our day's work done, to test what Pat had prepared for us during our absence. She knew quite well the need for conserving our scanty store of food, but she never failed to produce a tasty, four-course dinner, varying our supplies with the help of Mrs. Buller's cookery book and presenting us with never-ending varieties.

I wonder sometimes whether I am now looking with rose-tinted spectacles at those anxious, strenuous, exciting days—whether I have forgotten many a dark moment of hopelessness and terror that we sought to conceal from one another—but always I think back upon them with pride and happiness.

We had to keep careful check of the days, for we had no means of knowing which was Sunday and which was Monday unless I ticked each evening in my diary before retiring to bed.

We checked our watches by the sun, for my diary told me the time it set each day.

It was Pat's idea that Sunday should be a day of rest, with a gala evening at the close of it.

We had a simple service on those Sunday mornings. I was afraid it might be embarrassing with only three of us, but it turned out to be refreshing and quite natural. After Sunday lunch we would walk a little, although Pat insisted that we should rest as much as possible that day.

And then, after tea, would come the big event of the week. Robin and I changed into dinner jackets and Pat put on an attractive dress that she had salvaged from The Manor House. Dinner was cold, to save us cooking, but more generous and varied than upon other nights. I had six bottles of champagne, and one was opened with great ceremony upon each Sunday evening. We followed dinner with a dance to the gramophone and a game of cards, and Pat would say, as we said goodnight, "That's kept us civilised for another week!"

It was upon the Monday following the third of our gala nights when that startling sequence of events occurred: startling because they were totally disconnected from each other, and yet all three happened within a couple of hours.

Robin and I had gone to The Manor House to bring some coal across from the cellars. We were just slinging the sacks across our shoulders when suddenly, without warning, an old man came shambling out of the coach house with a spade.

We dropped our sacks in astonishment: I could scarcely believe my eyes—and the next moment Robin was shouting: "Humphrey!— my God!—it's Humphrey!"

The man stared dumbfounded: for a moment he crouched down in terror at Robin's headlong approach—and then he threw down his spade and took Robin's hand and began laughing and crying and muttering incoherent sounds: "Master Robin . . . Master Robin . . ." was all that I could understand.

He was an old man, past seventy I should say, small and wiry and wrinkled. He had lived in a cottage upon the far side of The Manor House and for twenty years had been a man-of-all-work upon the farm.

How he had survived we never clearly knew, for he was very hazy about it himself and the account of his adventures varied a great deal in each telling. He didn't "hold with" the dugout in Burgin Park, and on the fatal night had "just gone to bed." The noise of the storm had kept him awake until suddenly "the whole bloomin' house had fallen on top of him." He had wriggled beneath the bed and lain buried for "no end of a time." Eventually he had made his way through piles of debris and hobbled to The Manor House. Finding it deserted, he had made up a bed of straw in the apple store, creeping out occasionally to look for scraps of food in The Manor House larder, but lying for most of the time in the darkness, nursing an injured knee.

We helped the old man across the valley, and Pat was overjoyed to see an old retainer of her family. She gave him tea and a slice of pudding. Humphrey was obviously devoted to the boy and girl (he had, amongst other things, looked after their ponies when they were children), but the poor old fellow was so dazed by his sudden change in fortune that he could only mutter through his mouthfuls of pudding: "Anything I can do, miss . . . anything I can do . . ."

We elected him at once a member of our Community and gave him a job of his own. There was nothing that Humphrey did not know about farming. The home farm of The Manor House was upon high ground beyond the ravages of flood, and as the fields had been sown before the cataclysm, Humphrey was elected our farmer. He was to care for the crops, and bring the wheat along when ready. The old man was a little frightened by his heavy responsibilities and kept murmuring: "If only I had a cow . . . I'd bring you all you needed then."

"Maybe we'll find a cow one day," said Robin.

"You find a cow and a bull, Master Robin!—I'll do the rest!"

We were a little perplexed to know how to accommodate the old man. To take his meals and live with us in a social way would have been embarrassing both to us and to him, for although he was not actually a half-wit, there were obvious limits to his conversational powers. But fortunately he solved the problem himself by asking permission to live in the apple store, where he had made himself very comfortable.

"I've always lived by meself," he said, "and I'd like to now—if it's the same to you."

It was a spacious, well-built shed, very little damaged, filled with the sweet odour of stored apples and hay. We brought a mattress and blankets from The Manor House and made the place as comfortable as possible. Pat was reluctant to let the old man live like this, but he so obviously preferred it that I persuaded her from ill-spent kindness. He was to come over to my house for an hour each morning to make the fires, skin the rabbit, and do the work which I hated Pat having to undertake herself. He was to spend the rest of his day in the fields, receiving in return his meals and any comforts we could provide for him.

Although naturally I was glad to have the old man to help us, I must confess that I was a little offended by his general behaviour. He was so completely obsessed by a desire to "help Master

Robin and Miss Patricia" that he scarcely glanced at me, and when he replied to my questions, he spoke to me as if I were another servant instead of being the principal person. But he was, as I have said, a completely illiterate old man, and I made allowances for him.

We had only just left Humphrey to enjoy the comforts of his shed and were returning across the valley when the second, and infinitely more dramatic, event occurred.

Slowly, from the stillness, came a sound: the first man-made sound within a month to disturb the silence of the valley. At first I took it to be the purr of a motor-cycle a long way off upon the Mulcaster Road, but gradually it gathered power and fullness: the purr rose to a roar, and over the hillcrest came an aeroplane!

We behaved like maniacs: we ran up the slope, waved hats and handkerchiefs and yelled our heads off!

The pilot of the aeroplane did not appear to share our frantic excitement: we saw his goggled face peer down at us in complete unconcern: he gave no response to our waving hats, and it seemed at first as if he would leave us to our solitude. Then he changed his mind, circled around in search of a landing place, and dropped gently to the downs.

I will leave the reader to imagine the burning thrill and excitement of our scramble across to that shabby little monoplane. The discovery of Humphrey in the apple store was nothing compared with this. Humphrey was a slow-witted farm labourer: one of our own villagers who had nothing to tell us beyond what we already knew: but here at last was a messenger from the outside world!— someone of intelligence: someone who could, at long last, quench our desperate thirst for news!

The pilot was out of his machine and pulling off his goggles and helmet when we reached him. He was a tall, thin young man with a pale, grimy face and intelligent, deep-set eyes: he was wearing grey flannel trousers, an oil-stained leather jacket, and a red-and-blue-striped muffler.

Had I been in a normal state of mind I should have resented his casual, offhand reception of us. No doubt he was tired and I am sure that we must have appeared ridiculous and undignified as we raced up to him with outstretched hands, panting out joyful words of welcome and incoherent questions.

He accepted our handshakes abruptly and impatiently, although he favoured Pat with a thin smile and a slight inclination of his head. But while the eyes of all three of us were upon him with burning interest, he took little notice of us in return. He glanced around him and began to study a ragged map in his hand.

"What's this place?" he asked.

"Beadle!" we chimed in chorus.

He pored over the map in silence for a while, then raised his eyes and let them rove across our valley. Only then did I see how desperately tired they looked, with deep grey pits beneath them.

"Beadle . . ." he muttered. "I see. How many of you are there?"

"Three!" I said.

"Four!" cried Pat, "counting Humphrey!"

The young man produced a greasy little notebook and a stub of pencil.

"Beadle . . . four," he muttered as he wrote it down. Then he glanced up, dropped the notebook into his pocket, and nodded to us. "Thanks," he said—and to my astonishment turned and climbed back into his machine.

I was dumbfounded by his extraordinary behaviour. "But surely!" I exclaimed, "aren't you going to stay?"

He looked over the edge of his cockpit in surprise. "Stay? . . . why?"

I was growing angry. Only by an effort did I control myself and answer calmly:

"Don't you realise we haven't seen a soul . . . not a single living creature . . . since this happened? . . . Surely you realise we want to . . . to know something!"

He gave a short, hard laugh. "How much work d'you suppose I'd do if I stopped and gossiped with everybody I meet?"

"But we want news!" I cried.

"What exactly d'you want to know?" he answered.

For the life of me I could not frame a definite question: there were a thousand things that I wanted to know—a thousand questions tumbling over one another to be asked—but all that I could say was:

"Where's the moon?"

It was the young man's turn to look surprised.

"Don't you know!" he exclaimed.

"Of course we don't know!—we've heard nothing!"

"The moon's in the Atlantic. I thought everybody knew that," and he began to adjust the controls of his machine.

It was Pat's turn to play a part. She had remained quite silent until this moment, but now she came forward and laid her hand upon the edge of the machine. "You look frightfully tired," she said. "It isn't good to fly when you're tired. Come in and have some tea. It's ready now."

The young airman was tempted. He fidgeted with the control board of his machine, glanced at his watch, then braced himself abruptly to the call of duty.

"Good of you," he said, "but I've got to do the rest of Hampshire before it's dark."

"You'll do it a lot better after a cup of tea," suggested Pat, ". . . and a few chocolate biscuits," she added.

The young man's head came up with a jerk. "Chocolate biscuits? . . . where did you get those from? . . . looting's forbidden, you know."

His remark was no doubt meant in fun, but it gave me an unpleasant shock. I had most brazenly looted the grocery shop in the village and had probably laid myself open to a sentence of death.

"Come and try our loot, anyway," said Pat.

The young man gave way. "Ten minutes, that's all," he said, and climbed out of his seat.

Robin said afterwards that Pat had behaved like a shameless huzzy, luring the young man from his plane with a lot of cheap "vamping." But I knew quite well that she had done it for my sake, in order that I could satisfy my lust for news.

Pat went off to the kitchen to make the tea and the tired young airman sprawled himself before the library fire.

"You seem to have come out of it pretty well," he remarked, glancing around the room. "My name's Rooke-Glanville," he added.

"Mine is Edgar Hopkins," I replied.

I wished that I could have said "Sir Edgar Hopkins" or something of that kind. The patronising manner of the youth offended me, and I should have enjoyed giving him a gentle snub. He scarcely spoke until Pat returned with the tea. He apparently considered Robin and me of little consequence, and was awaiting the return of Pat in order to show off before her.

"Now!" said Pat, placing a cup of tea and a plate of biscuits beside him: "you don't go until you've told us everything. Start at the beginning and go on until the end."

The airman laughed, and pushed a biscuit into his mouth. "You want a ten-hour story in ten minutes!"

"All the more reason for starting at once!" rejoined Pat.

We had made a mistake in greeting the youth so eagerly, for he clearly belonged to the type that loves the taste of power and he made the most of it by playing upon our suspense. He stretched his legs to the fire as if the house belonged to him and began to prolong our anxiety with silly compliments to Pat about the tea. I could see that Pat shared my opinion of the young gentleman, but she played up to him against her will in order to get the story as fully as possible.

"I'm not an airman by profession," he began. "I'm really a scientist: the air was just my hobby. I was one of the scientists selected by the Government for their big dugout at Beaconsfield: the Government took careful steps to see that as many as possible of the best brains survived."

He winked heavily at Pat to make sure of her understanding this as a piece of wit.

"Beaconsfield is on high ground. It missed the flood and we came through safely. By eight o'clock in the morning we were having breakfast as if nothing had happened."

"I was walking about at six o'clock that morning as if nothing had happened," I put in. (It was a slight exaggeration, but I was compelled to keep the bumptious youth in his place.)

"Never mind what we all did!" said Pat. "Tell us what happened!"

"That's what I'm coming to," said the airman. "The scientists reckoned that if the moon struck the earth at the time expected—at 8:23 p.m.—it would land with a bang in the centre of Europe, and goodbye to the lot of us. Fortunately they were wrong: wrong to the tune of nine minutes, and those nine minutes saved us. The moon came over Europe like a huge meteor, falling in a slanting direction from the northeast: it was less than five hundred miles above you when it passed over this valley. . . ."

"We never saw it!" said Robin.

"Of course you didn't see it. It was too close to the earth to take the reflection of the sun, and in any case it was dragging that colossal dust cloud along with it. It landed at two minutes past eight-thirty, upon the western edge of Europe, just grazing our own island at Cornwall, the west coast of Ireland, and France and Spain."

The young man took a biscuit and crunched it noisily before proceeding.

"No scientist expected the world to survive, you know . . . that stuff about a 'graze' was just bunkum . . . just a sop to keep you quiet."

"We realised that perfectly well," I stiffly replied. "I am not altogether a country yokel, although I live in the country. I happen to be a member of the British Lunar Society and knew a good deal about all this—probably before you did!"

"Fancy that!" said the young man with a laugh. His conceit was so intense that the rebuff had no effect whatever.

"Go on," said Pat.

"Possibly the air pressure had something to do with it—possibly the resistance of the Atlantic—anyway the shock was not fatal to the earth: it performed some strange antics and the moon rolled into the ocean, like an enormous bagatelle ball into its pocket, and collapsed."

"Collapsed?" I exclaimed.

"Of course it collapsed," replied the airman. "The moon is a dead world, and the cooling of its inside had naturally caused great caverns. Practically speaking it was a hollow body with a thick crust, and the force of its landing made it collapse like a fat pancake. Have you got a map?"

I produced my *Encyclopaedia Britannica* and opened it upon the map of the world. The airman produced his stub of pencil and began to trace a rough circle that filled the whole of the North Atlantic, one side of the circle merging upon Ireland and Spain, and the other upon Canada and the United States of America.

"There's your new Map of the World," he said, handing the book to me. "The diameter of the moon was two thousand miles—the width of the Atlantic is three thousand. It was the moon's collapse that made it span the whole ocean from one side to the other."

Pat was staring at the map over my shoulder. "Then America is joined to Europe!" she exclaimed.

The young man nodded and pushed the last biscuit into his mouth. "You can now walk from Penzance to New York . . . if you want to. Could I have another cup of your excellent tea?"

We were silent while Pat filled the young man's cup. The news was bewildering, for I had thoroughly decided, in my own mind, that the moon had "grazed" us and disappeared into space.

"What are we going to do about it?" I asked.

"Nothing has yet been decided," he replied, with a meaningless wink at Pat which annoyed me.

"Perhaps," I said, "you will favour us with some news of how the world survived the shock?"

"There were three separate, independent forces of destruction," announced the young man as if he were lecturing to children, "the tornado, the earthquake, and the flood. The tornado was worldwide and we can only judge its havoc by our own experience. A lot of damn fools refused to go to the dugouts"—(it was my turn to exchange a wink with Pat)—"and most of these were killed, buried under buildings, or swept away. The flood was caused by the masses of water displaced by the moon when it fell into the Atlantic. Most of the water was forced north and south, over Greenland and towards the South Pole, but a huge wall of ocean was forced up the valleys of England and over the Continent."

"Within a few feet of this house," I said.

"It would have been about eight hundred feet high, receding gradually as it flowed inland. If you look at your map of England you can reckon that all the land coloured green was submerged for about two hours, and all the land coloured brown, over five hundred feet, remained dry like islands in an archipelago. There was a reaction—a 'back suction'—that drew most of it away, but it hasn't settled down yet: it still sways to and fro, running up the valleys and flooding all the low land every day or so."

"How did London fare?"

"London," said the airman, "is still underwater, covered by fathoms of mud. A good many people escaped, mainly those who were in the Underground Railways. They were led along the tunnels and brought out at Hampstead, which stood above the flood: as for the rest . . ." The young man blew a kiss in an offensive indication that they were dead.

"And what happens now?" asked Robin. The boy had scarcely spoken. His eyes had been fixed upon the airman in fascinated silence.

"The Government's been set up at Oxford," said the young man. "They are working like stoats and doing pretty well. Every town and community is looking after itself as best it can until the central control gets working. The Government is mobilising labour to clear the roads and engineers are getting the main services at work again. And now," he said, laying down his cup, "I must be off."

He stood up and reached for his helmet and goggles, and we walked with him across the downs to his machine.

"What have you got down there?" he asked, pointing to the *King Lear* in my meadow.

I explained to him, but he was not particularly interested. "There's a couple of battleships and a submarine on Salisbury Plain," he said, "you were in luck to get a luxury liner!"

"It may seem amusing to you," I tartly replied, "but that happens to be my meadow! If you are in touch with the Government I shall be obliged by you telling them that I want the boat removed with as little delay as possible."

"How do you suggest they move it?" he asked.

"That is not my business. I presume it takes to bits?" The young man stared reflectively at the huge, rusting hulk in my meadow: its great screws glittered in the setting sun.

"I'll tell them," he said, "but you can't expect them to take much interest. There's no Atlantic to cross any longer."

My heart sank. I had forgotten that the moon now blocked the sea passage to New York.

"Take my advice and keep it," he said. "One day you can turn it into a hotel."

"But it's lying sideways," objected Robin.

"Makes it more interesting," replied the airman. "Call it the Hotel Sideways: doors in the ceiling—windows on the floor—great novelty."

He climbed into his monoplane and pulled the goggles over his eyes.

"Scattered people are being told to make their way to the nearest towns." He pointed vaguely to the north. "You three had better pack up and trot along to Mulcaster—there's about a hundred people in the town. You'll be all right there. It's about six miles across the downs."

"Having won every important prize at the Mulcaster Poultry Show," I replied with biting sarcasm, "I know where Mulcaster happens to be, almost as well as you do." I was really angry at this absurd attempt to patronise me. "We have organised ourselves here without waiting for instructions. We are self-supporting and propose to stay in Beadle."

"Good!" responded the airman. "All the better!—Self-supporting—that's the great thing."

He reached over the cockpit and shook hands with Pat. "Thanks for the tea," he said.

"Thanks for all the news," replied Pat.

"Not at all," said the young man, holding Pat's hand with offensive familiarity. "A pleasure. Goodbye!"

"Goodbye!"

We watched the battered little monoplane drone away into the evening sky, and as we turned towards the house Pat glanced at me with a glint of amusement in her eyes.

"You weren't very polite," she said.

"Awful outsider!" exploded Robin.

"A cad, I'm afraid," I murmured.

"Anyway, we got the news we wanted. Strange to think we aren't the only people in the world, after all!"

Strange it certainly was—but stranger still was my own reaction to it. It would be absurd to suggest that I was not deeply glad to hear that many others had survived, but the news of people living as near to us as Mulcaster had somehow taken the edge off our gallant adventure and brought anticlimax to our brave determination to face the world alone. The dark moments of the past three weeks were forgotten now. I thought only of the happy, sunlit mornings as Pat waved goodbye to Robin the hunter, as he strode down the valley with his gun: as she waved goodbye to me the gardener, as I strode up the hillside with my spade. I thought of the evenings, with the day's work done, when we gathered in the dining-room to see what food Pat had prepared for us—and the nights, around the fire, as we talked over our adventures of the day, and planned the work ahead. It all seemed over now: and only now did I realise how intensely happy I had been.

I do not think that I was alone with these thoughts, for Pat and Robin were very silent as we returned to the house. It needed an hour to dinnertime. Pat went to the kitchen to prepare the meal: Robin, unusually reflective, sat down in the library and pored over the map of the world upon which the airman had drawn that rough circle with all its incredible meaning.

For the first time since the cataclysm I felt at a loose end. I called out to Pat that I was going for a stroll: I took my hat and walking stick and went out to encounter the third, and to me the most delightful and miraculous, surprise of that eventful day.

About half a mile beyond the ruined village, the valley closed in to a kind of narrow neck, and in this neck an immense pile of debris had collected as a result of the storm and flood. I had not, until now, had leisure to inspect this mountain of wreckage, and I decided to walk down and see whether anything of value had got stranded there.

I found it to consist mainly of broken trees, part of the Beadle cricket pavilion, and a large assortment of small, empty beer bottles, apparently from the Fox & Hounds.

I was poking about in this depressing rubbish when I was startled by a faint rustling sound. Noise of any kind was rare in our silent valley and my senses were immediately alert. After a while it came again—a little to my right, from amidst a thick mass of twisted branches—a furtive, uncanny stirring. . . .

I can face open, visible danger as well as anybody, but there was something in that feeble sound that clove my tongue to the roof of my mouth and dried my throat—the thought came to me of some half-drowned, half-living human body, horribly emaciated by weeks of exposure, and I knew that I was a coward. With Pat or Robin with me I could have gone calmly to investigate, but I was terribly alone—I was trembling—I was upon the point of stealing shamefully away, when something white upon the ground attracted me: a snow-white feather—fresh, unmuddied—and dry! In a flash I was beside the tangled branches, frantically pulling them apart: there was an alarmed flutter, a cackle of fear, and there was Broodie!—my beloved Broodie!—the finest hen that ever stepped in Hampshire!

How can I describe my feelings of wonder and delight? There stood Broodie, cowering in the arbour of branches where she had made her nest—and there behind her lay three eggs!

Never shall I know the epic story of Broodie's survival. I can only assume that when my chicken houses had blown away, Broodie was caught in this barrier of branches and saved from destruction. How she had lived through the past three weeks was a miracle, yet characteristic of this sterling hen. There was a pool of brackish water nearby—and for food she must have lived, literally, from claw to beak.

"Broodie!" I cried. "Broodie!—It's me!"

Poor Broodie did not recognise me at first, and I do not wonder, considering what she had been through. She cowered back in her wild, ragged nest, until I had made my way, with many jags and scratches, through the branches. I took her up gently and held her closely to my face.

"Broodie!" I said, "don't you know me?"

Broodie stared at me with a bloodshot, beady eye, and then grew calm and began the little crooning cry that I knew so well.

I carried her in triumph to the house. I held her up to the astonished eyes of Pat and Robin.

"Look!" I exclaimed.

"A chicken!" cried Robin. "Chicken for dinner tomorrow! Good for you, Uncle!"

I stared at Robin in amazement. The boy could not have hurt me more if he had struck me between the eyes. I realised afterwards that he did not know how revolting to me was the thought of having Broodie for dinner.

"It is Broodie," I cried.

The announcement seemed to convey nothing to Pat and Robin.

"How can you tell?" asked Robin. "They all look alike to me whether they are broody or not."

For answer I walked to the cupboard of my library, threw open the door, and pointed to the unique collection within—to Broodie's fifty First Prizes—to her ribbons, medals, and challenge cups.

"Those," I said, "are Broodie's prizes."

Pat and Robin exchanged scared glances. I think that, for the moment, they feared my mind had become unhinged, and then light dawned upon Pat.

"Oh!—she's yours! D'you mean she won all those prizes!—she must be a wonderful hen!—she *is* a wonderful hen"—and Pat was stroking Broodie's head.

I waved my hand once more towards the cupboard. "She won all those in nineteen months," I said.

"She's done something on your coat," said Robin.

I liked Robin, for he was a nice boy, but I frequently had cause to be irritated by his thoughtless and rather silly idea of humour.

But Pat was different: she understood. "How splendid to find her! Where was she?"

I told her.

"We must make her comfortable and give her a home . . . and something to eat."

It was growing dark and Broodie was very tired. She pecked listlessly at a few crumbs of biscuit and yawned. I fixed her up for the night in the tool shed; I laid a broomstick across the shelves as a temporary perch and decided to make a run for her next day.

Broodie's arrival had delayed dinner for a few minutes and Robin was annoyed.

"Lot of fuss over a damn chicken," I heard him say to Pat as I returned, and for the first time I lost my temper with the boy.

"We all take a pride in something, my boy. Broodie may only be a 'damn chicken' to you. To me she happens to represent the result of years of striving—years of work to produce the ideal chicken."

Robin looked at me in surprise. "Sorry," he said. And for the first time in our adventure he ate his meal in sullen silence.

It is a pity that so many of our happiest experiences are marred by some trivial squabble.

I lay sleepless for many hours that night, the joy of Broodie's return crushed by the fear that this little difference with Robin might widen into an irreconcilable quarrel, for I knew that Pat, in the long run, must take her brother's side.

But gradually the miracle of Broodie's return surmounted every other thought.

When we had appointed old Humphrey our farmer, he had sighed and said: "If only I had a cow and a bull, I'd give you everything."

In bed that night I tossed to and fro, murmuring again and again: "If only I had a cockerel—a good, thoroughbred cockerel, worthy of my Broodie!"

CHAPTER TWENTY-FOUR

With the advent of full summer came the "Epoch of Recovery," a wonderful period which lasted for well-nigh two years, until the autumn of 1948.

The sweeping power of it—the conquering energy of it—left even its leaders breathless and amazed. So pregnant were those years with the striving genius of man that even now, as I think back from the twilit wreckage of these final days, I feel a surge of pride that rides triumphant through my misery and weakness. My anger at the senseless destruction of that glorious Epoch has spent itself now. I seek only to live my last lonely days with the memory of what was great and fine, for that, I know, is the way that Pat and Robin would have expected me to face the end.

For two months the world lay stunned, but even with civilisation numbed beneath the cataclysm, people were groping back towards life in small communities—even in twos and threes, like Pat and Robin and me. Tiny sparks of life: twitching muscles in the prostrate body of humanity, determined, if need be, to rebuild the world with our own unaided hands.

But unbeknown to these struggling little communities, men in other places were gathering the threads of government, mobilising labour for work upon things wider in scope than mere self-preservation. Roads were cleared of wreckage, machinery repaired: communications re-established between town and town, and then, when radio sprang to life, between nation and nation.

It would need volumes to describe in detail that "Epoch of Recovery." I can only reveal its progress as it came to Beadle in sudden, surprising ways.

There was an afternoon in late July when I was disturbed from my work in the garden by a shout from Pat. I can still conjure up that picture of her, waving her arms from the library window and calling out: "Come here—quick!"

For a moment I could not understand the weird glow that filled the library: it was as if the sun were suddenly, abruptly setting in the middle of the afternoon. And then I realised what had happened: the electric light was on!

It was shining from every room in the house, for on the morning after the cataclysm I had gone vainly from room to room, pressing down every switch, and failing to get light, had left them on. Two months and fourteen days, and here was light again! My house seemed to blink in wonderment, like a blind man to whom suddenly the miracle of sight has been restored.

"Pity they didn't come on when it was dark," said Pat. "What a thrill if all the lights had just popped up as we were groping into bed!"

And then the day when a motor-cyclist came bumping down the village street. Bearing in mind the patronising manner of our young airman friend, I was careful not to be too effusive this time, but our visitor turned out to be a pleasant, freckled young man with a shock of red hair and a disarming grin.

"Beadle, isn't it?" he said—and then consulting a small typewritten paper: "Four of you, is that right?"

"Quite right," I said, with a sudden respect for the organisation. "Four of us and an excellent fowl named Broodie."

"Then one of these will be enough," he replied, drawing a folded paper from a haversack.

It was like a very roughly printed newspaper, headed: "Government Bulletin No. 1."

The young man refused Pat's offer of refreshment. "I've got a long round to make," he said, "but I'll be back next week, I hope—you'll have a bulletin regularly now until the ordinary newspapers get to work again."

We read that priceless little document from beginning to end a dozen times, taking it in turns to read in silence, taking it in turns to read aloud.

It was upon rough, grey paper, in type so blurred that parts were almost indecipherable, but it was a feast for news-starved people like ourselves.

It began with a brief summary of events that led up to and followed the cataclysm. This we knew to some extent from what the young airman had told, but it gave much detail that was new to us. It dwelt very little upon the dreadful destruction and toll of life, for that was over and beyond all remedy. It concentrated entirely upon an inspiring call for reconstruction.

The British Government had established itself in Oxford, partly because Oxford stood well in the centre of England and partly because that stubborn old city had suffered less than the majority from the tornado and the flood. The massive structure of its colleges had stood up to the shock as placidly as they had withstood the assaults of time and criticism. As a Cambridge man I could not but deplore the Government's choice, but Cambridge was no doubt severely flooded.

The ample buildings of Christ Church were now the Parliament House, and each Government Department had taken a College for its own use. The Exchequer was in Magdalen, the Home Office at Balliol, and the Ministry of Transport at St. John's. Wisely, they were not attempting to organise from this fountainhead downwards: orders had gone out for every town and community to form its own council to undertake urgent services of food and health and to clear their immediate localities to the best of their ability.

Each town was to provide one representative to a "County Parliament" to sit in the principal County Towns and organise their scattered communities. Above this authority was a council of representatives from the Counties themselves to sit in Oxford in close touch with Parliament.

The survivors of the Parliament sitting at the time of the cataclysm were mainly engaged upon National Reconstruction: of railways, water supplies, and affairs that went beyond the localised authority of the Counties themselves.

Money values existing at the time of the cataclysm were no longer legal currency because this would have led to the whole population wasting valuable time in a feverish hunt for cash amidst the ruins. A primitive system of barter and exchange of goods was organised pending the issue of a new currency by the Government—and examples were given for the guidance of organised communities:

4 potatoes = 1 egg
4 eggs = 1 rabbit
4 rabbits = 1 chicken, etc.

It was announced that radio programmes would begin once more upon the 1st September, and the bulletin even provided a column of domestic notes: "Reconstruction in the Home." Oiled muslin, it stated, if nailed across broken windows, would provide light and protection from rain until such time as glass was available!

The keynote of the bulletin was "work!—work!—work!"—and the whole country responded with excitement and joy.

One morning I was awakened by a steady clanging in the distance, and went down to discover a gang of men repairing the railway. Three days later a luggage train went through: a long, groaning train made up of every conceivable kind of truck. We shouted and waved from the hillside, and our greeting brought a grimy hand waving in reply from the engine cabin.

On another day a lorry came bouncing ponderously down the village street, and we went to meet three severe-looking gentlemen in mackintoshes, with blue armlets marked "RM." They were members of the "Reconstruction Ministry" and had come to investigate the future of our village. We could offer them no information concerning the baffling disappearance of the people of Beadle, and they could give me no promise as to the removal of the *King Lear*. After inspecting my house they informed me that no rebuilding of Beadle would be contemplated for the present at least. For purposes of organisation we were to consider ourselves citizens of Mulcaster. It was our first contact with Government officials and I was relieved when they departed, leaving us in peace.

Summer passed to autumn. The days were surprisingly, often distressingly hot, accompanied by heavy, tropical rains. Old Humphrey prophesied a bumper wheat crop and my own vegetables throve prodigiously in the steamy warmth that followed the torrential downpours of that strange summer.

Robin had made ingenious plans to guarantee fresh food supplies. With large quantities of wire netting he had constructed his own "rabbit farm" which he stocked from the burrows in Widgeley Copse, and by damming the river behind the church he had created his own "fish reservoir." Sources of fresh food were now close at hand in times of severe weather, and although we were getting rather sick of rabbit, we kept extremely fit and well.

But the little town of Mulcaster was the mirror through which we watched the steady stride of progress, for Mulcaster, in common with thousands of other towns throughout England and Europe, was hammering out its own destiny and forging its own primitive but effective scheme of organised life.

We soon established regular communication with the town. Robin had salvaged three old bicycles, and every Saturday we "rode to market," taking with us a bundle of rabbits, a can of fish, and any vegetables I could spare from the garden.

Although its roof had disappeared, Mulcaster Town Hall had been cleaned up and turned into an "Exchange Market." We would hand over our farm produce to the "Reception Officer," who gave us coloured vouchers in exchange. With these vouchers we could go around and purchase goods we needed from surrounding stalls. In place of our rabbits we would take back a slab of butter; our fish-can returned to Beadle full of milk; and I usually set aside the vouchers gained by my vegetables for small domestic necessities, such as darning thread for Pat, floor polish, new curtain hooks, etc.

There was a fine spirit of comradeship in the town; a spirit that compared most favourably with the local pomposities and smugness of pre-cataclysm days. Its two hundred survivors were mostly in youth and early middle age, for unlike a war that destroys the best and strongest, the cataclysm had weaned away the weak and the infirm, leaving only the sturdy ones to survive the tornado and the privations that followed it. No man passed another without a friendly greeting: every man and woman was busy from morning till night, for each, beside his own personal occupation, gave three hours of his day to "The Council of Reconstruction" for community work.

The destruction of the big combines and chain stores had brought individuality back to English life: the return of the craftsman and the master-man. It was a happy experience to walk down the main street—to hear the ring of the hammer and the hack of the wood-worker: to listen to sounds long silenced by the mass production of remote factories.

All through a scorching week of August we worked together in our wheat field. Humphrey and Robin scythed the corn while Pat and I stacked it into sheaves.

Humphrey threshed it himself in a primitive but effective manner, and by autumn the apple shed was stacked with twelve good sacks of golden grain.

We kept three sacks for ourselves, hired a wagon, and took the rest to Mulcaster. For our crop we received no less than nine red vouchers, the highest notes of currency, and as I locked the priceless little tickets into my bureau drawer I was able to say to Pat: "We are now bloated capitalists!"

I was able to turn part of our new wealth to excellent account. One morning in Mulcaster I was stirred by the sight of a dish of new-laid eggs in the Exchange Market: their price was prohibitive, but through exhaustive enquiry I traced the eggs to an old man who had by some means collected together enough poultry to run a small breeding farm.

I was so excited that I kept missing the pedals of my bicycle as I rode out to his farm, but I returned in triumph with a cockerel!

I had to pay the atrocious price of two red vouchers for it, but cockerels were naturally worth their weight in gold. It was a common-looking little bird, with mean little eyes and a conceited strut that betrayed its obscure descent. It was utterly unworthy of Broodie, and I felt ashamed to introduce it to my fastidious, blue-blooded old hen. Broodie looked him up and down with obvious surprise and distaste. She had never met a cockerel of this type before, and at first declined, very naturally, to make the slightest response to his advances. But after a night's reflection she realised her duties towards the shattered fortunes of the poultry world. She submitted with patient but thinly disguised revulsion to her ordeal, and when at last she presented me with nine mongrel but healthy little chicks, I was very pleased at the determination with which she prevented her vulgar little spouse from taking any part in their upbringing.

It was during one of my visits to Mulcaster that the mystery of the Beadle dugout was suddenly and unexpectedly revealed to me.

I had almost given up hope of solving the baffling problem of that solitary open door—the waterlogged dugout and the uncanny disappearance of the Vicar, Sapper Evans, Dr. Hax, and all the villagers.

In vain I had enquired of the people in Mulcaster and scanned the streets for a familiar Beadle face: in vain we had searched the downs for some clue to help us; and then one evening, as I was returning from Mulcaster Market to join Pat and Robin for our journey home, a little woman passed me with an armful of firewood.

Some of the faggots slipped from her grasp and fell into the road. I picked them up for her, placed them in her arms, and found myself looking into the wizened face of a Beadle villager!

The old lady stared at me as if I were a ghost. It was Mrs. Chaplin, wife of a labourer who had lived in a cottage upon the Widgeley Road.

"Mr. Hopkins!—'owever did you get out?"

"Out of what?" I asked.

"The dugout," she replied with a shudder.

"I didn't go to it," I explained. "I stayed at home"—and then in trembling fragments I drew from her the tragic story.

The fatal evening had begun quite well in the Beadle dugout.

Directly the doors had been closed, Charlie Hurst and his Trio had begun a programme of popular music and the Vicar had organised a small whist drive for those who desired to play. At eight o'clock there had been a light supper of coffee and sandwiches, and as far as Mrs. Chaplin could say, they had neither felt nor heard the hurricane raging above them upon the hillside. Towards nine o'clock, as they were arranging their blankets for the night's rest, they had felt "a sort of shudder": several coffee-cups had fallen over: one or two children had cried, and Charlie had called out: "That was the moon, that was!"

"The dugout seemed to dip down and come up again," explained Mrs. Chaplin, "but when nothing else happened, we begun spreading our blankets."

And so the people of Beadle had prepared for rest—unaware of the fatal wound in the structure above them. For it seems that the earthquake had brought a deep fracture to the chalky hillside:

a fracture that had distorted the concrete beddings of two of the doorways and forced open wide cracks in the chalk surrounding them.

Some of the people were already asleep, and Mrs. Chaplin herself was dozing when urgent cries of warning came from the men upon watch. The villagers had scrambled from their blankets to the nightmare of great streams of muddy water gushing down the steps of the two fractured entrances. The tidal wave was upon them.

Fiercely—desperately the men had worked under Sapper Evans—struggling to block the crevices with blankets and canvas sheets. But relentlessly the chalk had crumbled: one by one the men had been swept from the stairways by the increasing torrent. The mud upon the dugout floor was around their ankles—around their knees—it crept up to their thighs.

Then Sapper Evans had shown a last heroic resource. The third entrance to the dugout remained secure. To have opened it in an endeavour at escape through that awful flood would have been suicide, but the upper section of the stairway would form an airlock against the rising water.

Into this airlock the Sapper had forced the women and children—forty of them, huddled upon the fifteen steps with one man—Mrs. Chaplin's husband—who understood the mechanism of the door.

Mrs. Chaplin had only the vaguest recollection of the horrifying hour that followed, and I do not blame her. They had watched the water creep to the roof of the dugout: listened to the last sounds beneath them which mercifully their own cries helped to drown.

Within half an hour the atmosphere upon the steps was unbearable, and rather than face certain death by suffocation her husband had unbolted and thrown open the door. In a dream they had seen the pallid sky and the turgid flood receding.

For a while they had lain upon the slimy hillside, powerless to move and powerless to think. The village lay far beneath the tidal wave, but as dawn came they saw the ruined church tower slowly creep into view.

Her husband had tried in vain to open the jammed doors in the hope of finding someone still alive; then he led his little party of survivors away across the downs and came at last to the ruined town of Widgeley.

They had found shelter with the survivors of the town and settled there to live. Mrs. Chaplin had come to stay with a friend in Mulcaster but she did not think that any would have the courage to return again to Beadle.

I never told Pat and Robin of what I had learnt. They had almost given up the puzzle of the dugout and I saw no purpose in oppressing them with the thought of that tragic tomb so near at hand.

They found me very silent on our journey home that night: but even in my sadness I found pride in the memory of the gallant men of Beadle.

Autumn turned to winter. At one time I had dreaded the season of darkness, but it passed happily enough in Beadle Valley. A little petrol was now available and Robin doctored up the old Ford car for our journeys to Mulcaster. There was now a picture house that produced each Wednesday night a scratched old film of pre-cataclysm days, and it was strange to see those pictures of an age that now seemed so dead and far away. Every Saturday we stayed on after Market for the weekly Dance and Concert.

For my own part I should have been happy enough at home, but I encouraged every opportunity of going out for the sake of Pat and Robin.

With the beginnings of my new poultry farm the cup of my own contentment was filled, but I felt a growing concern towards those two loyal young partners of mine.

It was not natural for a boy and girl with the spirits of Pat and Robin to live in monotony and solitude. In the early days, throughout the spring and summer, gratitude for being alive and the need to work for one's very life swept all thought of other things aside; but as the dark evenings came—as life was gradually eased from its first primitive strivings, I knew that a longing must often have come to Pat and Robin for the life and companionship of young people of their own age. It was impossible to sit, night after night, and talk of our daily doings. Sometimes we would read aloud or play cards and I devised several amusing but rather childish games with dice and racehorses cut from paper in order to break the monotony. But often our conversation after dinner would languish into gulfs of silence, and at last, one evening, I summoned the resolution to voice the thoughts that were oppressing me.

Pat was at work upon some new curtains from material we had bought in Mulcaster that week, and Robin was curled upon the sofa with a book of adventure.

"I've been wondering for a long time, Pat, if you ever feel that you would like to go away from here."

I was looking into the fire as I spoke, but I felt those two young heads jerk up in surprise. I felt their keen eyes upon me and I continued with a leaden heart. I was sure that my words were going out to them as keys to freedom: that they would grasp them eagerly, and go. . . .

"Mulcaster is becoming quite a lively place now," I went on, "there's no doubt that both of you could find valuable work to do—more interesting and varied, perhaps, than here."

"What are you getting at?" came Robin's curt voice. The boy had an overbearing abruptness at times that irritated me, but on this occasion the challenging tone gave my heart a bound of hope: it seemed almost as if he were defending the home—against me!

"I'm getting at just this, Robin. The day after the cataclysm I invited you and Pat to share my home. But I distinctly said: 'until things get straight.' There's no question they are getting straight now."

Robin put down his book and rose from his couch. "You mean that you want us to go?" he said quietly.

"I want you to feel absolutely free," I replied. "I know that life must be very dull for you here . . . at times. In Mulcaster you might take a leading part in recovery and in the end find a place in the world more worthy of—"

"Do you want us to go?" demanded Robin.

Pat looked up from her work. "Robin! . . ." she began.

"I think it would break my heart if you went," I said. "I simply want you to understand that you must not stay for my sake. That's all."

I realised that despite all the consideration I had given to the words I should use, I had spoken them clumsily and hurt Robin's pride. I had suggested that the boy was not doing all that he should do in the work of recovery, when in fact he was doing magnificently. . . .

But Pat, with her deeper understanding, realised what I was trying to say. She rose and came to me and laid her hand upon my shoulder.

"It was good of you to say that, Uncle—to think of us like that. But Robin and I have talked it all over a good deal these last few weeks—we've known about it for a long time."

"Known about what?" I asked in surprise.

Pat laughed. "Known that you were bothered about us: by the way you've bundled us into Mulcaster for those funny little dances: by the way you've worked up all kinds of crazy little games for these winter evenings. I knew exactly why you did it, and loved you for it!—and Robin has, too . . . although he's too tough to say it!"

"My dear Pat!—" I began.

"You've had your say!" interrupted Pat, "and here's our answer. It's good to know that Mulcaster is getting along so well . . . good to know that we can go there when we feel like it—but it's better still to be self-supporting: grand to be independent and to make our way by ourselves. If Robin and I were to go away from here, it would be like cutting a slice off both of us. It would hurt like blazes, because we love this house, and the work we are doing. . . ."

I was almost overwhelmed by my relief. I could only press Pat's hand as it rested upon my shoulder and say: "Thank you, Pat . . . that's grand . . . that's grand . . . we'll have our last bottle of champagne for dinner!"

"The first sensible thing you've said this evening!" remarked Robin.

How gladly I would dwell for the rest of my story upon those happy days!—of the spring that came in a blaze of glory and that sunlit summer when progress towards recovery reached its zenith. In August 1947 it seemed as if we had cleared the last of the cataclysmic wreckage: the world was ready: upon the brink of an even greater epoch in which recovery would give place to creation. The Government published a magnificent "ten-year plan" for the rebuilding of our cities, the laying out of public parks, and the reconstruction of public services. A "ten-year plan" in which a new and finer Britain would rise from the ruins of the old.

In Beadle our progress can best be recorded by the news that we actually went for a two days' holiday!

The fashionable thing to do that summer was to take a "trip to the moon." The Railways displayed great enterprise in this respect, for the eastern edge of the moon overlapped Cornwall to within three miles of Penzance. Immediately the railway was sufficiently repaired the authorities announced their "Weekend Excursions to the Moon" that became remarkably popular that summer and autumn.

In this connection I am forced to confess to an error of judgement which occasioned me much heart-burning. It concerned a financial transaction that I had carried out before the cataclysm, the details of which the reader may remember.

When first I received the secret information that the moon was likely to strike the earth, I sold £2,000 of Debentures in the Great Western Railway (which seemed of little further value), and purchased in place of them 4,000 shares in Wigglesworth & Smirkin, the well-known manufacturers of china crockery. It seemed to me, with every reason, that a collision with the moon would cause sufficient destruction of crockery to create a boom in the above-mentioned shares and greatly enhance their value.

As it happened, my judgement was completely and disastrously at fault. Beyond question vast quantities of crockery were destroyed, but so also, unfortunately, was the firm of Wigglesworth & Smirkin, whose factory collapsed and was never heard of again. Not only were my crockery shares completely valueless, but owing to these railway trips to the moon I had the chagrin of seeing a boom in the Great Western Railway Debentures which I had sold!

However, it is no good crying over spilt milk, and I was sports-man enough to patronise the railway by purchasing three weekend excursion tickets to the moon for Pat and Robin and me.

*　　*　　*

It usually happens that "stunt" excursions of this type fall short of expectations and our "excursion to the moon" was no exception to the rule.

We went off in high fettle to catch the train at Winchester. It was a long, tiring journey, often at snail's pace over stretches of temporary line, and after spending a night in tents near the ruins of Penzance we were taken over miles of barren fields in a charabanc fitted with "caterpillar wheels" to negotiate the hideously broken countryside.

When at last we arrived, the anticlimax was pitiful. We had been burning with such excitement throughout the journey that nothing, I suppose, could have risen to our inflated expectations. All the same we at least expected some awesome, majestic sight—some towering lunar mountains and giant craters.

But when at last the charabanc pulled up, and the guide said: "Here we are, ladies and gentlemen," I looked around me in bewilderment. Only after careful study of the barren countryside did I observe that it sloped gently away and steadily upwards towards the west. We were only, of course, upon the "fringe" of the moon's broken surface, and all that we saw was what appeared to be the edge of an immense slag-heap of grey, broken slate stretching as far as we could see across the land and far into the distant sea like some gloomy, ghostly continent of primeval times.

Several members of our excursion openly expressed their disappointment. I think that the less imaginative expected to see an immense globe towering above them, with the familiar face of the moon upon it: one gentleman, in fact, went so far as to say that it was a swindle. "Have we come all this way to see that!" he exclaimed.

"I'm sorry, sir," said the guide, "but nevertheless, this is the moon." And he poked his stick into the edge of the slaggy plateau where it spanned the road.

"It's terribly smashed up," put in an old lady.

"Lucky for us it is," replied the guide. "If the moon hadn't broken up when it hit us, *we* might have been broken up instead."

Some of the members of the party expressed approval at this reasoning, and we followed the guide up a twisting, broken path until we came to a small tea shop labelled in large letters: FIRST HOUSE ON THE MOON.

We bought some picture postcards and a small fragment of the moon upon which was painted a little effigy of the moon's face as we had once known it. Around this effigy was written *What I was* and upon the slaty substance was painted *What I am*. It was an interesting novelty which I determined to keep for Aunt Rose if ever I should see her again.

"How horribly dreary," whispered Pat as we walked back to the charabanc.

I nodded in silent agreement, but to me there was far more than dreariness in that ominous expanse of grassless, treeless waste. There was something menacing and sinister in it that made me shudder. I wished that I had never seen it. I had led myself to believe that the moon was done with and harmless now that it had arrived and hit us, collapsed and settled down. I had grown to regard it as another Sahara, another Siberia that might in time become the haunt of animals, even, perhaps, of a few lonely human beings. But I went away from it with a strange, indefinable dread: a haunting conviction that the terrors of its arrival were trivial beside the horrors that it held in store for us.

CHAPTER TWENTY-FIVE

The first hint of impending trouble came to us one autumn night. During the summer Pat had been laid up with an injured knee, and I had called in a doctor from Mulcaster—a Dr. Cranley. Having assured himself that the injury was in no way serious, Dr. Cranley handed over the case to his son Peter, with happy if somewhat unconventional results.

Peter was a pleasant, cheerful boy. A medical student at the time of the cataclysm, he was now completing his training as best he could as partner to his father. Directly Pat was able to get up, Peter made a point of assisting her every morning upon a short walk across the downs, explaining that exercise to the injured muscle was essential. I observed that these "curative walks" became longer every day, and when, one morning, Pat announced her knee to be so far recovered that the doctor had suggested they took a picnic lunch with them, I naturally realised that something was in the wind.

One Sunday Peter came to tea, bringing with him a charming sister named Joan. Robin had affected to scorn Pat's behaviour with the young doctor, but upon Joan's arrival he suddenly woke up himself. He took her down to see his rabbit farm and presented her with three of his best fish to take home for supper.

Within a short time the four of them were firm friends and constant companions. They repaired the tennis court upon the lawn of the ruined Manor House: they danced together at Mulcaster and went upon long walks across the downs.

Although naturally this led to some lonely evenings for me, I was delighted that Pat and Robin had found such cheerful companions of their own age. Despite their staunch devotion to their work and home, I had long been worried by the monotony of their evenings, and the occasional loneliness that I now experienced was well repaid by the wider interests and greater happiness of my young companions. They even began planning an Amateur Theatrical Club in Mulcaster—and promised me a part!

But it is a sad irony that this new and happy companionship should have led to the ominous, disturbing night that I have already referred to.

One evening in late September, Dr. Cranley invited the three of us to dine at his home in Mulcaster, adding that Major Jagger, Parliamentary Representative for Hampshire, would also be his guest.

I shall never forget our journey to Mulcaster through the dusk of that lovely autumn evening. Perhaps, in reality, it was just an ordinary journey like many others: perhaps my memory has idealised it because it was the last evening of a precious span of happiness that nestled between cataclysm and final disaster, for never again did I feel the peace and tranquillity of that happy, twilit journey.

I remember how the sunset lingered upon the tarnished old windscreen of our car, how suddenly, as we dropped into the valley, the stars were glimmering in the pale, evening sky: how for a while we shouted jokes at one another above the rattle of the car, and how, as the moonless night enwrapped us, Robin's eyes became intent upon the rough, precarious road, and Pat and I lay back in silence with our thoughts.

I thought of this wonderful year that was drawing to its close: this year of striding progress—the peace and gathering prosperity of Europe. All the bitterness and hostility, all the suspicions and racial hatreds that had threatened and darkened the closing years of the old world had gone forever. The nations of Europe had arisen from the ruins of the cataclysm, cleansed of greed, drawn into harmony by a common disaster; determined to build a new world in friendship and mutual respect. The cataclysm had almost destroyed us, but from the ashes had arisen the United States of Europe.

But nothing gave greater cause for satisfaction than the progress and growing renown of my poultry farm. In the old days it was my hobby: today it was my profession. I had purchased two new cockerels of sturdier type and better blood than my first one. My long experience, and, I might say, genius in poultry breeding had enabled me to produce a fine, distinctive strain that was already known throughout all Hampshire as the "Beadle-Hopkins." The "Beadle-Hopkins" hens were fine layers, and with few exceptions careful and successful mothers, while the "Beadle-Hopkins" cockerels were eagerly sought after in Mulcaster Market for breeding purposes and fetched high prices.

People came in from miles around to secure a "Beadle-Hopkins" cockerel and I gained a great deal of amusement by sauntering about the market upon the days when my birds were on sale. If I heard anybody mention the name "Beadle-Hopkins" I would sometimes saunter up to them and casually introduce myself. It was a treat to see the expression on their faces: to hear them say,

"Hopkins?—not *the* Hopkins!" It was a simple, inexpensive way of giving people pleasure, and I never failed to secure a thrill at the thought of having given my name to a breed of domestic fowl that would endure long after I was dead.

It is easy to understand how happy and contented I felt that night. I was excited, too, at the prospect of meeting Major Jagger, a member of our new and energetic Parliament, for although I had met, at different times, almost every famous personality in the *Poultry Times*, my quiet career had not brought me into touch with eminent persons in other walks of life.

Dr. Cranley's house lay upon the outskirts of the town, in a broad, old-world avenue that seemed to have escaped the worst ravages of the hurricane. We were very impressed, as we drove up the drive, to see Major Jagger's car standing by the door, with its big yellow badge denoting its use by a high official of our new National life.

Robin parked our old Ford as far from the magnificent limousine as he could, to avoid odious comparison, but he could not tear himself away from the big new car.

"What a beauty!" he whispered. "One of the new ones from the Government Factory near Oxford. Just look at that glorious instrument board!"

"We've come to dine with Dr. Cranley," I gently reminded him, "not to stand gaping at his guest's car!"

"Wonder what the politician will be like?" said Robin, as we walked to the front door.

"Old and pompous and gouty," suggested Pat.

"He's probably young and handsome and romantic, and you'll fall in love with him!" I answered.

To think that we talked light-heartedly about Major Jagger!— to think that we strolled happily to the house, eager and rather honoured to meet him! How strange it all seems now!

I cannot define the feeling that came over me as I entered Dr. Cranley's drawing-room. It was such a bright, gay room; so charmingly prepared for us with fresh autumn flowers and blazing fire. Joan Cranley came forward and greeted us so happily, and Dr. Cranley handed us sherry with such friendship and welcome . . . and yet, in that same instant I had an overwhelming wish that I had not come.

All my life I have been acutely, abnormally sensitive to the personality of those I come into contact with. When I enter a room of pleasant, simple people I feel happy and at ease, even before I have said a word—even before I am introduced. But if a discordant, unpleasant person is there I feel it immediately: I feel uneasy and unhappy even before I have discovered which of the guests possesses the personality that has disturbed me.

Never have I felt this so acutely as upon my entrance to Dr. Cranley's drawing-room. I felt something near to panic—a helpless longing to escape—and I knew that the reason for it lay in the tall, stooping figure by the fire.

I never discovered why Jagger called himself "Major." Dr. Cranley told me afterwards that he knew him before the cataclysm as Professor of Philosophy at some northern university, where Jagger had been a very quiet, strange man, and something of a recluse. At the time of the cataclysm he was living in a big lonely house near Mulcaster, writing books, and becoming more and more of a hermit.

"The cataclysm seemed to alter his whole personality," the doctor told me. "He came to live in Mulcaster. His shyness changed to the complete reverse: he never seemed to stop talking—he was full of wonderful ideas—and he was the obvious man to elect as Parliamentary Representative."

And now, for a night, he had returned to Mulcaster in connection with the reconstruction of the town under the "Ten-Year Plan."

*   *   *

I can see him now as he turned to shake my hand: his thin, slanting mouth, the deep furrows of contemplation drawn downwards from its corners: the deathly pale face with its deep-set, burning eyes and the mane of black hair that waved back from the wide furrowed temples. He seemed so utterly out of place in that light-hearted party and I think that he realised it, for he made no endeavour to join the conversation. Until dinner was served he stood there by the fire, greeting a joke or a gust of laughter with a tired, patronising smile. Peter and Joan Cranley were apparently accustomed to him, but once or twice I saw Pat glance at the dark, stooping figure with shy, puzzled eyes.

During dinner, too, he seemed quite incapable of joining in the happy small-talk of the rest of the party. Once or twice Dr. Cranley attempted to draw him in with some question or other, but he would answer briefly and lapse into silence again. Once, in fact, when Joan Cranley asked him to settle a small argument as to whether an attempt would be made to revive the Olympic Games, he was so far away with his thoughts that he seemed unaware of being spoken to, and an embarrassing silence fell as we waited, thinking that he was considering his reply.

As dinner progressed we all, with one accord, endeavoured to sympathise with his mood by making no effort to draw him in. While we talked he sat hunched in his chair, toying listlessly with his food and sitting between courses with his long, thin fingers stroking his chin.

It was not until coffee was served and the butler had left the room, that Major Jagger became dominant: suddenly and startlingly dominant.

We were discussing (more, I think, out of compliment to Major

Jagger than for any other reason) the fine achievements of our new Government, and the splendid future that lay so near at hand.

"The cataclysm," I said, "was terrible. But it was almost worthwhile to have achieved this wonderful spirit of friendship and helpfulness between nations. Who would have believed, ten years ago, that a Permanent International Council would one day be sitting at The Hague, not to wrangle and snarl at one another, but to help one another in such splendid ways!"

For the first time in the evening Major Jagger laughed. His laugh was so sudden and unexpected that we all jumped with surprise. For my own part I felt angry at this strange reception of my remark. "You are a happy man, Mr. Hopkins. I hope you will remain so."

"I don't understand you, sir," I stiffly replied.

"I imagine we have good reason to congratulate ourselves on this new friendship between nations," put in Dr. Cranley.

There was a short silence. Jagger sipped his coffee, then turned his dark, mocking eyes upon the doctor.

"Do you imagine a cataclysm—or a hundred cataclysms—can change human nature?" he said.

"I think that the changed circumstances that have followed the cataclysm have definitely done so," replied the doctor.

There was another silence. I saw a puzzled look in the eyes of the four young people around me—a look of eager, questioning anticipation. Major Jagger slowly sipped his coffee. He relit his cigar with the deliberation of a man who loves an audience and knows when he has got it.

"The Muller-Henderson report is to be published on Monday," he announced. "I don't think that I shall abuse my position by referring to it."

Despite my aversion to the man I sat up and leant eagerly forward.

In the early spring a well-equipped scientific expedition had left Europe to explore the inland regions of the moon. Led by Dr. Muller, the famous Norwegian scientist, and Professor Henderson, of Cambridge University, the personnel had included experts in every branch of science and engineering: the best and most distinguished men of Europe.

The departure of this expedition had aroused great romantic interest when first announced: an inspiring journey of adventure and discovery such as this could scarcely do otherwise. Its progress into the moon's unexplored regions was reported, for a while, every morning in our newspapers and was read by everyone as though it had been an exciting new fantasy by H. G. Wells. And then a strange reticence had crept into the reports. We heard less and less about the expedition until rumours began to circulate that it was a dismal failure. Stories were even whispered that it had met with some terrible, mysterious disaster which the newspapers were breaking to us very carefully.

We did not even know that the expedition had returned, much less that its report had been submitted to The Hague Council and was now to be made public. It seemed very mysterious to me.

"When did they return?" enquired Dr. Cranley.

"In June," replied the Major. "They were away for five months. Their report has been before the International Council for nearly four." He glanced around the table with the ghost of a smile. "I'm afraid there's trouble. Serious trouble."

"Trouble!" I exclaimed. "Why trouble?"

The Major turned his dark, luminous eyes upon me. They seemed to bore into my brain. I felt myself struggling against a horrid, evil magnetism.

"You are a happy man, Mr. Hopkins. I hope you will remain so." I was startled by this strange repetition of his previous remark—angered by the impudence of it.

"I am pleased to say I am a happy man."

The Major smiled. "You have everything you desire?"

"I have," I retorted. "And I'm proud of it."

He turned from me and shrugged his shoulders. "I wish that you spoke for the rest of the world," he remarked.

Again there was a silence. I could think of nothing to say.

"Can you tell us something of the report?" asked Dr. Cranley.

"I can," replied the Major. "There were some 'experts' who declared that the moon would prove to be a dry, destitute mass of rock—dead and useless. Those 'experts' are going to look slightly foolish next week."

He reached for the matches. Slowly and deliberately he relit his cigar before proceeding.

"The Muller-Henderson report will announce that the moon is by no means destitute. On the contrary, it is immensely, incredibly rich. Rich in oil: rich in gold: rich in radium-bearing rock and rich in coal. The moon contains minerals sufficient to give wealth to this world undreamed of . . . iron—platinum—it has all been found . . . analysed and tested. . . ."

One could almost feel the silence in the room. For my own part I found myself groping desperately to fit these extraordinary pronouncements into my scheme of understanding. I frankly confess that, since the cataclysm, I had been far too busy with my own urgent affairs to give any thought to the future value of the moon. For a few months it had been a ghastly menace. Now it was happily out of harm's way in the Atlantic where, except for its inconvenience to shipping, it would never again be a factor in our daily lives.

I was still trying to realise the significance of Major Jagger's announcement when Dr. Cranley found words to break the silence.

"But this . . . this is the most amazing, wonderful news!" exclaimed the old man. "Is it not a fact that our earthly supply of many of these precious minerals was rapidly being exhausted?"

"It was generally accepted that our supplies of oil and coal would have been used up in a hundred years," replied the Major. "That probably applies also to our other precious minerals. We had made reckless, improvident use of them. We were, for example, burning millions of gallons of oil every hour—every day: oil that could not be replaced."

"And now . . . ?" began the doctor.

"Now the moon has presented us with ample supplies for many generations to come."

Again there was silence.

"It confirms my belief," said the old doctor, "that a divine providence lay behind this terrible cataclysm."

"As if," I exclaimed, "the moon, long ages ago, were wrenched away from this earth by a divine, far-seeing power that realised the greed of man!—that realised that he would squander the earth's wealth and find it out too late! And now the moon is given to us in the hope that we have learned our lesson and will take more care of our treasures in the future! We believed the moon to be an omen of destruction—it proves to be a gift from God!"

And once again Major Jagger gave that sharp, hard laugh.

"I envy your simple faith, Mr. Hopkins." For a moment his eyes were upon me: then he glanced around the table with a smile. "I wonder whether these younger people—this younger generation—shares your happiness?"

"I don't see that any normal person could do otherwise," said Peter Cranley, and I gave the boy a grateful smile. "Surely every normal person must realise what a wonderful thing this is!"

"Normal people are rarely in positions of power," replied the

Major. "Mr. Hopkins is a normal man. He is perfectly happy, rearing his poultry in Beadle Valley."

"One does not speak of 'rearing' poultry," I began, for I resented the impudent patronage of the man's tone, "one 'breeds' poultry." I was about to amplify my statement, but the man spoke on, right over me, right through me. . . .

"What does Mr. Hopkins care about the wealth upon the moon? . . . what does he care about the British Empire?"

I was so bewildered by this strange and completely irrelevant remark that I began seriously to doubt the Major's sanity.

"What on earth has the British Empire got to do with it?" I exclaimed, and I almost jumped out of my chair at the vehemence of the Major's reply.

"Good heavens, man!—don't you *see*! Have you never for a moment considered the matter, or have your chickens sapped all your powers of thought! The moon is in the Atlantic, man!—it has blocked our sea routes to America—to Africa—to India—to Australia!—the whole power and greatness of Britain depended upon our access to the sea! Today we are an impotent little island! Our ships can sail as far as Plymouth and no farther!—we are of no more strategic importance than Finland or Denmark—or Greece! Thousands of our own people are cut off from the Motherland in our Colonial possessions—in India and Africa. They depended upon the sea power of this island . . . and now they are at the mercy of vast native populations who are beginning to understand that the brain centre of the British Empire is suffocated!"

"You have made a remark to the effect that my chickens have sapped my powers of thought," I said. "I resent that remark, and demand an apology." I was really angry now, and had no intention of allowing the man to get away with this insult. But no one seemed to hear me—all eyes were upon that stark white face: those smouldering, fanatical eyes.

"Surely," said Dr. Cranley, "we must revise and adjust our ideas of the British Empire. The Empire was founded upon certain geographical conditions, but owing to our collision with the moon these conditions no longer exist. We must surely develop a new outlook upon world affairs to suit these new circumstances?"

"You suggest that we betray our people overseas?—sentence them to death ?—say 'goodbye and good riddance' to the Empire?"

"Dr. Cranley didn't say that!" I rejoined with heat.

"What can be done?" went on the doctor in a quiet voice. "Surely it has been considered . . . is there no plan?"

"There *is* a plan," replied the Major, pulling a map from his pocket and spreading it before us. All drew their chairs around and stared, fascinated, at the strange, unfamiliar map of the new earth. Even I myself edged a little nearer.

"This is known as 'The British Plan.' It was submitted to the International Council at The Hague last May, and was given a friendly, sympathetic reception.

"We proposed that the territories of the moon be divided amongst the nations of Europe according to each nation's size. Britain itself was prepared to forgo its full share on condition that we were given this 'corridor' of territory, ten miles in width, which would give us direct communication with Gibraltar, and thereby to the Atlantic and Mediterranean. By running a railway down this corridor, our communications with our Dominions and Colonies would be re-established."

"An excellent scheme," said Dr. Cranley. "You say that the other nations agreed?"

"They appreciated our vital need of access to the sea."

"Then what's the trouble?" I asked in a sharp voice, for I could not help feeling that the Major was making a great deal of fuss about nothing.

"The Muller-Henderson report is the trouble," returned the Major. "When the nations agreed to our 'corridor' to the Mediterranean the moon was generally believed to be barren and useless rock. All that they requested were certain rights of way across our corridor to their own slices of the moon so that in course of time they could explore and possibly develop. We naturally agreed to that."

He folded the map and put it carefully into his pocketbook. "But today, I am afraid, the situation has completely changed. The moon, instead of being worthless, is now proved to be immensely, immeasurably rich in precious minerals, and I repeat that the cataclysm has not altered human nature."

"I completely fail to see why this alters the British Plan to divide the moon fairly and evenly," I said. "In fact, it seems to justify this dividing up."

The Major turned to me with a smile of pity.

"There are one or two little details that possibly you haven't realised. The moon is not a cake with currants evenly distributed in each slice. The scientists report that the oil is all in the northern area of the moon—the area allotted in the British Plan to Sweden. Germany and France will not agree to that: they want the oil themselves. Italy demands the coalfields. Every nation in Europe demands a bigger slice than what the British Plan suggested for them. In fact, I am afraid there is not nearly enough moon to go round."

"But this is ridiculous!—childish!" I cried. "You surely don't suggest that the nations are going to quarrel about a gift! Surely they can agree!"

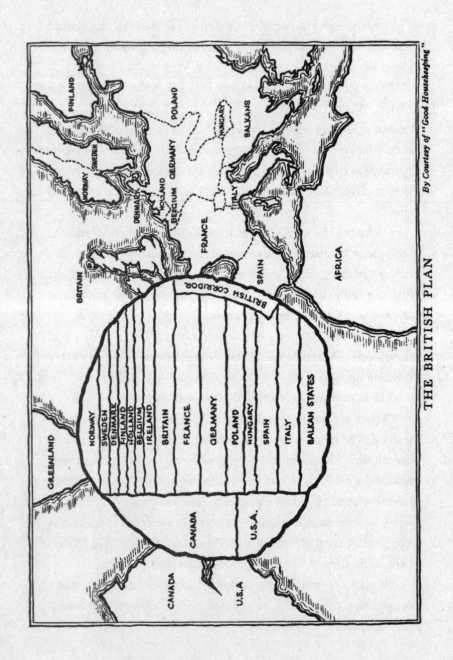

THE BRITISH PLAN

By Courtesy of "Good Housekeeping"

"They all agree upon one thing: they emphatically, fiercely agree that Britain must not have its corridor."

"A ten-mile corridor!" exclaimed Dr. Cranley. "Surely that isn't asking much!"

"It may only be ten miles wide," returned the Major, "but it happens to cut off other nations from direct communication with their own slices of the moon. We have agreed to give them freedom to cross our corridor without hindrance, but they declare it will give us too strong a strategic position: they fear we might fortify our corridor and cut them off at any time we wished to. They even declare we might, eventually, by means of our 'strategic corridor,' take the whole moon for ourselves. They say that the British Empire is not above doing that. They are resolutely against us. The whole of Europe."

Silence fell. Pat and Robin and Peter and Joan had scarcely said a word: they had scarcely moved except to strain forward over the map when Major Jagger had spread it upon the table. To me the whole evening had assumed a dreamlike unreality: we were playing a game of make-believe that had no kinship with real things.

"What is happening now?" enquired the doctor. The ruddy glow had passed from his cheeks: the old man looked tired and spiritless. Even his question seemed to lack demand for a reply.

"What is happening?" The Major shrugged his shoulders. "Deadlock. We refuse to give in. If we are robbed of our corridor and denied a clear open road to the seas, then the British Empire is finished."

There was a knock: the butler entered and handed the Major a slip of paper. I watched him read, and raise his eyebrows.

"You must excuse me, Doctor. A message from the Government. I must drive back to Oxford tonight for an urgent session."

We stood at the front door to see him go. For a moment the coachwork of the big car gleamed in the light from the hall, and then it was gone. I was never to see the man again—but how many times was I doomed in days to come to hear that horrid, strident voice, booming its "messages" over the radio! . . .

"I think perhaps we should be going, too," I said. It seemed impossible to revive the gaiety of the party now. There was something ominous in Jagger's sudden departure: almost as if he had been called away to defend our very shores from invading foreigners.

Dr. Cranley made no attempt to detain us. I think that he felt, as I did, a longing to be alone—to think and to try to understand.

Even the night had changed in concert with our mood: the stars were gone and a slight drizzle had set in. While Pat and Robin were raising the battered old hood of the car I had the opportunity of a last word with Dr. Cranley.

"Was Jagger serious about all this?" I asked. "I mean . . . it seems—impossible."

"He's serious," replied the doctor. "Dead serious. In his way he is a great man. He is leading a new opposition party against the Prime Minister. He told me about it before you came in. The Prime Minister wants compromise. He has a plan for giving up all claim to that 'corridor' to the Mediterranean. By establishing touch with Canada across the northern area of the moon, we could reach Australia—possibly India. That would mean peace with Europe but the end of half our Empire—the end of Gibraltar and the Sudan—Africa and the West Indies. . . ." He paused for a moment, his face hard and pale. "We can't do that—we can't desert and betray thousands of our people. We *must* have our corridor."

"So you are on the side of Major Jagger?" I said, "on the side that opposes a 'peaceful compromise'?"

"Yes," replied the doctor after a long silence. "I share your personal dislike of Jagger: he's not my sort of man, but I am with him in preserving our Empire. With him heart and soul."

The drizzle turned to a silent, ceaseless rain. It was intensely dark and the lights of our car were feeble and uncertain. Robin, straining over the wheel, was peering intently through the tarnished windscreen at the rugged, difficult road and Pat sat up beside him to watch for pitfalls.

I sat in the back seat alone, trying to believe that two hours ago we had driven this same road without a care in the world.

I wondered whether increasing years had made me a coward. I remembered how I had faced the cataclysm without a shadow of fear: how I had even exulted, at times, over the fierce excitement and danger of it. But now I was afraid—miserably, despicably afraid. I tried to fan within myself the spark of a new adventure—a flame of patriotism—a grim determination to face this new menace as I had faced the approach of the moon: to give up all that I had achieved in Beadle Valley: to take a gun, if necessary, and fight for freedom.

But it was useless. I had survived the cataclysm: by superhuman endeavour I had rebuilt my life. It was too much to ask of any man that he should face a second ruin and rebuild again.

CHAPTER TWENTY-SIX

I am in no sense of the word a politician. I have always preferred to leave politics to those who had no poultry farm or other keen interest to claim their attention, and I am fairly convinced that if it had not been for the politicians I would not now be struggling against increasing weakness to write the last tragic chapters of my story in the lonely twilight of a dying world.

Perhaps I am too hard upon the politicians. I may be judging them all upon the foul creatures that arose to destroy us. I admit that it was necessary to have some kind of Governing Body to lead us from the ruins of the cataclysm; and I also admit that our leaders performed wonders in the first two years.

But a strange thing happened, and it happened not only in England, but with uncanny similarity throughout the whole of Europe. The first Parliaments to be elected after the cataclysm consisted with few exceptions of hard-working, level-headed, modest men. It seemed as if the survivors of the disaster turned instinctively to this quiet type of man to lead them from the brink of famine and disruption. There was no thought of election campaigns—no time for pedantic speeches and gimcrack theories. When the people were told to select a man from amongst themselves to represent them in Parliament, they turned towards men of proved character and mature judgment—the country gentlemen—the local professional men—men who for the most part had been Mayors of Towns or Chairmen of Local Councils.

These were the men who set their countries upon the road to recovery and established international harmony of thought and ideals. These were the men who established the International Council at The Hague and were planning the United Parliament of Europe at Vienna when disaster overwhelmed them.

Disaster came through that fatal scientific report upon the riches of the moon. If these sane, level-headed men had remained in power, I am convinced that they would have reached agreement and divided this lunar wealth fairly and peaceably to the immense and lasting benefit of all.

But the strange thing is this. The news of the fantastic, owner-less wealth within the moon was the signal for a horrid swarm of political upstarts to appear in every nation of Europe. Some were fanatics devoid of all powers of reason and common sense, but most of them were worthless adventurers, greedy for wealth and power, their only claim to attention a loud voice and endless cascades of words.

These nasty creatures would swoop down upon peaceful, hard-working communities, upon people intent only upon rebuilding their shattered fortunes and living in quiet happiness. With clever, impassioned speeches they declared that their cowardly Govern-ments were allowing other countries to seize the lion's share of the moon's wealth. They frightened bewildered people into believing that if they did not arouse themselves and "stand up for the rights of their country" they would soon be living in poverty, slaves to a foreign power.

The quiet, hard-working men of the original Parliaments, exhausted already by their incessant labours, were no match for these maniacs and noisy upstarts. One by one, in different ways, the Governments fell, and with their passing the doom of Europe was sealed.

But I am wandering into the very trap that I have resolved so firmly to avoid. I am speaking of politics, and politics are no part of my story. Even had I the ability, I have no inclination to unravel and describe the network of intrigue—the cesspits of political chicanery that marked the Years of Decline.

I resolved, from the beginning of my narrative, to tell the story of these days as I saw them with my own eyes, and I shall do so until the end.

When I awoke on the morning after Dr. Cranley's party I found myself living once again the emotions of an autumn morning two years ago. My reactions were very similar to those after the meeting of the British Lunar Society, when the approach of the moon was first made known to me.

Once again I was drowsily, uneasily conscious that something unpleasant had happened: once again I tried to persuade myself that it was no more than a dream, and then, when at last reality forced itself upon me, I began to persuade myself that it was just a silly scare and that nothing serious would happen.

But this new menace was so different—so sordid compared with the menace of the approaching moon. Despite the horror of it, the news that Professor Hartley gave to our Society upon that other night was too fantastic to be sordid: it had carried a spice of romance with it: a breathless excitement—a secret and a mystery that had chilled and yet enthralled me. The approaching moon had been so remotely beyond human control that it drew humanity together in a bond of ennobling courage.

But what thrill was there in the menace that stalked us now?—the menace of human greed and suspicion? The thin, brittle crust of prosperity that we had built over the ruins of the cataclysm would never stand the weight of human strife. Under the strain of war it must collapse in unspeakable chaos and misery.

I feared my fellow creatures far more than I ever feared the moon. The crisis of the cataclysm had been calculated to a definite day: a definite hour. We knew that by the 4th of May it would all be over one way or another: that we should die or live. But who could measure the suspense—the awful possibilities of war with every nation at the throat of its neighbour?—a war that could only end in the slavery of all to the tyranny of a solitary victor?

As I dressed in the pale sunlight of that autumn morning I whistled a tune from *The Mikado*: I whistled away the menace of the previous night and ran cheerfully down to breakfast determined that Major Jagger and his mad stories of approaching violence should be treated with the contempt that they deserved.

At breakfast Pat and Robin were quiet and thoughtful: it was natural that their young and impressionable minds should be affected by what they had heard, and I wasted no time in debunking Jagger with a vengeance.

"The fellow's a menace!" I declared. "If he goes about talking as he did last night he ought to be locked up! Does he imagine anybody's mad enough to fight over a gift from God?—there's tons of moon—millions of tons of it: more than enough for everybody!"

Pat murmured agreement and poured out my coffee, but Robin was unconvinced.

"Of course, it's mad to think about fighting one another when we're all just getting on our legs again. But it's difficult. I never realised how difficult it was. I've been thinking about it all night."

"You've allowed a thing like this to keep you awake?" I exclaimed.

"I should have thought it would keep anybody awake," retorted the boy. "Look here. . . ." He drew from his pocket a sheet of paper, and I saw that it was a sketch, drawn from memory, of the map which Jagger had shown us on the previous night. To my alarm I noticed something of Jagger's voice in Robin's as he spoke: something of Jagger in the abrupt, decisive way in which the boy laid his map upon the table.

"England, Spain, and France are the only countries with a direct contact with the moon. Norway and Sweden might get to it around the north of Scotland, but how are the central European nations going to do it? How can Germany and Poland and Italy get to their provinces on the moon without passing through France and Spain? D'you suppose France and Spain will allow that?"

I had not thought of this. I looked at the map with a sudden loss of appetite.

"How can they do it?" demanded Robin.

"The big question at the moment," I replied, "is how we shall get our wheat and potatoes to Mulcaster Market. Shall we hire the municipal lorry and do it in one journey, or run it over in half a dozen journeys with the old Ford?"

I was afraid the boy would be angry at this bold and impudent change of subject, but instead his eyes lit up, and he laughed.

"You're right, Uncle," he said. "Let the politicians look after the moon and we'll look after the farm."

*　　*　　*

I went out to my morning's work, happy and reassured. Even if men were mad enough to fight about the moon, their insanity could never harm us here. The air was fresh and keen: the first frost of autumn was sparkling in the meadows and the threat of danger, remote though it was, acted as a spur to my pleasure in the happy scene before me: to my pride in our achievement. The threat of danger gave me a fierce, triumphant determination that, come what may, our little estate would stand inviolable.

I thought of this valley as I had seen it in the grey dawn that followed the cataclysm: the hideous wastes of slime and destruction: the hopeless ruin of it all—I looked upon it now with renewed wonder.

The muddy silt of the tidal wave had given new heart to the land, and in the spring the grass had broken through richer and more verdant than ever I had seen it. The hillcrest, swept bare by the hurricane, was already speckled by stripling trees sprung from the shattered roots of their fathers. Stretching for two broad acres beyond the house lay my vegetable garden with its strong green ranks of cabbages and leeks, celery and turnips, with its reddish haze of sturdy rhubarb in the background.

We now employed a boy named Jim: a good, willing boy who gave alternate days to me in my vegetable garden, Robin in his rabbit and fish preserves, and old Humphrey in the farm beyond The Manor House.

We were far more than self-supporting now. We sent regular and increasing supplies to Mulcaster Market and were accumulating a nice little credit with the new National Bank that opened in the summer. From this credit we bought new houses for my poultry farm, also our most prized possession of all, a cow and a calf. Humphrey had cleaned out and repaired the old dairy of The Manor House and Pat became expert at butter making. She was even experimenting, under Humphrey's direction, in the art of making cheese.

Robin had taken advantage of the lack of clothing materials to build up a thriving little business in rabbit skins for coats. For my own part, I sent an average of five dozen eggs to market every week and I have already referred to the eager and increasing demand for "Beadle-Hopkins" pullets.

We were a happy, vigorous little community, made happier by our increasing friendships in the town of Mulcaster. As the days drew on and the winter came, my belief in the emptiness of Major Jagger's scaremongering fully justified itself. The scientific report upon the wealth of the moon was duly published, became a seven-day wonder in Mulcaster, and was quickly forgotten. The town was far too busy with its reconstruction plans: far too engrossed with its growing prosperity to concern itself overmuch with the problematical riches in the bowels of the moon.

"Steel's what we want," said old Mr. Wilkins, the Market Manager. "Steel and cement to build our houses—and a bit o' good timber thrown in. There's plenty of that in old England—let them that wants gold and platinum go digging up the moon." And Mr. Wilkins expressed the sentiment of the whole of Mulcaster.

By Christmas the cement began to come from the Portland Quarries and by early spring a start was made upon the roads. Mulcaster was to be rebuilt in ten years upon a fine, inspiring plan. Broad avenues, with each house in its own half-acre of land.

Although I lived eight miles from the town, the prosperity of my farm and the fame of the "Beadle-Hopkins" pullets had made me a man of considerable importance in Mulcaster. My opinion was sought upon all serious poultry matters, and we began to entertain upon a scale that would have astonished me in my old pre-cataclysm days.

Dr. Cranley and his son and daughter were frequent visitors to dinner and the growing friendship of my "children" and his was a source of pleasure to both of us.

The days of loneliness that I had feared had not materialised, for frequently, when Pat and Robin were going to a dance, they would take me with them and I would dine with some prominent people in Mulcaster and stay there until Robin was ready to drive me home.

Most of the people were still living in temporarily repaired houses: some even in wooden huts, pending the rebuilding of the town, and everybody continued, voluntarily and cheerfully, to give two hours of each day in service to the community.

The first of January 1948 was the greatest day since the cataclysm: the Official Opening Day of the Ten-Year Rebuilding Plan throughout the whole of England. Luckily it kept fine. It was just like a Jubilee Day in Mulcaster, and we took a full day's holiday from the farm, driving in early to enjoy the celebrations.

At eleven o'clock the whole town assembled in the Market building, which used to be the old Town Hall. A platform had been specially arranged at one end, decorated with flags; a big cardboard shield, brightly painted with the town coat of arms, hanging in the centre.

Mr. Ponsonby, the Mayor, opened the ceremony with a remarkably good speech—quite inspiring, and not too long.

"We shall build a city," he concluded, "which will immortalise us here this morning to generations of Mulcastrians to come: a city that will stand for all time as a monument to the self-sacrifice, courage, and craftsmanship of all of us in this Hall today. A hundred years hence the citizens of this town may build a monument in the public gardens which we shall lay out for them: a monument with a simple dedication: 'To those heroic Mulcastrians who survived the cataclysm and built this noble town.'"

The speech had a wonderful reception, and the Mayor was followed by Captain Weeks, the Borough Architect, who unrolled a large coloured plan of the new Mulcaster and explained it in a most interesting way.

The new city was to be built on slightly higher ground to the west of the old town, and the old buildings were eventually to be pulled down to make a public park beside the river—all except the old Town Hall, which was to remain as a Museum.

The plan of the new city was bold and simple: a fine wide main street was to lead to the Market Square with the Town Hall and Public Buildings grouped around it.

"Never again," declared Captain Weeks, the architect, "shall the people of this town be herded together in stuffy rows of houses. Every dwelling, large or small, will have half an acre, in some cases a full acre of land attached. Mulcastrians will no longer be forced to walk a mile beyond the town to their vegetable allotments. Every man will have room in his own garden for all that he needs!"

When the meeting was over we formed a procession and marched with quite a lively little brass band to the site of the new city, where the Mayor cut the first square of turf from the place where the new Town Hall was to stand.

The sun shone gloriously over the happy scene and everybody was in wonderful spirits. By one o'clock we were back in the Market building where trestle tables had been rapidly laid for a celebration lunch. In the old days, when Mulcaster numbered 3,000 people, only the most important persons could have sat down to a lunch of this kind. Today the whole town—every one of the 436 survivors of the cataclysm—was able to sit down together, with 83 children in a big tent nearby. It is hard to realise what a difference this meant in the spirit of the town: everybody had a place at the table: everybody an important job—none were useless—none were unemployed. Distinctions of class were gone forever, and I sat with Mrs. Smithson, the wife of a plumber, and Miss Bingham of the drapery store, talking to them almost as if they were my equals.

When Mr. Ponsonby, in his after-luncheon speech, announced that there were twenty-three little newcomers to the population of Mulcaster since the cataclysm (eleven boys and twelve girls), the cheering nearly lifted the old patched roof of the building!

Life began afresh in Mulcaster that day. All the suffering and privations of the past were forgotten in the glorious promise that lay ahead. I try not to remember those happy, excited faces as we rose to drink the toast: "To Mulcaster!—to the new city!" The memory of them overwhelms me. In that moment of silence a vision came to me: the vision of broad, tree-girt avenues and clean white houses upon the green hillside beyond the Hall: of happy children in the shady Parks: fresh air—warm, friendly houses—peace—purpose—happiness. . . .

We drank the toast in the first cask of ale from the new-built Mulcaster Brewery. Even that was a symbol to conjure with!

In the afternoon I took advantage of the unusually big gathering to do a little business. I received orders for two dozen Beadle-Hopkins pullets from gentlemen desiring to start small farms of their own. I discussed with Mr. Johnson Betts, an old poultry acquaintance of mine, the possibility of reviving the Mulcaster Poultry Show in the spring. He considered it an excellent plan to stimulate the aesthetic interest in poultry, as distinguished from the purely commercial viewpoint, and I readily accepted his suggestion that I should act as Organising Secretary for the first show.

What a delightful evening I spent when I got home!

Far into the small hours I sat, all my old books and papers spread before me as I revived old memories of past triumphs! I drafted preliminary announcements: a list of events and classes:

a guide to judges in view of the inevitably poor quality of the first exhibits. I even conceived a new and novel departure—a veterans' competition! I determined to show my dear old Broodie, now almost five years old. How wonderful if Broodie, at her age, could win another prize!—her fifty-first First Prize!

A cock crew from the distant hillside: I glanced at my watch in astonishment—three o'clock! I went to bed in a drowse of happiness.

I pass to another evening, three months later. A grey April evening of scudding cloud. It had rained all afternoon, but at sunset the sky cleared for a while, and we ate our dinner, for the first time that year, in the last rays of the sun.

Robin and I had decided to walk down in the twilight to the rusty old *King Lear* to see if we could rig up one of the saloons as a ping-pong room for our friends. The Shipping Company had made no effort to take the liner away, and I saw no reason why we should not make use of it. As the liner lay upon its side it would, of course, be necessary to use the saloon wall as the floor, and the floor and ceilings as the walls, but Robin was very keen on fixing up some novel kind of amusement for our friends when they came to dine with us, and I agreed to go with him to see whether we could cover up the windows to avoid players falling through them as they ran about.

I had put on my coat. I was filling my pipe, preparing to light it. "Let's just hear the news before we go," said Robin.

He switched on the radio—I remember it so clearly—I was searching the mantelpiece for a match to light my pipe, but my pipe was never lit that night. I found it when I went to bed, forgotten in my pocket, for as my fingers ran along the mantelpiece the voice came through: the voice that spoke the end of all our strivings—that spoke the prelude to the last chapter of our days.

"This is the National Station of Britain. At five o'clock this evening the Government issued the following Bulletin:—

> After many weeks of earnest discussion, the International Council at The Hague has failed to reach agreement upon the division of the territories of the moon. This morning the Council, which has, in the past two years, performed such admirable work in International Reconstruction, was broken up, and its delegates returned to their respective countries.

"In ten minutes' time the Prime Minister, who returned from The Hague this evening, will explain the position of the British Government. In view of the vital importance of his message you are requested to warn all those within reach of you to listen."

There was dead silence in the room—broken long after the announcer had finished by a whisper from Pat.

"What does it mean?"

"I don't know," I replied.

I was bewildered by the news: numbed by a fear out of all proportion to the meagre and casually delivered announcement, but from my bewilderment rose one dreadful conviction: "It has come!—it has come . . . I knew that it would come!"

My memory rushed back to the party at Dr. Cranley's house three months ago—to Major Jagger. I saw it all once more as vividly as if it had happened an hour ago—and yet I had striven with all my might to drown it in reassuring thoughts of future happiness. I knew now what, despite myself, I had striven to ridicule. I knew that every word that Major Jagger had said that night was true . . . desperately true. . . .

I should have known it, long ere this, had I tried to understand. I should have read through the guarded newspaper articles: I should have seen through the veiled references in broadcast speeches: the hurried comings and goings of Ministers to The Hague—the urgent meetings of the Cabinet, always ending with "negotiations are proceeding well." "There is no question of serious disagreement"—"the matters involved are naturally very complicated and need further discussion." Always the note at the end: "All is well—all is well!"

Deep within me I had known the truth: in the depths of the night I had known it.

"This is the National Station. The Prime Minister."

I had not heard John Rawlings speak before. He had risen from a solicitor's office in a small country town to a minor post in the Government before the cataclysm.

The new Parliament had voted him Premier as a result of some good work he had done in organising the City of Oxford as the provisional seat of government. The choice had been justified, but while John Rawlings proved himself an excellent administrator of home affairs, it was whispered at the time, and loudly proclaimed afterwards by his enemies, that he was a weak negotiator and no match for the greedy opportunists who seized power abroad directly the wealth of the moon became known. And now his voice came to us, thin and desperately tired.

"It is vitally important that every citizen shall understand the crisis in which the British Empire stands today.

"The moon's position in the Atlantic Ocean has blocked our sea routes and isolated the British Isles from its Colonies and Dominions. Unless we have free passage across the moon to the Atlantic and Mediterranean, Britain is doomed. Without that corridor to the Ocean we shall be dependent for all time upon bringing our vital supplies through the lands of foreigners who can cut them off and starve us at their will.

"Before the moon's wealth was known to Europe, no nation raised objection to our corridor: all recognised it as our lifeline, and agreed to make it British territory. But new leaders have risen abroad—irresponsible adventurers who crave for the lion's share of the moon in order to enhance their prestige. They deny our right to a corridor: they reject our guarantee to preserve its neutrality and our promise to give them freedom to cross it, on the grounds that we might fortify it and one day claim the whole moon as our own.

"Britain stands today at its greatest crisis: either we must submit to the greed of others, forgo our right to the corridor, and take the road to servitude, or we must stand firm and assert ourselves, if necessary, by force of arms. No citizen of this proud, free country will hesitate in his choice: any sacrifice is better than servitude. . . . I and my Ministers are working day and night in our search for an honourable and peaceful solution . . . we do so in the knowledge that every man and woman of Britain will support us . . . will give their lives, if need be, in the sacred cause of freedom. . . ."

CHAPTER TWENTY-SEVEN

I have written nothing in these past three days. I have been ill with some kind of fever that must have come to me from the stagnant mists that rise from the undrained marshes of St. James's Park. I have lain upon my bed in a kind of dream, creeping out now and then for a little water from my store.

The fever has left me, but I find myself too weak to go any longer upon my journeys in search of food. Fortunately, when I was stronger, I set aside a little of the food that I discovered on my daily excursions and laid up a small reserve of water in the bath. The food is hanging above me, suspended in a sack from the electric light pendant—the only means of protecting it from the rats. There is sufficient to last me for a week, and I shall not leave this room again. The last pages of my story will be a desperate race—a desperate struggle against a weakness that consumes me day by day. I am writing with my thermos flask beside me. As each page is finished I roll it and place it in the flask. Should I feel the end suddenly upon me, my last act will be to seal my flask in order that posterity may receive at least the pages that I completed up to the moment of my collapse.

I hope and pray that my thermos flask will preserve them: that the hiding place will be discovered. It would be sad if all that I have done were proved to be in vain. . . .

But I have no time for moralising: I must hurry with my story: every page shall be a victory over the panic of encroaching weakness—over the panic of the dreadful silence that enshrouds me more deeply every hour.

How shall I begin the story of these final, nightmare years? Until the Prime Minister spoke on that April evening four years ago, we knew nothing of the storm that had been gathering throughout the winter. Desperate that nothing should disturb their laborious plans for rebuilding our cities, the Governments had deliberately kept us in the dark, no doubt appealing to the newspapers to support them. They knew how slight and precarious were the foundations of our new prosperity and they hoped that the international problems could be settled without disturbing us. But the crisis had overwhelmed them. On the morning after the Premier's speech the newspapers told us the whole fantastic, pitiful story.

The dispute over the "British corridor," critical though it was to us, emerged now as a mere side-issue to the chaotic problems that were tearing Europe to pieces.

The root of the trouble, as I have said before, lay amongst the ignorant, unscrupulous adventurers who had seized power. All of them realised the doubtful methods by which they had become leaders: all of them, with one accord, set out to strengthen their precarious positions by glorifying themselves in the eyes of the more ignorant of their followers. Their way to glory lay in clamouring for a bigger slice of the moon than anybody else got—the whole of it if possible. They cared nothing for those whom they professed to lead: they cared only for power and riches for themselves.

The scientific expedition had naturally explored a small part only of the moon. Riches had been found, but vast areas still awaited investigation. The "leaders" were torn between playing for safety and claiming the wealth already known, and gambling upon large claims upon the unexplored sections. They had no defined policy: they changed their plans and increased their demands from hour to hour. Unfortunately, the northern part of the moon had so far proved more fruitful than the south, and the north had been assigned by the British Plan (before the wealth was known) to the Scandinavian countries. Naturally this led to uproar. Italy demanded the coalfields in Denmark's area. France clamoured for the oil wells in Sweden's territory, and all without exception shouted for the gold fields reported in the strip assigned to Holland.

When I speak of "France clamouring" or "Italy clamouring," or any other nation "clamouring," I mean that the leaders "clamoured." The poor, bewildered people knew little and cared less about their "rights" upon the moon. All they desired was leave to rebuild their houses, to grow their corn and to graze their cattle, to feed their pigs and to sit in the evening sunlight when the day's work was done. All that they desired was peace, and the dignity of quietness.

The quarrel extended in further and even more bewildering directions. The "leaders" in central Europe demanded free and uninterrupted approach to the territories which they had claimed upon the moon, for as Robin once pointed out to me, central Europe was cut off from the moon by the territories of France and Spain that lay sprawled in their way.

A demand was accordingly made for "corridors" through France and Spain, but these old and stubborn nations had no intention of splitting their territories into pieces with "corridors" swarming with Germans, Dutchmen, Hungarians, and Poles. They rejected the demands and refused to discuss the matter.

To make the problem worse, America suddenly became truculent and extremely difficult. The Council of European Nations, in a special session at The Hague, had formerly declared the moon to be part of Europe. As America had so frequently declared her wish to take no part in European troubles, it was naturally assumed that America would have nothing to do with the moon.

America, however, had strong opinions to the contrary. A new and upstart President of the United States dropped a bombshell by declaring that the fairest way of settling matters was to divide the moon according to the respective sizes of the nations concerned. As America was as big as Europe, America would take the western half of the moon and leave the eastern half for Europe to divide or fight for as they wished.

That, briefly, was the situation when The Hague Council broke up in disorder upon the 7th April. The Deputies returned to their own countries, declaring that they would "take whatever steps were necessary to safeguard their rights."

It all came flooding through to us over the radio—flaming its way to us across the pages of the newspapers. Speeches: leading articles: special reports . . . diehards . . . pacifists . . . compromisers . . . they all came swarming back like unwholesome ghosts from the old world before the cataclysm. Major Jagger was right . . . human nature had not changed.

For my own part I discovered, to my pleased surprise, a new strength within me: a strength engendered by two years of self-reliance: a sturdy independence that sprang from my conviction that we had built in Beadle Valley a little self-supporting Empire of our own. Bread and vegetables, milk and eggs, poultry—rabbits—fish: we had everything to support life and plenty to spare to sell or exchange for boots and clothing. The man who needs nothing from his fellows has a fortress impregnable: impregnable even against universal lunacy.

The downs and the valley were lovely in those early summer days: our farm a picture. The bluebells found protection once more beneath the stripling trees whose branches were now broad enough to shade them. The louder our dangers were bawled across the radio, the more contemptuous I grew: the more determined I became to have nothing to do with it—to ignore this lunacy and get on with my own work.

The brave old town of Mulcaster shared my views. They were sane, hard-working people; proud of their town, eager for its reconstruction. They listened to the radio and read the news and returned again to work. "It'll all blow over," they said, "political scare."

One evening, early in July, a gleam of hope emerged. John Rawlings, our Premier—the sole surviving statesman of the "old school"—spoke over the radio again. He announced that he was proposing a sweeping new Plan to all nations concerned. To end the drift towards disaster he proposed that every nation should give up all individual claim to the moon and its wealth: that the moon should be explored and its wealth exploited by a Permanent International Commission: that the wealth be pooled and divided amongst nations in fair proportion with their needs and population.

He spoke very well: he explained the complicated details simply and straightforwardly and as I listened I breathed a sigh of thankfulness. Nobody, not even a demented fanatic, could deny the fairness and common sense of the "Pool."

There was a week of silence, and then came the news that every "leader" in Europe had rejected the plan as "humiliating."

When my bewilderment had passed, I realised the truth. There was no difference, in the vocabulary of the Leaders, between "fairness" and "humiliation." To them it was one and the same thing. The weaker their positions, the more moon they needed to justify themselves in the eyes of their followers, and as all of them were weak, it would have needed at least seven moons to satisfy the aspirations of them all. The vital issue to every Leader was not so much the amount he got, but how much more than the others he was able to snatch.

Our Premier's plan was destroyed and our doom was sealed. Events now happened with such fierce rapidity and bewildering complexity that I cannot hope to relate them in logical order.

One evening—(it was August, because I remember the days were beginning to draw in)—I was startled from my work of collecting the eggs by an urgent shout from Pat. She came running from the front door, waving her arms and shouting: "Jagger!—quick!—Major Jagger!"

For a horrid moment I thought the man had called upon us in person. I hastened towards the house, and to my relief discovered that he had just been announced to speak over the radio in ten minutes.

"'Very special—great importance,' they said!" Pat's eyes were alight with excitement. She was still so charmingly young; so thrilled at the prospect of hearing over the radio the voice of a man whom she had actually met.

"What's he doing on the radio?" I asked. I did not share Pat's excitement. I did not like the sound of it at all.

"I don't know," replied Pat. "I switched on just as the news was ending—just in time to hear them announce Major Jagger."

Robin came hurrying in. He seemed unusually disturbed and excited. He lit a cigarette and paced the room in a silence that seemed to last an hour.

It took me quite a while to recognise that voice again: it seemed deeper and more resonant over the radio—possibly because the thin, twitching face was hidden from us. But gradually that overwhelming personality came bursting through. I stood by the mantelpiece—Robin by the window: Pat beside the table, and we listened to the most astonishing speech I had ever heard in my life. We stood because the incredible, fanatical intensity of the speaker held us rigid. . . .

I cannot attempt to record the whole of that amazing flood of words: it lasted, I imagine, for half an hour and left us weak and exhausted as if some giant vampire had sucked us dry of vitality.

The old Government, our sane, hard-working old Government, had fallen. A reactionary party had, that evening, taken power, and Jagger was "leader"!

He began with a disgusting, shameless attack upon John Rawlings, the fallen Premier. He accused Rawlings and all his Ministers of cowardice: of attempts at compromise with the Leaders of Europe.

"Rawlings, with his spineless compromise—his ignominious retreats—his futile arguments—has made our country the laughingstock of Europe! He disguised his terror of his opponents under such words as 'reason' and 'sanity'! To reason with these men is insanity itself! A few more weeks of Rawlings' 'reasoning' and the British Empire would have been wrecked beyond repair!"

We heard him take in a rasping breath that sounded like the ripping of a piece of canvas.

"One thing alone will regain for Britain the respect of Europe's Leaders," he shouted—"a good big dose of their own medicine, which I—Roland Jagger—propose to give them! I shall give them a double dose!—a treble dose!—a dose big enough to keep them on their backs until Britain, by her own power, has assured peace in Europe and a fair division of the riches of the moon!

"I have no intention of claiming the whole moon: no intention of claiming more than a just and rightful share. What I do claim is the right to trample on and suffocate these ridiculous little Leaders and give peace to the honest, decent people of the whole of Europe!

"Europe today is plunging towards a destruction more hideous than any that was threatened by the moon itself! One hope alone remains to us! One nation must take the lead: one nation must gain such powerful ascendancy that it can call all other nations to heel and enforce them to accept peace. That nation must be Britain! With God's help I shall remain your Leader until the great salvation is completed!

"The people of Britain shall be the crusaders! I depend upon you, one and all! Man and woman, young and old, shall dedicate themselves to our great crusade! I am confident that none will hesitate: none will show themselves as cowards! Day by day I shall call upon you: I shall call upon you in the name of peace!—the name of sanity!—the name of Britain!"

The voice was so intense, so vibrantly overpowering, that I almost expected it to cry out: "You, Mr. Hopkins!—what about you!"

The awful part of the speech was the reason of it!—the wild, raging reason of it! With things in their existing, hideous chaos, one nation *must* sooner or later take the lead. There were but two alternatives: either leadership must emerge after a long and horrible war: one nation an exhausted victor over a stricken Europe—or it must emerge *now*, and make a desperate bid to save not only Europe, but the world. Jagger was right. I loathed the man more than ever before: I hated his bombast: his truculence: his colossal conceit, but I knew that all of it was necessary—that the man himself was necessary. The only way to stamp out this pest of "Leaders" in Europe was to produce one ourselves, worse than any of them, and stronger. . . .

After his speech was over, we went to bed. I don't think that anybody, after listening to that speech, could have done anything else but go to bed. I think Jagger must have gone to bed himself.

CHAPTER TWENTY-EIGHT

I have had much time for reflection in these last years of deepening loneliness. Often, in the sleepless hours of night I have reviewed my own conduct during the days when we hovered upon the brink of disaster. I have wondered whether I could have done anything, by word or deed, to have saved my country—or, at least, my home.

Perhaps it sounds conceited for an obscure, retiring man even to consider the possibility of guiding his country away from that abyss; but history tells us of many such men who rose up in the darkest hours to guide the destiny of their fellows. If I had raised my voice in the sacred cause of sanity, could I have done anything? If I had clothed myself as a prophet, taken a staff, and gone from village to village preaching the gospel of self-preservation, could I have gained sufficient followers to defeat the submerging madness? Always I come to the same conclusion. If I could not save my own home, I could not have saved the world.

After a night's rest I was sufficiently recovered from Major Jagger's speech to think coherently once more. It was useless to deceive myself any longer. Jagger was not bluffing. It was no good pretending that it would "all blow over." Jagger meant business: he had proclaimed his fateful decisions to the world, and I knew the man well enough to realise that nothing would divert him from his ruthless purpose.

My own course of action was quickly settled. I had a clear-cut, inflexible conviction of the right and patriotic thing to do. It happened to be a Saturday, and every Saturday morning it was the custom of our small community to meet together in the granary of The Manor House to decide upon the produce that we should take to Market that day.

This was an excellent opportunity to declare my policy, for it saved the disturbing necessity of making an "occasion" of it by calling a special meeting.

"You have seen this morning's papers," I began. "Some of us listened last night to Major Jagger's speech. I'm afraid we have some very black days ahead of us, and I think we should be unanimous upon the proper understanding of our duty."

Old Humphrey, who was nearly eighty and very deaf, had probably not seen the papers, nor heard a word of Jagger's speech, and Jim, although a willing boy, was only sixteen, and slow in the uptake. I scarcely expected either of them to grasp what I was talking about, but by speaking, apparently, for the benefit of our farm hands, I was able to let Pat and Robin know my views without restraint.

For Pat and Robin were of an age to understand: reliant enough to form their own opinions. They might have resented any attempt of mine to influence them had I spoken to them privately, and I desperately hoped that they would understand me, and stand by me in all that I had planned.

"In the next few months," I said (with my eyes upon the goggling Jim, and the corners of them upon Robin), "we may hear many radio appeals: we may read in our newspapers of what we ought to do to serve our country. Let us do what we know to be right and patriotic! In times of great stress it sometimes happens that those in authority overlook the less spectacular, but no less vital needs of mankind. They may seek to throw all of us into the front line and forget that, without good food, a front line must soon collapse! Our duty in Beadle Valley is clear. We must work with all our strength: redouble our energies and supply the food that leads to victory. If the farmers desert their farms because it seems more heroic to carry a gun, then not only their fellow soldiers, but thousands of women and children will face famine in the winter. Are we all agreed to turn a deaf ear to panicky appeals and do our duty in Beadle Valley?"

"It ain't too late to put another acre under turnips," said old Humphrey.

I was surprised that the old man understood. "Splendid!" I exclaimed. "For my own part, I'll put in another ten rows of late potatoes. I'll keep those new pullets out of the market to increase our winter egg supplies."

I glanced towards Robin, hoping for a response, but the boy was impatiently looking at his watch.

"It's nearly ten," he said. "We'd better load the car."

When we arrived at Mulcaster Market we found the town bewildered and dismayed. I had hoped that a short respite at least would lie between Jagger's speech and the day when Jagger began his "drive"—but I was quickly disillusioned.

On the previous night, the town had been jubilant at the long-awaited arrival of a trainload of steel girders for the new Town Hall. At dawn next morning, when a gang of workmen had gone to unload, they discovered to their astonishment that the train had disappeared. Under cover of darkness, in accordance with urgent orders from the Government, the train had been shunted out and its load of steel girders taken away to an "unknown destination for special military use."

It was a crushing blow to Mulcaster. They had waited weeks to get those girders and the whole progress of their "Ten-Year Reconstruction Plan" depended on them. To me it was damning proof of Jagger's headlong stupidity. However much he needed the girders for tanks or guns, he should never have called them back when once the people of Mulcaster had set eyes upon them. It was pitiful to see that brave little town, by one stupid Government order, cast from the heights of optimism to the depths of disappointment and despair. I left the town as early as possible that day. I could not bear to see those loitering, aimless people whose employment had gone with such tragic, unexpected swiftness.

We got home early enough to hear the evening radio news: to hear that Jagger had that day despatched an army of 10,000 men to garrison the British corridor across the moon to "protect our vital interests." We also heard an impassioned speech by a man I had never heard of: a Mr. Justin Wheelwright, new Minister of War. He appealed for 200,000 men to volunteer at once. They were to proceed to the Military Training Centre at Aldershot.

Two days later we heard that fighting had broken out in Normandy, upon the northeastern fringes of the moon. The war was on.

Military historians, in days to come, may take the task in hand, but it will need men of superhuman genius to give sense and logic to that tangled, fruitless war.

The news we received was heavily censored. We were told of "magnificent victories" and "astonishing progress." One evening, with a blast of official jubilation, came the news that our Army of the Corridor had reached the Mediterranean and established touch with the survivors of the Gibraltar garrison. "Britain reaches the sea!"—"The British Empire saved!"—"A glorious peace in sight!" cried the radio. "Our mighty purpose is all but achieved!" boomed Jagger. "The corridor is ours! We shall build a bulwark of Blood and Iron: a mighty bulwark of British courage will starve greed and suspicion into surrender! As guardians and trustees of the moon's great wealth we shall dispense fair play and give equal shares to every nation in the world!"

I must admit that even I was thrilled by the news and stuck out my chest. I was proud to belong to a great people whose crusade for peace and justice was carrying all before it. For a space dejection lifted from the town of Mulcaster: they hung an old Union Jack from the unfinished skeleton of the new Town Hall.

But that was in the summertime. Autumn came and winter loomed through a haze of menace and gathering suspense.

It was clear that Jagger had taken Europe by surprise and carried all before him in the opening campaign, but news crept through by way of foreign radio, and we learnt of the "Confederated Army of Europe."

It seems that Jagger's dramatic rise to power had impressed the Leaders of Europe so deeply that they made friends with one another. They came to the unanimous conclusion that the destruction of Jagger was essential before they could proceed with their long-looked-forward-to destruction of each other.

One morning an aeroplane scattered pamphlets over Britain, and a copy came down in the garden of Mr. Wilkins's house in Mulcaster. It was addressed to "The People of Britain" by "The Confederated States of Europe." It told us not to lose hope, because the Confederated States had solemnly agreed to destroy Jagger and release the British people from the toils of a mad usurper who was leading us to destruction. The people of Mulcaster did not consider this quite fair upon Jagger, but it certainly made them think.

A few weeks later a broadcast in English was given from Amsterdam. It announced that the Confederated Army had forced its way across the British corridor and cut our forces into two. "The Southern Army is isolated and starving into surrender. The Northern Army is in retreat to Britain."

The news stunned us. It was vigorously denied by Jagger, but the denial lacked conviction. With the news came winter and the grinning spectre of famine.

Desperately I sought to drown my misery in work upon my farm, and those who toiled beside me were staunch and loyal. The Poultry Show that I had striven so hard to organise, was cancelled. The heart and soul had gone from Mulcaster. For a while they had hoped for victory and peace by autumn: they had desperately hoped to start once more upon the reconstruction of their town. But now their fine roads, begun with such brave endeavour, lay derelict and weed-grown—the wind sighed through the rusting framework of the new Town Hall and men walked the streets with bowed heads and hollow eyes.

Voluntarily I gave one-half of all our produce to "The National Pool." Once a week we drove to Mulcaster with all that we could spare, and the pale, dejected people watched our fine brown eggs and succulent vegetables loaded by soldiers upon Army lorries and driven off to the training camp at Aldershot.

Throughout that winter our fragile civilisation clung together by a miracle. There was hunger and misery: insistent calls for men: urgent and still more urgent calls for courage and renewed resolve.

"The Confederated States" swept our army from the corridor, and sometimes, in the long, dark evenings, creeping up that silent valley, came the sound of guns.

By Christmas we learnt that the Confederation had collapsed. The leaders of it had come at last within grasping distance of the wealth upon the moon, but as they stretched forth to clasp it, they began to knock each other's hands away; they began to argue about their rights once more: they began to fight. By June the fighting had spread through the limbs of Europe like disease through a weak, resistless body.

Autumn came once more, and with it the day I dreaded: the day that I had known for a long time must come.

It was in the twilight of an October evening when Robin came to me. I was closing the hatches of my chicken houses as he came up the slope of the downs. He stood there for a little while, talking of casual things: of the way the seedling trees had grown that summer—of how the sunset caught the windows of our house and made it seem as if every light were on within it. And then he turned his head away, brushed his hair back from his forehead with a characteristic little movement that always betrayed him in embarrassment.

"I don't know what you'll think, Uncle—but I've got to go."

"Go?" I echoed. My heart fell with the weight of lead. For many months I had known that this must happen; yet now that it had come it seemed unreal and dreamlike. . . . "Go where?"

"I wrote last month . . . for a commission in the Infantry Army. The reply came this afternoon."

I held the thin, shabby strip of paper in my hand. I read the words through a quivering mist of unreality. *Robin Parker: appointed Lieutenant—the 14th Expeditionary Battalion.*

"Robin! . . ." I began, but he stopped me with a weary, impatient gesture of his hand.

"I know. I know exactly what you're going to say. We agreed that our job was to stay here. But that was over a year ago . . . in the days when everybody believed we'd win easily in a month or two. It isn't like that anymore. It may sound silly and . . . and sentimental, but I still believe terribly that we are the people who must get this beastly thing put right. My people were always soldiers. D'you suppose my uncle would have stayed at The Manor House and grown potatoes with the country in this awful danger?"

Many a time I have regretted my passionate outburst. I was not angry with Robin: I was furious at the senseless folly of it all: furious at the impotent devilishness of it. . . .

"You're a fool!" I shouted. "A senseless young fool! D'you imagine you're serving your country by walking out like this! You're not! You're just playing into the hands of a beastly crowd of money grabbers who don't care a damn for England or anybody else! One day when these upstarts have cut each other's throats, the world will turn to people like us and bless us for keeping a few corners of a madhouse free from lunatics! D'you realise that the only way to save a few shreds of humanity upon earth is for people like us to stand firm and carry on! D'you think you'll save women and children from starvation by going off and playing soldiers with a lot of other fools!"

I stopped. I was exhausted. I sobbed for breath, and I was alone. Robin was walking slowly down the hillside.

It was quite dark when I returned to the house. For nearly an hour I wandered to and fro, ashamed to go inside.

Through the library window I could see Robin. He was writing at the desk, but I could not go in to him. Quietly I went up to my room. The door of Robin's bedroom stood open and the light was on. Pat was moving between the bed and the cupboard by the wall. I went in to her, puzzled to know what she was doing.

On the bed lay the cadet uniform that Robin had worn at Eton: Pat was brushing it and cleaning a stain from the sleeve. She looked up at me almost guiltily, with a shy, embarrassed smile.

"When is he going?" I asked. "He's told you?"

"Yes."

A shadow of relief passed across the girl's face. "He hated telling you," she said. "We talked it over and over a hundred times. It was all so terribly difficult."

There was a little silence. The old clock in the hall was striking seven. "He's going tomorrow," said Pat. "He's got to get to Canterbury somehow—his regiment is waiting there." She saw me looking at the old worn uniform upon the bed. "I'm afraid he's grown a lot since he wore this at Eton, but they say there aren't any uniforms at Headquarters anymore. They've got to take anything they can. I've let the sleeves out as far as they'll go."

"How long have you known about this, Pat?" My voice sounded hard and dull—I could not bring a spark of life to it. The loss of Robin was in itself well-nigh unbearable: my shame at the way I had behaved towards him had numbed me.

"For over a year," replied the girl. "Ever since they first called for men he was tortured by a . . . a sort of urge. He knew that his work here was important: he knew how much you depended on him . . . but when things began to go so terribly badly . . . he just had to go."

"Did you never think of consulting me, Pat? . . . did you never feel that I could help?"

"We thought of that—always," replied Pat. "You've been so good to us—but you had so many things to worry you. We just couldn't bring ourselves to throw the decision upon you."

For a moment her fine, clear eyes were upon me, and then she glanced unhappily away towards the windows. The wind was rising: it came in little moaning gusts across the downs. Upon the dressing table lay Robin's underclothes, neatly, in little piles—pitifully threadbare now—pitifully inadequate, I thought, to face the grim menace of this winter. Beside them lay a few of Robin's little treasures that Pat and he had selected to take with him—an old pair of binoculars that Colonel Parker had carried through the Great War of thirty years ago—a pipe that I had given him last Christmas—a clean towel—two slim volumes of Kipling.... I thought of this dear, devoted girl—quietly, secretly planning with her brother the things that he would most need in that groping, twilit journey to his duty.

"He just felt it . . . it was the right thing to do," said Pat in a low, trembling voice. "However silly it seems—whatever we think of the men who have brought us to it—it's still our country, isn't it? . . . it's still worth giving everything we have to save it." Once again her eyes were upon mine. "Are you very angry with him?" she asked.

I looked down at the empty haversack upon the floor, opened in preparation for tomorrow's journey. I took Pat's hand and turned my eyes away.

"No," I said. "I'm very proud."

A solitary train crawled through Beadle Station at six o'clock each evening. Two years ago there used to be as many as half a dozen, all stacked with building materials for the new towns, but now there was no need for them, and this one old train meandered through on its aimless way to Winchester and London. Robin was to go by this train to London and thence to Canterbury as best he could.

He cycled into Mulcaster that morning to say goodbye to Joan Cranley, whose brother had left some weeks before to serve with the Medical Corps of the Expeditionary Force. He returned to lunch, and in the afternoon we went for a last walk around the farm. I had asked his forgiveness on the previous night, and on that last walk he became the charming, carefree boy whom I knew and loved so well.

"I've taught Jim all I know about the fish and the rabbits: old Humphrey will keep an eye on him: they'll carry on all right till I come back." We stood for a few moments, watching the dark little shadows whisk to and fro in the clear, slowly moving water.

"You've made a wonderful job of this, Robin," I said.

We walked up to the ruined Manor House—to Colonel Parker's grave beneath the old cedar whose splintered trunk was already a haze of green again. We went on, over the downs to the eastern crest where the great plain lay beneath us in the pale autumn sun.

"Remember this place?" said Robin.

There was a lump in my throat, and I could scarcely speak. "The place where I first met you and Pat . . ."

"I came climbing up the slope with Pat's flabby little hat . . . and you were there. What years ago it seems!"

He turned away: he took my arm and we walked back to our house.

Tea was ready: a big substantial tea of eggs and fried potatoes. There was no telling when the boy would see hot food again.

"Come on, Robin!" called Pat. "You'll miss either the tea or the train if you don't hurry up!"

Robin came down from his bedroom and stood before us with an awkward, boyish grin.

"Do I look very funny?" he asked.

He was in his uniform. In a smart cadet parade at Eton he might have looked funny in a uniform three sizes too small, but to me, at that moment, he looked splendid. I had not realised how tall he had grown in the past two years: the tightly fitting tunic enhanced his height and suddenly he seemed to tower above me.

"You've done marvels with these sleeves, Pat: nobody'll notice how short the trousers are so long as I keep the puttees on."

"It fits perfectly," I said. "You've grown upwards—not outwards."

"And they'll give you Lieutenant's badges when you join the Battalion," put in Pat. "You'll look an awful swell!"

Pat and I tried valiantly to eat in company with Robin. To me it seemed utterly unreal—utterly impossible. The little room was darkening with the setting sun: pale beams of sunlight lingered upon the table and slowly fell away: the memories of all our happy evenings came whispering through the twilight: the strange, exalting evening when the three of us first gathered here on the night that followed the cataclysm—when Robin had knelt before the fire, coaxing it once more to life. Evenings when we had read aloud around that glowing fire—evenings when we had woven our dreams of all the splendid things that lay ahead.

Twilight still lingered around the lips of the valley as we went down to the station. The wind had fallen and it was very still and peaceful. There was just the faintest rustle in the brown leaves of the stripling trees that lined the lane.

We must have looked a strange little party upon that weed-grown, derelict station—Pat in her old Burberry coat and "flabby little hat"—I in my old patched plus-fours and walking jacket—Robin, the young soldier going out to war. To an onlooker, deceived by our pitiful attempt at gaiety, we might have been a father with his daughter, seeing his tall son away to school. We rattled an empty old automatic machine with a rusty label marked MILK CHOCOLATE: Robin banged against the window of the empty Booking Office and called out: "Three Excursion tickets to Blackpool, please!" We scared a family of starlings from their nests in the ruined signal box with our gay laughter, and all the while my eyes kept turning towards the cleft in the valley where the sunset lingered—the cleft from which the train would come.

A dull haze of smoke tarnished the sky: a faint, weak whistle drifted through the twilight. "Here it is," I said.

Suddenly, with one accord, our laughter died. I saw Robin stoop to pick up his haversack. He slung it over his shoulder and turned to Pat. In that last moment I knew that I should never have come to the station that night. I should have remained at home, for I felt like an eavesdropper upon a moment sacred to that boy and girl. I knew their devotion to one another: I should have given them this last moment alone. The boy's hand lay upon her shoulder: with lowered head she groped and held her brother's leather belt.

"Steady, old girl," I heard him whisper, "it won't be for long . . . I'll be back in no time, really."

"Take care of yourself, Robin. . . . I'm . . . I'm so proud of you. . . ."

I walked down the platform and drew out my torch to signal to the train, for they never stopped at this ruined little station unless you signalled to them.

The engine was just panting into the cutting—a precious minute still.

From the distance I saw the boy lower his head to kiss the girl beside him. Through the gathering night I saw her arms around him, and my memory raced through the years to far-off days when boys of my own generation had gone to another, far different war. They had gone in the morning sunlight—gone in fresh uniforms and glittering badges—gone to a fluttering blaze of flags and the

brave music of bands—to cheering crowds and waving handkerchiefs. They had gone to finely ordered regiments, well-clothed,
well-fed: gone, above all, with a clear and definite purpose: with
burning faith in the triumph of a cause.

And now Robin was going: going from the darkness of a derelict, wayside station into a deeper darkness from which reason
and purpose had long since died, knowing nothing except that the
land of his birth was in the toils—feeling nothing save an aching
desire to do what he believed was right.

The engine driver had seen my waving torch. He signalled a
grimy hand to me and the shabby train came slowly to a halt.

"So long, Robin!" I cried. "Write to us!"

"Your sandwiches!" cried Pat, thrusting the little packet
through the window.

"My heavens!—I nearly forgot them."

For a long way we could see Robin's waving handkerchief. A
tiny, solitary white speck, blotted now and then by the smoke of
the train.

We scarcely spoke as we walked home through the night. My mind
was numbed to the thoughts of the boy who had left us. I was
thinking all the way of a silly, irrelevant thing.

There had been scarcely anyone in the train, but as it had drawn
away I had glimpsed through a window an elderly, red-faced man in
a dinner jacket! A man with the heavy, wine-red face of a country
gentleman, in a trilby hat and dinner jacket! Where on earth was
he going, in a meandering train through a land quite barren of
dinners demanding jackets?

It puzzled me and puzzled me. When Pat had gone to her room
I sat for hours alone by my library fire, wondering about it. I have

wondered since whether that old man in his dinner jacket was shown to me by a divine providence: a merciful drug to numb a pain beyond my bearing. The pain of the first evening without Robin sitting there by the library fire.

It was in the week after Christmas—on New Year's Eve—when Pat said "goodbye" to me.

An urgent call had been made for girls prepared to serve as nurses with the Expeditionary Force in Europe. Heavy fighting all that winter had made the need a desperate one, and Pat was going with her friend Joan Cranley.

On the afternoon of New Year's Eve I helped to strap her luggage upon the back of Robin's old bicycle, for the chain of her own had broken with age.

I walked with her to the crest of the downs. I waved to her until she was out of sight upon the road to Mulcaster, and returned to my home alone.

CHAPTER TWENTY-NINE

My story is over. Strange things have happened in the years since Pat and Robin left me: food for vivid narrative if the man experiencing them had been alive to them as well. To me they have left but a blurred and senseless jumble: neither food nor inspiration to my pen, for when Pat and Robin went away they took my very soul along with them, leaving a numbed, bewildered creature that I dimly recognise as "Edgar Hopkins."

I remained alone in Beadle Valley for close upon two years. It is true that old Humphrey and Jim the boy were there, and a woman named Miss Tomlinson whom Pat had brought from Mulcaster to keep house for me, but never had I known such loneliness as came to me in those last days. All my life I had been a solitary man, but solitary through inherent shyness rather than desire. The coming of Pat and Robin had brought a breath of life and gaiety that I had never known before. Despite our hardships I can truly say that those were the happiest days of my life, and the passing of them brought a solitude deep and terrible.

For a little while I sustained myself with one grim resolve. Fiercely I told myself that Pat and Robin would soon return: fiercely and desperately I worked to keep our little estate clean and prosperous and worthy of their homecoming. I told myself that they might return quite unexpectedly—if only for a few days' leave, and I devoted my whole life to that one abiding thought. At whatever time they returned, whether it be at dawn or midnight or in the full sunlight of noon, they would not catch me unawares: they would find their home as they had left it and know that I had kept, through all my loneliness, a stout heart.

Twice I had letters from Pat, and once from Robin. Pat was working in a big derelict factory, converted into a hospital, at Antwerp: she, too, was lonely, although I only read that through the lines. Her friend Joan Cranley had been sent elsewhere and most of Pat's companions were French and German girls. *We are terribly busy,* she wrote, *and horribly short of the things we need. Nobody seems to know who is fighting whom, but all the armies are moving eastward now—away from the moon—and we hear the strangest rumours. . . .*

Robin sent me a brave, cheerful letter from "somewhere in Austria." It was written on a scrap of tattered, dirty paper. *We are an awful-looking crowd of ragamuffins . . . there's been some kind of alliance, because there are Germans and Spaniards and Frenchmen all fighting with us . . . we had our first scrap yesterday . . . a crowd of black men came swarming out of a forest . . . our guns are awful, but we put up a good show . . . I could do with a couple of good fresh Beadle eggs . . . I'm longing for the day when it's all over and I come home. . . .*

I spent hours in those winter evenings writing long letters to Pat and Robin. I told them all manner of little details: some so trivial that I felt almost silly to write them down, but I felt somehow that it would amuse and cheer them.

It was impossible to lose hope entirely when springtime came to Beadle: we struggled valiantly through that summer and on towards the autumn, but as winter approached I could no longer blind myself against reality.

I was fighting a hopeless, losing battle in Beadle Valley. Old Humphrey never disguised from me that his whole life and soul were devoted to "Miss Pat" and "Master Robin." By instinct and tradition he was the devoted feudal retainer of "the Parkers of The Manor House." I meant nothing to him whatever: he treated me as a fellow workman rather than as a master.

For a little while he, too, lived for the day when his young master and mistress would return, but as the weeks stretched to months and the months to years he gave up all hope of seeing them again. I did my utmost to cheer him: I showed him the three letters I had received, pretending that they were new ones: I pretended to read paragraphs, imaginary paragraphs saying that Pat and Robin would soon return; but when nothing happened his indifference to me became hostility—he avoided me and I left him alone. His wheat field lay derelict: he turned into something hardly human—a very old, very dirty animal that brooded over a log fire in the granary, murmuring songs of days gone by in a cracked senile voice, baking potatoes to keep the clinging spark of life within him.

During that winter the last semblances of organised life passed into memory: the towns were back once more in the chaos that followed the cataclysm: back again, but now without the urge or energy to rise from it. The Mulcaster electricity supply was gone for lack of fuel and my radio died with it. I used to send Jim the boy to Mulcaster now and then in the hope of securing news: I sent him with a few eggs or vegetables in an endeavour to exchange them for candles and oil, but usually he returned empty-handed with vague rumours that the army was fighting "black men" and getting beaten every day. Government control had gone with the collapse of communications and the silencing of radio, but the "War Ministry" still scoured the country with lorries in a hunt for able-bodied men. One day I sent Jim to Mulcaster and he did not return.

I do not know when the conviction first came to me that I must leave my home. It may have been upon that bitter January morning when I ploughed through the snow to find my dear old Broodie dead beneath her perch. The passing of Broodie seemed to break my last link with Beadle, for day by day I grew more certain that my sanity depended upon escape from this overwhelming solitude.

I had hated Miss Tomlinson from the day she came to me. She was a dreary, unwholesome creature without any eyelashes, who never disguised the fact that she remained because there was nowhere else to go. She was unclean in her work and ruined my fast receding stores of food with careless cooking.

I scarcely exchanged a dozen words with her a day, and spent the long dark evenings reading in my library. I would doze and awake, thinking I had heard Pat's gay laugh outside my door: I would start up, trembling with excitement, and hurry to the bleak deserted passage. I knew that when this endless winter passed, I would have to go.

The idea came to me quite suddenly, and I wondered why I had never thought of it before. Uncle Henry and Aunt Rose! They were old before the cataclysm five years ago, but they were the kind of people who might quite well survive. I had often rebuked myself for not enquiring after them, but in such universal and far-reaching chaos the fate of two aged and remote relatives had not seemed of great importance.

I would go to London!—to Notting Hill—to the house of Uncle Henry and Aunt Rose! There were certain to be some people in that great city: there would be news: possibly some semblance of organised society.

After long months of drifting despair the thought of my adventure put new life into me. I spent the whole spring in preparing for the journey—making a list of what I should carry with me, clearing up my affairs, and locking away my valuables in the hope that I might one day return.

It was no use trying to send a letter in advance and our solitary train had long ceased running. I would have to walk, but I would do so leisurely, taking ten days to cover the seventy miles. I fixed upon the first of June, when the days were long and the nights were warm.

I sent Miss Tomlinson off to Mulcaster a week beforehand and spent the last days entirely alone. On my last night I wrote a long letter addressed *To Pat or Robin* telling them where I had gone, giving them my address in London and asking them to come to me upon their return. *Then we shall all come back together,* I ended, *and Beadle Valley will be like it was before you went away.* I pinned the letter on the library table, drew the shutters over the windows and groped up the dark stairs to sleep the last night in my home.

I said "goodbye" to Beadle Valley in the dawn of a clear June day. I saw it through a dream: remote and unreal to me as I went down the hill to the lane that led me to the old Winchester Road.

Luckily the excitement of the adventure spared me the heartbreak of that last view of my beloved valley. Memories were crowding in upon me: they were threatening to overwhelm me when mercifully I began to wonder whether I had packed my slippers. I was just closing my garden gate at the foot of the hill when the doubt came to me. I had sat upon the drawing-room sofa to put my walking boots on, and I could not for the life of me remember putting the slippers into the haversack. What a relief it was to find them there!—how awful to retrace my steps and enter that dim, curtained house again! Had I done so, I believe my iron resolve may have broken down: some little, forgotten relic might have unleashed a flood of memories from which no escape would have been possible, and I would have remained in Beadle Valley till I died.

The tarred surface of the main road had long since worn away: over the hills it ran, straight as an arrow—spangled with young nettles and wild tufts of grass: empty and derelict, just as it was in the dark ages after the Romans left it sixteen centuries ago: empty and derelict as it settled down to sleep through the dark ages that were upon us once again.

I would like to dwell upon that lonely, leisured journey had I the strength and time. I think of it as a little oasis of repose and happiness in the arid months that lay around it. In a canvas sack I carried food: two boiled chickens, the last of my proud "Beadle-Hopkins" breed, conveniently cut before leaving home into joints that needed neither knife nor fork: a parcel of hard but nourishing wheat cakes: baked potatoes and some hard-boiled eggs. Enough, I reckoned, for ten full days.

In my thermos flask was sealed the last of my favourite vintage of claret. A change of clothes in my haversack, my pipe and slippers, and three favourite books completed my luggage, and as I trudged between those wild and lovely fields of cornflowers I dreamed sometimes that tragedy had never come—that I was back in the far-off days when, as a young schoolmaster, I found happiness upon the open road in days of holiday.

The nights were warm, spangled with stars and sweet with the scents of boyhood. Sometimes I slept in ruined cottages or barns, but mostly beneath some derelict haystack with the field mice rustling around my ears.

It was lovely to awake in the dawn of those June mornings: to lie and watch the clouds float overhead: to know that, even if an age were dying, this countryside would remain in all its beauty though centuries might pass before man came to it again.

I avoided the towns for fear of the things that might sadden and oppress me: I passed few people on the roads and those that I met would come and go with lowered heads and a wistful smile.

Once I was startled by a cloud of dust and a horrid, discordant jangle in the distance: I hid in the undergrowth to watch a dirty, battered lorry clatter by. It was using some crude oil that made a filthy smoke and a horrid stench, and was filled with tattered, bearded soldiers. I took them to be soldiers, for they were all in freakish cartoons of khaki uniform. I imagine it was a "recruiting" lorry, for there was a boy amongst them in a dirty open cricket shirt and wondering, childish eyes. I remained in hiding until it was out of sight, for although I was well past military age there was just a risk of being pounced upon and whisked away.

I spent two peaceful days with an old railway signalman who was living in his signal box upon the deserted line near Windsor. He had served this box, he told me, for nearly twenty years: twelve years before the cataclysm, when he had signalled as many as a hundred trains a day: two years after the cataclysm, when the trains began again. It was now over a year since he had signalled through the last old luggage train to Oxford. He had waited hopefully for several weeks, sitting for hours beside the little bell that would tinkle the approach of another train. But none had passed that way again.

I had developed a bad blister on my heel and the old man gladly offered me the shelter of his little home. He had a small vegetable garden and a few chickens, and we slept in the box beside the signal levers which he still kept oiled and shining.

It was pleasant to sit out in the fading sunlight of those two restful evenings, smoking our pipes and watching the old man's chickens roam beside the rusty, silent rails. I discovered that he had shown Bantam hens in a small way before the cataclysm and was very proud of having won a Second Prize at Windsor! This gave us much in common to pass the hours away but I did not tell him my name lest it should embarrass him and prevent him from talking with such disarming freedom of his own little triumphs in the poultry world.

I felt quite sorry when the outskirts of London told me that my happy, carefree journey was drawing to its close. I saw more people now: ragged, dejected people whose heads seemed permanently bent forward in a ceaseless search for food. I saw a few working in the fields—a few tending their own vegetable plots and chickens, but for the most part they seemed bereft of all creative energy: they just wandered in their unending, dreary search for food.

I crossed the Thames by the old, weed-grown lock gates at Teddington and followed the northern bank of the river towards the city. The tidal waves had thrown vast quantities of silt across the boroughs of Hammersmith and Chelsea, and for one whole afternoon I plodded across a plateau of flat, sun-baked mud, threading my way between the chimney stacks and church spires, guiding myself by the course of the sun.

Towards sunset upon the twelfth day of my journey I climbed the steep, narrow road to Uncle Henry's house. My heart was pounding with excitement: the houses were in good condition here and smoke wreathed from an occasional chimney. I had met quite a few people on the last stage of my journey: some working in little gangs to clear the debris from half-buried provision shops.

At every step my hopes of finding my aunt and uncle alive had risen higher. I reached the secluded little house. It was concealed between higher buildings and it was not until I was right upon it that the familiar red-brick front revealed itself.

I knew in a moment that my uncle and aunt were no longer there. The wrought-iron railings were almost buried in wild, rank weeds and I had to climb over the rust-jammed gate. I could see in a flash that my aunt's fastidious old fingers had long since fallen from the ragged, dejected curtains of the windows.

The front door was locked and bolted: I forced my way through the undergrowth to the tradesman's entrance and found a mildewed fragment of paper, secured by a large stone upon the doorstep.

It requested, in Aunt Rose's bold round hand, that the milkman should leave a pint of milk "if possible." I remembered the faulty catch upon the pantry window and clambered inside. I drew the dusty curtains from the morning-room windows: breakfast things for two were neatly laid upon the table in readiness for my uncle and aunt's return from the dugouts five years ago.

I went all over the house, opening the windows to the warm, summer evening breeze. Packed snugly away between bigger, taller buildings, the little house had come almost unscathed through its ordeal.

I opened the French windows of the upstairs drawing-room, drew a chair onto the verandah, and sat down to think.

It was better, after all, that my Uncle Henry and Aunt Rose were no longer there. It would have been very hard to have two old and failing people upon my hands, for by the look of things I should have my work cut out to keep myself alive.

From the balcony I could see a long stretch of the Bayswater Road, with the shadows of the Park beside it. Why had I left my house in Beadle Valley? Loneliness had driven me to leave, yet in this ruined city I seemed lonelier than ever.

But at least I had the advantage of new surroundings here. Even the labour of living might offer a new and diverting occupation. Desperate and derelict though the great city seemed, I might find little communities hidden away—even some remnant of social life to pass the hours.

Twilight came: an old man drove two cows across the road from Kensington Park and through the open doors of a bank. He closed them in for the night and went away. Two people came from the Park with bundles of wood and pails of water, and then it was too dark to see any more.

I groped for one of the spare candles in my haversack. I lit it and explored the house. There was some tinned food in the larder including condensed milk and coffee: there was still some wine left in the cellar. I cleared one place away from the breakfast table and ate a substantial meal. I took a book from Uncle Henry's library and read for a little in a silence broken only by the distant baying of dogs—and then I went to bed in the room that was always reserved for me in days gone by.

I have no power to record my day-by-day existence through these final days. My hopes of finding a remnant of organised social life faded with my first day of exploration, and by force of necessity I fell into the strange routine of those around me. There were, at that time, perhaps five thousand people in London—scattered over its length and breadth—but only a few in each district. They lived a scattered life because it was easier that way. Food was the one absorbing factor of existence and although sufficient could still be found in ruined shops there was only enough so long as we lived well separated from one another and gained by mutual consent our own individual hunting grounds.

I found a little district that seemed to belong to no one: a row of small shops hidden away behind the Camden Road. One was a fried-fish shop, and amongst the debris I discovered some tins of oil and fat that served for my lamp and occasional cooking. A little grocery store adjoining had completely collapsed. I spent a week in clearing away the wreckage and my labour was well rewarded in sardines and tinned spaghetti. This little hunting ground served me without fail for the best part of six months, and it was not until the winter that I had to search farther afield, with gradually diminishing success. Sometimes I met with little families hunting together, but mostly they were people like myself, hunting quite alone.

It was the custom of the people in my neighbourhood to meet, towards sunset, in Kensington Gardens, where we went to draw our daily bucket of water from the Round Pond. On fine evenings we would set our buckets down, stroll amongst the trees, and pass the time of day.

We were a strangely assorted little community of about fifty people, varying in appearance and condition according to our temperaments, ability to hunt well, and our will to live. One old gentleman, with snow-white hair, invariably wore a buttonhole and always appeared, by some miracle of resourcefulness, sprucely dressed and immaculately clean. He had been a stockbroker in a very big way, I was told, and still lived amongst the ruins of his Park Lane mansion. In contrast came an old woman in whose hunting area must have lain a well-stocked wine store. She appeared every evening at the Pond, bleary-eyed and garrulous, her voice too blurred and thick to understand. But for the most part they were quiet, wistful people who talked and moved as if they were taking part in some ghostly charade. All of us were in middle age, for the "recruiting lorries" had long since carried away the few young people that remained.

It was by the Round Pond that I met Professor Bransbury, and from him that I learnt all about the man who called himself "Selim the Liberator."

Bransbury had been at Cambridge a few years before me, but we found much in common and several mutual acquaintances of our far-off student days. It became our custom to wander off together, to find a seat amongst the wild, unkempt shrubberies and to talk till twilight came.

He had been a Professor of Economics at London University— a man of wide reading and deep culture—Robinson Crusoe–like with his long matted beard and straying locks of iron-grey hair. He wore a tattered morning coat with an open-necked cricket shirt and carried an old fur-lined motor rug that he had made into a kind of cloak. He told me the scraps of news that drifted into the ruined city, and one evening he casually remarked: "I hear that Selim is in Berlin."

"Selim?" I enquired. "Who is Selim?"

Bransbury stared at me with wide, incredulous eyes. "My dear fellow," he began. "Selim!—surely you know!"

"I know nothing," I replied, "for the past two years I have been buried in the country—completely isolated—without a word of news."

"You've never heard of Selim!—good heavens, man. . . ."

"Tell me who he is," I said.

My request for information pleased the old Professor. His instinct for teaching was awakened—he leaned back in the rotting Park seat and began in a dreamy voice—with faraway eyes.

"You amaze me. I thought the whole world knew of Selim by this time. Selim, as far as I know, is a Persian, the son of a small local official who lived in Teheran. Apparently he was known in a small way for some years before the cataclysm. He was a revolutionary—possibly an anarchist. He preached against the exploitation and oppression of the Eastern peoples by the white nations of the West.

"But it was the moon that made him. Whether he is a divine leader or a rank charlatan we shall never know. The fact remains that his magnetic power amounts to genius. By some means he discovered the secret of the moon's approach before it was evident to the naked eye. He declared to his followers that the moon was the God of Oppressed Peoples: that very soon the Moon God would descend upon the earth to destroy their hated white oppressors.

"I imagine his followers took it with a pinch of salt at first, but when it became evident that the moon was actually growing bigger and brighter every night, Selim's name was made. His fame spread like a forest fire to every corner of the Eastern world, and he lost no time in cashing-in upon the superstition of those ignorant millions. He trained the best of his followers and sent a hundred young disciples to spread the word. To millions Selim became a god himself: a divine messenger from the silver god that was rushing to their aid from the skies above.

"He had a big stroke of luck when the moon landed in the Atlantic. It would have been a different matter if it had landed on Selim himself, but he was able to announce that the Moon God had arrived: that it had crushed the white tyrants of Europe, leaving a miserable remnant for the oppressed peoples themselves to destroy as a sacrifice in honour of their deliverance. He called upon his followers to prepare for the Great Pilgrimage.

"But Selim has a level head. He knew that Europe was by no means destroyed as completely as he had announced to his followers.

All through those two years when Europe was re-gathering its strength and struggling back to life, Selim was collecting his hordes upon the plains of Turkestan. They came in their thousands to his camp—from the mountains of Afghanistan and the jungles of Africa—from China and Abyssinia—from India and the deserts of Arabia.

"He trained them in discipline and in the use of arms, but he need not have gone to so much trouble. By the time his Holy Pilgrimage was ready to start, our silly little leaders in Europe were busily at work destroying one another.

"The Selimites swept in seething hordes across the Steppes of Russia and the eastern hills of Turkey: they were across the Volga—into Poland and the Balkans before our European leaders came to their senses.

"A Congress of startled little Deputies met at The Hague about a year ago and patched up a hasty alliance against what they called 'The Eastern Menace.' Even then they squabbled for months as to who should be 'Leader-in-Chief.' In the end a Dutchman named van Hoyden took command. . . ."

Dusk was coming. It was almost dark beneath the trees of the Park, and we were quite alone.

As Bransbury had been talking I had watched our small community file through the Park gates with their pails of water . . . dejected little animals, they seemed, in tattered clothes and grotesque, shapeless hats, creeping back to their ruined homes for another lonely night. The Professor's story, strange though it was, had not surprised me. For a long time I had known instinctively that some deeper menace must have arisen to account for the hopeless collapse of our organised life. It explained two other things to me: Pat's reference in her letter to our soldiers moving eastwards—Robin's mystifying account of a fight with "black men" in the forests of Bohemia . . .

"What happened then?" I asked.

"Who knows?" replied the old man. "There is no news—no touch with our men in Europe: only vague, scattered rumours come to us here. Van Hoyden, by all accounts, is a brave leader, and he has brave men to follow him. But what can a few thousands do against these seething millions?—a few thousand starving, bewildered, worn-out men who have fought each other and worn their guns out upon each other for three desperate years?

"Last week I heard that the Selimites were in Vienna and Berlin—that they had sacked Venice and Milan. There was talk of van Hoyden making a stand upon the Rhine, but I heard the guns quite clearly last night . . . much nearer than the Rhine. . . ."

"It need not have happened," I whispered. "If Europe had remained united, we could have scattered them to the winds. . . ." I was past all anger now. I had listened to Bransbury as if he were relating some legend of the Ancient World. I was living as those around me were living: in a fantasy of dreams that had no further kinship with this earthly world. "It need never have happened."

"Many things need never have happened," returned the old man in a low, patient voice. "It's nearly dark. I think we ought to go."

A young family of rabbits scuttled through the wild undergrowth as we walked in silence to the gates of the Park. I bade "goodnight" to the Professor and hurried as fast as possible up the steep lane to the shelter of my home, for the baying of the starving dogs came ominously through the gathering darkness.

*　　*　　*

Until Professor Bransbury told me of "Selim the Liberator," I had never quite lost hope. Always in the background of my thoughts lay the prayer that this tragic interlude might pass away: that reason would return and peace would come once more to our stricken earth.

I began my story when I returned from the Park that night. For over a year my determination to complete it has given me the will to live. Nothing more has happened save a bitter winter that has left me almost alone, and day by day I have watched the shadows close upon us. Night by night I have written through an unearthly silence, broken only by the clatter and fall of a decaying roof, the hooting of owls, and the howls of wild, starving dogs. Selim and his men are no doubt upon the moon by now—probably building upon it a Temple of Deliverance. They have not disturbed me here. Once a great black aeroplane hovered overhead, buzzing like a bloated autumn bluebottle. It circled around and came again next day—then disappeared towards the east and left us alone.

My story is finished. By the setting of the sun this evening I would say that it must be November. Another winter is at hand. My flask stands beside me in readiness for the last page of my manuscript: the bricks lie on the floor beside the recess that I have made to conceal it in. I pray that it may someday be discovered: "The Hopkins Manuscript" that will light these dark ages for the men who may one day live in another era of happiness and culture.

Just beneath these windows, in Uncle Henry's small wild garden, stands a seat beside an old twisted cherry tree. Tomorrow I shall go to it and sit there for the last time: it brings happy memories to me . . . memories of a seat beneath the elms of a village cricket ground where once, long years ago, I sat with Colonel Parker, and

Pat, and Robin . . . as we watched the moon wane over us in its last course above this earth.

It is long past midnight and I am very tired. From the blackness of the city comes one solitary, flickering light . . . one fitful little gleam from a house in Ladbroke Square. . . . I wonder who it is?

ABOUT THE AUTHOR

R. C. SHERRIFF was born in 1896 and worked as an insurance clerk after leaving school. He joined the army shortly after the outbreak of the First World War, and from 1917 served as a captain in the East Surrey Regiment. He saw action at the battles of Vimy and Loos and was severely wounded at Ypres. After the war, he returned to his desk job and spent ten years as a claims adjuster. It was an interest in amateur theatricals that led him to try his hand at writing. His most famous play, *Journey's End*, was based on his letters home from the trenches and was initially rejected by many theatre managements. In December 1928, it was given a single performance by the Incorporated Stage Society, with a young Laurence Olivier in the lead role. The play's enormous subsequent success enabled Sherriff to become a full-time writer. In his mid-thirties he fulfilled a long-held dream and went to Oxford to study history, but gave up his degree when he was invited to write scripts for Hollywood. His screenplays include *The Invisible Man* (1933), *Goodbye, Mr. Chips* (1933), and *The Dam Busters* (1955), while his best novels include *The Fortnight in September* (1931) and *The Hopkins Manuscript* (1939). He spent most of his life living quietly with his mother in Esher in Surrey; his autobiography, *No Leading Lady*, appeared in 1968. Sherriff died in 1975.